THE
LATE
HIT

ALEXIS BUXTON

Other Titles

CTU Eagles

The Late Hit

The Christmas Scramble

The Change Up

Author's Note

Dear Readers,

Thank you for picking up a copy of The Late Hit. Writing has always been a passion of mine. I've always dreamed of becoming a writer and it's finally happening.

After becoming a mom, twice, and approaching my 30th birthday, I went through a major identity crisis. With a big push from my husband and a few close friends, I just started writing. And here we are, nine months later.

I hope you love Central Texas University and the fictional characters I've spent many nights talking to as much as I do.

Love & Hugs,

Alexis Buxton

Playlist

Party Girl - CharlieOnnaFriday

Icky Thump- White Stripes

Believer - Imagine Dragons

Humble - Kendrick Lamar

Seven Nation Army - White Stripes

Goosebumps - Travis Scott

Mo Bamba - Sheck Wes

I Think I'm Okay - MGK & YUNGBLOD

Ophelia - The Lumineers

Daylight - Shinedown

Take Me Away - New Medicine

More Than Friends - Aidan Bissett

Broken Halos - Chris Stapleton

Wrecked - Imagine Dragons

Collide - Justine Skye ft. Tyga

Body - Megan Thee Stallion

In The Air Tonight - Phil Collins

Scotty Doesn't Know - Lustra

What's Your Fantasy - Ludacris

Missed Calls - Mac Miller

Careless - Arden Jones

Over - CHVRCHES

The Loneliest - MANESKIN

Best Friend - Ingrid Michaelson

Here With Me - D4VID

Can't Help Falling in Love - Haley Reinhart

ALEXIS BUXTON

Ho Hey - The Lumineers
Grow Old with Me - Tom Odell
I Got You - Ciara
Best Day of My Life - American Authors

For the complete soundtrack, search 'THE LATE HIT' on Spotify

Before You Read

This book does feature a few trigger warnings. Please read on with caution as these triggers may be considered spoilers.

This book contains adult material including the death of a loved one (off page), grief, and depictions of non-nurturing parents who do not provide support and cause emotional and psychological distress. The Late Hit is an open-door romance with explicit sexual content, strong language, as well as college-aged main characters drinking, smoking, and partying.

I hope that I've handled these topics in the care that they deserve. Readers, please be advised.

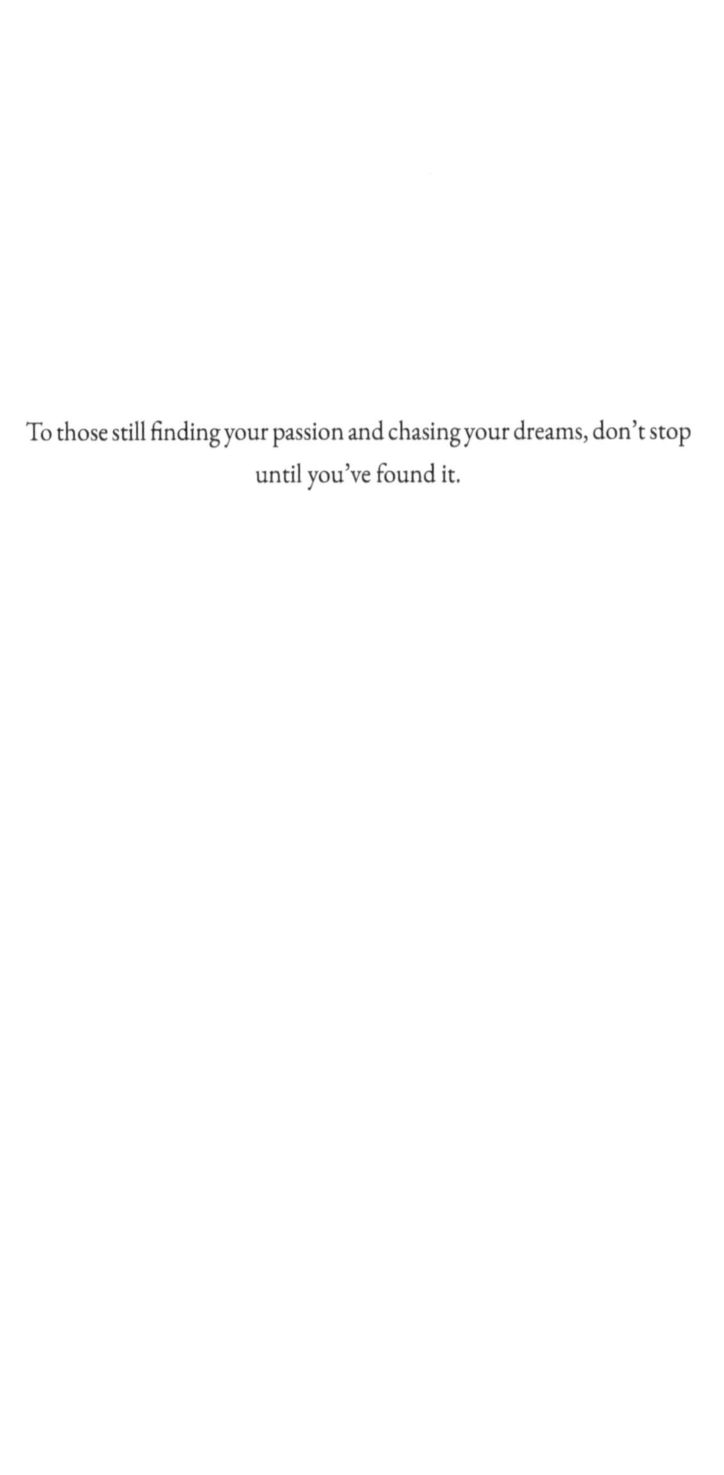

To those still finding your passion and chasing your dreams, don't stop until you've found it.

To my husband, thank you for encouraging me to chase my dreams.

To my kids, never stop chasing your dreams.

To my family and friends that were cheering me on along the way, you made this happen.

I love you all so much! xx

THE LATE HIT

CHAPTER 1
Brynn

I'M NEVER DRINKING AGAIN.

The soft chirp of birds fills the silence around me as the sky is slowly starting to wake. Steadily, I begin to rise from bed, only to be met with the pounding in my head that is trying to consume me.

Another morning, another hangover.

Glancing around the room, I search for my clothes. There is no way I am making the trek to my car in only a borrowed Central Texas Eagles football shirt that looks more like a dress than a shirt on me.

I throw the covers off me, sitting up slowly, trying to avoid the inevitable feeling of the room spinning and the need to empty my stomach.

"The sun isn't even out," Quinton groans from the makeshift bed on the floor.

"I've got class," I reply, jumping out of his warm bed. It's either I get up now, or I'll cave in and spend all morning lying in bed. "Besides, don't you have to get up soon for weightlifting?"

"Coach pushed weightlifting back until eight o'clock, thank god," Quinton replies.

"Lucky you," I say. "Meet me at the Student Union at eleven thirty for lunch?"

"Yeah, see you later," Q says, rolling over and bringing his blanket up to his chin. He looks so comfortable. I wish I could say the same about myself. Why did I want the best professor for my Psychology 3600 class? And why does he only teach eight a.m. classes?

Locating my clothes on his desk chair, I throw off Quinton's T-shirt, toss it in the pile of clothes that I assume are dirty, and pull on my clothes from last night. I'm always thankful when parties are casual and not themed. It makes the next morning less awkward. Cutoff jean shorts, a cute tank, and Converse don't scream "walk of shame" quite like a tight dress and heels.

Stumbling over to the nightstand, I pick up my round, tortoise-framed glasses and pop in a piece of gum. Gum will have to do until I make it back to my townhouse to freshen up. The inside of my mouth feels like I licked the mat that holds overflow draft beer at bars. *Gross!*

Stepping out of Quinton's bedroom, I notice that the house is calm and quiet, the total opposite of last night. But before I can take in my surroundings, I am met with the stench of weed, sticky floors, and littered beer cans.

God—this house is a disaster.

Dubbed the Football House around campus, Quinton's house is a three-story brick colonial. His parents purchased the house for his older brother to live in while he was in college. Once Damien graduated, Quinton moved in with some of his teammates and younger brother. The Football House is the place to party on campus. They're known for throwing the wildest parties. But since a lot is riding on the line for all the guys that live here, the parties are usually invite-only to keep the crowd under some control.

Since I don't live nearby, Q lets me crash in his room after parties, as long as he isn't hooking up with some chick. On the nights he's got a lady, I crash in the third-story movie room. The couch isn't as comfortable as Q's bed, but it gets the job done. And it definitely gets the job done. It's the most comfortable bed I've ever slept on. It's like lying on a cloud. There's no way I'd give up sleeping in this bed if it was mine. But Quinton does every time I stay over. He never sleeps in the bed with me, he always takes the floor.

Quinton Boyd is not only a Power Five running back for the CTU Eagles, but he's a potential first-round draft pick in the NFL. With Q's stats, it's a no-brainer that he will go first round, top ten. He's insanely talented, can bench and squat an ungodly amount, and makes defenders look stupid. While he may have the NFL's eye, he also has the campus eating out of the palm of his hand. The guys want to be him, the ladies want under him, and I'm lucky enough to call him my best friend.

Football season kicks off next weekend. Every September, the team kicks off the season and the new school year with their weekly Thirsty Thursday party. The guys always say their Thirsty Thursday nights are going to be low-key, but the parties are far from laid-back. Last night's party got a little carried away.

That's what happens when people start talking about a party, especially one at the Football House.

Carefully, I make my way down the old, hardwood staircase, stepping over a few bodies of passed-out partygoers, and walk straight into the kitchen. For some reason, during the party, I ended up taking my Converse off, and now I have no idea where they are. This brings me to a better question than where, but why would taking my shoes off in *this house* even cross my mind?

Pulling a kitchen chair to the refrigerator, I stand and look to see if someone put them on top. Nope, not there. Glancing around the open concept kitchen, dining room, and living room, I see a lot of random things, but no Converse. My eyes keep scanning and snag on something hanging from the patio. Stepping off the chair, I make my way to the kitchen window and peer out over the yard. And there they are. My shoes are dangling from the patio roof. There's no way I'm going out to get them now. Deciding to let them hang, I make my way to the front door barefoot.

It's six o'clock in the morning, my head is pounding, and I got four hours of sleep, but I can't help but take in the quiet campus. I don't think there's anything better than the morning on campus. Even hungover, I can truly appreciate the historic campus that makes up Central Texas University, a one-hundred-fifty-year-old university. The school hasn't lost any of its charm over the years and somehow, like a fine wine, keeps getting better with age.

The mature trees line the sidewalks and are flourishing. Instead of paved streets, CTU features a majority of brick-lined streets. The buildings that make up the campus are all original with stunning architectural designs.

Attending CTU had always been my brother's and my dream. I'm so glad I decided to attend, even though his plans changed. Thankfully, I met Quinton. He helped ease the guilt of being at CTU.

Quinton and I met freshman year. But we weren't instant friends.

The first week of school was 'icebreaker' week. Each day, we were assigned mandatory activities. Quinton and I were assigned a lot of the same activities. My team kept beating Q's team, and apparently, he's a sore loser.

Then at the end of the week, we were both at the same party. Q and I were paired opposites in a beer pong game. He and his partner were on their ninth game-winning streak, when my partner and I beat them. We continued our winning streak and won the little tournament that was going on.

My cockiness might've shone through as I ran my mouth to all of his friends about how much he sucked. I might have been a little—okay, a lot—drunk.

Karma would then come around and bite me in the ass when we both had the same mandatory freshman class. The only open seat was beside Quinton, which made us partners for the semester. It ended up being a blessing because we quickly became best friends and have been inseparable since.

Making the ten-minute drive to my townhouse, I park in my designated spot. I share a three-bedroom house with my two best friends, Chloe and Macy. Before I get a chance to open the front door, I'm forced to halt my entrance as Macy opens it with a tall man behind her. He looks familiar, but I can't quite place where I recognize him from. Story of my life.

"Well, looks like it's a good morning for you," I greet Macy and her friend.

Her face flushes red as she lets her friend out the front door.

"Gregg, this is my roommate Brynn Wilder. Brynn, this is Gregg Carlton." She introduces us as Gregg reaches his hand out for me to shake. "Thanks for last night, Gregg," Macy says, turning her attention back to him.

Gregg leans down and kisses Macy on her cheek, her face turning even redder.

"See you around, Macy."

He turns and walks down the three steps off our front porch and heads down the sidewalk toward the guest parking.

Shutting the door after I walk inside, Macy turns to me.

"I could say the same about you," Macy retorts.

"Oh please, you know I stayed with Quinton," I reply, placing my keys on the hook by the front door before heading into our kitchen.

As put together as I try to be, if I don't put my keys on the hook right away, I'll be tearing the house apart trying to find them. Once I put them in the freezer, and it took four hours to find them.

Macy is right on my heels, and we both make our way to the Keurig. Coffee is essential this morning. Caffeine is vital every morning, but especially today. I will never understand people who don't drink coffee. That first sip of hot coffee rolls through my veins and warms up my black heart. It's the absolute best.

Reaching up in the cabinet above our coffee cart, I pull down two mugs. One is a yellow mug that says *"My anxiety is chronic, but this ass is iconic"* and the other is a blush-colored mug with *"Have fun. Don't do stupid shit. Study hard. Go to class, Call Home"* written on it. The mug is definitely not from my collection. While I'm grabbing the mugs, Macy is loading the Keurig with Death Wish coffee. Turning to me, she grabs a mug from my outstretched hand, places it under the drip, and resumes our conversation.

"When are you two going to give in to all of that sexual chemistry? I see it. Chloe sees it. Cody sees it. Everyone sees it but you two," she says, leaning against the counter.

A sigh escapes my mouth as my eyes roll in a dramatic fashion. Grabbing my mug from under the Keurig, I take my first sip.

Ahh that first taste is like the perfect hit.

I can feel my soul waking up, putting Bitch Brynn to rest.

"Mace, I'm going to stop you right there. I'm too hungover to have this conversation with you for the hundredth time. Q is my friend. That's it. End of," I say, turning to head out of the kitchen. Before I make it all the way out of the room, I turn over my shoulder and say, "I've got to shower and head to class."

Macy just stands there, leaning against the counter with a smirk on her face.

Quinton and I are constantly getting asked why we aren't together. Even in college, people can't understand our relationship. He's my best friend.

Do I find him attractive? Of course. I have eyes and a pulse. He's stunning, there's no denying that.

Quinton Boyd has flawless, medium-brown skin marked with black ink. Tattoos line his left arm from his shoulder to his wrist. Across his strong chest is a giant eagle with its wings spread open, stretching from one pectoral muscle to the other. Inked down his rib cage on his right side is a detailed cross. His black hair is kept in a tight fade on the sides, with longer curls on top. A gold chain always lays around his neck with a small cross at the center—it was a gift from his grandma Cleo.

And his smile. Goddamn, Quinton Boyd has a panty-dropping smile, perfectly straight, white teeth and the tiniest dimple on his lower cheek, but only on the left side. The dreamiest brown eyes that remind me of rich dark coffee are outlined with an umber-brown ring.

But what makes him most attractive is his personality. He's cocky, yet charming and protective, with a wild side. He's a man of few words. The quiet one who sits back and listens. Quinton would give the shirt off his back for a stranger, and he's the first person to help an old lady cross the road. Believe me, I've seen him do it many times.

But the thing is, I value our friendship too much to ever even think about crossing that line.

And I'm too damaged to be in a relationship, especially with someone as good as Quinton.

The next hour flies by as I shower and get ready for Friday classes. It's the end of the first week, and I only have two classes. I throw on a black pair of bike shorts and an oversized graphic T-shirt with a pair of dad-style tennis shoes. Since I don't have time to fix my hair or makeup, I settle for tossing my blonde hair in a claw clip. I am forever thankful to whoever decided to bring back claw clips—y'all are the real MVPs.

Quickly, I apply a small layer of mascara. It's the only makeup I have time for. Before I leave my room, I put on my gold bar necklace that has the letter 'B' engraved on it. This necklace is my favorite possession, and it only comes off when I shower. I try to never leave the house without it.

Running down the stairs, I stop at the entry closet and pull out my backpack and grab my keys off the hook. Sitting on our entryway table is a cup of on-the-go oatmeal and a note.

B,

Didn't mean to upset you this morning. Have a kick ass Friday.

XO,

M

PS- Say this out loud and put that shit in the universe. "I am worthy of an amazing life"

Macy is all about manifesting. She says things are more likely to come true if we speak it out loud to the universe.

Taking a deep breath in and exhaling slowly, I close my eyes and look up to the ceiling before repeating: "I am worthy of an amazing life."

And with that, I rush outside to my car.

Finding a parking spot on campus after nine a.m. is a challenge, but before nine a.m. is a piece of cake. There's a spot two rows in and five cars in. Doing one more glance at my appearance in the rearview mirror, I decide it's as good as it's going to get. Thankfully, my glasses help hide some of the dark circles under my eyes. Why did I sign up for such an early class? Oh yeah, hot Prof. Peters. Grabbing my bag, I exit my car, locking it as I head toward all of the walking zombies, I mean students, who are looking as tired and hungover as I am.

I enter Rogers Hall, finding the elevator and stepping on with others. Pushing through the bodies and standing shoulder-to-shoulder until the doors open on the third floor. I follow the rushing crowd to Lecture Hall 302, one of the largest lecture halls on campus. It's a three-story auditorium and holds a couple hundred students.

Descending the steps, I walk toward the middle of the room. Glancing around, I finally spot a familiar person and head toward him. He must hear me coming, because Cody glances up with a questioning look before a smile takes over his face.

"Yo, B, I'm glad to see someone I know in this class," Cody says as he shuffles his backpack out of my way.

Cody Jacobs is a pitcher on the baseball team, and the two of us run in similar crowds. Like Quinton, Cody is one of my best friends. No, I'm not a jersey chaser, I just prefer hanging out with the jocks. Plopping down in the seat next to him, I fold my arms on the desk and rest my head on my arms. There are about ten minutes before class begins and I'm planning on taking full advantage of the calm.

"Ohemgee, Cody, why does Peters have to teach the Friday morning lecture?" I whine.

"What's the matter, B? A little hungover?" Cody asks with a chuckle as he spins his pen on his fingers.

I don't even bother with an answer, just look at him with my eyes squinting.

He lets out a chuckle. "Let me guess, you're taking tonight off?"

"I'm hungover, not dead," I answer. "I think we are heading to The Eagles' Nest for happy hour and wings."

"Dude, I'm in. The Eagles' Nest has the best wings around."

The Eagles' Nest, yes the bar is named after the CTU Eagles, is a local campus essential. While the Football House is the place to party on campus, The Eagles' Nest is the spot to be when you need to unwind off campus. They serve cheap food and cheap beer. There's always some kind of local band on Friday nights. It's the place to be around campus. The owner loves football, and Q can usually get a few tables reserved for us.

"I'll have Q add you for the total," I say, finally pulling my head off my arms and reaching into my backpack to pull out my iPad and stylus.

"So, B, you and Q?" Cody begins before I cut him off.

"Don't even think about finishing that question, Cody."

"Just making sure nothing has changed," Cody replies with a smirk.

I shake my head. Cody has been trying to get me to go out with him for a while, and for some reason, I just can't bring myself to say yes. Cody is a good guy, the best guy, and he'd be a good time—at least, that's the rumor on campus—but that's all it would be, a good time. And I prefer not to mess around with close friends. It always makes everything awkward, and then all of our friends are in our business. I'm all about that "no strings attached hook-up."

Before we have a chance to finish our conversation, the first-floor door opens, and Professor Peters walks in and slams the door. Peters is a second-year professor and he's not much older than we are. He is hot, hot, hot. As in, model hot. He's like that guy on Instagram you stumble upon and immediately become obsessed with. Tall, lean-built, but not skinny, more like a swimmer's build. He has dark hair, dark-green eyes, and a golden tan. Not to mention a permanent five o'clock shadow that he keeps groomed to always look a little disheveled.

"Good morning, this is Psych 3600," Professor Peters greets the class. His eyes look around the lecture hall. "If you're not a psych major, you shouldn't be in this room. This isn't a GenEd course." He pauses, making sure no one gets up to leave the room.

Reaching over with a tissue, Cody says under his breath, "Here, B, wipe the drool from your mouth."

"Oh shut up, Cody," I reply with a chuckle and a one finger salute. Because, yeah, I was totally staring and picturing Peters doing some "not safe for school" activities.

Why yes, Professor, I do need some extra help. Oh, meet in your office during office hours? See you then.

CHAPTER 2
Brynn

AT FOUR FORTY-FIVE, MACY, Chloe, and I are rushing out the door and climbing into the Uber Chloe ordered. All three of us are dressed in ripped jeans, some kind of casual top, and flip-flops as we make the drive to The Eagles' Nest. Macy and I have convinced Chloe to put down her book and join us. Chloe is our third roommate and a Texas native. Where Macy and I are tall, Chloe has a petite build. She might not be the tallest, but her southern attitude makes up for her height. Both Chloe and Macy enjoy a night out to party, and both know their limits, while I haven't discovered mine yet. My motto is to live fast, and theirs definitely isn't.

Crammed in the middle, I feel my phone vibrate in my back pocket.

"OMG, B, please tell me that was your phone and not vibrating panties," Chloe says.

The Uber driver's eyes bounce up to the rearview mirror. His eyes are as wide as saucers as they make contact with mine. Giving the driver a wink, I pull out my phone and wave it around.

"I wear vibrating panties one time, and you never let me live it down," I reply, and check my messages.

Reading the message from Quinton, I quickly thumb out a reply.

Q: Ordered a pitcher for us and Mace a spicy margarita. Hurry your asses up!

Me: Pulling up!

"She's not going to let you live it down because we were in the middle of a group study session, and your ass was vibrating. The whole room knew what was going on." Macy laughs.

"Whatever. You bitches are just jealous with your vanilla sex life."

We arrive in front of The Eagles' Nest, and I'm all but pushing Chloe out of the back door. I need a beer, and I need to move my body. The Eagles' Nest is having my favorite alternative cover band Ecstasy and I'm so ready to dance this first week away.

College is fun. It's an absolute blast. If I could study partying, I totally would. Classes aren't my thing. It's not that I'm not smart, because I am. I just think it's ridiculous. All of this money is spent sitting through hours and hours of boring lectures. But isn't real-life experience so much more valuable? I think so. Hands-on experience makes a person better, not studying the influential people who created parts of psychology.

In typical Friday night fashion, the bar is packed. There's a line outside the doors to get in. The bouncer recognizes me and nods his head for us to enter. I could seriously kiss Q for having his connections to get us a reserved table.

Walking through the front doors, I take in my favorite bar on campus. It's nothing spectacular, but it feels like home. The bar is made up of worn, tiled flooring and wood-paneled walls. TVs hang everywhere, high-top tables are scattered around the bar, and vinyl booths line the perimeter. Straight ahead of the front doors is a large L-shaped bar. Following the long part of the bar is the stage, and next to the stage is a separate room with multiple glass doors that lead to a private room with large tables, a pool table, and dart boards.

Pushing through the standing bodies, the girls and I make our way to the first set of double doors that lead to the private room. There are twenty or so people already congregated in the room. Q spots me before I see him. He stands up and waves us over and points to the pitcher and full glass he has waiting for me.

"Hey, beautiful ladies," he greets us, pulling us all in for a hug. "We've got pitchers coming nonstop, and I ordered a spicy marg for you, Macy."

"You're the best, Q," Chloe and Macy say at the same time.

Over the next hour, pitchers are continuously brought to the table, and baskets and baskets of wings are placed around us. Conversations are flowing, laughter rattles the walls, and the first week of school is forgotten. Before I know it, I hear the opening chords to The White Stripes' "Icky Thump." My foot starts tapping, my head starts moving, and I'm glancing out the doors toward the stage.

Standing up, I grab the pitcher of beer, fill up my cup, and glance around at my friends.

"Well, friends, it's that time."

Will Davis, a senior safety on the football team, makes eye contact with me and jerks his head toward the stage. I don't respond, just give a smirk and a wink before turning and making my way to the dance floor.

Will's hot. He's your typical boy next door with light-brown hair that he keeps cut tight on the sides and longer on top and amber eyes with flecks of gold that are so stunning you just want to get lost in them. At a few inches over six feet tall with trim muscles, his tight clothes always seem to show off how built he is. And I've had the luxury of counting his eight-pack abs...with my tongue. While Will is every girl's dream, his personality isn't always the greatest. But I don't hook up with Will because of his personality.

Will and I have had many shared moments together over the last year. He's a repeat hook-up since he actually knows what the hell he's doing and can get me off more than once. And it looks like tonight might be another one of those moments.

This is my third year at Central Texas, and Ecstasy has been playing for as long as I've been attending. I try to make it my mission to attend their shows. Now, I wouldn't call myself a groupie, but if the guitarist wanted to strum something other than his guitar, I wouldn't tell him no.

I stand there, letting the music move me. My hips start moving to the beat, the lyrics are flowing from my mouth, and I feel Will Davis slide in behind me. His hands skim up my thighs before settling on my hips, pulling me into his hard body. There will never be a time that I willingly pass up a hot, hard body pressed up against me, especially if he knows how to use his physique inside the bedroom.

Sweat drips down my body after dancing nonstop for the past hour and a half. Will has been keeping my beer full, and I'm well on my way to being drunk. Ecstasy takes their only twenty-minute break to head out back and smoke. The guitarist makes eye contact with me and jerks his head to follow.

"Did he just tell you to follow him?" Will asks over the house music.

"Yeah, I think he did," I answer, watching the guitarist slide off stage and head our way.

The guitarist stops right in front of us and leans in toward me. I feel Will tense behind me as the guitarist shouts in my ear. "Hey, I've noticed you before at other shows."

Leaning toward him, I shout back, "Hell yeah. I'm a huge fan!"

The guitarist grins, looking me up and down. "Come out back for a smoke?"

I nod my head yes at the same time that Will grips my hips.

"I'll be back," I tell Will.

"Seriously, B?" he asks, jealousy skating across his face.

"Green isn't your color, Will," I say, patting him on the arm. I follow the guitarist down the hallway that leads out back for a smoke.

He opens the back door for me. I step outside into the stifling Texas air and follow behind the guitarist while he leads us to the van where the other members are toking up.

"Yo, guys, this is—" The guitarist pauses his introductions, looking over at me, realizing we haven't exchanged names yet.

"Brynn," I supply, introducing myself.

"Guys, this is Brynn. Brynn, these are the guys—Neal, Maddox, Bear—and I'm Max."

The guys all give me a nod, checking me out. Most girls would be uncomfortable in a dark alley with four guys in an alternative band, but not me. There's not much that makes me uncomfortable.

Bear takes a drag on the joint he's holding, blowing out the smoke, and handing it over to me. I nod my head and place the joint between my fingers, bringing it to my lips, for a long inhale. Breathing in the smoke, I hold it. The weed, mixed with the multiple beers, makes the buzz rush straight to my head.

"This is good shit," I say, exhaling a plume of smoke.

"Only the best," Max replies, taking the joint from my hand.

We stand there, passing the joint back and forth, shooting the shit for who knows how long. The back door bangs open.

"Are you guys coming back to play?" a balding man asks the band.

"Hold your fuckin' horses," Maddox shouts back.

Bear finishes off the joint before we all head back in. Max steps in line beside me before moving aside to let me enter first. Once we are inside, he looks me up and down one last time.

"See ya around, Brynn," he says, flashing me a panty-dropping smile and hitting me with a wink before jogging back on stage.

What the hell just happened?

I'm standing there stunned with a smile on my face. Slipping my poker face back on, I follow the hallway back to the bar. The dance floor is packed, and I scan the room for a familiar face. Will is leaning against the bar, watching the hallway with a beer in his hand. Making my way over to him, I slide my body up against his, taking the beer out of his hand, and downing half of it. He wraps his arm around me, settling his hand in my back pocket.

"Have fun?" he asks.

Most men wouldn't be willing to share their girl, but I have a strong feeling Will wouldn't be one of those men. At least, he's always given the vibe he wouldn't mind sharing, as long as he's involved. But tonight, his actions are saying the opposite.

Slipping my arm around his neck, I pull his face to mine, letting our lips touch. Our kiss turns heated, and I open my mouth for him. He accepts the invitation. Before things get too out of hand, I pull back.

Smirking at him, I finally answer his question. "Not as much fun as we're about to have," I purr.

Dragging me back to the side room where everyone is, he can't keep his hands off me. His body is pressed against me, hands skimming the exposed skin above my jeans.

Chloe sees me first. She takes one look at my appearance and shakes her head with a knowing grin on her face.

"You two getting out of here?"

"I'm going to his place," I answer. "Just letting you know."

"Be safe," she replies.

And with that, Will and I make our way to the exit and back to his place.

CHAPTER 3
QUINTON

"**B**OYD, GET YOUR HEAD out of your ass," Coach Campbell yells from the sideline.

Coach is right, my head isn't on the field this morning. It's back to last night in that damn room, watching Will and Brynn. His hands were all over her. His tongue down her throat. Will's a douche, but Brynn can't seem to see it. Or maybe she does and just doesn't care. But I care. I care that he gets to touch her and share her space.

This morning's practice is mild compared to normal practices. Thank God. I can't stay focused. My mind is all over the place. This season is going to be huge for me, and the pressure is sitting like a weight on my shoulders.

Tyler Harris calls for us to huddle up.

"Dude, what the fuck?" He points the question to me.

"I'm here," I say to him.

Harris calls out the next play. It's a pitch to me.

"Q, you've got this, man. I know a lot is riding on this season, but stay focused. I've got you," Harris says, slapping my helmet.

The remainder of practice goes off without a hitch. My mind stays on the field. Walking toward the tunnel, one of the equipment girls tosses me a water bottle. I lift it in the air and squeeze a long stream of water into my mouth, quenching my thirst. This Texas heat is no joke. I'm sweating my balls off. I'm pretty sure my sweat is sweating, that's how fucking hot it is out. Thank god our season doesn't start for another week. Hopefully, Texas will get a clue that it's about to be fall. But who am I kidding? We have months until it cools down.

Making my way into the locker room, I start peeling my practice jersey off. It's stuck to my skin from all the sweat. All I want to do is get out of these damn clothes, shower, and sit my happy ass in the air conditioning for the rest of the day. Oh yeah, chilling in the air conditioning sounds incredible.

My thoughts are interrupted by the sound of Will Davis. That mouthy cock sucker constantly gets under my skin.

"Dude, that girl can *fuuuck*," Will draws out. "Last night, when she went out with that Emo freak, I thought my chances were shot, but she came back in ready to get down."

Standing in front of my locker, I try to tune out the asshole. Brynn's hook-ups are her own business. I just don't want to hear about it. Grant Campbell—yeah, Campbell, as in the coach's son and my closest teammate and friend—senses my mood.

"Dude, you just gotta ignore it," Grant says, trying to calm me down. "Will just likes to run his mouth." Grant is one of my closest teammates and friends.

Reaching into my locker, I pull out my shower bag. Moving my neck side to side, I feel the muscles pull and hear the cracks. The season hasn't even begun, and my body is sore.

"And the way her body moves, it's like a work of art," Will continues. "And don't get me started on the way her ti—"

The sound of my locker slamming shut silences the room.

"Shut the fuck up, Davis," I say, my shoulders tensing. "Shut. The. Fuck. Up."

"What's the matter, Boyd? Jealous I've screwed her now—how many times? Compared to your zero?" Will retorts.

The two of us stare each other down, my chest rising rapidly.

Grant moves between Will and me.

He looks at me and mutters under his breath, "Not here. Q, just walk away. He's not worth it."

Taking a deep breath, I move away and head toward the showers.

A cold shower is all I need. I just need to cool off and find some food.

Climbing in my Tesla, I slip my phone out of my pocket, checking my messages before I head home.

There are two texts waiting from Brynn.

Wilder: You picking fights in the locker room now?

Wilder: Swing by?

Reading her texts does nothing to calm my mood. I'm all worked up. Maybe I just need to get laid? Closing out Brynn's text thread, I look over my recent messages to see if there's anyone I can text for a quickie. No one stands out.

Tossing my phone in my cup holder, I push the ignition button. "Sicko Mode" blares from my speakers, making me jump. Reversing out of my spot, I turn right out of the parking lot and head toward Whataburger. To turn this day around, I'm spoiling my nutrition plan with a double Whataburger, fries, and a strawberry malt. If I show up to Brynn's empty-handed, she'll have my balls. I'm positive she already wants to rip into me. I don't need to give her another reason.

"Before you say anything," I pause, shoving the malt toward Brynn. "I bought you a malt. It's strawberry."

Shaking the cup, I watch her face for any hints of emotion. Brynn is a closed fucking book ninety percent of the time. And today, I guess the book is slammed shut. Taking the Styrofoam cup from my outstretched arm, she moves aside. Cautiously, I step in. There's a weird vibe in the air. I'm screwed. I can feel it. Never in our years of friendship have I got in the face of anyone who might be warming Brynn's bed. She's free to do whomever she wants.

"I'm not mad, Q," she finally says after a few silent moments of her inhaling her strawberry malt.

The first time B got upset, she told me that there was nothing ice cream couldn't solve, and a strawberry malt would make it go away. It's also her go-to when she's high. Scanning her face for any clues, I come back empty.

"You're not?"

She laughs. "Of course not. I assume Will mouthed off? He's a douche." She shrugs. Moving past me, she heads up the stairs.

Looking over her back, she asks, "You comin'?"

I stare at her, a quizzical expression stretching across my face. Slipping off my shoes, it takes me two steps to catch up to her. She leads us to her room and plops down on her bed. I'm so confused.

"Are you gonna stand in the doorway, or are you going to come in and watch a movie with me?"

This girl. She never fails to surprise me. Of course, I'm staying and watching a movie. It's been too long since B and I just got the chance to chill. No roommates, no friends, and no one looking to hook up interrupting us.

Holding the remote up, she clicks on Disney+. "*Thor: Love and Thunder* or *Black Widow*?" she asks, taking another gulp of her malt.

Bringing my hand to my chin, I act like I'm *really* pondering this.

"Hmm," I begin. "Watch you gush over Hemsworth or watch me gush over Johansson, hmm."

"You won't be the only one gushing over Scarlett. She's a babe."

Snapping my head at her, I let out a chuckle. "Black Widow it is then."

Both of us smile at each other before turning our attention to the movie. I settle against the pile of pillows Brynn has on her bed. and she snuggles closer to me. This is my favorite way to spend an afternoon off.

The weekend passed by in a blur. I swear it was just Saturday afternoon, and Brynn and I were arguing about who had the better chance of shagging a superhero. She says Hemsworth wouldn't be able to pass her up, and I said Scarlett would be stunned to see me. It was a silly argument full of hypotheticals, but that's our game.

Instead of chilling in bed, I'm tossing my phone, a.k.a. my alarm clock, on the floor. Five o'clock comes way too damn early. The team has a mandatory six a.m. lift Monday through Thursday. It's Coach's way of making sure we get our asses up for classes.

Stumbling into the bathroom, I flip on the light and rub my hands over my eyes to get the sleep out of them. Sliding the curtain back, I turn on the shower. A cold shower in the morning is how I start the day. I step out of my boxers before reaching into the closet for a towel. Tossing the towel onto the toilet seat, I jump in the waiting cold water.

"Fuuuck," I draw as soon as the cold water hits me.

Grabbing my body wash and pouring some in my hand, I immediately start scrubbing down my body. A cold shower is the only thing that can jolt me out of sleep, but damn it's so cold. I finish showering in roughly four minutes before hopping out and drying off with my towel.

I'm excited about this week. It's another week of classes, and unlike most, I enjoy my classes. There's just something about sitting in lectures and learning about the body. While most athletes, especially those looking to go pro, pick fluff majors, I picked a major that I would *actually* enjoy doing if football doesn't pan out. Leaving sports forever would never work for me, so I decided on athletic training.

I've had some incredible trainers throughout the years of sports, but my high school trainer was the absolute best. She was fun, she was nurturing, and she could read our bodies like we came with manuals. No one likes to sit out and miss games and practices. Ms. Fox knew when we were hurting. It was like she could use her eyes to scan us and diagnose the problem. It's what made her a helluva trainer.

One time in my junior year, I took a nasty hit and tweaked my hip. Whenever a coach or personnel would pass, I would suck it up and overcompensate to make it look like nothing was bothering me. Ms. Fox caught on. After practice one day, she asked me to come into the training room and point-blank called me out.

"Boyd, how am I supposed to help you when you don't tell me that your hip is bothering you?" she said, staring me down.

Ms. Fox was a petite lady in her midforties. But when she stared you down, that lady made you feel small. Like a damn child. It was humiliating. Well, maybe not humiliating, maybe humbling.

"I don't know what you're talking about," I lied, looking anywhere but at her.

"Quinton Boyd, you're full of it. I've been watching you gimp around all week. Now, lay back, and let me check it out," she said, sliding her stool closer to the training table. "Give me any pushback and I'll tell the coaches. But neither of us wants that."

Turns out it was just a bruised muscle and, with some of her magic, she was able to get it feeling close to normal by that Friday's game. I think she was a wizard in her past life, like someone from Harry Potter. She had insane healing powers.

Halfway through my freshman year in college, I called up Ms. Fox to let her know that I was going into athletic training. She was so excited to hear from me. The whole time on the call, she kept spilling secret after secret of her wizardly ways. Before we ended our call, she told me how proud she was that I made it, and that she always knew I would. It was an unusual way to end our conversation. But six months later, it made sense. Ms. Fox died of stage four cancer that she had been secretly battling.

While I know she's not physically here to cheer me on, I know that wizard is watching down on me. And I'm going to make her proud.

After finishing up the normal morning routine, I slip into a pair of mesh shorts, a fitted, sleeveless CTU Eagles, and tennis shoes. Grabbing my workout bag and backpack, I head downstairs.

"Morning, sleepyhead," my roommate, Jeremiah, greets me.

I grunt in acknowledgment.

Our house only has one blender, which is stupid, but none of us ever think about buying another one. So each morning, it's a race to get downstairs and get to the blender first. Most mornings, I beat my roommates. Today, I was too slow.

"Lucky for you, I made extra," he says over the whirring of the blender.

Shutting off the blender, Jeremiah pours the chocolate peanut butter protein shake into two separate cups and hands me one.

Grabbing the drink, I set it on the counter next to my phone before moving over to the pantry to grab some snacks for the day.

"Thanks, man."

"No problem. Is Xavier up?"

"No clue. But I'm not waiting around to find out," I answer.

Xavier might be my brother, but I'm not his babysitter. He can set his own alarm and make sure he's up for practice. I'm not going to coddle him like our mom does.

Heading back over the counter, I grab all of my shit and head to the garage. As I am throwing my bags in the back, Xavier makes his way out, looking rough.

"Dude, what the hell happened to you?" I ask, pausing with my hand on the back door.

"Might've stayed up too late entertaining a lady and her friend." He shrugs, a smirk sliding over his face. I just shake my head. "Can I get a ride?"

"Yep, let's go," I answer before shutting the back door.

Xav tosses his bag in the back before tossing himself in the front seat. The house clears out, everyone in their cars, and off to hell we go.

Leaving the weight room, I make my way toward campus. I slip in my AirPods as a smile stretches across my face. My legs may be dead, but I'm damn happy. It's Monday. The first Monday of the football season. It's game week. And a big game waits for us on Saturday.

This is what I live for, and nothing and no one is going to bring me down. It's time to get focused. I'm taking my team to the 'ship and bringing home the hardware. My hands are itching to feel the cold stainless steel of the National Championship trophy. My arms are aching to raise the fifty-pound trophy above my head.

My dad might think this is all his doing, but he didn't put in the blood, sweat, and tears. I did. I've been busting my ass to make a name for myself. He's not taking the glory from me.

I'm three songs into my playlist when I feel a presence beside me. Glancing to my left, I see one of the jersey chasers. Internally, I groan. I refuse to acknowledge her, just give her a look. Only she interprets my 'go away' look as a sign that I want to talk. I don't.

"Hey, Q, baby," she purrs in her fake seductive voice, moving her body right in front of me. My eyes are rolling in my head. "You've got a big game this weekend. Need some help relaxing?"

"Nah, Jaz, I'm good." Turning up my music, I step around her.

She doesn't take the hint and keeps walking with me. Girls like her are so predictable. She thinks that walking next to me will stake a claim, and other girls will back off. Only too bad for Jaz, I don't do jersey chasers. I'm no saint, but I know the difference between a jersey chaser and a girl that's looking to hook up for a quick release. Jaz is a thirsty jersey chaser and looking to trap a guy.

Doing my best to ignore Jaz and her incessant chatting, Siri announces I have a new text. Reaching into my pocket, I pull my phone out.

Wilder: Need me to cut a bitch?

My eyes scan the quad before I find the bright blonde hair that belongs to my best friend. She's sitting outside the Union, puffing on her vape pen, looking fierce.

Me: Why? You know someone?

The dots appear quickly, letting me know she's typing.

Wilder: *middle finger emoji* Buy your own breakfast, twat waffle.

I chuckle at my screen, watching her get up and head inside. Jaz sighs heavily beside me, causing me to flinch. I forgot she was still standing here.

"She's trash," Jaz states.

"Find some other free dick to ride," I snap, leaving her there with her mouth wide open. I'm not a mean person. I keep a lot of shit inside, but I don't put up with mean girls. Mean girls are catty, full of gossip, and cause nothing but problems. I don't need that shit in my life.

Opening the doors, I enter the Union, scanning the mostly empty space for Brynn.

"Wilder," I yell, still scanning the room. That's when I see her head pop up and look toward the doors. "Breakfast is on me."

She breaks out into a wide smile.

Yeah, it's going to be a great week.

CHAPTER 4
Brynn

"WAKE UP! WAKE UP! Wake up!" Macy screams as she comes barging into my room. I was still sound asleep with my sheets barely covering my body in a pair of tiny sleep shorts and a tank. "It's the first game of the season, bitch. Wake up!"

Groaning, I lift my sleep mask to see Macy standing beside me with a Jell-O shot in one hand. Our annual tradition is to kick off game day with a morning shot, followed by spending a couple of hours drinking coffee and getting ready, and then we head to the game. This year, the first game of the season is a night game, which is always trouble for us, but the atmosphere of a night game can't be beat. Not only are night games a blast, but this year we are having a rematch of last year's playoff game, which we lost. Tonight's game is a huge deal.

"Morning," I grumble.

Taking the shot from Macy, I dip my tongue into the cup, sliding around the rim of the plastic, breaking loose the Jell-O before sucking it down. Mmm, cherry Jell-O shots are my favorite. Before getting out of bed, I reach over to my phone, check the time—it's nine forty-five—and pull up my text messages.

Me: Good luck today, Q! Kick some ass

Q: Hell yeah!

Q: I'm so hyped!

Me: Meet you after the game in our spot!

"Q ready for the game?" Macy asks.

"Oh yeah, he's pumped," I answer, climbing out of bed and heading over to my bathroom to brush my teeth.

Since I was the one to find the townhouse, the girls gave me the master suite. Both of their bedrooms are upstairs, as well, but they share the guest bathroom. It's not that big of a deal since we all get ready together. Usually, that's in my room since it's the biggest.

"Chlo ran out to grab donuts," Macy says while I brush my teeth.

She heads out of my room while I finish my morning routine—brush my teeth, bathroom, wash my face. You know, the typical stuff.

By the time I make it downstairs, Chloe had returned with the donuts. She picked up a dozen glazed donuts decorated in CTU colors, along with three red, white, and blue Eagles lattes, which are only available during football season. The drink features our school's team colors, and the latte is a combination of white chocolate, raspberry, blueberry, milk, and espresso. It's really good, but I only drink them on game days. I much prefer my coffee black and, if I'm feeling adventurous, I add a splash of cream.

"Okay, so what's the game plan?" Chloe asks, shoving a donut in her mouth.

Reaching around Chloe, I grab myself a donut and sit down on a bar stool at our island. College GameDay is blaring on the TV from the living room behind us. Before answering, I take a swig of my iced coffee, but not before I shake the ice around for a couple of seconds, because it obviously makes iced coffee better when you shake it around first.

"Get ready, get drunk, get food, and get rowdy?"

Macy looks up from where she's painting her nails in OPI's shade Color So Hot It Berns.

"I'm down for that plan. The baseball house is having a party, and I'm sure we can find somewhere to eat at the tailgate."

"Oh, I forgot. Q said he told his parents we would be stopping by their motorhome for a barbecue."

Quinton's parents and I have a like/dislike relationship. Mr. and Mrs. Boyd are CTU royalty. Mr. Boyd set the sack record for the Eagles before playing fifteen years in the NFL. He just recently retired and has become a heavy presence in the athletic boosters. His wife was also a CTU legend in basketball. While she didn't go on to play in the WNBA, she holds the CTU record for most rebounds in a season. After graduating, she put her business degree to use and is a Chief Financial Officer at one of the largest Credit Unions in the state. The Boyds are a well-respected family, and that's why I believe they think I'm not good enough to call Quinton my best friend.

But what can I do? I am who I am.

"I can't wait to see what the Boyds bring for their barbecue spread. I wonder if they hired a professional," Mace responds.

"Knowing Mrs. Boyd, I'm sure it's catered with some kind of decorator coming to set up the motorhome and the outdoor tents," Chloe says, standing from her seat. "I'm going to grab a shower while your nails dry, Mace. Meet in your room in an hour, B?"

"Sounds good! I still need to figure out what I'm going to wear. It's going to be hotter than hell today."

Early September in Texas is always hot. Throw in outdoor tailgating and standing in a crowd of a hundred thousand people, and it gets *really* hot.

After an hour, we all met in my room for hair and makeup. The best thing about living with girls is that we all have unique strengths and weaknesses when it comes to getting ready. Now we can all do our own makeup and hair, but it makes it more fun to have girl time and do it for each other. Chloe is the hair goddess, Macy the makeup guru, and I always provide the killer soundtrack.

Macy is a fashion major and each year she makes us custom shirts to wear to the games. She finds vintage shirts, cuts them, and combines them to make unique combinations. For the first game, she found vintage CTU T-shirts, cut them to be tube tops, and sewed elastic in the top and the bottom. This way the shirts would fit snugly on our bodies and would prevent any wardrobe malfunctions. Nobody wants a nip slip. Well... one that isn't intentional.

Our outfits are the same, aside from the colors of the shirts. Chloe is wearing blue to bring out her blue eyes, with white denim shorts, and brown leather sandals. Macy has white to contrast against her tan skin, paired with ripped denim shorts, and red Converse. I'm wearing red to pop with my platinum-blonde hair, opting for a denim skirt, and my new boots.

"You guys! Look what I ordered for this season!" I scream, running to my closet and pulling out my most prized purchase.

I slip on my new Glitz Cream Lucchese Priscilla boots. Walking out of my bathroom, I'm met with squeals from the girls.

"Shut up! Girl, you look amazing!" Macy screams.

I've been talking about buying these boots for a year. Finally, I bit the bullet and put them on my parents' credit card. It's the least they can do since we haven't seen each other in almost a year. If they won't show me their love, they can buy it.

Five years ago, our family dynamic changed. It was never that great, but the events from five years ago nailed the coffin closed. Each year, the time between our communication gets longer and longer. It's been a year since we've seen each other, a year since we've spoken. I didn't even bother flying home for the holidays. They still live in my hometown, a suburb of Chicago, and I'm here in Texas. If one of us needs to communicate with the other, it's done through text or email. As long as they keep the credit card balance cleared, I'll take their bought love. It's fine. I've accepted it.

That's why my relationship with Chloe, Macy, Cody, and Quinton means so much to me. We aren't family by blood, but our love is deeper. And that's what matters to me.

B, enough, we aren't focusing on them today. Today is about you. Today is about the girls. Today is about Quinton.

Shaking my head, I go over to my phone and pair it with my Bluetooth speaker. "Believer" by Imagine Dragons starts playing and all three of us crack open our Coors Lights.

Game Day 2022 has begun!

At a quarter past one, the three of us emerge from my bedroom with our hair and makeup looking fabulous. Grabbing our clear belt bags, we make our way to the parking lot to wait for our Uber driver.

Campus is buzzing.

Cars are trying to park. Students are walking with backpacks that you know are full of beer. Fans are decked out in their red and powder blue Eagles gear. The sun is shining, and even though it's going to be a hot one, I love it.

These are the days I live for. There's nothing better than football in the fall. As excited as I am, the first game always brings with it some sadness. My brother should be here with me. We should be celebrating the first game together. Shotgunning a beer in the parking lot after the game, just like we did in high school. Yeah, yeah, I know, but it's what we did.

The Uber driver stops in front of the Baseball House. There's no more street parking, and the cars behind us are honking. The three of us climb out and head up the sidewalk toward the house. Tables are set up in the yard for Beer Pong and Flip Cup. There's music coming from speakers.

Scanning the yard, I recognize one of the guys playing beer pong. "Isn't that the guy from last week? What was his name?"

Macy looks around before responding, "Gregg. Yeah, that's him."

Stopping abruptly, Chloe grabs Macy's arm. "Wait, you slept with Gregg? Why didn't I know about this?"

Macy shrugs. "It was after the Thirsty Thursday party at the Football House. It wasn't a big deal."

"Small dick?" I ask.

Chloe snorts and Macy glares at me.

"No, it wasn't small. It was just a one-time thing."

"Gregg is relationship material and a serious dater. He doesn't just hook up. If he hooks up, he wants more," Chloe says as we make our way over to the cooler to grab more beers.

"Guess his streak is going to stop with—" Before she can finish her sentence, Gregg interrupts her.

"Hey, Macy! How's it going?" Gregg asks, leaning down and grabbing another beer for himself.

"Hey, Gregg! I can't complain. How about you?" she replies as he pops that tab on his beer, sliding next to her.

And that's my cue to go check out the rest of the party. As much as I'd love to stay and watch Macy get out of that whole situation, I've got people to see and drinks to drink.

Macy is a dater, even though she claims she isn't. She had a boyfriend our freshman year but found out he had been cheating on her the whole six months they were together. Since then, she's decided college isn't for relationships, and guys suck. She's not wrong, but she's a relationship girl. It was hard to see her so defeated and broken after that douchebag.

The inside of the house doesn't look much different than the outside. There are people gathered everywhere. I didn't realize this was going to be such a party before the game. I'm the definition of a party girl, but if *your girl* is going to make it to a seven o'clock game and stay up to, *hopefully*, celebrate a big win with the guys, then I've got to pace myself. Reaching inside my belt bag, I fish out my phone.

> **Me: Are you at your house?**

> **Cody: Yep. Upstairs in the game room. Come up.**

> **Me: Be right there! Need a beer?**

> **Cody: We've got a cooler. Thanks.**

Cody lives with three other guys on the baseball team. Hudson Larsen, centerfielder; Ty Billings, third baseman; and Niko Vega, shortstop. Much like the Football House, they also have a large house and turned their attic into a game room with couches and an eighty-inch TV. Making my way up the two flights of stairs, I push open the door to the attic. Whistles and catcalls fill the room as I enter.

"Goddamn, Brinley Wilder, warn a guy before you enter," Hudson rasps out, choking on his beer. I ignore his reaction.

"Damn, Brynn, you look smokin'," Cody says, pulling me in for a hug as I sit down on the couch next to him.

"Thanks, guys. It's not too much?" I ask, curling into Cody.

Glancing up, I notice the five guys in the room scanning my body from my boots to my face—well, they don't make it up to my face but stop at my boobs.

"Not at all, but if I was Q, I'd never let you out in public," Ty says, finally pulling his eyes from my boobs and back to the game that's playing on TV.

"Why would you think Q has any say in what I do?" I retort.

"You two aren't together?" Ty asks genuinely. He's a new transfer who arrived over the summer from the West Coast.

"Um, no. Just friends."

Before I have a chance to elaborate any further, Cody jumps in. "Yeah, dude, if she was with Q, there's no way I'd be curled up with her like this. Dude would beat my ass. Hell, he still might."

"So why aren't you guys downstairs partying with everyone else?" I ask.

"Shit, if I started this early, I'd be passed out before kickoff," Cody says. "We've got a cooler of beer and water, snacks, and other games to watch until we make our way to the stadium around five."

"Same. I'm hoping there will be a big celebration party somewhere tonight," Hudson adds.

There's no denying the campus is eager for the game tonight. Everyone is hoping for some revenge against The University of Loganville Raiders.

Every year, the college football playoffs come down to the same six or seven teams all vying for their chance to make it to the National Championship game. And for the past three years, we've come up short by either not making it into the playoffs or losing in the first round of playoffs. It's aggravating.

Fans are annoyed. The team is frustrated.

But most of all, the team is hungry for a win.

My seat begins to shake.

Holy shit, is it an earthquake? Wait, does Texas have earthquakes? I don't know my geography.

My body is now moving, and I can feel my heart rate start to increase.

"Brynn? Brynn, wake up," Cody whispers in my ear.

What? Why is Cody whispering in my ear?

Jerking upright, I realize that I'm curled up on Cody's shoulder with my hand... oh god, my hand is on his crotch. "Oh my god," I jerk away. "Did I fall asleep?"

Cody laughs before standing up to stretch. "Yeah, about thirty minutes ago. Your phone chimed and I saw it was Chloe checking on you. I told her you dozed off. She said to let you sleep until it was closer to us leaving."

I stand up and straighten out my clothes.

"I'm so sorry. I can't believe I did that," I answer, embarrassment spreading across my face.

"Brynn, it's fine. Really. I didn't need to go anyway, I was just watching the Georgia game," Cody says.

"Shit, what time is it? Q told his parents we'd be over for their barbecue," I ask, standing up and adjusting my clothes.

"You have plenty of time. I woke you up a few minutes before you girls needed to leave so you could freshen up. Come down to my room and you can use my bathroom." Cody leads the way out of the game room, which I just realize is empty and walks to his room.

Reaching his door, Cody types in the code to get his door unlocked. This is my first time in Cody's room, and it's surprisingly clean. He has a navy comforter and gray sheets. Above his bed is a panoramic view of Truist Park, home of the Atlanta Braves. His desk is organized with textbooks, notebooks, and his MacBook. On his dresser are a few framed pictures that I walk over to check out. I pick up a picture of him with a younger girl. She looks to be about fifteen with long brown hair, hazel eyes that match Cody's, and braces.

"That's Leah, my sister," he says, answering my unasked question. "And the picture next to it is my two buddies from high school. We started playing baseball together when we were six. Now we play against each other."

"It's a cool picture. My brother had a picture on the baseball field with his two best friends like this. It's a special bond," I say, nostalgia taking over my voice. If I don't snap out of it, I'm going to start crying. "Mind if I use your restroom real quick?"

"Go for it, B," he says. "I'm going to change real quick."

Standing at the sink, I take in my appearance in the mirror. Taking a deep breath, I let the memories of Bryce, my twin brother, leave my mind. Searching through Cody's cabinet, I find a bottle of mouthwash. Swishing it around my mouth, I spit it out and have instant fresh breath. Reaching into my bag, I pull out my holy grail of long-lasting lipstick, Maybelline's Innovator, and reapply. This shit is a game changer. Nobody wants red lipstick that smudges or doesn't last a whole night out.

Feeling like myself again, I make my way out of the bathroom. Cody and I head downstairs and reunite with Chloe, Macy, and, surprisingly, Gregg. Hell, who am I kidding? This is not surprising. It's typical Macy. I knew she couldn't go all year without dating.

CHAPTER 5
Brynn

T HE BOYDS KNOW HOW to tailgate. After weaving our way through many tents, we finally found the Boyds' RV. It's a massive blacked-out motorhome with a silver design on the side. Outside of the RV is a party tent with tables, chairs, centerpieces, a TV, and wait—

"Is that a freaking chandelier?" Macy asks, her jaw dropping open.

"The Boyds don't skimp out," I answer, approaching Mr. Boyd. "Mr. Boyd, how are you doing?"

Glancing up from what I presume is his Old Fashioned, Howard Boyd has a powerful presence. At six feet, four inches tall and two-hundred-fifty pounds, with muscles on muscles, he can be intimidating. While I know they're not my biggest fans, I've learned that Mrs. Boyd has a bigger issue with me than Mr. Boyd.

"Brynn," he greets, stretching his arms out for a hug. "How are you doing?"

Stepping into his arms, I give him a warm hug back.

"I'm doing great. It's the first game of the season!" I pause, taking a look around. "It was so kind of you and Mrs. Boyd to invite us to join you for dinner."

"You're always welcome to join us, Brynn. Abigail always plans way too much food for these tailgates. This week, she hired a pitmaster to do our barbecue. Now, you guys go and help yourselves." He gestures toward the door of the motorhome where I know all of the food is prepared. "Oh, and Brynn, it's Howard and Abigail, not Mr. and Mrs. Boyd," he says with a wink, and I just smile back.

Macy, Gregg, Chloe, Cody, and I make our way inside the motorhome, where we are greeted by the delicious aroma of smoked meat. Spread across the large counters are all of the food—brisket, pork ribs, chicken wings, macaroni and cheese, baked beans, coleslaw, cornbread, and an assortment of cupcakes decorated in CTU colors.

"God, it smells so good," Cody says.

"Thank you," I hear Mrs. Boyd respond from behind us.

I feel my body tense and my butthole clench. I was hoping my run-in with Abigail would be after we got our food and were back outside among the crowd. The more people we are around, especially her friends, the friendlier she is, especially when Quinton is not at my side. Turning her gaze to me, Abigail looks me up and down. The disapproval over my outfit radiates off her. That's fine. I don't need her approval.

"Brynn," she greets me. "Howard said you arrived with friends."

"Hi, Mrs. Boyd, thank you so much for extending the invitation to us. You remember my roommates, Macy and Chloe." I gesture to each of the girls as I introduce them. "This is Gregg, Macy's friend, and this is Cody Jacobs—he's on the baseball team."

Mrs. Boyd, Gregg, and Cody exchange pleasantries. "Go ahead and help yourselves, there's plenty. There are coolers under the tent with drinks."

"Thank you," we all respond, grabbing heavy-duty paper plates.

Rumbling. There's rumbling beneath my feet as I make the long descent toward the first row of the student section. The fans are starting to fill Valor Stadium, and the crowd is getting eager.

Eager for kickoff.

Eager for redemption.

Eager for the start of the best time at Central Texas University.

It's a sea of blue and red. Pump-up music blares through the stadium speakers. The cheerleaders are performing stunts, hyping up the rambunctious crowd even more.

And now we wait. Biding our time to hear the band fire up our fight song as our team comes running through the tunnel.

This is the atmosphere I crave.

It's chaos, and it's loud.

It sends chills down my body.

There's nothing better than the first game of the season.

We all make our way down the aisle until we get to the first row. Quinton pulled some strings to get these seats reserved, and I'll love him forever for it. In case he enters the draft early and this is his last season, Q wanted me to have the best seat in the student section to watch him kick some ass. I can't help but notice the girls around us giving us dirty looks. Jealousy does not look good on them.

"We need pictures!" Chloe yells over the crowd.

She turns to the person behind us to have him take our pictures. We all turn our backs to the field, and Chloe pulls Macy and me into her sides for our first set of pictures. The three of us take a variety of photos in different poses. Once the three of us have our fill, it's time for others to join in.

Obviously, we've gotta do it for the 'gram.

Kickoff is about to start. The mini photo shoot took up enough time to run down the clock.

The announcer comes on over the speakers, and we turn our attention to the big screen. A hype video fills the screen as "Humble" plays. The crowd goes wild. As the video ends, the CTU band fires up with the fight song. Next to the tunnel, flames shoot up in the air, and the team comes running out with Quinton, Will, and Tyler—our three Captains—leading the way.

The student section erupts when the team starts running out. It's mayhem. I'm jumping up and down, screaming. I already know that I'm not going to have a voice tomorrow, and I'm perfectly fine with that. Sundays are recovery days, especially since I don't have a class until Monday afternoon.

The White Stripes' "Seven Nation Army" fills the stadium as the Eagles line up for kickoff. All around me, students begin to jump up and down on the bleachers with that all-too-familiar chant as our kicker runs to kick off the football.

Game one of the season is underway.

At the end of the first half, the Eagles are down by a touchdown, and it's fourteen to seven. Quinton scored our only touchdown on a thirty-seven-yard run.

"I'm going to run to the bathroom and grab more beers," I announce, standing to make my way into the halftime crowd.

I don't know why I wait until halftime. It's always packed, but I just can't bring myself to miss any of the game.

"I'll come with," Chloe says.

The line to the bathroom is forever long. I stand there, nursing the remaining beer in my bottle, and listen to the chit-chat surrounding me.

There are girls in dresses, talking about parties and who they want to hook up with tonight.

Older women are eyeing the younger girls in disgust over their conversations about who's sleeping with who. I chuckle to myself, because these women would have a heart attack if they knew what *actually* goes on in college. Hell, they'd die if they knew half the things that I've done in my three years at CTU. College is all about experiencing life before the real world sinks its claws in us and drags us down to a lifeless nine-to-five job and endless responsibilities.

I say "hell yeah" to these girls embracing their sex lives. Women are held to such a high standard. Manners always, and heaven forbid we have sex.

News flash, women have needs too, Linda. It's not all about pleasing our men. Women deserve to be pleased too, dammit. And not by our battery-operated friends. I'm talking about being pleased by a guy who knows what the hell he's doing down there, and not one where you constantly have to remind them "a little to the left."

"Excuse me, are you Brinley Wilder?" a girl asks from behind me.

"Hi, yep, that's me!" I respond, eyeing the girl, and trying to put a name to her face.

I don't recognize the blonde. While I meet a lot of people at parties, I can usually remember a face, even if I can't remember her name.

"Ohmygosh, I thought that was you." With a smile, brighter than the sun, she introduces herself. "I'm Monica. We have psych together with Professor Peters."

Moving with the line, I return her smile, mine more fake than hers. "Oh, hi! I'm sorry I didn't recognize you."

"It's totally fine. I usually sit a couple of rows behind you," she says. "This might be a little bold, but are you dating Cody Jacobs?"

I laugh because, seriously, what is it about being seen with a guy that people immediately think that you're dating.

"Nope, Cody and I are just friends. Why? Are you interested?"

She blushes and places a strand of hair behind her ears. The girl is shy, but it almost feels like an act.

"Um, yes. We've had a few classes together, but I've never talked to him before. I wasn't sure if you two were together, and I didn't want to step in."

Okay, wow, there are not a lot of girls who would have the respect to do that. While I can't grasp how I feel about her, I decide that it's not my decision. Just as I'm about to carry on more of this conversation, a stall opens up.

"Monica, come sit beside me next week, and I'll introduce the two of you!"

Finishing up, I glance at my reflection in the mirror. I tug on my ponytail to fluff it up and give it some more volume. This humidity is killing my hair. Sweat glistens from my face. Thank God glowy skin is in. Making my way out of the bathroom, I find Chloe waiting for me. The two of us make our way to the beer garden to grab more Coors Lights, the classy beer for college students.

CTU's band is just finishing up when we find our seats. Macy looks awfully cozy next to Gregg. So much for Macy not wanting to get serious with a guy and trying to break Gregg's serial dating reputation. I knew she wouldn't be able to go without a relationship this year.

There's a part of me, deep in the back of my mind, that misses being in a relationship. That misses the comfort of one man. But that ship has sailed, and I can't go down that path. Not today and not ever.

The second half begins, and our defense forces Loganville three-and-out, after Jeremiah Prince, our defensive back, secures his second sack of the game. Xavier catches the punt and returns it fifty-five yards to put us in excellent field position. The adrenaline is pumping through my veins, and I've got a feeling that we are going to come out on top.

"E-A-G! L-E-S! EAGLES! EAGLES! EAGLES!" I chant along with the rest of the crowd.

Thanks to a handoff from Tyler Harris to Quinton for a diving three-yard run, the Central Texas Eagles secure their revenge against the Loganville Raiders. Freaking finally!

"Holy shit! Holy shit!" I scream, grabbing ahold of Chloe. "We did it!"

Everyone around us is going crazy. High fives are given as beer sloshes everywhere. We were down by six points with five seconds left. From kickoff to the buzzer sounding at the end of the fourth, it was a thrilling game that had all of us standing, waiting to see what would happen in front of us. Somehow, we were able to pull off the win. All thanks to a crazy diving run by Quinton. Seeing Quinton dive across the goal line was exhilarating, as it showed off his raw athleticism. He looked like Superman flying over the defensive line.

Slowly, excruciatingly slowly, the fans start to retreat back up the stairs on the way to the exit. Before we have a chance to exit our row, a security guard that I recognize from my visits to the stadium approached us.

"Excuse me, Miss Wilder?"

Turning around I smile at Gary. "Hi, Gary! Hell of a win, wasn't it?"

He smiles. "It sure was. Best one I've seen in a while, and I've been here for ages."

"Oh please, Gary, you don't look a day older than twenty-five," I respond with a wink.

"Now, I didn't peg you as a liar," he says, blushing. "I'm sorry to interrupt you, but I was instructed by Mr. Boyd to escort you to the athletic hallway."

A shocked expression slides across my face, because I can't imagine that Mr. and Mrs. Boyd would request my presence after our awkward cookout. "Of course."

Turning to look at my friends, I give them a shrug.

"Want us to wait for you?" Cody asks. "I don't like the idea of leaving you behind."

"I'll be fine, Code," I assure him. Giving him a hug, I whisper in his ear. "Just make sure the girls get back okay. I don't know this Gregg guy."

"I've got 'em, B." He goes to exit our row as the rest of our group follows, giving me hugs as they pass by. Cody turns over his shoulder and calls, "I'll save a shot for you!"

Gary leads me across the wall separating the stands and the field until we get to a gate. He uses his badge to unlock the gate and escorts me down the stairs, across the field, and into the tunnel. I've been down here multiple times, but knowing I've been summoned has a sense of dread crawling up my skin. Weaving our way through the tunnel, we approach the athletic hallway where a few other family members, friends, and girlfriends wait. The girls spot me first and, of course, are the first to give me displeased looks. Of course, Tiffani, a well-known jersey chaser and campus mean girl, is waiting with her girl gang. I wonder whose bed she's warming tonight to end up in the tunnel. To wait outside the locker room, you have to be on an approved list that the players or coaching staff submits. It keeps the jersey chasers at bay. Well, it's supposed to, but Tiffani is here, so obviously not it doesn't keep them all out.

"Quinton asked me to bring you here to wait for him. Tell him I said 'good game,'" Gary says before turning away and leaving me standing in this hallway.

There's not one ounce of me that wants to make conversation with parents or these bitches, so I do the universal signal of 'leave me the hell alone.' I pull out my cell phone.

Roomies

Chloe: What do Q's parents want?

Macy: ^^ Yeah! WTF?

Me: Not Q's parents…Q wanted me to wait for him.

Chloe: Oh…that's strange??

Me: Yep! I have a feeling he doesn't want to be with his parents tonight.

Me: Also, who is Tiffani with?

Macy: Um…

Macy: Will…

Me: WTF???

Chloe: They went home together last night...

Me: Of course they did.

Macy: You okay?

Me: Yeah. It's not like Will and I are anything.

Chloe: She's just looking for a jersey to grasp on to so she can secure her M-R-S degree.

Macy: Chloe... you mean her trophy wife degree?

Me: Guys, stop! I'm smiling like an idiot over here.

Macy: Maybe they'll just assume you're watching porn? *shrug emoji*

Chloe: *laughing emoji*

Chloe: But seriously, you deserve better than Will, B!

Chloe: *kissing emoji*

Will has a reputation on campus. He's a playboy. He hides behind his reputation, putting on this fuckboy personality. Everyone has their secrets and relies on their masks to hide behind.

Me included.

CHAPTER 6
QUINTON

T HE LOCKER ROOM IS hyped. A full freak-out mode. We just beat Loganville for the first time in five years. Damn, it feels great. Fucking fantastic. And the best part is, I scored the winning touchdown. The NFL scouts are going to love that shit.

"Settle down! Settle down! Settle down!" Coach Campbell yells over all our excitement. "Guys, give me five minutes, and then I'll let you have this night to celebrate."

J.P. turns down the music that he had blasting through the speakers, while the rest of us gather around Coach.

"Now, that was one hell of a game. I'm so fucking proud of you boys. You've worked hard all week. You were hungry for a win, and you hunted those Raiders down and persevered to get the W. Defense, you put up a big stop at the end of the fourth quarter that allowed our offense to go out and show Loganville that we are superior. Now, where's Boyd?"

Coach looks around, searching the crowd for me. Grant pushes me toward Coach.

"Boyd, that was one hell of a run! Holy shit, I've seen you jump, but that was top-notch. Not only did you score the game-winning touchdown, but you put up two-hundred-twenty-seven rushing yards."

Everyone starts whooping and hollering before Coach continues.

"Today's game ball goes to you. Keep putting in the work, and it'll keep paying off."

Coach Campbell hands me the game ball and slaps my back.

"That goes for all of you," he continues over the cheers. "This is going to be one hell of a season. Now go celebrate. Don't do anything stupid but go have some fun. Y'all earned it!"

Helmets hit lockers as Harris begins our chant. "Whose house?"

"Our house!" the rest of us yell.

"Whose house?"

"Our house!"

"Eagles on three. One! Two! Three!"

"Eagles!" the team responds as JP hits play on his playlist. "Win" by Jay Rock blares throughout the locker room.

My body is still jittery. The adrenaline is still coursing through my veins. The only way I'm going to settle down is to see Brynn and celebrate at the house. Unlacing my shoulder pads, I watch as some of the guys dance around the locker room. Grant steps up next to me to help pull the tight, sweaty jersey from my hot and sticky body. Removing a jersey post-game is such a process. Once I'm finally free, I toss the jersey into the hamper the team provides. Thank God for team laundry.

I'm going to miss these guys when the season ends if I decide to go pro. It's hard to believe how fast these three years are going. I know there are always going to be other teams and teammates, but there's something special about the bond we've formed here.

Xavier breaks my train of thought. "You going to see Mom and Dad?"

Barely making any eye contact with him, I answer with a strong, "Nope."

My relationship with my parents is a roller coaster. I know they both love me, but sometimes they're just suffocating. My brothers and I are gifted at football, but I'm the only one of us who has had college scouts stalking me since high school. Both of my parents want me to skip my senior year of college and enter the draft. Skipping my senior year was never my goal. Truth is, I like school and I want to finish my degree. If the cards line up for the possibility that I go first round, then I'll consider it. I'd be stupid not to. But it's going to be my decision to make.

Dad enjoys the attention that comes with having a son 'follow in his footsteps' and Mom wants me to find some hoity-toity princess to have on my arm. That's not my style. Damien didn't even play after high school. And while Xav is good, he's only a sophomore, and he's got a lot of work to do.

And for some unknown reason, my mom doesn't approve of Brynn, and that shit isn't going to fly.

"What am I supposed to tell them?" Xavier asks, not taking the hint that this is the last thing I want to talk about. I don't want this high to fade.

Wrapping a towel around my waist, I finish stripping my boxers off. I grab my shower stuff and start walking toward the shower before turning over my shoulder.

"I don't give a shit what you tell them. Tell them I'm going to celebrate my fucking win without their goddamn nagging."

Making the walk into the showers, I find an open stall. Stepping into the shower, I remove my towel and turn on the water. Standing under the faucet, I let the hot water beat against my skin. Every muscle aches, and I could use an ice bath and a massage, but I'm not sticking around for that shit tonight. Tonight's party will have plenty of willing participants to rub down my body. Grabbing my all-in-one wash, I scrub the sweat, dirt, and grime off my body.

Toweling off, I make my way back to my locker, and slip on a fresh pair of boxer briefs. Grabbing my navy joggers and powder-blue long-sleeve, I get dressed. Coach requires us to wear suits when we arrive, but team apparel is acceptable when we leave. Thank God. Putting on a suit is the worst after a game.

"Party at your house, Q?" Riggsby asks, slapping a hand on my shoulder.

I give a sly grin before responding, "Hell yeah! Baseball guys are getting it set up."

The baseball team and some of the football players have worked out a system that whenever one of us wins a big game, the other sets up the party. Attending a big campus like this has its perks. There's always some wannabe DJ who is down to spin some tracks. All our parties are BYOB because we're not paying for kegs and being responsible for others. It's bad enough that we've got to be somewhat responsible since we host. A few of the backup linemen play security guards at our parties to keep the crowd under control. Fighting isn't tolerated unless it's deserved, but really, it's not tolerated.

The locker room begins to empty out. Everyone is ready to celebrate. As I get closer to the door, I hear voices rising from outside the door.

What the fuck?

"So which one of your many men are you waiting for tonight?" a girl asks in a high-pitched, Valley Girl voice.

It's a voice I can easily recognize as Tiffani's. She's the campus mean girl. Not only is she a major jersey chaser, but she's a cleat chaser, puck bunny, or whatever gets her closer to one of us athletes.

"Will," I hear Brynn quip back.

Like hell she is waiting on that prick, especially after I heard him bragging about his night with Tiffani before the game.

Turning the corner, I spot Brynn leaning against the wall. Her body is on full display and looking like sin in that red crop top, and denim skirt that barely covers her ass and makes her legs look even longer, especially with those white cowboy boots.

Goddamn, she's trouble.

Tiffani scoffs, but before she can respond, Brynn continues. "Oh no, wait, I heard you've moved on to my sloppy seconds." Continuing, she looks Tiffani in her eyes. "I guess it's time for me to choose from other available men." Brynn rolls her eyes at Tiffani and her attempt to slut-shame her.

"It's amazing you haven't passed a disease around campus," Tiffani replies in disgust, which is rich coming from her.

Will is in front of me, taking in the scene. He must have put Tiffani on the list after their hook-up last night. And a few feet from Brynn stand my parents, who I did not put on the approved list. Dammit, Xavier. This is not going to go well.

"Well, if I'm crawling with diseases, enjoy my leftovers. Now move along, I don't have time for you." Brynn gives her the brush off by pulling her phone out of her back pocket like she doesn't have a care in the world.

Only deep down, I know she cares. There is nothing wrong with the way Brynn lives her life. If she were a guy, she'd be constantly getting high fives. Hell, every guy in our locker room is getting high fives and constant praises over our conquests. Body counts are the new football stat.

Fucking double standards.

And Will just stands there, letting Tiffani attack Brynn, knowing damn well who Brynn is. I mean, Jesus, he was just with her the week before.

As that thought leaves my mind, Tiffani turns and sees Will. She runs and jumps in his arms, causing Brynn to roll her eyes.

"Baby, great game!" she squeals, and we are lucky there aren't any windows around to break. Will places Tiffani back down on her feet, and the two of them take off, hand in hand, with Tiffani's minions following close behind. I'm just about to approach Brynn when Tiffani turns back over her shoulder. "Q, you might want to double wrap it before you jump in bed with that." She says, her nose wrinkling in disgust.

"Bitch," Brynn mutters, but not quiet enough for my parents to miss.

I hear my mom gasp. I take a deep breath because I know I'm going to hear about this later.

"Really, Brinley?" my mother hisses. "It's appalling, the way you talk."

Turning her attention to my mom, I can see the smoke coming out of Brynn's ears.

Throwing her arms out in exasperation, Brynn claps back. "You stood right here and enjoyed the show of her running her mouth about me."

Making her way over to me, my mother gets closer to Brynn before saying something that shocks even me. "Well, Brinley, your reputation certainly implies that you should visit the health clinic more often. Thank God, my baby is smart enough not to go crawling in bed with you."

"Mom—" I cut in just as my dad says, "Abigail."

But the damage has been done. Brynn turns and storms off toward the exit. That's when I notice that even more players have filed out of the locker room to watch the shit show unfold. I turn to see Grant give me a sad, knowing look. He knows that I feel more for Brynn than I let on.

Without even acknowledging my parents, I turn and go after Brynn. I hear my mom yell my name, but there's no way in hell I'm choosing her over Brynn. Not after all that.

"B, wait up," I yell after her.

She stops with her back to me, waiting for me to catch up.

"I'm sorry about my mom."

I sling my arm around her shoulder, pulling her into my side. Leaning down, I kiss the side of her head. She's quiet, and I know she's processing. She allows me to lead her through the exit to the staff and player parking lot.

I swear, if my night is fucked, I'm going to go off on every single person who mouthed off to Brynn. All I want to do is celebrate a win with my friends. A win that I fought hard to get. A win that *I made* happen. But nope, they've got to constantly fuck up everything good that happens to me and make it about themselves.

"Q, just give me a minute. I need to breathe."

She pulls away from my grasp and reaches into her bag and pulls out her vape pen. Bringing it up to her mouth, she wraps her lips around the tip and sucks. My body twitches as I watch her. It's getting harder and harder to ignore my body's reactions to Brynn.

"Oh yeah, and that's the way to breathe," I mutter, giving her the space she asked for.

"Don't start with me, Quinton."

She takes another inhale on her pen before she starts walking toward my blacked-out Tesla Model S. Following her, I get to her side of the car first and open the door.

"I know, B. I'm so fucking sorry for that. That's not why I invited you down to the hallway."

Leaning down to get in the car, Brynn looks up at me through her long eyelashes. She looks so fucking good today. I finally get a chance to fully check her out. A tight, distressed denim skirt, a barely there crop top that has my number on the back, and those boots. Goddamn, those boots. I can imagine what those white boots would look like wrapped around my dark skin.

Fuck, get a grip, Q.

"I'm not mad at you, Quinton." She tilts her head toward my seat, her crimson red stained lips smiling up at me. "C'mon. Let's go celebrate."

Closing her door, I make my way around to the driver's side of the car. Opening the door, I slide into my seat and start up the car. "Goosebumps" erupts through the speakers. It was the last song I was listening to on my phone, and, thanks to the Bluetooth, it starts right up.

"Want to grab Whataburger?" I shout over the music.

Brynn looks over at me with a smirk that I swear makes my blood rise. "Do I want to grab food from Whataburger? Q, c'mon, you know that answer."

Whataburger it is.

An hour later, both of us are stuffed from our meal and pulling into the garage of my house. I'm surprised I was able to get into the driveway with the crowd that's gathered. People are spilling from the house, taking residence in our yard and surrounding yards.

As I'm opening my car door, Brynn grabs my arm before I'm able to climb out. "I didn't get a chance to tell you earlier, thanks to the shit show in the hallway, but I'm so proud of you Quinton. Great game tonight." She leans over the center console, giving me a very awkward hug and kiss on the cheek.

It might have been an awkward angle, but I'll take it. There's nothing I love more than this girl. She's my best friend. She makes me happy, makes me laugh, and drives me absolutely crazy. I hate that her night was ruined by comments that don't fit her.

Flinging open her door, she jumps out, taking off running toward the garage door, yelling, "Last one inside has to take a shot."

My lips turn up in a smile, and my Brynn is back to herself.

Letting her win, I enter the door as cheers erupt from the partygoers. The DJ flips the track to "Mo Bamba," and I see Brynn standing next to the kitchen counter, surrounded by Chloe, Macy, Cody, Riggsby, and a few others, with a shot glass in her hand.

This girl is going to be the death of me.

Cody pours everyone else a shot of tequila - *Lord help us all.*

Raising our glasses, Cody starts chanting "E-A-G L-E-S" while the rest of us chant "Eagles! Eagles! Eagles!" and down our shot.

The night is a blur. Girls are all over me, drinks are flowing, colored lights flash around us, and the party is wild. I lost sight of Brynn and her friends a while ago. I'm surprised I'm still standing. Well, I guess I'm leaning against the wall, but I'm still upright, so that still counts.

The dance floor is packed with sweaty bodies gyrating against each other. Glancing around, I see a few of the guys. Meeting each of their gazes, we tilt our heads in a bro nod.

"Q," one of the girls, Keisha, I think is her name, whines in my ear. She's one of the girls that's nestled up to my side. "Asia and I want to know if you're ready to go up to your room...maybe do some celebrating together?"

She looks up at me with pouty eyes and a seductive smirk. Her friend inches closer.

Glancing around, I spot Brynn and Will grinding against each other on the dance floor. Internally, I roll my eyes. They have the most fucked up relationship, friendship, whatever you want to call it, but Brynn's a big girl.

Wrapping my other arm around the second girl, I lead them both over to the stairs. As soon as we make it up to my room, both girls start exploring my body.

Tonight, I'm going to celebrate with these lovely ladies.

CHAPTER 7
Brynn

The next couple of weeks seem to fly by. October is officially here. Classes are starting to get busier, homework is starting to pile up, and I'm finding myself in the library a lot more than normal.

After the first home game, the next three games have been away, which means I've barely seen any of the guys from the football team, including Quinton.

Am I avoiding him? I wouldn't say yes but I wouldn't say no.

Rumors circulated that he had quite the threesome during the first game celebrations. While I'm far from a prude, obviously—Tiffani and Mrs. Boyd calling me a whore ring any bells? —Q having a threesome shocked the hell out of me.

I don't even know why.

Maybe because he just fucking dropped me at the party and disappeared. One minute I'm dancing on the dance floor, the next minute Will's hands are gripping my hips as he sidles behind me, pulling me closer for a dance. The whole time we were dancing, he admitted that he had Tiffani waiting on him to make me jealous. Will isn't happy with our 'friends with benefits' situation and wants to take things to the next step.

Why? Why do people have to change a good thing?

By the time Will and I were finished with our conversation, Q had disappeared. Which is ridiculous for me to be upset about. I'm a big girl, for god's sake. I don't need Quinton by my side the whole damn night.

Ugh, why am I being so dramatic?

Is my period coming?

Yeah, now that I think about it, that bitch Flo is about to make her appearance.

But also, *don't ever be late Flo, please and thank you!*

Studying has never been an issue for me. Surprisingly, I get good grades. I enjoy school, and I enjoy writing papers. There's just something so calming about sitting down with my AirPods, lighting a candle, drinking endless amounts of coffee, and letting words fly from my fingers.

It used to be easy to sit at the townhouse and focus on homework, but lately, it's a distraction. Macy is officially dating Gregg and they bang 24/7.

Ah, that new relationship bliss.

Don't get me wrong, I'm happy for my bestie, but damn, take a fucking break to come up for air every now and then. But according to Macy, it's the best dick she's ever had, and I'm not about to be a cockblock.

Then there's the whole "sitting in my room" issue. My mind is constantly wandering about being back home, especially with October thirteenth getting closer. Five years later, and that date still gets to me.

This is why I've been choosing to let Wednesday nights be my late night on campus to work on any homework. Nothing happens on Wednesdays. Mondays are for Monday Night Football on TV. Tuesdays are Taco Tuesdays at the Mexican restaurant. Thursdays are Thirsty Thursdays. And then, it's the weekend, which means endless football.

Leaving the Student Union, where I grabbed a quick bite to eat—burger and fries—I begin my trek to the library. Why is it that the library is the farthest building on campus? Wouldn't most schools put it right in the center of campus to encourage students to do their studying? Nope, not at Central Texas University.

Walking along the concrete sidewalk, I let the songs coming through my AirPods lull me into a trance. The campus is busy for it being six o'clock in the evening. Groups of students are gathered on the sidewalks. A handful of students are speed-walking to get to class on time. The trees on campus are slowly starting to change colors as fall weather is taking her sweet time getting here. Being from Chicago, I miss the changing of leaves, but Texas doesn't get the memo like the Midwest.

Still lost in my head, I don't notice the large person standing in front of me until I nearly run into him. Quinton grabs ahold of my arms to keep me from running completely into him. Jumping in panic, I remove one side of the AirPods.

"Jesus, Q, I didn't even see you there."

He laughs. "No shit, Brynn. Where the hell were you just now?"

Tucking a piece of hair that had fallen from my claw clip behind my ears, I chew on the inside of my cheek before answering. "I was thinking about Chicago."

A knowing look passes Quinton's face. Even though Quinton is my best friend, there are still some parts of my life that I've kept hidden from him. I know it's shitty, believe me. I know that, if I'm going to call someone my best friend, then I need to be open and honest with him. But there are some parts to our stories that are just plain hard to talk about.

"Are you heading in to study?" I ask, gesturing toward the library.

Still staring at me with a sympathetic look, which I freaking hate, it takes him a second before he answers. "Yeah, some of the guys are meeting for a study sesh, per Coach's orders." Rolling his eyes he continues, "Some dumbasses are letting their grades slip, so now we all have mandatory study sessions. It's bullshit."

Both of us turn toward the library doors, and we finish our short walk to the entrance. Quinton opens the door wide for me to enter before following me.

"That sucks. But at least you get your work done."

Even after three years of attending Central Texas and visiting the library a handful of times, I'm still amazed at the pure beauty that makes up The Benjamin Liberty Library. The Liberty Library is original to the campus with beautiful brick craftsmanship. The east wall has a variety of stained-glass windows that give the building such a classic look. Vintage chandeliers take over the ceiling, casting a warm and inviting glow. The center of the main room is completely open to the ceiling, with tables for studying and a large antique desk that the head librarian sits behind. Around the sides of the library are floors housing books on different topics. On each floor, you can find individual cubbies, small group tables, and rooms that can be reserved.

Once again, I let my mind take over as I look around, soaking in the glorious library. I don't even realize that I have stopped walking until Quinton whisper-yells my name.

Shaking my head, I face Q again. "Sorry," I add, catching up to where he's standing off to the side of the stairs.

He's standing there eyeing me up and down, and it's at that moment that I know he knows I've been avoiding him. "Seriously, B, what the fuck is going on?"

Bypassing him, I start walking up the stairs, but he's right on my heels. "Nothing is wrong. I'm fine."

Placing my hand on the handrail, I make sure to let it help guide me up the stairs. No one wants to cause a scene and trip walking up a flight of stairs in a quiet library.

It'd be so embarrassing...no, it'd definitely be embarrassing. I made that mistake freshman year, thinking I was so cool and could just walk up the stairs without the handrail. I didn't realize that my tennis shoes had come untied until I tripped over the laces and ate it. It was loud, and everyone on the first floor turned to the stairs to see what had happened. Oh, you know, just a clumsy idiot freshman falling on her face, no big deal.

Changing the subject, I stop on a landing and ask, "What floor is your study room?"

"Fourth floor," Quinton responds.

Turning to continue walking up the stairs, I let him lead the way, deciding to study on the same floor. Moving off the stairs, I weave my way through bookcases until I find a single cubby outside Quinton's study room. Before he moves past me, Q stops and wraps his arms around me. Just that connection makes me want to cry.

Seriously, screw you, Flo. You're making me a weak bitch, and I hate it.

"Love ya, B," he whispers before leaving me alone.

Settling in at the desk, I open up my backpack and pull out my MacBook, planner—yes, paper planners are far superior to digital—and my psychology textbook. Reaching into my pocket, I grab my AirPods and turn on my alternative study playlist. "Ophelia" fills my ears, and I zone out the world.

After what feels like forever, I've written a paper for my social psychology class, and I've completed my reading for *Psychology of Personality*. Glancing down at the clock in the right-hand corner of my screen, I realize I've been here for almost two hours. Seriously, that flew by.

Pulling up my email, I want to double-check that I'm caught up before my Thursday classes. There's an email from my mother. Thinking back on it, I haven't heard from my mother since the middle of summer.

Do I open it now? Or do I wait?

Ugh, just get it over with Brynn.

Hovering over her email address, I decided to just rip off the Band-Aid and open it.

To: brinley.wilder@ctu.edu

From: carolynwilder@cabotpres.com

Subject: Five Years

Brinley,

*The fifth anniversary is approaching. Your presence is **required** Friday, October 14 through Sunday, October 16, as the high school is doing a tribute. We **must** be a united family front and I **expect** you to be there.*

*See attached for your flight information and let me know **ASAP** if this works for your schedule.*

-Dr. Carolyn Cabot-Wilder

I reread the email. And for shits and giggles, two more times. The nerve of that woman to require that I attend some bullshit ceremony and look like we are a loving family. That ship sailed five freaking years ago. Even before that, a happy family was far from what we were. The only people happy in that family were Bryce and me.

Not only does she require my presence, but not once does she even ask how I'm doing. The audacity. This shouldn't surprise me. It's typical Carolyn Cabot-Wilder.

Sitting here, I can feel my blood pressure rise and my chest tighten. The anxiety is creeping in. Not only does dealing with my mother bring out the bad in me, but she's so nonchalant with it being the fifth anniversary. How can she be so cold?

You know what, let her sweat it. I'll reply to her later. Slamming my laptop shut and shoving it in my backpack, I quickly gather all of my things before storming down the library stairs.

Moving through all the students, I'm in a daze as I make my way from the library to the opposite side of campus where my car is parked. Fuming, I cannot get over how cold this woman has become. There used to be good times with my parents before the shit hit the fan, and our lives were changed. Right?

"Mommy, Mommy!" I call out. Closing the front door, I began searching our large house for her. "Kitchen, Brinley." I hear her voice from the back of the house.

Running, I make my way into the kitchen where the smell of freshly baked cookies greets me. Standing in front of the oven, placing freshly baked sugar cookies on a cooling rack, is my mom. She's still dressed in her scrubs from work, and her hair is tossed haphazardly in a messy bun at the top of her head. Mommy looks tired, and her smile doesn't quite meet her eyes, but I know she's excited to see me.

Pushing a bar stool next to her, I climb up and reach out to grab a cookie. With a 'thwack,' my mother gently smacks my hand with the spatula.

"They just came out of the oven, baby."

"But sugar cookies are my favorite," I whine.

Leaning down, my mother places a big kiss on my forehead. "There's some sugar to hold you over." We laugh. "Now where is your brother?"

Shaking my head, I push the memory out of my mind. That was the last time I remember my mother baking cookies for Bryce and me. We were seven. Any other time we wanted cookies, we would have to ask Isabella, our housekeeper, to put a request in with the chef. Because shortly after, my mother was promoted to chief resident at our family's hospital, Cabot Presbyterian.

Finding my polar white Mercedes Coupe and placing my thumb on the door handle to unlock it, I climb inside. I let my body relax against the black leather as I reach inside the center console for my vape pen. Bringing the pen to my lips, I take a long drag, letting the inhale expand my lungs. Holding the vapor in, I close my eyes before releasing a long plume of vapor. Before I think about it, I'm bringing the pen back to my lips for a few more deep inhales.

In and out. In and out.

The act slowly brings my body into a state of relaxation.

Why did I let her get to me? Why are they having a tribute and making this whole situation another publicity stunt?

Thinking of the tribute only brings me pain. And the sense of peace is now gone. Pushing the automatic start, I switch my playlist over to my 'in my feels' playlist. "I Think I'm Okay" by MGK and YUNG-BLUD blasts through the speakers. Reversing out of the parking spot, I start my ten-minute journey back to the townhouse.

During the drive, my phone continues to notify me of text messages. The alerts coming through my speakers every two to four minutes are really annoying.

Can't people take a hint? If I don't respond right away, I'm not interested in talking.

The parking lot of the townhouse complex is surprisingly not full, and I'm able to score a parking spot close to our unit. Putting the car in park, I climb out and sling my backpack on my shoulders. I can see the lights are on at home, and I can't decide if I'm happy to have my roommates home to distract me, or if I just want to wallow in self-pity alone.

Storming into the house, the door slams behind me. Three heads whip in my direction from the couch—Chloe, Macy, and Gregg. Not bothering to acknowledge them, I go straight to the kitchen. Alcohol is calling my name.

"Woah, you look like shit," Chloe calls from the couch.

My middle finger flies in the air instead of a response. Digging through the fridge, which needs to be cleaned out, I grab a Coors Light. Shutting the door, I make my way back into the living room where sounds of one of the *Housewives* shows fill the room. Plopping down in the armchair, I swing my legs over the side and make myself comfortable.

"It's cute she's already got you whipped enough to watch the *Housewives*," I snark, taking a long pull of my beer.

"Someone's in a bitchy mood tonight. Not getting laid enough this week?" Macy quips back.

Staring at the TV, I add, "Nope, it's about to be shark week, and I got an email from my mom."

"That explains the mood," Chloe adds.

Silence ensues in the room as we watch the housewives fight, and one of them flips over a table. Seriously, why is someone always destroying dinner, especially when there's hired help at the dinner party?

Wouldn't that be so embarrassing to show your ass in front of the help?

For the next half hour, I find myself zoned out staring at the TV, nursing my beer.

"Brinley, you ungrateful, spoiled brat," she says, and I roll my eyes. It's two forty-five in the morning, and I'm just coming in from another party. You would think that, given what happened six months ago, a party would be the last place I'd be, but we all grieve in our own way.

"Look who decided to be a mother," I crack, slurring my words. "Did you finally remember that you still have a child?"

Smack. Her hand flies across my cheek. I can't even say that I'm shocked. Did I deserve to be smacked? Probably. Am I surprised she did it? No.

Carolyn Cabot-Wilder is the picture of the perfect woman. She's climbed the ladder at the hospital. No surprise there since it's our family's "legacy," a legacy I have absolutely no desire to continue. Even if I wanted a career in the medical field, being under the scrutiny of the Cabot name is a big fat "fuck no." She wears her fitted dress with her perfectly poised attitude while clutching her precious pearls. But what most people don't know is that Carolyn is a ticking time bomb.

Every woman in this society has her secrets.

And Carolyn Cabot-Wilder has many.

"Did that make you feel good, Mother?" I ask, rubbing my cheek. "Does it make you feel powerful to hit your daughter?"

"Do you really think you're the first daughter to be slapped? Get over yourself, Brinley," she scoffs. "It's about time for you to grow up and

start preparing to join your family's legacy. Lucky for you, you've got two legacies to choose from."

I laugh, actually laugh, at the audacity of this woman.

"Please Mother, like I'd join either one of the family legacies." Making my way to the fridge, I pull out a water bottle and start guzzling the ice-cold liquid. "Do I take after the adultering mother and her many conquests? Or the crooked politician who floats to whichever side has the most money?"

"Speak ill about your father or myself one more time young lady and see where that gets you. We will not allow you to disgrace our family's reputation any longer," she snarls.

"Bryce lucked out," I whisper.

"Why couldn't it have been you?" she mutters, knowing it was loud enough for me to hear. And, oh how she hit her target with that shot.

On the six-month anniversary of losing my brother, my twin, and my best friend, I lost the remaining respect for my mother. I was hurting. I just wanted to feel loved. And she told me she wished I was the one to have died in that accident, not her son.

That night, I lay in my bed, wearing my brother's favorite hoodie and cried myself to sleep. I dreamed of more time together. Of the time I fell and cut my leg. Bryce sat next to me with his arm wrapped around me, wiping my tears, just like I wished he would do for me tonight.

Only this time, in my memory, I can feel him.

I feel him wrapping his arm around me. I feel him brushing the tears from my cheek with his thumb. I hear him trying to console me. "Wilder!"

Wait...Bryce never called me Wilder.

"Wilder! Wilder, stop crying. Hey, Wilder."

Waking up, I look over to find Quinton squatting in front of me. He lifts me up from my spot on the armchair before taking my place and pulling me tight against his chest. I was so lost in my memory that I didn't even hear him come in.

Wait, how did he even get in?

Scanning the room, I realize that the space is empty aside from me and Quinton. The Housewives are still on the TV, but everyone else is gone. Clutching Q's shirt, I pull him close to me as the tears continue to fall. Quinton doesn't say anything. He lets me cry, rubbing my back and whispering consoling words.

"What the fuck happened, Brynn?" Quinton mutters. "I saw you take off in the library. I've been trying to call and text you, but you won't respond. What's going on?"

Leaning up, I wipe the tears from my face. Pulling my hands away, I see that they're streaked with the black mascara that's running down my cheeks.

Jesus, I'm a freaking mess.

Looking up, I ask, "Why are you here?"

"Why am I here? For fuck's sake, Brynn, it's me. After you stormed out and didn't respond, I texted Chloe." He stares at my tear-stained face. "You blew past Cody in the quad. He said you looked like a ghost and didn't even acknowledge him when he said your name."

"I didn't even see him," I mutter.

"No shit, you didn't. He said you looked like you were in a trance, so he texted me to see what was wrong with you. That freaked me out more. All I kept thinking about was you drivin' home in a trance, wrapping your damn car around a pole." Taking a breath, he continues. "Then I show up here, and you're staring at the TV, sobbing. Brynn, you don't cry. At least, I've never seen you cry. Stop avoiding me, and fucking talk to me."

Shock eclipses my face as I look up at him.

"Yeah, I know you've been avoiding me. That's somethin' else we need to talk about, but I need to know you're okay."

Clearing my throat, I look away toward the window. Still staring out the window, I feel around the chair, and under the pillow for my vape. Feeling the hard pen touch my fingers, I pull it out from behind the pillow and bring it to my lips. I start to inhale, but it's batted out of my hand.

"What the fuck, Quinton?"

"Don't *what the fuck me.*' Quit using that thing as a crutch to avoid talking."

Groaning, I force myself out of his grasp and up off his lap.

"Don't come to my house, demand I talk to you, and lecture me. You're not my parents."

"Thank God for that. They suck," he quips.

"Yeah, they do."

"That's what it is, isn't it?" Quinton stands and walks over to me. "Brynn, what did they do now?"

Sighing, I stand there with my arms crossed, looking up at Quinton. I can see the worry lines etched across his face. There aren't many days where we fight. Sure, we have days where we bicker, but that's because we spend too much time together. He knows my likes and dislikes, my quirks, that I can eat as many wings as most men on the football team. He knows my secrets—well, most of them—my fears, my dreams, and my ambitions.

While he knows most of my secrets, he doesn't know everything. Some things in my past are just hard to talk about. It was ingrained in me at a young age that what happens in our family, stays in our family. Not only could it hurt my dad's political career, but it could hurt the precious family legacies. Our family legacies not only affected my brother, my parents, and me, but all of our relatives, the generations before us, and the ones to come. Secrets are what keep our family mighty.

"I have to go home next week. It was *demanded*, not requested."

"Okay," he drags out, not quite getting what the big deal is.

Inhaling, I continue. "The high school is doing a tribute during the football game. Then on Saturday attend some kind of formal event. That was all the information I got." Pausing, I run my fingers through my tangled hair. "She sent me a fucking email after not hearing from her in almost four months."

I can see the moment it clicks, and he looks down at me. "Five years."

"Five years," I sigh.

Quinton pulls me in for a hug. He drags his hand up my back and starts rubbing the turtledove tattoo I have on the back of my neck.

"You're lucky," he says.

Jerking my head up, I look at him in shock. After everything I just said, I can't believe he just said that to me. He just grins.

"We have a bye week. There's no way in hell I'm letting you go alone."

"Thank you, Quinton."

"Anything for you, Wilder." He squeezes me before releasing me from his grip.

It's in this moment, with his arms wrapped around me, I'm clued into how different this hug feels. This hug isn't a brotherly hug. In fact, if I let myself accept the truth, his hugs have never felt brotherly. The heat between us is rising within me, like lava about to erupt, as he holds me, caressing my skin with his gentle touch.

What if I look up? Will I find him looking down at me? Would his eyes be darkened with lust? Would my own desire be reflected back? And where did these feelings come from?

With his grip released, I take a much-needed step back. Shit just got way too serious. With a pep in my step, I turn toward the kitchen.

"Ice cream and a movie?"

"Grab the ice cream, and I'll go up and pick something," Quinton answers, giving my butt a love tap as he bypasses me.

Startled, I jump in surprise at his contact. Fire spreads throughout my body.

The rest of the night is spent lying in bed with my best friend, watching *Anchorman*, eating ice cream, and laughing.

It felt good to have the old Q and B back, laughing our asses off, and quoting a movie we've seen too many times to count.

CHAPTER 8
QUINTON

"**H**ELL OF A GAME today, boys!**" Coach calls from the front of the locker room. "It feels pretty damn good to be five and oh!"

Cheers and hoots erupt.

Truth is, it does feel pretty damn good to be undefeated. Our season is halfway over, and next weekend is a bye week.

"It's a bye week. While we don't have a game, there are still some things that we need to work on. But, if we work hard this week, I'm prepared to give you Friday through Sunday off from practices. Just do some kind of workout on your own. Check your emails for the updated practice schedule for the week. Now, hit the showers and get the hell out of here."

More cheers come from the team. Turning to my locker, I strip out of my uniform and grab my toiletry bag. The game was an early one, which means we have the rest of the day to kick back.

"What's the plan for the day, Q?" Grant Campbell asks, following me toward the showers.

I enter my stall, turning on the faucet to let the water heat up.

"No idea, man. I think I'm just gonna chill." Standing under the faucet, I let the hot water pour over my body. I'm starting to feel some aches and pains. I need to meet with the team's PT for a good full-body massage. There's still a lot of season left, and I can't get injured.

Yesterday, I had a call with my agent Eliza. She likes to call every couple of weeks with an update on the draft. Even if she doesn't have anything major to talk about, she still likes to check in and let me know that she's watching my games and recognizes the year I'm having.

It's nice to have these kinds of conversations with her.

The firm that Eliza works for is based out of New York, and they are pretty amazing. Some of my previous teammates had put me in contact with them, and it's nice to know that my dad didn't find them for me. He tried to push me on a firm that I knew was just going to kiss his ass, do whatever he wanted, and not what I wanted. That's why I chose to work with Eliza.

At our first meeting, my parents came, of course. When Dad started to showboat and talk about himself, Eliza put him in his place, telling him this meeting wasn't to discuss a former athlete, but the potential of someone who's going to be bigger and better than him. He shut up real quick, sitting with his arms folded, pouting, the rest of the meeting. A tiny smile had my lips turned up the remainder of our appointment.

That was the day I signed my contract to work with Eliza. I didn't need to hear anything else during that meeting. If a woman, a woman barely over five feet no less, could stand up to Howard Boyd, I knew I needed her in my corner.

She hasn't let me down once.

"Quinton, mate, things are looking good this year!" she exclaims on the phone in her thick Australian accent.

"Thanks, Eliza," I reply. "What all have you been hearing?"

Pacing around my bedroom, I can't help but let my mind wander.

Going pro has been a dream for as long as I can remember. As a boy, my dream was to be like my dad. What boy doesn't look up to his dad? Then in junior high, I fell in love with the dream even more. As a sophomore, college scouts started coming to more and more games. I always thought it was a favor to my dad, until I realized that I actually had the potential to go pro.

That was all on me. Not my dad. My numbers spoke for themselves. I kept my head to the turf, got good grades, and busted my ass.

Interrupting my thoughts, Eliza continues. "Mate, I'm tellin' ya, things are lookin' good. First round, good. Especially at the pace you're going."

"Damn, Eliza. Are you serious?" *I ask in disbelief, rubbing a hand down my face.*

"Darlin', I don't joke," *she says.*

Eliza is tough. She has to be tough to work with hard-headed, arrogant athletes. I don't think I've ever heard her crack a joke, or hell, even laugh. She's as professional as they come.

"Let's just say, your top three teams are looking at you."

"Holy shit," *I mutter as she continues.*

"That's all I've got. Just wanted to check in and letcha know you're doing a great job."

Shaking my head in disbelief, the reality starts to sink in. There's a really good chance I'm selected early in the first round for one of my dream teams.

"Thanks, Eliza. Talk soon." *She disconnects the call without a goodbye.*

"Yo, Q," Grant yells from the stall next to me. Lost in the memory of yesterday's phone call, I had completely zoned out. Eliza is the only one I can talk to about the draft. Making the decision to stay or go has been incredibly difficult. I know I'll have the support of my teammates and coaches, but the truth is, I'm not ready to announce. I want the focus to be on this season, not next season. For now, I'm keeping this secret between me and Eliza.

Rinsing the soap off my body and grabbing my towel, I dry off before wrapping the towel around my waist and stepping out.

"Sorry, man." I step out of the stall with my toiletry bag in hand, getting out of the way for the next guy. "What were you saying?"

Grant chuckles. "I was saying, Dad and I are heading to Arizona over the bye weekend to see my sister. She hasn't been home since Christmas, so Dad and I are going to surprise her."

"Surprising her? Dude, is that a good idea?"

Reaching my locker, I slip on my boxer briefs, tossing the towel across the room to the laundry bin.

He just chuckles before responding. "I tried to tell Dad that, but he doesn't see what the problem could possibly be."

I'll never understand why people surprise others. Nobody likes to have someone show up out of the blue, or have people jump out and shout at them. Growing up, I hated going to surprise parties. Once in elementary school, a classmate had a surprise party. The kid was terrified of his own shadow, but his parents thought it'd be a great idea to invite his whole class to a surprise party. He shows up, we all jump out yelling "surprise," and the poor kid pissed his pants, right there in front of the whole class. He never lived that shit down. People still talked about it through high school. No thanks.

"You have plans for next weekend?" Grant asks.

Both of us finish dressing and turn to walk out of the locker room.

"Yeah, I'm going to Chicago with Brynn. She's got some family stuff at home, and her parents suck. No way in hell I'm letting her deal with them on her own."

Grant just looks at me.

We've been buddies since the beginning, when both of us lived in the same dorm on campus. Our rooms were next to each other. Whenever we had down time, we were chilling together. Madden tournaments on our floor were weekly occurrences. He chose not to live in the Football House our sophomore year, opting to rent a townhouse in the same complex that Brynn lives in.

Last year, after a wild party, I might have drunkenly confessed my feelings for Brynn to Grant. Yeah, I spilled all the dirty details. Mostly, that I have more than friendly feelings toward the one girl who is supposed to be my best friend. Grant, being the good guy that he is, has never once called me out on it, aside from acknowledging it the morning after my drunken tirade.

But judging by the look on his face, he's going to bring it up.

"Don't look at me like that, man."

The locker room door shuts behind us. Neither one of us has anyone waiting for us this week. As we head toward the exit, the only sound is our shoes on the linoleum. He's not saying anything, but the look on his face tells me enough. Grant has been rooting for Brynn and me to get together since we all met, even before the words spilled past my lips.

I just can't. I can't bring myself to risk our friendship. Brynn isn't the relationship kind of girl. She likes her "no strings attached" relationships, and I can't say that I blame her. College is for fun times, for flings, for finding yourself, especially when you have no idea where you're going to be after graduation.

"Look, man." Grant grabs my arm, stopping me from climbing into my car, interrupting my thoughts. "We've never talked about that night, but I'm just going to say this once. I've never seen you both smile bigger, laugh harder, and just be yourselves like you do when you're both together. Don't let her slip through the cracks."

Nodding, I brush past Grant and climb into my car.

Don't let her slip through the cracks.

After parking in the garage, I grab my football bag and takeout bag from my favorite barbecue place, Hog Heaven. I'm starving after that game, but nothing that a Hog Heaven sampler platter—pulled pork, brisket, ribs, and all the sides—won't fix.

Football and barbecue are two of my favorite things.

Although Brynn is starting to make her way higher on my list. Don't get me wrong, she's always been at the top of my priorities, but lately, she's consumed more and more of my headspace. The girl drives me wild.

Can I keep these feelings to myself? Does she feel them too? Does her body spark with awareness when I walk into the room like mine does to her? Do her fingers twitch with the need to touch me when we are sitting side by side? When she closes her eyes at night, does she picture me lying next to her? As her hand trails down her tight stomach, slipping inside her—

My phone buzzes in my pocket, the vibration snapping me from my thoughts. But I don't pull my phone out. Instead, I sit down at the bar and pull out my food, forcing myself to stop thinking about Brynn lying in her bed.

As I dive into the perfectly tender ribs, my phone buzzes again. Knowing it's probably my parents, I ignore it. But I secretly hope it's a feisty blonde.

What's with you, Boyd? You're like a damn teenage girl with her first crush.

Brynn isn't my first crush, she's far from it, but she's the first girl that I can picture having a future with.

Whoa, where'd that thought come from?

I don't date. Ever. I've never had a serious girlfriend. Football has always been my first love. But Grant's parting words come rushing back to me like a tidal wave.

Don't let her slip through the cracks.

What will I do if she starts dating? What if I blow the only chance I have with her? But what if I take a chance, and she doesn't feel the same way? Will our friendship be forever changed? Why is she avoiding me?

This week we had a breakthrough, and she actually showed some of her cards, but there's still something she's not telling me. Laying in her bed, trying to cheer her up, I could tell there was more on her mind than going home the next weekend.

Stabbing my fork into the pulled pork, I take a huge bite. The smokey flavor and rich barbecue sauce explode in my mouth. Goddamn, this is good. I take the next several minutes going from pork to brisket to ribs before diving into my sides. Good barbecue requires good sides: homestyle macaroni and cheese, green beans and ham, and sweet spoonbread. Nothing better.

Pushing the empty containers aside, I pull my phone out of my pocket and thumb through the notifications. Three missed calls—one from my dad, one from Grant, and one from Brynn, too many social media notifications, twenty-two texts—friends and family congratulating me on the win, and five text messages from Brynn. Brynn's are the only ones I care about at the moment, the others can wait. Tapping on her name, I bring our conversation up.

> **Wilder: 3 touchdowns…my bestie is a baddie!**

> **Wilder: Congrats on the win, Q!**

> **Wilder: Seriously so proud of you!**

> **Wilder: Sidenote…talked to my mom's assistant *gag emoji* about next weekend. Friday is casual attire, but Saturday is cocktail. Think you can wear a black suit and a white shirt.**

> **Wilder: I love you forever. Thanks for coming with me. I don't know what I'd do without you. *heart emoji kiss emoji***

I type out a quick reply, taking a sip of my water.

> **Me: It's all good, Wilder. I'll make sure my suit is ready.**

Before I even get a chance to sit my phone down, it's buzzing with multiple texts. I chuckle at the onslaught of messages. Brynn is the short-multiple-text sender, rather than the long-paragraph sender. And the girl gets pissed with one-word answers. I learned that the hard way.

> **Wilder: This week is going to be SO busy… 3 exams.**

> **Wilder: Flight has been adjusted to a 1:57 flight.**

> **Wilder: It's a 2.5-hour flight and I've got a car ready for us.**

> **Wilder: We'll have to change quickly at the house and take a car to the stadium.**

> **Wilder: Just wanted to prepare you. Have fun celebrating the W**

> **Me: Sounds good. I'll be prepared.**

> **Me: Good luck with your exams.**

Stuffing my mouth with the last bite of spoonbread, I shove off the bar stool and head to the third-floor game room to park my exhausted ass down for endless hours of football.

And that's how I spent my remaining Saturday and all of Sunday.

Sunday night, I fell asleep with an assortment of images of Brynn doing things best friends don't do.

Fuck, I'm screwed.

CHAPTER 9
Brynn

"**B**EFORE YOU GO TO Chi-Town, we are having a girls' night," Macy announces during breakfast Wednesday morning. The three of us are gathered around our kitchen table, drinking coffee and munching on our breakfasts—a blueberry muffin for Chloe, waffles for Macy, and cereal for me.

Is there anything better than cereal? Like, it's the perfect meal.

Need breakfast? Cereal.

Need a snack? Cereal.

Don't want to cook dinner? Cereal.

But none of that healthy shit. Give me the Frosted Flakes with another teaspoon of sugar.

Taking a heaping spoonful of the sugary goodness, my head snaps to Macy.

"Ready to come up for air from dear ol' Gregg?" I ask around a mouthful of cereal, milk dribbling from my mouth.

"Chew first, you heathen." Macy tosses me a napkin. "And, as a matter of fact, Gregg is busy, and I miss my girls. It's not my fault you don't know what it's like to be in a relationship."

Oof, that stung. Because, just like Quinton, my closest girlfriends have no idea about my last relationship. The last time I loved someone.

Sensing my mood change, Macy apologizes. "Sorry, B."

Bringing another spoonful up to my mouth, I take another big bite, nodding my head in acceptance of her apology. There is nothing worse than conversation while eating cereal. Soggy cereal is shit, and anyone who disagrees is a psychopath.

Chiming in from the other side of Macy, Chloe asks, "What'd you have in mind, Mace?"

Macy's face lights up like a kid on Christmas morning.

"For starters, no boys allowed. No texting, no surprise visits, nothing. This is a girls' night only." Taking a breath, she continues. "Let's do a spa night with facials, mani/pedis, and hair treatments, while eating junk and watching early 2000s chick flicks!"

Out of the three of us, Macy is the girliest and, honestly, I can't even complain because she keeps me in line. If it wasn't for her, my nails would be a hot mess with chipped polish, and my face wouldn't have the healthy glow it has.

"Can we get Chinese food?" Chloe asks as she makes her way over to the kitchen sink to wash up a few dishes.

"Chinese sounds fantastic," I add, getting up and getting more coffee.

"Yes! Text me your orders, and let's plan on five o'clock."

"Sounds good, see you guys tonight."

Exiting the kitchen, I make my way to the front door to head to campus for my classes.

At five o'clock on the dot, the Chinese food delivery driver shows up with our food. Macy has the living room set up when Chloe and I walk in from classes. A pedicure spa tub, bowls of popcorn and chips on the coffee table, and a variety of beauty products are scattered around. Thank God Macy knows everything there is to know about beauty products because I am clueless. I'm no stranger to beauty regimens but growing up in an elite family meant I had appointments made for me with professionals who would take care of my hair, skin, and nails.

"I thought we could go ahead and do our hair masks while we eat, and then we can do facials, pedicures, and then manis. How's that sound?"

Chloe and I look at each other, neither one of us having an opinion on the matter.

I answer, shrugging. "Yeah, sounds good to us."

Macy stands there, clapping before tossing us each a bottle of hair treatment.

"Run up and wet your hair, apply the treatment, then come back down."

We do as we are told, returning to the living room a few minutes later. The townhome we share is very modest. It's a recent, new build with modern finishings. Our living room is a large rectangular space that is separated from the kitchen and eat-in area by the staircase. The townhome association made a smart decision by incorporating light and luxury vinyl flooring. Not only does it go perfectly with the warm, white walls, but it's easy maintenance.

The girls did all of the decorating. deciding on neutral colors with pops of yellow sprinkled throughout the house. Our leather couch and armchair are both extremely comfortable. So comfortable that someone is always falling asleep on them. But most of the time, you'll find us sitting around the coffee table, eating. Like we're doing now.

We dig into the assortment of containers—egg rolls, crab rangoon, fried rice, beef with broccoli, sweet and sour chicken, orange chicken, lo mein noodles, and steamed veggies. I'm pretty sure Macy ordered everything off the menu. *A Cinderella Story* is playing on the TV while we eat.

"So B, a friend of Gregg's is interested in taking you out on a date. What do you think?" Macy asks.

Taking a drink of my lime margarita, I savor the strong, cold liquid, letting the tequila burn the whole way down.

"I'm not interested in blind dates, Mace, you know this."

If I had a dollar for every time someone voiced concern or questioned my love life, I wouldn't have to pay for college. Seriously, it's absurd. What's wrong with a girl being in a non-committed relationship, or just hooking up with the opposite sex? Guys do it all the time. The whole double standard is archaic bullshit. It's 2022.

Where are all my promiscuous girls at?

"I know, I know but I thought I'd ask. I still think you should take Cody up on his offer. He's perfect for you," she replies, stabbing a piece of fried chicken.

Mulling over her comment, I know what I say next is going to shock the hell out of them. So I wait until Chloe is taking a drink of her marg.

"*Actually*, I've thought about it."

Macy half chokes on her chicken as Chloe snorts the margarita out of her nose.

Yes, just the reaction I was hoping for.

"Jesus, Chloe, you got margarita snot all over the table."

Sputtering, she grabs a napkin to clean up her mess. "You literally just shocked the hell out of me."

Macy chimes in. "Are you serious? Because if you're serious, I'm going to force you to text him right now."

"Ohmygosh, you guys are ridiculous."

Turning my attention to the TV, I can't help but appreciate a young Chad Michael Murray before *One Tree Hill*. Wasn't he everyone's dream guy growing up? Feeling eyes on me, I glance back at my friends who are still looking at me like I have two heads.

"What? Is there something on my face?" I ask, knowing damn well that's not why they are staring at me.

"Get your phone out, and text him right now," Macy demands.

Who does this bitch think she is?

Laughing, I turn my attention back to the TV again.

"Brinley Carolyn Wilder, do not ignore me."

Looking at my shocked bestie, I play dumb. "What Macy Marie?"

Pointing to my lap where my phone is, she barks, no, more like demands, "Get your phone out, text Cody right now, or I'm calling bullshit on you taking him up on a date."

Realizing that I'm not going to win this battle, I reach in my lap, grabbing my cell. Before I text Cody, I look Macy in the eyes.

"I thought you said no texting boys?"

Chloe stares at me. There's a look on her face that I can't quite decipher. It almost looks like she's upset at the prospect of me going on a date with Cody. And honestly, there's no way I'm going to go on a date with him. He's one of my best friends, and that's where things are going to stay.

I need new friends.

Scrolling through my messages app, I find Cody's name.

> **Me: So I've been thinking…**

Leaving the text vague, I hit send. Not even thirty seconds later my phone chimes.

> **Cody Jacobs: And what could you be thinking about in that beautiful head of yours?**

I grin and shake my head. Always a flirt.

> **Me: What's a baseball player do when his eyesight starts to fail him?**

Hitting send, I wait. And wait. And wait. The bubbles appear, notifying me that Cody is responding. Then they disappear. Appear again. Then disappear.

Ping, my phone chimes.

> **Cody Jacobs: What's he doing?**

> **Me: You really thought hard on that one.**

> **Cody Jacobs: Shut up and tell me.**

> **Me: He takes a job as an umpire.**

> **Cody Jacobs: *palm to forehead emoji* Good lord.**

> **Me: *laughing emoji***

> **Cody Jacobs: That was random.**

> **Me: It's girls' night at home tonight**

> **Cody Jacobs: So there's tequila involved.**

> **Me: Obviously!**

> **Cody Jacobs: Have fun, B!**

Turning the phone around, I show the girls my conversation with Cody.

"Happy?" I ask.

Macy grabs the phone from my hand, but Chloe just takes a sip of her margarita, avoiding the phone. My eyes narrow at her.

Note to self, circle back and figure out what's up with Chloe.

"You brat," Macy squeals, tossing my phone back.

I throw my head back and laugh. "I'm not going on a date with Cody!"

I watch as Chloe's shoulders relax. I toss her my phone, so she can read it.

Sitting around laughing with my two best friends is just what the doctor ordered. The evening is spent reminiscing on our friendship. We laugh at the story of when Macy got locked out of her dorm room and had to go floor-to-floor in a tiny towel, trying to find an RA to unlock her room.

Chloe reminds us of when we became friends with the football guys and how they called *dibs* on us when we met Cody. As if they could call dibs on us. The boys just had to learn to share and, thus, a beautiful friendship developed between the football and baseball teams.

Am I taking credit for their bromance? Oh, hell yeah.

A lot of margaritas are consumed, causing even more giggles.

There really isn't anything better than surrounding yourself with your tribe.

Growing up, I was never without a crowd. There were always people wanting to hang out with me. Those people called themselves my friends, but the truth is they were just using me for status. That's the problem with living where I grew up. It's full of fake people needing clout to make themselves feel important. Getting out of Chicago, and the toxic dynamic that surrounded my family and their "friends," was the best thing that I ever did. To this day, I'm so glad I chose to continue the dream that Bryce and I had in junior high. We both wanted to see the country, but we didn't want to do it without the other.

Little did we know that I would be doing it alone.

And, in just two short days, I'll be catching a flight back to Chicago to honor my brother's memory.

CHAPTER 10
Brynn

"**I** CAN'T BELIEVE THAD got us tickets to the Colts–Patriots game!" Bryce exclaims, running into the living room where I'm curled on the couch watching a movie with Asher.

Thad is our older cousin on our dad's side. He's a cousin who is closest in age to me and Bryce. We haven't seen him in a while, not since he graduated high school and spent a year in rehab.

"Dude, I'm seriously so jealous," Asher says, folding his arms across his chest.

Thad scored 50-yard line tickets and asked Bryce and me to go with him.

Pushing myself up in a sitting position, I look up at Asher and glance over at Bryce.

"Why don't you go with them?"

"Are you serious?" Asher asks me, eyes widening in surprise.

Smiling up at him, I say, "Yeah, you should go with them. Make it a guys' night, and you can crush on your man, Tom Brady."

Grabbing my face between his hands, Asher leans down and gives me a kiss that makes my toes curl. Every time he kisses me, I swear he makes my cheeks flush and my blood pump harder.

"Would you two knock it off?" Bryce says, making a gagging noise. "I'm still having a hard time seeing you two together."

Asher looks me in the eye and smiles against my lips before replying to my brother. "Seriously, dude, it's been almost two years."

Making his way farther into the room, Bryce plops down on the other side of the sectional.

"Yeah, seriously. That's my sister. It's weird to think about my child-hood best friend and my sister making out and..." he trails off, his body shivering at whatever thought just crossed his mind.

Pulling away from me, Asher gives me a wink. I know that smirk on his face. He's about to make my brother and me uncomfortable. Running his hand up my thigh in a slow, seductive movement, Asher looks over at Bryce.

"And what, Bryce? Cuddling and touching—"

Asher's voice is immediately cut off as a pillow hits him directly in his face.

"Dude, shut the fuck up."

I laugh at the two of them, even though my cheeks are red. It's only been a couple of months since Asher and I took things to the next level in our relationship. He waited until my sixteenth birthday this summer before surprising me with a sleepover. The night was perfect. The moment was perfect. And Asher was perfect.

Pounding sounds in the distance.

What the hell? Where's that pounding coming from?

More banging, and it's getting louder and louder.

"B, you're going to be late!" Chloe yells from the other side of my door.

Jerking up from my dream, I reach for my phone on my nightstand. Shit, I overslept. Ripping off the covers, I jump out of bed. Racing off too quickly, I stub my toe against the metal bed post.

"Ow, fuck!" I scream. "Shit, shit, shit!"

Hopping on one leg, I rub my toe and stumble into my bathroom. Flicking on the bathroom light, I quickly pee, flush, and wash my hands. Pulling out my toothbrush, I swiftly clean my teeth before brushing out my hair and tossing it up in a messy bun. There's no time for makeup. Instead, I strip out of my pajamas, leaving them lying on the bathroom floor.

Let's face it, that's not because I'm running late. I'm the worst at leaving clothes lying around, even though I have a super cute hamper.

Not all of us girls care about the whole "tossing the clothes next to the hamper and not in the hamper" situation.

Turning off the bathroom light, I head back into my room in search of clothes. Slipping on my glasses, I find a pair of black bike shorts and an Eagles Baseball tee. Bouncing from foot to foot, I get my socks and tennis shoes on, my toe still throbbing. Grabbing my phone off the charger, I take off running down the stairs.

"There's a protein bar and water on the table by your keys," I hear Chloe yell from her room.

"Thanks, Chloe! You're the best!" I yell back, swiping the protein bar off the table and tossing it into my backpack that's sitting on the floor.

Tucking the water bottle in the outside pocket on my backpack and grabbing my keys from the hook, I take off out the door toward my car, hitting the automatic start on the key fob. I have twelve minutes until class starts.

I make it to campus in seven minutes—don't ask me how. Getting out of the car, I hit the lock on my fob before taking a jog toward

Rogers Hall. My phone chimes in my pocket and I pull it out, trying to read the message while avoiding running into anyone.

Cody Jacobs: You coming to class?

Me: Almost there. Running late.

Of all days to oversleep, today wasn't the day. Today is already stressful, and I just added more stress to myself by having to rush. Rushing immediately overwhelms me, and my body breaks out in stress sweat, which is the worst type of sweat.

Throwing open the doors to Rogers Hall, I jog up the stairs, making sure I don't trip over a step. Slowly opening the door, I slide inside, hoping not to disrupt Professor Peters. He glances up from the front of the room as I make my way to the middle of the rows where Cody is saving me a seat. I slide into the desk next to him and reach inside my backpack to pull out my laptop.

"I wasn't sure if you were going to show," Cody leans into me and whispers. "Here, I brought you a coffee."

"Thanks, Cody," I whisper, taking the coffee from him. "And no, just running late. Since we had girls' night Wednesday, I had to spend all day catching up on assignments. I underestimated how late I'd be up finishing a paper for next week. Q and I leave this afternoon for the Chicago trip."

Nodding his head, he bumps my shoulder, a grin spreading across his lips.

"Go show Chicago the badass Brynn."

We make eye contact with each other as a slow smile spreads across my face.

"Excuse me," Professor Peters yells, bursting the bubble Cody and I are in. "Not only do you show up to my class late, but you are distracting those around you with your talking."

Cody and I both turn our faces to the bottom of the lecture hall, my face flushing with embarrassment. Someone must've peed in Professor Peters's cereal this morning, because he continues humiliating us.

"After reading your papers this week. I have decided that today we are going to do a little introduction and find others with like-minded career prospects. Tardy, you can kick us off. Please stand, introduce yourself, and tell us your career plans."

Of all days to show up late, it had to be today. And of all days to talk about our career plans, it had to be today. Clearing my throat, I slide out of the desk and stand.

"I'm Brynn—" I start before I'm rudely interrupted.

"Speak louder, it's a big room."

Exhaling, I start again. "I'm Brynn Wilder, a junior. After graduating, I'm planning on continuing into the master's program with plans to become a youth grief counselor," I finish, eyeing Professor Peters.

"Ambitious," he responds. "Youth grief is a tough career. What makes you want to make that your career?"

Looking around the lecture hall, I see that heads have turned to watch me talk. Public speaking is not my forte. My heart rate is accelerating while my palms grow damp with sweat.

"I'd rather not answer that to a room full of strangers."

He doesn't like that answer, and honestly, I don't care. Most of my friends have no clue about my history, I'm not about to share with a room full of strangers.

"You show up late to my class, and then decide that you don't want to answer. I can't say that I'm impressed."

You know what, screw this. Might as well raise my defenses now, since they are going to be on high alert this whole weekend around my parents.

"And with all respect, I don't care. We all have our demons, and you pushing me to share because you have authority is deplorable."

Pausing, I reach down and stuff my laptop back in my bag, zipping it up as I spill my past.

"I want to become a grief counselor because, five years ago, my twin brother was killed. Not only did my twin die but, along with him, I lost two other people I was extremely close with. No one was there for me. No one cared about my grief. I was alone. I want to be there for someone who, unfortunately, has to go through what I did but, unlike me, they won't be alone. And if that's all," I pause, throwing my backpack over my shoulder. "I have to catch a flight to honor my brother and friend in a memorial tonight. Thanks for the humiliation, Prof."

And with that, I hightail it out of the hall, working hard to keep the moisture pooling in my eyes from spilling over.

At a quarter till one, I'm packing the last of my bags. After getting back to my room, I decided to take a nice, long soak in the bathtub, since I had extra time, thanks to storming out of my class. It might have been childish and immature, but my mind is all over the place today.

Every year, I struggle with the anniversary of my brother's death, but this year, I'm going to be home. I haven't been home around the anniversary date in three years. Pushing the thoughts out of my mind for now, I wheel my suitcase down the stairs. My roommates aren't home. I grab a piece of paper and write out a quick note for them and leave it on the counter. Making sure I have everything, I head to the front door. Just as I approach the door, there's a knock.

When I open the door, my eyes widen in surprise to see Quinton standing on the other side. He's standing there with his hand in the pocket of his dark wash jeans. A tight athletic shirt stretches tightly across his broad, muscular chest. The black ink from his eagle tattoo barely peaks out from the neckline. His dark-brown eyes grow darker as he watches my perusal of his body.

Mouth going dry, I find myself needing water.

He clears his throat and I snap my gaze back up to him. Quinton's eyes are waiting for me, a smirk stretching across his lips. That perfect dimple makes its appearance.

"Hey, I thought I was picking you up?"

"JP is going to take us," Quinton answers, gesturing over his shoulder toward Jeremiah's black, crew cab, pickup truck that's parked out front.

"Oh awesome, thanks," I say, wheeling my suitcase to the door.

Looking behind me, I grab my backpack purse that's doubling as my carry-on, and step onto the stoop with my suitcase. Quinton reaches down and picks up my suitcase while I shut and lock the front door.

"Ready?" he asks.

"As I'll ever be," I mutter as we head down the steps.

Quinton leads me to the passenger door, but before he gets a chance to open the door, I stop him.

"You sit up front, I'll sit in the back."

He gives me a look before opening up the door behind him. Him sitting up front while I sit in the back goes against every chivalrous bone in his body. Climbing up in the back seat, I toss my backpack next to me. Glancing up in the rearview mirror, I find JP's eyes waiting on mine, concern lacing his gaze.

"Thanks for the ride, Jer," I say with a smile while Quinton loads my suitcase into the covered truck bed.

Jeremiah gives me a small, knowing smile. All of my friends here know that I hate going home. They might not have the whole story, but they know that I rarely make the flight home.

"There's a little something in the cup holder for you," he says, as Quinton climbs into his seat.

Quinton snaps his head in my direction before directing his attention back to Jeremiah. His eyes bore daggers into the side of Jeremiah's face. As Jeremiah pulls out of the parking lot, I reach for the cup holder. A cold, skinny pen brushes my hand. I pull it out and see a plant sticker on it. Holding the device in my hand, I look up to find Jeremiah watching me. With a slight nod of his head, I know what kind of pen it is. I mean, I could've figured it out based on the sticker, but his nod confirms my hunch. He rolls down my window for me as I bring the pen to my lips. Leaning my head back on the headrest, I take a nice long drag from the weed pen and my eyes fall close as I inhale. Holding my inhale, I let my mind relax before exhaling the plume of vapor out the window.

One long drag is all I take.

A little something to take the edge off. A little something to get me through the next few hours. A little something to forget that I'm going home—a home that hasn't felt like home in what feels like forever.

Twenty minutes later, Quinton and I are wheeling our suitcases into a busy Austin-Bergstrom International. Making our way through security, we find our terminal, which is chaotic. Everyone must be heading to Chicago. Most of the chairs are occupied, but we manage to find two empty seats, collapsing next to each other. My head drops to his shoulder as I inhale a deep breath. His hand finds my knee, and he squeezes. His touch is all I need. It's calming and comforting. But this time when he squeezes, I feel flutters in my stomach trailing lower.

Well, that's new.

"Have I ever told you about the time I snuck into the Dallas cheerleaders' locker room?" Q asks.

I shoot up, eyes turning into saucers at his random comment.

A low, rumbling chuckle escapes his lips before he continues. "Dad was playing for Dallas when I was ten. I thought I was going into the football team's locker room, but I got turned around. Turns out I was in the wrong wing. I walked right into the locker room that was designated for the cheerleaders. They were all in the process of changing." He pauses, adding drama to his story. *"Tits everywhere."*

A cackle bursts from my lips before I have a chance to stop it. Heads turn toward us from the surrounding people. There was just something about the way he said "tits everywhere" as if it's just another everyday occurrence to Quinton. Hell, it might be.

"Oh my god, Q. So ten is when your fascination with tits began?"

"Shit, B, it was probably sooner, but damn, seeing those ladies with their tits out in those tiny cheerleading shorts. I was in fucking heaven." He laughs, eyes rolling up to build up the sexual encounter. "I just stood there staring at headlights. Dallas cheerleaders are every boy's wet dream, and here I was, in their damn locker room."

"You're such a perv," I say, appreciating the distraction.

And this is what I love most about our relationship. Quinton can read me like a book. He knows what I need to get out of my head. Somehow, he has a way of knowing if I need a laugh, if I need to go to a party to drink away my thoughts, or if I need a movie day in bed. I didn't come with a manual, yet somehow, Quinton is able to figure me out. Which is saying something, because half of the time, I don't even know what I need.

A few minutes later, our flight is announced. The perky attendant greets us, taking our boarding passes from our outstretched hands as she scans the barcode.

"Have a wonderful time in Chicago," she says, handing our boarding passes back.

Quinton thanks her for the both of us. His hand finds my lower back. And dammit, there are those flutters again. What is happening right now? Guiding us into the jet bridge, I feel the movement as Quinton's hand moves from my back and finds my hand. His fingers intertwine with mine. My eyes snap to our connected hands. Quinton squeezes before leaning down, his lips finding my temple. *Swoon.* I could melt into a puddle at that simple gesture. Quinton is going to make a fine husband someday and, whoever the lady is, well, she's damn lucky.

Because that's the thing about Quinton Boyd. If you have the good fortune to find yourself in his close circle, you're truly one of the lucky ones. Quinton doesn't let a lot of people in. But when you're in, you'll be loved hard and cared for.

Climbing into our first class seats, I buckle my seat belt before resting my head against the window.

I'm coming home, brother.

The flight from Austin-Bergstrom to O'Hare goes off without a hitch. Thank God. Flying is not my favorite. I always break out in a stress sweat. Quinton spends the three-hour flight studying and watching a

30 for 30 documentary while I zone out and watch a few episodes of *Schitt's Creek*. There's nothing like a little bit of Alexis to forget the world. I mean, seriously, the Roses are so dysfunctional, yet hilarious.

After gathering our bags from baggage claim, we make our way outside. My parents have sent a private driver to escort us to the house. Walking outside, we are greeted with the crisp air of Chicago in the fall. I take in a deep inhale. Being in Texas for so long, I have forgotten what it is like to be in the Midwest in the fall. The air is cool and crisp, there's a sense of calm—yes, even in the crazy Chicago environment—leaves are falling, and life is hibernating before it is born again in the spring. The weather is starting to cool, summer has faded away, and there's always a breeze, especially closer to the lake.

I feel at home.

I feel at peace.

If only the rest of my trip could be spent reminding me of the love I have for my city. Instead, I'll be forced to fake a smile, hide my grief, and be the prim and proper daughter my parents hope to have raised. This weekend isn't for me. Hell, it's not even for Bryce. It's for my parents. It's for status and image. It's for showboating. It's sickening. And I'll have to endure it all. A part of me really wanted to skip everything this weekend. I debated multiple times on just saying "screw it." But I'm doing it for Bryce. He would've told me to suck it up, to be the bigger person. So, that's what I'm doing. It's not for my parents, that's for damn sure.

But at least, I'll have Quinton next to me.

My head whips from one direction to the other, scanning the cars. I spot the blacked-out SUV with the driver standing next to it, holding a sign that reads "Miss Brinley Wilder."

"Looks like we are over here," I tell Quinton, pointing toward the Tahoe.

"Damn, didn't know I was hanging out with royalty," Quinton jokes, nudging my shoulder as we wheel our suitcases.

I ignore his comment. Out of the two of us, he's more "royal" than I am. His dad is a well-known professional athlete, his mom is known because of his father's celebrity, and he's on his way to being a first-round NFL draft pick. I'm no one. I'm the daughter of a crooked politician and an unfaithful surgeon. Hell, both of them are unfaithful—vows mean nothing to Mr. and Mrs. Wilder.

"Miss Wilder?" the driver asks.

"Hi, I'm Brynn. This is Quinton. Thank you for picking us up."

Our driver opens the back door before placing our suitcases in the back. Fastening my seat belt, I inhale and exhale a deep breath.

Forty hours until I can head back to Texas.

CHAPTER 11
Brynn

A FTER A QUICK STOP at the house to change, Q and I are back in the car heading to my high school for the tribute. Our stop at the house was quick. We only had twenty minutes to freshen up and change into warmer clothes before we needed to head to the stadium. Nights in Chicago are a lot cooler than nights in Texas.

Friday nights in the fall are liable to get very cold, and after checking my weather app, I see that tonight won't be an exception as temperatures drop into the fifties. As much as I'd love to wear a pair of leggings, a hoodie, and sneakers, I don't want to deal with the disappointment of my parents right off the rip. So I choose to dress up, opting for a pair of black jeans, black booties, and gray sweater, topped with my camel trench coat. Warm, cute, and not overdressed for a high school football game. I'm seriously so jealous of Quinton since he can wear more casual clothes—black ripped jeans, a black hoodie, sneakers, and his olive utility jacket with a flat bill on. Q's hoping to go unnoticed, but I don't have the heart to tell him that there's no way he's going unrecognized. He's too damn attractive to fly under the radar.

Our driver pulls into the parking lot of Lincoln High, and everything comes rushing back. The memories are flooding my head. Oh god, the memories.

My breath becomes rapid. I can't seem to get enough oxygen.

Is the car spinning?

An elephant is sitting on my chest. Air can't get into my lungs, and I'm about two seconds away from a full-blown panic attack.

Why did I think I could do this? I could barely bring myself to come to Lincoln to finish out my last two years of high school. I begged my parents every day to let me transfer, to take online classes, anything to prevent me from coming back to this place.

Oh god, I can't do this.

Just as I'm about to tell the driver to pull away, I feel him. He's wrapping his muscled arms around me, pulling me against his chest. His hands are rubbing circles against my back.

"Brynn," he says, continuing to rub circles. "Brynn, look at me."

I feel Quinton lift his hand and drag it from my back, gently resting it under my chin. With slow movements, he raises my head.

Slowly, slowly, I bring my eyes to him. I must look like a maniac. But I can feel myself starting to calm down. I look into Quinton's eyes. His rich, brown eyes remind me of a steamy mug of black coffee, my favorite way to start my day. Q's eye contact soothes me, just like my morning coffee soothes my soul at the start of my day.

"Brynn, you're not alone. I'm gonna be right by your side."

My rapidly rising chest begins to slow as my breathing returns to normal. Before my mind has a chance to catch up, I throw my arms around Quinton's neck, pulling his body flush against mine.

"Thank you," I say with my face smashed into his neck. "You're always there to bring me back."

"And I always will be."

He reaches up and lightly grips the back of my head, pulling it away from his shoulder. Pressing his lips to my forehead, he smiles down at me. Smiling back, I pull myself from my best friend and reach inside my purse, pulling out a cannabis pen.

With a small chuckle, Quinton shakes his head before asking, "When the hell did you have time to get that?"

Bringing the pen to my lips, I smile before taking a long drag. "Nadia, our housekeeper," I answered on an exhale.

The driver of the car just eyes me through the rearview mirror.

Taking another long inhale, I continue. "Nadia has been getting me weed since high school. She's got a hook-up for the good shit. She used to supply Bryce and me with weed and alcohol for parties."

Letting out a large cloud of smoke, I smile at the memories. "She was always so protective of us. Nadia came from a wild background. She knows how high schoolers can be, especially ones with unlimited funds. She said that, if we were going to smoke or drink, she would supply us with it so she would have peace of mind that we weren't smoking laced shit. Our parents might not have given a shit about us, but our staff always did. Hell, our staff was our family. Before we left tonight, she tossed it to me, knowing that I would need all the vices I could get to get through this weekend."

Quinton just shakes his head with a smirk. "Damn, B, I wish I would've known you in high school."

"You wouldn't have liked me." Giving him a wink, I fling open the door, and dump the pen in my purse. "Let's get this show on the road."

The two of us fall in line behind all of the fans making their way to the entrance gates. Lincoln High is a large, private school with only around one thousand students. The school is a large brick building that was remodeled in the 1990s. The three parking lots merge into one long walkway centered between flower beds with arborvitae trees that leads to the football field. Tonight must be a big game. There's a buzz in the air, and the students are excited. You can feel the electricity.

Making our way through the gates, not having to pay since we are honorary guests for the tribute ceremony—ugh, I hate saying that—I see that the athletic director is waiting for us. He greets us at the entrance, guiding us up the stands to the closed suites. Lincoln isn't a college, yet they still try to be with their exclusive VIP suites.

Before we enter, I slow my pace and reach my hand back behind me, searching for my anchor. Quinton takes the hint, grabbing my hand. I feel the gentle, yet reassuring, squeeze.

He sidles up behind me, whispering in my ear, "I'll always bring you back."

I smile to myself before coming to a complete stop right inside the suite. The first person I make eye contact with makes me suck in my breath. Asher's mom is the first person I see. He was my high school boyfriend, until he wasn't. I haven't seen his parents since I moved to Texas. It feels like minutes pass by as we stare at each other, when it's only been seconds. She moves first, closing the gap between us.

"Brinley," she gasps, pulling me into a hug.

Quinton slips his hand from mine as I wrap my arms around my second mom and the only woman who ever felt like my actual mom.

"Hi, Mrs. Nelson."

She scoffs, pulling me back. She looks me up and down, appraising me.

"Oh honey, when have you ever called me Mrs. Nelson?"

She smiles, taking me in, almost like she can't believe I'm standing before her. With her eyes locked on mine, I swear that woman can read me like a book. She can tell my head is in the clouds at the moment. Grace gives me a small smile, one that doesn't meet her eyes, before patting my cheek.

"It's so good to see you, my sweet girl."

"You too, Mama Grace," I respond, pulling her in for another hug.

Once upon a time, I thought she was going to be my mother-in-law. But a week after Bryce died, my boyfriend died too, and everything I ever dreamed about shattered to pieces. Selfishly, I cut the two people who could have saved me out of my life. But it hurt too much to be around Daniel and Grace Nelson. Asher's parents reminded me too much of him, too much of our memories, and too much of the future that would never happen.

Grace looks past me, taking in the handsome man towering behind me.

"Pardon me," she says, looking between Quinton and me. "Who do we have here?"

Smiling, I introduce the two. "Grace, this is my friend, Quinton Boyd. Q, this is Grace Nelson, Asher's mom."

And it's at this moment, I realize that I've made a huge mistake. I've never *never* mentioned Asher to Quinton.

Shit.

"Hello, ma'am. It's nice to meet you," Quinton says, reaching out to shake Grace's hand.

He looks over Grace's shoulder, his eyes finding mine. Oh, I can read the questions written in his eyes, but Quinton plays along, not voicing anything.

A throat clears behind me, sending chills down my body. Goose bumps spread across my skin and my bones instantly chill. I would be able to recognize that throat clearing in the middle of a concert. Spinning on my heels, I turn and face the woman who birthed me. She looks older than the last time I saw her. Small bags puff below the same blue eyes that mirror my own. Wrinkles are prevalent, which shocks me as she's always kept regular Botox appointments.

"Brinley, nice of you to finally show up," Carolyn says in her fake, overly polite voice, but I can pick out the distaste in her voice. The sound makes me cringe.

"Carolyn," I mutter.

"Be nice," Grace whispers under her breath.

Before we have a chance to continue our conversation, an assistant to the athletic director approaches us, announcing the ceremony is starting and we are needed on the field. Daniel and Grace Nelson follow the assistant with my parents right behind them, but I can't bring myself to follow. I can't get my feet to work. I'm frozen. Quinton steps into my view, placing his hands on each side of my face, forcing my glazed gaze up to him.

"Quinton, I can't do it."

"Wilder, you can get through this. You know why?"

"Why?"

"Because you're one of the strongest girls I know," he says with a wink. "And because I'll be waiting for you on the other side of the fence."

My hands reach up, and I grip his jacket, pulling him into me as I wrap my arms around his middle. Without hesitating, he embraces me in his big, comforting hugs. He leads me down the stairs, catching up to the others. Before I follow everyone onto the field, Q spins me around, pulls me in for one more hug, and kisses the top of my head. My body warms at the affection. Not even the crisp, fall air can cool me down.

"Good evening, everyone, and thank you for coming out to support our Lincoln High Riders," the Athletic Director announces into the microphone. "Before we kick off, tonight we are going to be paying tribute to two amazing souls who lost their lives all too soon. Five years ago, we lost Bryce Wilder and Asher Nelson, two incredible young men both on and off the field."

I zone out for a few seconds, seeking out Quinton, letting the athletic director's voice fade away. When I find him in the crowd, he's staring back at me. Our eyes meet, and he mouths, "You've got this."

"Looks like you've found yourself a good one," Grace whispers in my ear.

I look up to find her watching the two of us. Guilt instantly swims in my stomach.

"It's not like that, Grace. Quinton is just a really good friend."

She lightly squeezes my forearm and gives me a motherly look that tells me she doesn't believe what I'm saying. And after everything today, I'm starting to doubt myself too.

"Tonight we unveil a new victory bell with the quote '*Set your heart on victory.*' The new bell will be featured at the top of the hill next to the entrance, where, underneath, we will have a plaque with Asher's and Bryce's names and jersey numbers. They may be gone, but we will never forget their spirits and the lives these boys touched," the athletic director states. "And with that, I'd like to introduce Asher's parents Daniel and Grace Nelson, along with Bryce's parents Philip and Carolyn Cabot-Wilder, and Bryce's sister and Asher's girlfriend Brinley Wilder."

The crowd gives a standing ovation, and a tear slips down my cheek at the sight in front of me.

After our introduction, we are handed the plaque that will rest underneath the victory bell. Flashing lights swarm my vision, blinding me momentarily. The photographers click away on their cameras at the broken families in front of them.

"Excuse me," I announce to no one.

My feet start moving of their own will. They're leading me to him, and Quinton is waiting. With outstretched arms, he wraps me in close. Another flash from a camera catches my attention, and I hope that Q's hat keeps his cover discreet.

Not bothering to look toward the field, or at the people staring at us, I allow Quinton to wrap his arm around my shoulder and lead us back to our waiting car. Tonight, I'm hoping Quinton lets everything he's learned over the last hour go. Just for tonight. I need to get a handle on everything before I tell him. Tomorrow I'll tell him all of my secrets. He'll learn my whole story and finally see the damaged Brinley Carolyn Wilder.

Maybe he'll finally understand why I'm so fucked up.

CHAPTER 12
QUINTON

"How the hell can you eat so much and still be so damn skinny?" I chuckle, watching Brynn shovel french fries dipped in cheese sauce into her mouth.

After we left the high school, she decided she wasn't ready to head home yet, so instead, she instructed our driver to take us to the closest Steak 'N Shake. The drive to the 24-hour diner is quiet. Both of us are lost in our own thoughts from the ceremony. We've been friends, hell, best friends for two years. Never, not once, has she let on that she lost more than just her brother in that accident.

Blindsided. That's how I feel. And I've *actually* been blindsided by a two-hundred-fifty-pound defensive end.

Tonight's revelation hurt worse.

"Are you judging me, Quinton Alexander?" She looks up at me with her textbook smirk.

Grabbing her strawberry milkshake, she wraps her luscious lips around the straw, sucking up the creamy, thick drink. Something swirls in my body, rushing straight to my dick. Subtly, I reach down to adjust the chub forming in my pants.

"Hell no, I'm not judgin'. I'm just wondering which one of my teammates I should have you compete against in an eating contest?"

Picking up my double steak burger, I take another bite. The team nutritionist would have a fit if she could see my meal, but it's a bye week, and I'll work it off, no worries. There was no way I was passing up a delicious Steakburger, fries, and a cookie dough milkshake. Especially since it's what Brynn needed after the emotional whiplash she just endured. Watching her stuff bite after bite into her mouth brings a smile to my face.

I'm not mad at her. I'm bothered that she couldn't trust me with the whole story. A part of me wants to question our entire friendship. Was it all surface level for her? What else hasn't she told me?

Hell, she knows everything about my struggles with going pro, with my parents, and the lackluster relationships I have with my brothers thanks to my parents. The weight of the world is resting on me. Yeah, it might be a bit dramatic, but I'm constantly having conversations with the devil and angel on my shoulders. Constantly trying to unscramble what my hopes and dreams are, not the dreams that were planted like little seeds in my brain since birth.

"Hmm, if I were to have an eating competition with anyone on the team, who would I choose?" She ponders, bringing her hand up, as her skinny finger taps against her chin. The chin I love to grip between my fingers. "Harris. Yeah, definitely Harris."

I bust out laughing, garnering looks from the handful of other customers. Harris is our quarterback, and he's an animal when it comes to food. I don't know how the hell he can stay as fit as he does while consuming the amount of food he does. I once watched him eat a large pizza, twenty-five wings, and an order of breadsticks by himself.

"All right, after we win the Natty, I'm setting up some kind of eating competition between you and Harris."

"Deal," Brynn replies, reaching across the table to pluck a couple of my fries from my plate. She dips them in her cheese sauce before bringing them to her mouth.

Her fingers slide between her lips before she sucks them clean. *For fuck's sake.*

Our waitress appears back at our table. She slides the check onto the table while giving me another long perusal, a seductive smile spreading across her face.

"I hope everything was to your satisfaction," she says, talking to only me, not sparing Brynn a glance. "They'll separate your orders at the counter. I hope you'll *come* again."

Before she has a chance to walk away, Brynn chimes in. "Honey, here's a tip for you." The waitress pauses, turning back to our table excitedly. "Oh, I don't mean a monetary tip. I mean a life tip. Next time you serve a table with two people, don't flirt with the man. Believe me, that will not get you a bigger tip. It'll end up biting you in the ass one of these days."

"Excuse me," the waitress retorts, walking even closer to our table.

Which just spurs Brynn on. My girl doesn't hold back.

My girl? Where'd that come from?

Brynn reaches into her purse and pulls out two pennies. I know where this is going and Bitch Brynn is about to come out. Leaning back, I cross my arms waiting for the show to start. She places the two pennies on the table, sliding them toward our waitress.

"Here's my two cents for you. Next time a guy and girl are sitting at a table together, try to keep it in your pants and pay attention to the girl, not ogle her boyfriend. Believe me, the woman will control your tip. Oh, if you want a good tip, don't leave your phone number on the bill. That's *definitely* a ho move."

"You've got a lot of nerve—" our waitress starts before she's interrupted by Brynn again.

Brynn stands up, waving her pointer finger back and forth.

"Ah ah ah," she starts. "The customer is always right. Next time, drink a glass of water instead of looking so thirsty."

I can't help it, I laugh a deep hearty chuckle. Reaching down, I grab the check and place my hand on Brynn's lower back—where I notice her shiver—and gently, but firmly, move her toward the counter before there are more words. Bitch Brynn is feisty, and she's entertaining, but I'm not looking to get into any fights tonight. We leave our waitress standing there with her mouth floundering like a fish.

"Thirsty ho," Brynn murmurs under her breath.

After paying our bill, we climb into the car and head back to her house, much to Brynn's dismay. The ride home feels normal, a lot more normal than the drive to the diner. But I can't help but replay the conversation Brynn exchanged with our waitress. She called me her boyfriend. Never has she called me her boyfriend. We've had many encounters where girls flock to the two of us, it comes with the territory of being a star player at a D1 university. But she's never acted territorial before, and I kind of like it.

Shit, what's happening to me.

Brynn has always been the wild, easygoing, "never take things too serious" girl, but seeing her so vulnerable is doing something to me. Those feelings I've worked so hard to drown out are floating back up to the surface.

Get it together, Q. She's your best friend, that's all. You're here to be her emotional support friend, that's all.

Our driver pulls in front of the Wilders' home, and, after putting the car in park, he makes his way to Brynn's door and opens it for her. She thanks him before turning to walk up the front steps. I follow her inside, taking in the large expanse of the home. When we first arrived, time was not our friend so I didn't get a chance to check out the estate. This place is insane. A two-story foyer greets us with a large chandelier in the center. There's a grand staircase leading to the upstairs with an open railed runway across the foyer, connecting the two wings. Board and batten accent the walls, making the home feel lavish.

"C'mon," she says, nudging me along. "There's a room I know you'll like." My mind goes straight to her bedroom. If Grant were here and he could hear my thoughts, I have no doubt he'd smack me or force me to tell her my feelings.

"Yeah, it's nice," she says, not stopping to watch me check out her home. "C'mon, there's a room I think you'll like even more."

Following her into the kitchen, I watch her remove her coat, and my eyes immediately drop to her ass. I can't help but appreciate the way it looks in her tight black jeans. Brynn's hot, I'm not blind. There've been many opportunities for me to notice her body, and oh have I. Hell, I am a guy after all. When a girl who looks like Brynn is in your eyesight, you appreciate her. Brynn is the type of girl who's blessed with good genetics. She's not one to work out, but somehow manages to keep her body toned.

Snapping back to reality and following her lead, I take off my coat and drape it across the back of the same barstool where Brynn placed hers. The kitchen is just as luxurious as I'd imagined. A French country design with creamy white cabinets, large black-paned windows, champagne hardware, and Sub-Zero appliances, it's a true chef's kitchen. The stove sits in a concave space with arched woodworking and a brick backsplash and there's an oversized island with a smaller sink in the center.

It's incredible. I'm used to fancy houses, but there's just something about this house that makes it special. It's the difference between old money and new money. Nothing in our home has character. It's all modern and cold.

Brynn leads us through another doorway, which I discover leads to the butler's pantry. Not as elaborate as the main kitchen but still huge. She reaches into the fridge and pulls out two Stella Artois and two bottles of water.

Handing me the beer and water she finally speaks. "Stella is all we have, but I figured beer is beer." She pauses, sucking in a breath before slowly looking up at me, vulnerability and exhaustion are etched in her features. "I know there's a lot we need to talk about. A lot was thrown at you tonight, stuff I should've told you about a long time ago, but for tonight, can we just pretend?"

"Pretend what?" I ask, holding her eye contact.

It's there that I see the pain, the darkness she tries so desperately to hide under her mask. This is the real Brinley. The happy-go-lucky girl is just a facade that she uses as a disguise. Only I'm not everyone, and I want to see the real her. The Brinley Wilder that has warmed her way into my heart and my soul.

"Pretend that I haven't just kept a huge secret from you for the past two years. Pretend that I'm not as fucked up as I *really am*."

Pulling her into my arms, I hold her, feeling her body slump against me. It has to be exhausting to keep this inside, and then have everything unravel at your feet years later. Seeing her interact with her parents—which her dad didn't even acknowledge her tonight—it all makes sense on why she avoids Chicago.

"Yeah, we can pretend."

Seeing her so broken would have me agreeing to anything she wants. If pretending is what she needs, I'll agree. I'd do whatever I need to to get my Wilder back.

"Thank you," she whispers, squeezing me tighter before letting me go.

"Wilder," I say, before she has a chance to walk away. She doesn't turn around, just glances over her shoulder. "You're not fucked up. And I don't want to hear you call my best friend that again." My comment leaves her speechless.

Walking toward her, I run my thumb over her cheek. A breath catches in her chest. I see her pulse quicken.

Sliding past her, the two of us make our way out of the butler's pantry and into another room. It's the only room on this side of the house, and I can see why. It's a large media room with an oversized black sectional, a movie theater-sized projector, a table with a popcorn maker and snacks, and movie theater posters lining the wall.

"If it's alright with you, I thought we could just watch a movie tonight."

"Hell yeah! This room is sick."

Brinley grins before walking to the back of the room where a computer is set up.

"How about *Get Out*?"

"Fuck no! I'm already in the white one percent, I don't need that shit jinxing me." I shudder.

I hear her laugh, knowing that she's fucking with me.

Brynn's face is lit up by the screen, and it's the only light except for a couple of dimmed canned lights in the ceiling. I wander over to the snack cart where I discover fresh popcorn and a variety of movie theater boxed candy.

When did she have the time to get the popcorn made?

I fill a bucket with popcorn and pour melted butter on top. Once the bucket is full, I grab a few boxes of candy—Twizzlers for Brynn and Reese's Pieces for myself.

Making my way to the couch, I find a very comfortable Brynn curled up in the middle of the sectional, a fort of pillows nestled under her head and a fuzzy blanket covering her body. She looks spent—physically, mentally, and emotionally. I hand her the bag of Twizzlers before settling the bucket of popcorn down next to her. I take my spot on the other side of the couch. Toeing off my shoes, I make myself comfortable.

The opening credits of *Cabin in the Woods* start playing. Of course, she picks a scary movie. I've never met a girl as obsessed with scary movies as Brynn is.

Tonight, I'll let her have her way, but tomorrow is a new day. Tomorrow, I'm breaking down the walls I didn't know were still standing. Tomorrow I'm getting answers.

A heavy weight is across my chest. My nose fills with the scent of vanilla and citrus as I inhale.

What the fuck?

Blinking open my eyes, I take in the semi-dark room. Light, almost white, strands of hair tickle my chin. That's when I realize that Brynn is sprawled out across my body, my arms wrapped around her body. And that's also when I realize that my morning wood is tenting my pants right next to her stomach.

Reaching my hand down, I tuck my boner in my waistband, willing him to go away.

I try to think of something, anything, besides the fact that Brynn is sleeping soundly curled up with me in only a tiny pair of sleep shorts and a sports bra. I swear she had a baggie sweatshirt on earlier. She must've gotten hot and decided to strip. Brynn stripping. Now that's something to imagine.

No, dammit Q, get it together. Thinking of Brynn stripping is not going to get rid of your current predicament.

Grams stripping.

Gag.

JP's gym bag.

Double gag.

Now that did it.

Do I wake her or let her sleep?

Shit, maybe I should close my eyes for a little bit longer. I can't remember the last time I actually got to sleep in and not wake up to a five o'clock alarm. Early morning strength training is kicking my ass, and we're only halfway through the season. I love weightlifting. There's nothing better than pushing my body to its limits, but there's also nothing better than getting to rest. During the season, my body screams for sleep. Between workouts, practices, meetings, classes, and maintaining somewhat of a social life, sleep always falls to the back burner.

Deciding to shut my eyes for a few more minutes of rest, I've just about dozed off when someone comes into the movie theater room. After last night's awkward encounter with Brynn's parents, I decided to pretend I'm sleeping. Footsteps get closer, and I hear a long sigh along with a woman muttering.

"Seriously, Brinley," her mother snaps, nudging Brynn's shoulder.

Brynn starts to stir under my arms and, again, I think it's best to pretend I'm still sleeping. Slowly, Brynn lifts her head from my chest before darting into an upright position.

"Shit. Mother?" she says.

That's when I decided to open my eyes.

"Yes, it's your mother. What the hell are you doing?" she retorts, eyes bouncing from Brynn's half-naked body to me.

Knowing exactly what Mrs. Wilder must be thinking, I move to sit up as well.

"We fell asleep watching a movie. What's the big deal? You've walked in on me doing far worse."

"I *definitely* don't need a reminder of that, Brinley," her mother snaps again.

This is getting awkward. Clearing my throat, I run my hand over the back of my neck.

"Sorry Mrs. Wilder, we did fall asleep. Nothing suspect is going on under your roof," I speak up.

She glances over at me before her eyes dart back over to her daughter.

"I just wanted to remind you that you are to be at the Bellaire at six for cocktail hour. Hair and makeup will arrive at three. Be ready for them," Mrs. Wilder says in an exasperated voice before turning to leave.

My eyes track her hurried movements, making sure that Mrs. Wilder has left the room before turning back to Brynn. She's sitting upright with her legs folded in front of her, the blanket abandoned on the floor, her perfect handful-sized tits are on full display. I will my dick not to focus on how perfect they look in her tight bra. Her hands are folded in her lap. I watch her take lots of deep breaths and wonder what's going through her mind. I want so badly for her to let me in. All the way in. What I would give for a few minutes to deep dive in that beautiful mind of hers.

"Wilder, what does the receptionist at a sperm bank say as clients leave?"

She just looks at me, squinting her eyes with a dumbfounded expression painted on her face. I love when I stump her.

"Thanks for coming!"

She laughs. Like full deep laughter. Seeing that smile stretch across her face is like seeing the sun after a storm.

"I'm sure glad you decided to break the ice with a joke instead of me asking you about your camping trip this morning." She smirks.

"My camping trip?" I ask, puzzled. What the hell is she talking about? "Are you high?"

Another laugh. "No, I'm not high...I'm talking about that impressive tent you pitched this morning. No wonder the ladies keep throwing themselves at you."

I groan, dropping back against the couch. "Oh god, sorry about that. It's morning."

"I'm well aware you men can't control yourself in the mornings. Enough about your dick, we've got a big morning ahead of us."

"We do?"

"Yep," she says, popping the p. "Go get ready in something casual. I'll meet you in forty-five minutes?"

Forty-five minutes later, I'm dressed in a pair of gray joggers, a navy hoodie, white sneakers, and a flat bill CTU Eagles hat, waiting on Brynn. One of the best things about Brynn is that she's far from high maintenance. Again, another reason why the two of us hit it off so easily. She's as down-to-earth as I am. I'm chilling in the front sitting room when she emerges dressed in a cropped gray hoodie, leggings that hug her delicious ass, a bag slung across her body, and her camel-colored coat. She's dressed casually, but damn, does she look hot.

Hell, here I go again, ogling her body.

"Ready?" she asks, dangling a set of car keys in her hand.

She doesn't wait for my answer as she slips out of the front door, skipping down the front steps toward a detached garage. She hits a button on the fob, and one of the four garage doors rises. Inside is a new cherry red Tesla S-APEX. Brynn hits the fob again, unlocking the car. Looking over at me, she gives a shit-eating grin.

"Climb in. We are heading into the city."

Holy. Fuck. This is one badass car. I mean, I drive a damn Tesla, but this is like the mother of all Teslas. I thought I overheard her dad talking about it to someone last night, but I didn't believe it. Now I'm seeing it with my own eyes. She's a beauty. And now I'm wondering if her dad has any clue that she has the keys to his car.

Hesitating to get in, I look over at Brynn, but she's already climbing into the car. She stops, sensing my pause.

"Q, get in the car." I do as she says and get in the car. Adjusting her seat, I watch her get comfortable behind the wheel. Wilder would make a fine model for cars. She looks sexy as hell behind the wheel.

As hesitant as I was about making this trip, I'm glad I told Brynn I'd be her emotional support date. There's not much I wouldn't do for this girl.

Now it's time for the truth; I've let her stall long enough.

But first, I'm going to enjoy this ride.

CHAPTER 13
Brynn

NAVIGATING THE TESLA INTO the city is an absolute blast. Dad's car is fast. Like really freaking fast; I feel like I'm flying. After I heard him brag about his new car to Asher's dad and him failing to acknowledge me last night, I decided to be a little spiteful this morning. The key card was just sitting on the counter, calling out to me. I grabbed them, and then left a note on the counter.

Gosh, it's the most fun I've had so far, aside from waking up in Quinton's arms. Wait, why did I say that was fun? That wasn't fun, it was weird, or was it? My feelings about the situation are all screwed up. Maybe that's the problem, I haven't had a good screw lately.

Yeah.

Yeah, that's what it is.

As many times as I've stayed in his room, we have never, ever fallen asleep together. But waking up in his arms, it felt...it felt good. It felt surprisingly right. And to be honest, that scares the shit out of me.

Quinton Boyd is my best friend, my emotional support date, my partner in crime. He's my *best friend*. That's it. End of discussion.

Whipping through the hustle and bustle of Chi-Town, I finally reach our destination. This morning, I woke up deciding that today's heart-to-heart would need lots of good food. And comfort food is always a good idea. Grant Park Bistro is one of my favorites when I come home, which isn't often, but I always make sure that I can grab brunch when I can. I pull into the valet parking lane at the hotel next door. Exiting the car, I tip the valet when he slips us our valet ticket. Quinton and I make our way to the restaurant, taking in the craziness of Chicago on a Saturday morning. It's busy, full of groups heading to brunch and tourists exploring the city. I'm grateful I thought to book us a reservation last night. While I'm busy checking out the city, I notice that Q is glancing around too. It's his first time in the city, and I'm glad I get to be his tour guide.

He pulls open the heavy door to the restaurant for me.

"Are we underdressed?" he asks, as we step inside.

"Athleisure is in, Q," I say with a smile, my eyes cascading up and down his body, stopping to admire the way his gray joggers accent his body.

He's working with a very good asset, which I felt stabbing me in my stomach this morning. My mouth goes dry, but I can't help myself from staring. It's just right there. Men in gray sweats should be outlawed in public.

"Wilder, if you don't stop staring at my dick, we are going to have a very embarrassing repeat of this morning," he whispers.

Immediately, my eyes snap up to his, as heat spreads up my neck, and a pink blush settles on my cheeks.

"Good morning, welcome to Grant Park Bistro," the hostess greets us. "Just the two of you?"

"Yes, please," Quinton answers, placing his arm over my shoulders.

Clearly, he doesn't want to have a repeat of last night when I bitched out our waitress. Oops. This might be one of those "sorry, not sorry" moments.

"Oh, we have a reservation," I announce a little too loudly. I'm flustered. My nerves are shot. On top of that, I'm having weird feelings for my best friend, and I'm about to spill my deepest secrets that no one outside of Chicago knows. "It's under Wilder."

The hostess takes a minute scrolling through her iPad.

"Yes, there it is. Mr. and Mrs. Wilder, please follow me."

My stomach flutters at the hostess's slip-up, but neither Q nor I correct her. She leads us to a booth near the window, setting down our menus, and letting us know our waiter will be right with us.

Silence falls over the table as we peruse the menu. When it comes to eating out, I'm so predictable. I find something that I love, and I don't usually stray from it. Which means I'll be getting the Land Benedict—Eggs Benedict served with ham—a side of breakfast potatoes and a cup of fruit. Oh, and of course, a mimosa. Who can pass up a mimosa? Especially at brunch. Closing my menu, I place it at the edge of the table, the universal sign that I'm ready to order. While I wait for Q, I look around the space.

There's a couple at the table next to us, and you can definitely get that early dating vibe from them. Both are a little jumpy and a little awkward. While I can't see her face, I can see his, and his eyes say that he's nervous as hell, but he's smitten with her. There's a warm glow in his eyes. It's sweet, and I can't help but smile to myself as I watch them. It reminds me of a memory I've long since forgotten.

"Happy birthday to you. Happy birthday to you. Happy birthday dear Bryce and Brinley. Happy birthday to you," everyone sang around our table.

Bryce and I looked at each other before bending over to blow out two birthday candles on our piece of cheesecake.

Today is the day that Bryce and I finally turn sixteen. We can officially get our licenses. Hello, freedom! We've been waiting for this day, well, since we learned the significance of turning sixteen. Not only is today my sixteenth birthday, but Asher has a whole night planned for just the two of us to celebrate. I can't help but think that tonight is going to be the night, you know, the big one. We've done just about everything else, and all signs are leaning toward sex.

Just thinking of sex makes my cheeks flush. I quickly glance around the table, hoping that no one is paying attention to what I'm thinking about. Only my eyes snag on a pair of piercing blue eyes that are getting darker and darker by the second. Asher is watching me with intensity, and nervousness, but it's like he can sense my inner thoughts. The thoughts of the two of us finally losing our virginity, together. My cheeks flare, and I have to look away. Only I look the wrong way, catching my twin brother watching us.

Busted.

Bryce wraps his arm across my shoulders, leaning over to me to whisper in my ear. "I swear, Brynnie, you two need to chill out. It's written all over both of your faces. And I don't want to see that shit. You're my *sister, and he's my* best friend. *I've barely gotten used to the two of you playing tonsil hockey, I don't need to think of anything else going on between you two."*

I lean in to add to the conversation. "How about you worry about you, and I'll worry about me, brother? The whole school hears about your sexcapades, which means I hear about them," I shiver. "Not to mention the girls who come up to me *wanting me to pass on what they want to do to* you. *Makes me want to swallow bleach."*

Bryce and I hold eye contact before we are interrupted by our parents.

"Kids, your dad and I have to stay in the city tonight for business. The Nelsons are going to drive you back home."

It's all I can do not to look at Asher. Instead, I bring my lip in between my teeth, biting back a smile.

Tonight is going to be the *night.*

"Brynn? Yo, Wilder?" I hear Quinton, breaking me out of the flash-back.

Shaking my head, I look up at him, realizing our waiter is standing at our table.

"Shit, sorry," I mutter. "What did you ask?"

Our waiter looks me up and down before smiling at me and repeat-ing his question of asking what I'd like to drink.

"I'll take a mimosa and a black coffee please."

He walks away and I realize that Q had already ordered, which means I was in quite a fog. While we wait for the waiter to return, silence falls over our table.

"Q, what goes in hard and dry then comes out wet and soft?" I ask the super inappropriate joke.

He just stares at me, blinking. It's almost like he's in shock that I would tell such a naughty joke.

"Gum, duh! What'd you think it was?"

Looking at me, he just shakes his head laughing. I just smile back at him.

Our waiter returns and sets down our drinks and takes our or-ders—the usual for me and steak cooked medium, eggs over easy, breakfast potatoes, and a side of fruit for Q.

"Where'd you go just a few minutes ago?" he asks, eyes full of concern, but his expression isn't one of annoyance.

A smile slowly stretches across my face. I imagine it looks like the Joker, a little crazy, a little unhinged.

"I was looking around and spotted the couple next to us," I say, gesturing my head toward the couple I'm talking about. "Watching them, I can tell they're on a date and it's new."

He squints his eyes looking at me with a questioning look.

"How do you know they aren't just friends? You blew up at our waitress last night for assuming we were just friends, which we are. Why are you assuming they're together?"

"Well, first of all, it's better to assume two people are together than that they aren't, that's just common sense. Second, look at his body language. He's nervous as fuck, but when he looks at her, his eyes flare with desire."

I watch Quinton watch them. He's seeing what I see.

Turning back to me, he folds his hands, placing his elbows on the table, resting his chin on his hands.

"Okay, say you're right, that doesn't explain why you just disappeared."

Inhaling a deep breath, I pick up my coffee, blowing on it before taking a sip. I take another drink, savoring that first taste of caffeine. It's my favorite thing in the morning. Placing the mug back on the saucer, I look at Q.

"Watching him all nervous made me think of my sixteenth birthday. Our parents and Asher's parents surprised us with an early dinner here in the city. Ash had plans for us to be *together* when I turned sixteen," I say, giving Q a look that he should understand what kind of *together* I was referring to. "Anyway, watching the nerves roll off that guy made me think of how nervous I was that whole dinner because I was *finally* sixteen."

He nods his head in understanding, but he doesn't keep eye contact. He's frustrated, and I can't say I blame him. I just want to get through breakfast, and then I'll spill my story. Taking another gulp of my coffee, I decide to change the subject.

"How's it feel not having football this weekend?"

Changing the subject was a good call. I watch his shoulders ease and he relaxes in his chair, bringing his coffee up to his lips for a drink. Only I can't take my eyes off his lips. The way his thick, full lips contrast against the white mug. Nervously, I bring my lip in between my teeth and nibble.

What is wrong with me? Who is the doe-eyed girl?

CHAPTER 14
Brynn

Brunch goes off without a hitch. We laugh, joke, and converse. No more zoning out and getting lost in the memories.

Getting up and pushing in our chairs, we navigate toward the exit. The city has only gotten busier while we were eating brunch. It's a beautiful fall day. The birds are chirping, the sun is shining bright, and the weather is a perfect sixty-five degrees. As we head toward Grant Park, Quinton soaks in the city. During that ten-minute walk, my mind starts wandering. Internally, I'm psyching myself up to open myself up and spill my heart.

There's a vacant park bench overlooking Buckingham Fountain. It's there that I decide to tell my story. Sounds of children screaming while their parents chase them surround us, joggers run past us, and groups are gathered around taking pictures.

Settling onto the bench, I look straight ahead, watching a little boy and girl run around playing.

"He was my best friend," I begin, sensing Q turn his head toward me. "Our moms met when we were five. They were both working on a charity fundraiser for the hospital. Asher's mom always loved party planning. From her first meeting with my mom, the two just hit it off, becoming fast friends. This was before my mom's personality shift.

"From then on, the two were inseparable, which led to Bryce and me becoming best friends with Asher. More often than not, when

Mom had a shift at the hospital, we would go to the Nelsons' instead of staying home with the nanny. Grace wasn't able to have more kids after Asher. She always wanted a large family, so Bryce and I became like her kids." I pause, letting a tear go.

Talking about Grace and how she took us in like we were her own children riddles me with guilt. Guilt over the fact I haven't seen her in too long. Quinton, sensing my need for comfort wraps, an arm around my shoulders, placing his other hand on my thigh. Still unable to look at him, I keep staring ahead, watching the kids run around before continuing.

"Grace would always joke that Asher and I would end up married and then Bryce and I would officially be family. As we got older, Friday nights became family nights with pizza and games. Holidays were spent with the Nelsons. Once we hit seventh grade, Grace fixed up a guest room to be my room. She said that we were getting too old to have coed sleepovers." I chuckle, a small smile spreading across my face.

"You two had already kissed, hadn't ya?" Quinton asks with a twitch of his lips. Turning to look at him, I smile bigger. "Yeah, at the sixth-grade end-of-the-year dance. We were slow dancing to Taylor Swift. How cliché."

Quinton chuckles.

"Nothing progressed after the dance. Bryce saw us kiss and was pissed. He had words with Asher. I was so mad at my brother. I thought he had ruined my chances of having a boyfriend. Then in eighth grade, I got my first boyfriend, but it wasn't Asher. Asher was pissed, so he got his first girlfriend. This cycle continued throughout the whole year. You know how dating was in junior high. So at the eighth-grade end-of-the year dance, he cut in while I was dancing with someone and kissed me. Anyway, that was the day everything changed.

Asher and I started dating. Fast forward to sophomore year. My cousin, Thad, had gotten three tickets to the Indianapolis Colts–New England Patriots game in Indy."

"*Thad*?" Quinton interrupts.

Ignoring his comment, I continue. "It was supposed to be Thad, Bryce, and me going to the game. But Asher loved Tom Brady, so I told him to go in my place. And that's the night everything changed." I pause, too shaken up to continue.

Quinton gives me the time I need, squeezing my thigh and my shoulder with his hands, letting me know that he's here for me. Inhaling a deep breath, I turn to face Q.

"Thad was driving them home, and when he stopped to get gas he took a cocktail of pills. He had a reaction to them while he was driving with the cruise control set. Thad was overdosing as the car went through the median and into oncoming traffic. A semi hit the passenger side. Bryce was in the passenger seat, and Asher was in the backseat, passenger side."

"Oh god," Quinton says quietly, wiping the tears from my face.

"Ash and I were supposed to be endgame. He gave me a promise ring for my sixteenth birthday. It was supposed to be forever. And I know, *I know* we were young, but it was like the stars had aligned for us."

All the emotions come rushing back to me, hitting me like a tsunami. I turn my head into Q's shoulder and let the sobs take over.

FIVE YEARS AGO

The sound of the doorbell wakes me. Rushing down the stairs to open the door, I don't bother looking to see who's at the door. Asher had texted me that they were on their way home, and we had been texting on his ride home until I fell asleep. Assuming Bryce forgot his key again, I open the front door. A huge smile is on my face, as I anticipate the stories from the game. I've been jealous of them, but I know I made the right decision letting Asher go see his idol.

I jump as I take in the two uniformed policemen standing on our front porch. Immediately, I know something is wrong. Clutching the door, I stare at the two men.

"What happened?" I croak out the words.

"Miss, are your parents home?" one of the officers asked.

"Is it my dad or my brother?" I ask in a whisper.

Dad was staying in the city, which he often does during the week. My parents have a condo in the city where they often crash, depending on their schedules.

The other officer removes his hat and lowers his head.

"Miss, is your mom home?"

"Yes, I'll go get her," I responded, opening the door wider. "You can come in."

The officers come into the house, closing the front door, while I turn and run up the stairs to my parents' room.

Mother was asleep with her sleep mask covering her eyes. Going around to her side of the bed, I start nudging her shoulder, trying to wake her, hoping that tonight wasn't a sleeping pill night.

"Mom! Mom, the police are here." I rush the words, trying to get her to wake up.

That does the trick, and she jumps up with a start. Glancing at me beside her, she climbs out of bed, slipping on her silk robe. The two of us descend the stairs, not saying a word.

The first officer acknowledges us first.

"Ma'am, we are sorry to stop by so late. Unfortunately, there's been an accident." Mom grabs my hand, squeezing it, as the officer continues. "Your son was involved in an accident on Interstate 65. He's been air-lifted to—"

I zone out, feeling like my head's underwater as my knees give out, and I collapse to the floor. The other officer squats down in front of me trying to talk to me, but all I hear is the teacher's voice from Charlie Brown. I can't process any of it. The officers never said anything about Asher. Oh god, Asher.

Snapping out of it, I look the officer in the eyes. "What about Asher? Asher Nelson was in the car too. He's my boyfriend."

"He's been airlifted as well."

Pulling myself out of Quinton's embrace, I stop the memory from playing in my mind. I have to get the rest of the story out.

"Bryce and Asher were airlifted to the hospital. The doctors did emergency surgeries, but both were put in medically induced comas, hoping that rest would help them heal faster. Mom had the best of the best flown in to treat them, but it didn't matter. Bryce's body was too weak from the direct impact, and he passed within a few hours of the accident..." I pause, wiping the tears and snot with the back of my sleeve. "Asher showed progress, and we all got so hopeful. A few days later, the doctors decided to bring him out of the coma. He woke up," I end the words with a sob.

"He woke up. I was the first person he saw when he woke up. It was the best moment of my life. The next three days were spent at his bedside, lying next to him. He told me how much he loved me, and how he couldn't wait until we were eighteen so we could start our lives together. On the fourth day of him being awake, I had to lay my brother to rest. I promised him I'd be back as soon as I could…" Another sob racks through my throat.

My mind goes right back to that hospital room. Seeing my sweet Asher awake, kissing me goodbye, telling me how sorry he was that he couldn't be there with me. Grace and I had left to go to the funeral while Daniel stayed behind with Asher. No one wanted to leave him alone once he was awake. While Daniel stepped out of the room, my life was forever changed…again.

Wiping my tears, I straighten. Sensing that I need some space, Q slightly slides away, just leaving his hand on my thigh.

"Asher died twenty minutes after we put Bryce in the ground. A blood clot dislodged and traveled to his brain. He was gone instantly. There was nothing anyone could've done or prevented it. Within a week, I lost my brother and my boyfriend. My two best friends were gone. Just like that"

"Jesus, Brynn," Quinton gasps out. Using his free hand, he rubs the back of his neck. "Why didn't you ever tell me this?"

"Because who would want to spend time with the fucked-up girl?" I throw up my hands, exasperated.

Before I can continue, Quintin is interjecting. "What'd I tell you about calling my best friend fucked up?"

"But Quinton, I am," I answer. "I've been floating through life sleeping around and partying to keep the demons from surfacing."

"You don't get to survive alone. I'm here for you, and you have an entire support system at CTU that is here for you, Wilder," Quinton adds, pausing to get my attention. "It's time for you to stop running on survival mode and start living. Live for them. Live for the ones who can no longer live. But most importantly, live for yourself. You have a beautiful soul that deserves to thrive. Open yourself up to more, open your heart to love. Because whoever gets the chance to be loved by you, and I mean fully, deeply, loved by you, is the going to be the luckiest son of a bitch."

Taking a moment, I wipe away the stream of tears that is spilling down my cheek. Looking up at the clear sky, I will the tears away.

"I don't let a lot of people in. It took me until I met you to even consider having a best friend again."

"But why?" he asks, still not getting it. "Why not let people see the real you? Why not date and find love again?"

"Don't you get it? The last two people I loved with all my heart died. Died together. I can't go through that again or curse someone else." I whisper that last part.

But he hears it.

Crystal clear.

"You blame yourself, don't you?"

"Of course I do. It's my fucking fault. Asher went because I gave him my ticket. If I had gone, I would've driven. I was always the driver, the responsible one. By choosing not to go, I sealed their fate."

"God, Brynn," he says, and I hear the emotion in his voice. "That's the most fucked up thing I've ever heard. It wasn't your fault. It was your piece of shit cousin who decided to ingest a mixture of pills and then drive. That's on him. Not you."

"Just stop. I've heard it all before. I've accepted it. You deserved the whole story, and that's the whole story."

I go to stand up, but before I can, two big, corded arms wrap me up in a hug.

Quinton squeezes me before whispering in my ear, "People deserve to see the real you. I love the real Brynn." I shake my head against his body. Before I pull away, he murmurs into my hair, "You deserve happiness, Wilder."

Pulling back, I give him a small smile. I can't talk about this anymore. I know how I feel about it, and while I appreciate his words, that's all they are to me. I'll forever live with the guilt, and that's something I've accepted.

CHAPTER 15
QUINTON

To say I'm in shock over this morning's events would be the understatement of the year. Jesus, not only is she dealing with the death of her twin brother, but her boyfriend too. And then there's her cousin. He caused her to lose her closest people, but his death had an impact on her too. Anger courses through me as I think about how he got off easy. He didn't have to pay for his actions.

Talk about a fucked-up situation. This is the shit you see in movies, not *actually* live it. Fuck, I can't get the image of her defeated body telling me this story out of my head. Part of me has always wondered why Brynn is as wild as she is, and clearly, she's living for herself, her brother, and her high school boyfriend.

She finished telling me the story, wiped her eyes, and then went on like it wasn't the most tragic story I'd ever heard. Brynn wore her signature smile, her mask back in place, and took us sightseeing for an hour. Leaf peeping through the park, watching a few boats on Lake Michigan, and a selfie in front of 'The Bean,' before she took us on a white-knuckle ride back to her parents' house in her dad's car.

I still can't believe she stole her dad's car.

Actually, I can.

Brinley Wilder is the craziest girl I know, and the more I'm with her, the more I crave her. Her spunk. Her smile. Her wild side. But there's more to her than that. She's passionate. She's caring. And she's a fighter.

We've been back at her parents' house for an hour. Both of her parents were gone by the time we got here. It's been weird. Despite them requiring that she be here, there hasn't been any real conversation between Brynn and her parents. Now I see why she hates coming home. My parents and I don't always get along, but there are always conversations—I might not like what we talk about, but they care enough to speak to me.

I make myself comfortable in the media room, turning on ESPN, while Brynn goes upstairs to start getting ready for the gala. I still have time before I need to change, so I reach into my pocket to pull out my phone. There's a text message waiting for me.

Cody Jacobs: How're things with B? She won't text me back.

Me: It's been a chaotic morning.

Cody Jacobs: Why? What's going on?

Me: Ok. There's more to the story. It's fucked.

Cody Jacobs: ????

Me: She's been keeping a lot from us.

Cody Jacobs: Dude...WTF?

Me: I've gotta let her tell her story when she's ready. It's fucked up.

> **Cody Jacobs: Well shit. Take care of our girl.**

She's not our *girl. She's my girl. Mine.*

Resting my head across the back of the couch, I let my eyes drift shut.

Sometime later, I'm woken up by a voice clearing. Slowly blinking my eyes open, I see Nadia, their housekeeper, standing next to me.

"I'm sorry to wake you, Mr. Boyd," Nadia begins. "Miss Brinley asked that I let you know that it's time for you to get ready."

Shaking out of my haze, I drag my hand down my face, standing up.

"Thanks. Sorry about that, I didn't realize I had dozed off. I'll head up now," I respond, reaching beside me to grab my trash.

"Leave it, I have to clean in here," Nadia says. She places her hand on my arm as I go to walk past her. "Thank you for taking such good care of my girl. She's a strong one, but she's still grieving."

Placing my hand over Nadia's, I respond "Always will. She's the best. I just wish she would've told me the whole story sooner."

Nadia's lips slightly turn at the corners, and she nods her head. I leave her standing in the media room and head to the guest suite to shower.

The hot water cascades down my body from the rain showerhead. I let the hot water pour over me. Lowering my head, I close my eyes, but my mind wanders to a place it hasn't gone to before, not fully.

With my eyes closed, I picture Brynn in the shower with me. The image conjured in my mind is so clear, it feels real.

Steam billows around her as hot water cascades down her creamy skin that's tinged pink from the heat of the water. My body reacts to the images playing in my head. Keeping my eyes closed, my hand trails down my stomach until I grab hold of my thickening erection. Wishing my hands were Brynn's, I begin stroking my ever-growing cock. She's standing here, the pink shade on her cheeks growing deeper, eyes growing darker with lust, as she watches me pump myself.

Licking her lips, she slowly slides down to her knees. Running her hands up my thighs, she pushes my hand out of the way. Eyes widening at the size of my erection, she brings her heat fueled gaze up to mine, looking at me from under her lashes. A smirk spreads across her lips as she sticks her tongue out, running it across her luscious lips. Keeping her gaze locked with mine, she lowers her chin, taking my cock in her mouth. A moan escapes her, and I feel the humming around my cock. She doesn't stop until I'm hitting the back of her throat. It's impressive that she engulfed my whole length in one go, most girls have to work their way to the base. Her cheeks hollow inward as she sucks me, bobbing her head.

Her gaze finds mine again, and I just stare down at her. Watching her use her hand to rub her sensitive center while she swirls her tongue around the head of my cock. Using my other hand, I grab the back of her neck, groaning at the sight of watching her coming undone while she brings me to the brink of nirvana. She takes me deeper as my grip tightens, and I'm fucking her face.

A guttural groan leaves my lips as ropes of my cum shoot against the tiled wall. Never have I come so hard from fucking my fist. But it wasn't because of my fist, it was because I pictured my best friend down on her knees, taking my dick.

I'm fucked.

Truly fucked with these feelings for Brynn.

Splashing on a dab of my cologne, I take one last look in the mirror. Brynn didn't tell me what to wear, just that I needed to bring something nice that I'd wear for a game. I opted for a pair of black dress pants, a white shirt, a black bow tie, and a burgundy jacket trimmed in black satin. I adjust my bow tie one last time before stepping out into the hallway. Looking up, my eyes immediately look across the landing and find Brynn standing in the other wing.

My mouth dries. Jaw dropping to the floor.

Not only did I just get myself off thinking about her, but there she is looking fine as fuck. Brynn is wearing a short, long-sleeved, gold sequin dress. Her white-blonde hair is curled in waves.

Perfect for me to wrap around my fist while I watch her take me in her mouth.

And those goddamn legs. Her dress is *short*, and those gold stilettos make her legs stretch for days. The gold of her dress makes her bronze skin look even more sun kissed. I wonder what she would look like with those golden legs wrapped around my waist.

Shit, Q. Stop ogling your best friend.

I need to get laid. As soon as we get back to campus, I'm finding the first girl who will give me the time of day, and I'm burying myself in her until these thoughts of Brynn leave my mind.

We both stand there for what seems like hours, scanning each other from head to toe and back up. I can't get my brain to function. She's officially made me short-circuit.

"Damn, don't you clean up well," Brynn says first, strutting her way toward me. Her hips sway with each step. "I love when you wear this jacket," she adds, running her hands down my lapels.

"You look beautiful, Wilder." I grab her hands from my chest, holding her out to look her up and down one more time.

She pulls her hand away and does a small twirl, which allows me to get a glimpse at the open back of her dress that exposes her minimal script tattoo that runs the length of her spine. It reads "live a life you will remember," and it's the most perfect tattoo for her. Drool collects in the corner of my mouth. Her long, toned body is mesmerizing, especially in this dress.

"My parents are going to die when they see me, but I don't care." Reaching back, she grabs my hand again. "C'mon, we're going to be late."

I let her lead us down the grand staircase. Nadia is dusting in the entryway when she spots us.

"Oh my heavens," she says, clutching her heart. "Miss Brinley, hand me your phone so I can get a photo of you two. Both of you look like you should be on the cover of a magazine."

"Thanks, Nadia, but if anyone is going to be on the cover of a magazine, it's going to be Q when he gets on the cover of *Sports Illustrated*."

The two of us spend the next five minutes posing in various positions that Nadia instructs. It feels like we are getting ready for prom instead of attending a gala to raise money for The Asher & Bryce Foundation—a scholarship foundation that was created in memory of them.

"Okay, there are lots of options, not that you two need options. You're both beautiful." Nadia hands Brynn her phone back, pulling her in for a hug. She whispers something in her ear that I can't make out, but it's enough to make Brynn pull back and kiss the housekeeper on the cheek.

Nadia pulls away and turns to me.

Wrapping her arms around my neck, the older woman pulls me into a fierce hug before she whispers in my ear. "Take care of our girl tonight. Don't let her get too out of control."

I pull back and give her a wink before leaning down and kissing her on the cheek as well. This woman is like a mother to the girl who holds the key to my heart. I'd do anything to make both women happy. Nadia leads us to the front door, opening it for Brynn and me.

Brynn leads the way to another town car where the driver is waiting to open the door for her. I follow her, my eyes staring ahead at her ass. Brynn's got a good ass. I might be her best friend, but I'm still a man who appreciates a good ass. It's curvy and round, but firm. I can only imagine what it would feel like to grab a handful. She enters the open door as I stride around to the driver's side, sliding into the back seat.

As the driver gets back in the car, I watch Brynn reach into her purse, pulling out the same weed pen she had last night. Moving my hand, I grab the wrist that she's holding the pen in.

"Quinton?" she asks, flinging her head to mine.

"Not tonight." I speak softly. "Use me. Let me be your crutch."

She searches my eyes. She must see the sincerity in them, because she places the pen back in her purse.

"Thank you." She nods with a smile.

The two of us ride in silence, both of us looking out the window as the city nears.

"What should I expect for tonight?" I finally break the silence.

She turns to me, twisting her hands in her lap.

"It'll be a lot of the who's who of Chicago, anyone with deep pockets will be there. We'll be sitting at a table with my parents, the Nelsons, and another couple—the table seats eight. Once dinner is over, the band will start. We can dance if you want, but some of us will sneak off and play games."

My brow furrows before asking, "What kind of games?"

She just smirks, patting my leg. "The wild kind."

I have a feeling tonight's going to be interesting. I'm not sure that I'm prepared for the events that are about to happen.

CHAPTER 16
Brynn

THE BELLAIRE IS DECORATED exquisitely. I'm in awe of her beauty. Located downtown, it's a historic building that used to be a theater. Over the years, it has been renovated with modern decor that still honors the original charm. The entryway features the most elegant crystal chandelier that dazzles, drawing your eyes up. Columns and delicate woodworking line the walls. I've always loved attending events here. I'm a sucker for historic charm.

Wrapping my arm through Quinton's, I let him lead us along with the crowd as we enter the dining hall. Fifty circular tables are set up in the room with white linens and floral arrangements. There's a stage in the front of the room where a band is playing soft music. After dinner, the music will transition to lively tunes, encouraging guests to get up and dance. A long bar is set up in the back next to the tables of baskets, services, vacation getaways, and other items that have been donated by local businesses to be raffled off at the silent auction.

"Breathtaking," I gasp, taking in the room. No matter how many times I attend galas here, I'm always taken aback by the beauty of the Bellaire.

"Yeah, breathtaking," Quinton repeats.

But when I look at him, his eyes aren't focused on the room before us, they're focused on me. I feel a blush spread over my skin.

"Let's get a drink." I gesture toward the bar.

Quinton steps in line behind me, his hand finding my lower back. It's an open bar, because why not? What better way to loosen purse strings than by encouraging the guests to overindulge, even though a table costs two thousand dollars?

There's a small line of guests dressed to perfection when we make it over to the bar. Quinton stands quietly behind me, never removing his hand from my back. His thumb caresses the exposed skin of my open-back dress. Goose bumps spread across my body.

"People cannot take their eyes off you, Wilder. You're the most stunning woman in this room."

That damn blush returns, making my whole body hot, especially the skin where his thumb is kissing my skin.

"Ah, Ms. Wilder, it's been a while. What can I get you this evening, sweetheart," the bartender asks.

Q gives me a puzzled look. George has been doing events for us for a long time. When I was in high school, he'd always slip me a glass—or two—of champagne. In middle school, he'd make me the best Shirley Temples, with extra cherries.

"Hi, George." I lean over the bar, planting a quick kiss on the old man's cheek. "I'll have a glass of champagne, and my handsome date will have—"

"Bourbon, on the rocks, please."

George starts making our drinks.

"Bourbon tonight?" I ask, turning to face Quinton, leaning my back on the bar. The cold material cools my heated skin.

"Thought I'd try to be a little classy tonight, Miss Champagne."

I just smile. Grabbing our drinks, we move through the crowd of people. Eyes follow us everywhere—shocked to see the missing Wilder child. Our table is in the front where we are joined by my parents, Daniel and Grace Nelson, and two empty chairs.

"Darling, there you are," mother greets us.

Quinton slides my chair out before sitting next to me.

"Mother," I greet, downing the rest of my champagne. "Daniel, Grace, it's wonderful to see you both."

"Hi, sweetie," Grace chimes in. "Quinton, how are you enjoying the city?"

Quinton's tongue escapes his mouth, using it to wipe the remaining bourbon from his lips. Stretching his arm, he places it across my chair and begins skating his thumb across my shoulder. My eyes track the movement of his tongue, my panties no longer dry.

Well that's a new development.

Wiping his mouth from his sip of bourbon, he places his arm across my chair, rubbing my shoulders.

"Wilder took us for quite the ride this morning," he says, and a small chuckle escapes my mouth.

Father grunts before chiming in. "I imagine she did, since she stole my car."

Rolling my eyes, I fold my hands, resting them in my lap.

"Oh Daddy, you call it stealing, I call it borrowing. What were we supposed to drive? It's not like I have a car here."

"Any other goddamn car," he grumbles before Mother changes the subject.

"How long are you here for?"

Signaling to a waiter, I point to my empty glass and hold up two fingers while Quinton holds up one finger for himself.

"Our flight is at six thirty tomorrow morning."

She harrumphs. I can only imagine that she's counting down the minutes until the problem child is out of her hair.

"So soon?" a voice from behind me interjects, pulling out the seat next to me.

Glancing up to see who so rudely interrupted this riveting conversation, my breath stalls.

"Tristan?"

I stare at the boy, now a man, who sits down beside me. So many of his features match his cousin's. It's like looking at a ghost.

"Hi Brinley," Tristan says, leaning in for a hug.

Tristan Nelson is Asher's older cousin. Growing up, if Asher wasn't with us, he was hanging out with his cousin. All of us spent a lot of time together when we were younger.

"You look stunning," he adds, perusing my body.

"Thank you." I blush. "Tristan, this is my friend Quinton Boyd."

Both men give each other an appraising look, but it's Quinton who reaches his hand out first.

"How's it going?"

Tristan shakes his hand, still looking at Q.

"Quinton Boyd. As in star running back for Central Texas University?"

A proud smile stretches across Quinton's face, and I can see the cockiness slip into place. There's my Q. This whole super polite, posh Quinton isn't the Quinton I love.

Love?

Yeah, like love as my bestie. Yeah, that's what I mean.

"One and the same. How do you know my girl?"

My girl. *My* girl.

Tristan takes a sip of his bourbon before answering. "Asher was my cousin."

Quinton's face drains. "Shit, man, I'm sorry."

Our waiter approaches with our fresh drinks, and a second server is right behind him with our appetizer—a simple greens salad with walnuts, apple, and raspberry vinaigrette.

Unrolling my napkin, I place the ivory-colored fabric in my lap. Scooping up a bite, an obnoxious voice to my left catches my attention.

"Sorry, baby, the line was so long," the voice says as long fingers come into my line of sight, placing a martini glass down next to Tristan.

"It's fine. Madeline, look who's at our table." Tristan glances from his date to me.

Glancing up, I met the eyes of the She-Devil herself. Madeline Sanchez, high school mean girl, head cheerleader, and all-around pain in my ass.

"Brinley, you remember Madeline?"

Reaching for my champagne, I take a sip before answering. My sip turns into a gulp, and that's when I feel a hand brushing up my right thigh. His touch is electrifying, and I can't help the way my body reacts to his touch.

Someone should really look into turning the air conditioning up.

My eyes find Q's, as he leans down to press a kiss to my temple.

Shit, why does that simple act calm me instantly? And why does his every touch, every glance, every action feel like a current running between us?

Turning back to my left, I look at the She-Devil, hoping I don't turn to ash. "Madeline, gosh, I almost didn't recognize you."

"You look just the same as high school, Brinley," she replies, eyeing me with that bitchy smirk on her face. "Always looking for attention," she adds under her breath.

"You didn't let me finish," I added. "I didn't recognize you, what with your lips the size of your face. Guess you needed the extra suction for all the ass kissing you do."

To my right, I hear Quinton and Grace chuckle quietly. Madeline's face drops and she's about ready to clap back, only Tristan stops her by whispering "don't" under his breath.

What the hell is he doing bringing this bitch as his date? Does he not remember all the problems she caused? All the bullying she did? She didn't just bully me, but *his* cousin too. I'm lost in my head when I feel Q's hand on my thigh again. I suck in a breath and finish my salad.

"Madeline, dear, this is Quinton," my mother chimes in. "I guess I'll do the introductions since Brinley clearly has no manners."

My eyes roll before I can stop them, and my mom catches it. She glares daggers at me.

"Hi," Madeline chirps. "Brinley and I go *way* back. How long have you two been together?"

"They're just friends," Mother answers for us. Even though it's the truth, this is one of those instances where I totally would've played into a fake relationship, like in one of the books Chloe is always talking about.

At girls' night, she couldn't stop talking about a book she just finished where the super hot football player pretends to date a girl on the team's PR staff. I guess he reads all the sexy scenes she has highlighted in her books so he can learn what she likes in bed. Talk about freaking hot. And *go him* for taking the initiative to learn how to please her.

Madeline starts eyeing Quinton like he's her dinner tonight. It's super awkward, especially since her date is sitting next to her.

Tristan clears his throat, bringing Madeline's attention back to him instead of eye-fucking Q, but not before she mutters, "That's quite a shame. A guy like you shouldn't be single."

Thankfully, we are interrupted by a server coming to pick up the salad plates.

The rest of dinner goes off without a hitch. Quinton and I are lost in our delicious main course of filet mignon, garlic mashed potatoes, and asparagus. Once dishes are cleared, Quinton leans in close to me, brushing my hair off my shoulder. His breath is warm on my neck.

"Want to go dance?" he whispers against my ear.

Chills erupt, and I try to hold in a shiver. You would've thought he asked to get me off with the way my body is reacting. I look up at him through my eyelashes and give him a sultry smirk and nod.

With my hand in his, I let him lead me to the dance floor where a few other couples are dancing. The band begins a cover of a slow Chris Stapleton song, and I melt. Quinton pulls me against his body. Flush. No space between us. I can feel every inch of his hard, defined body. He places his hand on my lower back and starts moving us to the music.

"You doing okay?" he asks.

I nod my head. No other words are spoken between us. We just let our bodies move to the beat as I soak up his touch.

There's something new brewing between us.

And I don't think I mind it.

"Oh my god," a girl shrieks.

I slowly turn to look for the voice.

"Taylor?" I ask, my mouth dropping open.

Taylor Shields was my best friend from fifth grade through high school. The two of us have grown apart since I left for Texas, but we'll always hold special places in each other's hearts. I take in the hottie in front of me. Taylor was never overweight, but she wasn't skinny either. The dress she's wearing hugs her curves. She looks healthy, happy, and hot. Her dirty-blonde brown hair is now shoulder length, a shiny brown with caramel highlights.

"Damn, girl, you look smokin'!"

She rushes me with a huge hug before pulling me back at arm's length, checking me out.

"I should say the same about you. But you've always been one sexy lady. Let's grab a drink and catch up!" She wraps her arm through mine, pulling me toward the bar before I have a chance to respond. "Can you believe the turnout?"

"No, I can't. It's weird, Tay," I say, looking around the crowd.

Pictures of Bryce and Asher line the wall behind the silent action. Taylor watches me take in the room.

"Is it hard being back?"

With a big sigh, I answer. "You have no idea. I miss them both every day, but being back here just brings all the pain to the surface."

"At least you've got some sexy arm candy to keep you company," she says, wiggling her eyebrows and gesturing toward Quinton who's standing in the corner talking to a guy who looks like the high school football coach. "Damn, B, you have the best luck."

"Oh stop it," I say, rolling my eyes. The She-Devil is in front of us in line at the bar. She turns to look at me and Taylor.

"Well look who it is, Porky Brewster and the slut."

"Aren't we a little old for high school shit Madeline?" I ask, stepping in her face.

"Please, it's not like you've changed," Madeline scoffs. "Still hopping on any willing dick? How long is he going to stick around? We all know your luck with—"

"You bitch," I cut her off, knowing damn well where she was about to go, stepping even closer, just as Tristan slides in between us.

"Ladies, ladies, ladies. Let's take this to another room." He gestures toward the back room before turning to the bartender. "Kind sir, can we get two bottles of champagne and a bottle of tequila, please?"

I feel him before he speaks, his warmth spreading down my back, just as his hands run down my arms.

"Everything good?"

"Yeah, Q, everything is good." I look at him before glaring at Madeline. "The fun is about to begin."

We make our way to the back room, which is a smaller room down a hallway from the main room. This is the room all of us usually hang out in during these events, especially when we were underage. We'd sneak lots of booze from the bar, and someone would always pass out joints before we played games to kill time. Looks like we are reliving the past.

Tristan has gathered up some others so there is a small crowd around a table. Quinton pulls me in his lap to make more space. Someone turns on their phone, and a throwback hit starts playing.

"Alright, the game is Truth or Dare," Tristan announces. "Rules are whoever is picked asks next. You pass, and you take a shot of tequila. Let the shit hit the fan, and let's get fucked up." He holds his drink in the air, and we all follow suit before taking a drink. "I'm going first," he says, looking around the table before a slow smile spreads across his face. "Brinley, truth or dare?"

I set my hands on the table, palm side down as I lean over the table. My new position causes Q to hiss through his lips.

"Dare."

He grins, leaning back in his chair.

"I dare you to go out and pinch the school board president's ass."

"Done," I say, standing up and taking a sip of my champagne.

Swinging my hips, I head toward the door with Tristan on my heels to witness. Standing in the main room's doorway, I quickly spot the school board president talking to a small group of people. He's facing me, so as I make my way over to him, I make sure to sway my hips and nibble on my lower lip. Sliding up behind him, I pinch his ass as I keep walking, keeping my hips swaying. He jumps, looking over his shoulder. I can feel his eyes on me. I glance over my shoulder, making eye contact with him, before giving him a wink. His eyes darken as I saunter back to where Tristan stands.

"Damn, Brynn." He chuckles. "You haven't changed a bit."

"Life's too damn short," I answer, making my way back to the group.

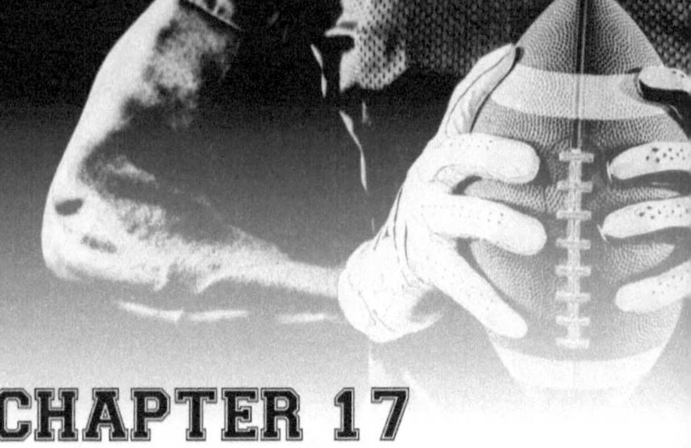

CHAPTER 17
QUINTON

TRUTH OR DARE HAS been going on for what feels like forever. Luckily, I haven't been subjected to anything too crazy. This game seems to be a passive-aggressive way for the girls to work out their shit and for the guys to make the girls do slutty things. All I have to say is that Madeline is a real bitch. I'm waiting for Brynn to leap across the table and punch her.

A new, upbeat song starts playing on someone's phone. Brynn's body starts moving to the beat against my lap. Christ, it feels good. My feelings are getting harder and harder to hide. And speaking of harder, my dick is twitching, appreciating the attention Brynn is unknowingly giving it.

Settle down, man.

The beat drops and Brynn starts to *really* get into the song. Her pussy is hovering right above my dick.

I wrap my arms around her middle, pulling her back against my chest.

Leaning into her, I whisper into her ear, "Wilder, if you don't stop moving that fine ass on my dick, I'm going to need a change of pants."

Her breath stutters and her face blushes. Making her blush is my new favorite thing. I love watching her cheeks tinge pink. She shuffles to the side, her body seated on my leg and not so much in my lap. Then she looks at my crotch, and slowly brings her gaze back up to meet my eyes. Her blue eyes start to take on a navy shade as a blush highlights her cheeks again.

"Oh god, sorry about that. I didn't realize—"

"It's fine," I interrupt. "I didn't say I minded, just wanted to let you know that either I'm going to embarrass myself or we need to find a closet."

She gasps, "Quinton?!"

"Um excuse me?" Madeline interrupts our thought. "You two need a minute to bang or are you ready to play?"

Have I mentioned how much I dislike this chick? The pink color spreads from Brynn's cheeks to her neck. Before turning her face to Madeline, her eyes shooting daggers. Seriously, if looks could kill, Madeline would've been dead now ten times.

"I asked Quinton Truth or Dare," Madeline repeats the question I never heard, too busy watching Brynn's body twerk in my lap.

"Dare," I answer, just as an evil smile takes over Madeline's fake as fuck face.

She looks between me and Brynn.

"Perfect. Quinton, I dare you to make out with Brynn. Right here. In front of all of us."

My hands tighten against Brynn's hips as her body tenses. I can do this, kissing Brynn isn't going to be a problem. The problem is does she want me to? And what's going to happen with my feelings once my lips meet hers?

"I didn't peg you for a voyeur Madeline. What's the matter, can't get anyone to kiss your giant lips, you need to watch others?" Brynn snaps at Madeline.

"I can get plenty, isn't that right, Trist," she purrs at Tristan, while I internally gag.

Moving my hands from Brynn's hips, I move her so that she's closer to me. Brynn places her hands on my shoulder while I rub my thumb against the skin on her thigh. She watches me brush my thumb against her before slowly dragging her eyes up to meet mine.

"We don't have to do this, Q," she whispers, and I smile at her, licking my lips. "If you don't want to take the shot, I will."

Keeping my left arm wrapped around her waist, I bring my right hand up to her neck. Wrapping my hand around her neck, I brush my thumb against her cheek, watching that pink blush spread over her body that I crave so much. She closes her eyes as I bend toward her, brushing my lips gently against hers.

Electric shock.

Fireworks.

An explosion racks through my body.

And from the gasp Brynn lets out, she felt it too. Taking advantage of her gasp, I slide my tongue inside her mouth. Tasting her. Battling against her tongue. Savoring the way her mouth feels against mine. My grip tightens against her as her hands travel from my shoulders to the back of my head, pulling me closer and letting out a moan. Her moan spurs me on and our tongues tangle with each other. Her hips grind against me, and my dick is hard as steel.

Cheers erupt around us, causing Brynn to pull away. She's flushed, her chest heaving. It's at that moment that I realize how fucked I am. I'm falling for my best friend.

Lying in the guest bedroom, I'm replaying the events of the night. That kiss is burned in my brain. And the way Brynn's legs looked in that dress. Goddamn. I knew she had great legs. But tonight, in that dress with those heels. I think I died and went to heaven.

Things were a little awkward between Brynn and me on the ride home. She bolted off to her room as soon as we got back to the house with an excuse that she was tired. Tired my ass. I was dying to get out of my suit. After changing into a pair of sweats, I make sure that all of my bags are packed for our morning flight, leaving out my morning essentials and a travel outfit. And after thirty minutes of no Brynn, I threw off my undershirt and climbed into bed, scrolling ESPN on my phone.

The highlights are playing from the day's games when my phone chimes in my hand.

Mom: YOU'RE IN CHICAGO?!

Mom: You're in Chicago with that girl.

Mom: And you didn't bother to let your parents know you left the damn state.

Me: How'd you know?

Me: And she's not 'that girl'. You know her damn name.

Mom: It's all over the internet. The two of you wrapped up in each other all night. It's not a good look, Quinton Alexander! Especially the way she's dressed. Does she not have any class?

Mom: Don't you dare use that tone with me.

Me: Goodnight.

I don't bother with any other responses. I'm so over her treating Brynn the way she does. She acts like every girl is bad news unless she hand-picks her for me. I don't want some little submissive housewife. I want a girl with a wild side, who doesn't take shit from anyone. Who makes me laugh until my sides hurt, who pushes me to be the best. I want a girl who looks good on my arm, but still has a mind of her own.

And with that thought, I just described Brinley Wilder.

Why is she avoiding me? Did she not want me to kiss her? Running my hand down my head, I squeeze my neck as a frustrated sigh leaves my lips.

Closing out the ESPN app, I set my alarm for four thirty, rolling over to try and get some sleep. With my back to the door, I'm almost asleep when I hear the door click open. Knowing it's Brynn, I don't make any movement, waiting to see what she does. She stands there, staring at me. I can feel her eyes scanning over my naked back. I can just imagine her twisting her hands together while chewing on her lower lip as she runs through a million thoughts in her head.

"You're thinking is keeping me awake," I finally say, breaking the silence.

She lets out a gasp. "I thought you were asleep."

"That's a little creepy," I murmur. Rolling over, I sit up against the headboard. "No, Wilder, I was waiting to see if you were going to stop hiding."

"Pssh, I wasn't hiding," she says, knowing full well we both know that she was, indeed hiding. "We kissed tonight, Quinton."

"Yeah, Wilder, we did. I can't get that damn kiss out of my mind."

She slowly places one foot in front of the other, erasing the space between us. I sit up and grab her hand, pulling her toward me. Her body flails across mine, landing on the bed. A breathy gasp leaves her lips. I chuckle at the shocked expression that takes over her face. Her body rests against mine and I slowly bring my hand up to brush away the loose tendrils of hair that's covering her face.

"Quinton, wh-wh-what are you doing?" she stammers, her eyes bouncing between mine.

I watch her eyes, before bringing my forehead to hers.

"I don't know, Brynn. I don't want to think, I just want to do what feels right."

Without hesitation, Brynn brings her mouth to mine. I open for her, letting her slip her tongue into my mouth. Pulling her body as close to mine as I can, I move us so that we are both lying on our sides. Our hands slide up and down each other's bodies.

Touching. Exploring. Allowing ourselves the freedom to touch each other.

My hand skates her hip, slipping under her oversized shirt. My hand continues grazing her skin until I hit her hip, it's at that moment I realize she's not wearing any pants. I groan.

"Fuck, Brynn. Where are your pants?"

"I hate sleeping in them."

Moving my hand from her hip, down her thigh, and toward her center, my finger grazes the apex of her thighs. It's there I feel the moisture pooling in the center of her panties. All of that is for me. She's wet *for me*. Another groan slips free as our tongues collide and duel against each other. My cock is throbbing. Never in my wildest dreams would I have imagined that I'd be lying in bed with Brinley Wilder, tongues battling like there's no tomorrow.

She moans against my lips as my fingers rub against her center. With much hesitancy, I pull back with much reluctance from her. We are panting, out of breath, chests rapidly rising and falling.

"Brynn. Brynn. What are we doing?"

She rubs her hand over my chest, skating her finger across my chest.

"Not thinking, just doing."

And in the next moment, she's flinging her leg over my waist, pushing me down onto my back. Her pussy hovers over my dick that's straining against my sweatpants, begging to be released. My mind is focusing on how soaked she is, and the only thing separating us is a tiny scrap of fabric.

She rests her arms on my chest, tracing the lines of the eagle tattoo. Slowly, she brings her lips down to mine. Her tongue runs against my bottom lip, coaxing me to open. And I do. Our tongues tangle, and I devour her taste.

Gripping the back of her head, my opposite hand grips her hip before flipping us so that her back is pressed into the mattress, my body resting on top of her, my bent arms keeping my weight from crushing her. Biting and licking soothing kisses down her neck and over her collarbone, I allow my hands to wander over every curve. Slipping my hands under her shirt, I slowly peel it away from her body. Lifting it until her arms are almost free. She keeps her arms stretched above her head with her shirt tangled against her hands. Finding her smooth skin again, I continue my assault down her body, trailing nips and licks until my chin is resting on her pussy. Groaning against her wet heat, my fingers trace the edges of her lace panties before I'm ripping the thin material from her body.

She gasps. "Quinton!"

My response comes without words. Eyes finding hers, she watches as I dive down, planting a kiss at her center. A moan escapes her lips as I swirl my tongue in a figure eight against her bud. Her body is writhing beneath me, but I don't stop tasting her. I can't stop. Sampling her sweet pussy has me reacting like a man starved.

Running my finger through her slit, I slip a digit inside her. Watching her reaction, I see the moment she's close. Her eyes snap shut and my finger slides out.

"Wh-wh-what the fuck?"

I watch her heaving chest before answering. "Eyes open, Wilder."

She nods her head, my mouth lowering to cover her pussy. This time I slide two fingers inside her. Pumping in and out, in and out. Tongue lapping up her sweet taste. Brynn's arms are still tangled in her shirt, resting above her head. Taking the hand that isn't pumping inside her, I reach up, tweaking her nipple in between my fingers. Twisting, flicking, and pulling while lapping and pumping inside her. I feel her walls tighten against my fingers.

"Oh, oh, oh god, Quinton," she screams, body coming off the bed as her climax erupts.

Sliding my fingers from her, I give her one last lick from top to center. Sitting up on my knees, I bring my fingers to my mouth, cleaning them off. Enjoying one last taste of Brynn.

"Holy fuck, Wilder."

Brynn moves her hands around and pulls them out of her tangled shirt. She could've easily done it earlier, but I think she enjoyed not being able to move her arms. Freeing her arms, they find the back of my neck. She's pulling my mouth to hers, tasting herself on my lips. Moaning, she slides her tongue inside me and laves at my mouth before pulling away with a quick peck.

"Does my dirty girl like tasting herself on me?"

Nodding her head, she reaches down, and grabs hold of my throbbing cock.

Batting her hands away, I shake my head. "Not tonight. Tonight was about you." With one last peck, I bring myself down on the bed next to her.

"Can I stay here tonight?" she asks sheepishly.

"Hell yeah, you can."

Brynn relaxes, moving back until her back is flush with my front. She wriggles around until she gets comfortable, which seems impossible with my dick rock hard and poking her in the back. Once she gets comfortable, I toss the covers over us, wrapping my arms around her.

"Are you sure I can't take care of your *situation*?" she asks, rocking against my cock.

"Maybe another time," I answer, squeezing her even closer. "Tonight I wanted to make you feel good."

She doesn't say anything after that. Both of us lie in silence. It's not long before I feel her drift off, her soft snores surrounding us.

Tonight I'm falling asleep with my girl in my arms and a smile on my face.

CHAPTER 18
Brynn

THE FLIGHT HOME WAS uneventful. After the weekend we had, a quiet flight was much needed. Both of us were exhausted from the little sleep we got last night. Quinton and I left my parents' house with no word from either one of them.

Honestly, a small part of me was surprised they didn't even say goodbye to us. My dad barely looked at me and only said a few words to me. We've never had a relationship. Not like my mom used to have with us kids. Dad was always busy climbing the political ladder. He had high expectations for what our family was supposed to be like. Bryce was being groomed by Dad to get into politics like he had. Only that wasn't what Bryce wanted to do. A part of me wonders if that was why he was pushing to enlist so badly.

It shouldn't bother me. It really shouldn't. But it does. I feel emotionally drained and empty every time I come back from a visit. I never know if I'm going to get the parents who ignore me or the parents who want to pick apart my life. Is it so bad to want parents who love me for me? Quinton could tell that my thoughts were consuming me, but this time he let me soak in them which I appreciated.

Not only was I dealing with my parents' issues, but also with the whole reason for our trip home. I didn't even go visit Asher or Bryce. What kind of sister—and girlfriend, ex-girlfriend, I don't even know what it's called when your boyfriend dies—doesn't go visit them? I'm too chicken shit to make the trek to the cemetery. It doesn't feel like they are there, buried beneath the earth. I've only visited Bryce twice, when we lowered him into the ground and when we lowered Ash into the ground. That's also the only time I've been to visit Asher. Those two meant so much to me that I can't even try to make sense of talking to a piece of stone.

Oh, and let's throw in a wild night of Truth or Dare where my best friend kissed me.

Quinton Alexander Boyd freaking kissed me.

That was one of the most heated and passionate kisses that I've ever had. It was the type of kiss you dream about. Raw, passionate, and hungry. No, it was fire, heat, and desire. It's like he's been wanting to do that for years. And I felt that damn kiss all the way to my toes. There was so much behind that kiss. When the two of us made it to the house, I went straight to my room. I didn't know what to say, instead I went to hide. But I couldn't go to bed. So much was left unsaid that there was no way I was falling asleep without seeing him.

And the escalation of what happened in his room was not what I was expecting when I walked into his room.

But there he was, lying in bed in nothing but those damn low rise, gray sweats. I couldn't pull my eyes from him. Seriously, does he own any other color besides gray? His dark, smooth skin was on display, making his black tattoos call me forward. The look in his eyes when he saw me was heated, and the spark ignited something in my stomach. It felt like lava, and I melted right there for him.

What the hell do I even do?

After a night of Truth or Dare, everything changed. But is it enough for me to put my past behind me and move forward?

I'm lost in thought as the Uber driver is pulling up in front of my townhouse. Our ride from the airport is coming to an end, forcing us back to reality. Climbing out of the back seat, Quinton follows after, asking the driver to wait while he helps me to my door. He hands me my suitcase from the trunk, and the two of us head up the walkway to my front door. Digging my keys out of my purse, I slide them into the lock before turning to face Quinton. His eyes are trying to mask his thoughts, only I can read him better than anyone.

He's worried.

He's worried that last night changed everything. I can't lie and say that it didn't, because it did. We crossed over into new territory. But I'm not going to run, which I know he's worried about.

My arms wrap around his middle, pulling my body flush into his.

"Thank you so much for coming with me, Quinton," I say into his chest. "I wouldn't have gotten through this weekend without you."

"I'm glad I was there for you," he answers.

Slowly, he starts to pull away, but before he can, my hands reach for the nape of his neck. My hands are pulling his mouth down to mine. My lips find his. He's stiff at first, the reaction shocking him. But with one swipe of my tongue against his full lip, his body relaxes.

I'm freaking kissing Quinton.

Of my own will. No dares.

Just doing what feels right. And oh, does it feel right.

I finally release Quinton, and we both take a step back. Heat spreads across my cheeks, and I can only imagine how red my face is. Pulling my lip in between my teeth, my eyes slide up to meet his burning gaze. He's searching my face, both of us find what we're looking for as wide, ear-to-ear smiles stretch across our faces.

"See ya later, B," Quinton says, his long stride leading him to the waiting Uber.

Turning back to the door, I unlock the door, push it open, and step inside, dragging my suitcase behind me. Pressing my back against the closed door, I bring my fingers up to my lips. Lips that are bruised and swollen from Quinton.

"What the actual hell?!" Chloe gasps from the kitchen, startling me.

She's sitting at the kitchen bar, a coffee mug paused halfway to her mouth.

My head swivels in her direction as I grasp my racing heart. I didn't expect my roommates to be awake. There's no sense in hiding. Clearly, Chloe saw the whole thing from the window by the front door. Inhaling a deep breath, I head into the kitchen.

"Macy up?" I ask.

If I'm going to tell this story, I'd prefer to tell them both at the same time.

Chloe nods her head before yelling Macy's name. Macy comes tromping down the stairs, sleep lines still marking her face.

Sliding into the kitchen, she asks. "Where's the fire?"

"In Brynn's pants," Chloe quips.

Macy's eyes widen. "Shit, girl. Do we need to get you to urgent care? I'm sure it's a treatable one."

Chloe throws her head back with a huge cackle. "Not that kind of crotch fire."

Turning her back to me, her hands slap against her thighs as her laugh continues. "Our Brynn was just seen kissing a very attractive, very sweet CTU running back on the front porch."

I internally smack my palm against my forehead. These bitches aren't going to make this easy.

"What?" Macy screams. "You two this whole time?"

Before answering her, I reach up to grab a mug from the cupboard beside my head. Pouring a hot cup of freshly brewed coffee, I savor the delicious aroma. Grabbing the Bailey's next to the coffee maker, I pour a heavy shot or two into my mug. I'm going to need coffee with a kick to get through this conversation.

Hopping up on the counter, I turn and sit. It's time the girls learn my story, the whole story. Starting with losing my brother and boyfriend.

A soft knock sounds from my bedroom door. Sitting up, I feel a strand of drool slide down my cheek. *Gross.* Using the sleeve of my hoodie, I wipe off the drool. The last thing I remember was curling up under my blankets to watch a sailing reality show. A nap wasn't on my agenda for the day, but, apparently, my body had other plans.

Telling the girls brought out a lot of emotions. Tears were shed by all of us. Both of them were justifiably hurt that I kept something of this magnitude from them, but it's not a story I open with. And as time went on, it felt like it was too late to share. Eventually, they understood my reasoning, especially when I shared the crazy turn of events from my weekend with Quinton.

"Where do you two go from here?" Chloe asks as concern laces her expression.

"That's the thing, Chlo, I have no idea." Releasing a sigh, my head falls backward to rest against my headboard. "We never discussed what happened. And while things were happening, we left it as we were doing whatever felt right. There's no way we are just a hook-up. That'll ruin everything, but I don't date."

"Yeah, there's no way just a hook-up will end well," Macy added.

"What's your heart saying?" Chloe asks.

Out of the three of us, Chloe is the emotionally deep one. She's always trying to figure us out. You'd think that'd be me, the future psychologist, but I never think about intuition. She feels all the feels. She's always asking us the hard questions, really digging into our emotions to see how situations make us feel. While I'm the one who wants to be a counselor, I don't ever dig deeper. It's not because I'm self-absorbed, I hate when my friends are hurting. My instinct is to shut down and process, while Chloe's is to not let emotions fester like an open wound, but to work on healing.

"My heart is saying it'll only end up hurt in the end, with more pain I don't have the strength to endure. My head is telling me to really think it through..." I pause, letting the words settle around us while I gather more thoughts. "And then my body is telling me to screw everything and get his hands back on me."

The girls both give a small chuckle, but it's Macy who responds first. "That good, huh?"

"Yeah, Mace, that fucking good."

Silence falls over the room, no one having more to add. Both girls know I need more time to process everything.

"I didn't realize I fell asleep," I say, reaching over and checking the time on my phone. "Shit, I slept for like four hours."

"Yeah." Chloe laughs. "You needed it." We both look up at each other. She's concerned for me. And I appreciate it because, deep down, I'm concerned too. "I just wanted to let you know that family dinner is going to be about ten of us."

My eyes snap to my hairline.

"Okay. Who all is coming?"

Every Sunday night, the girls and I host a family dinner. It's open to any of our friends, we just ask that you give us a heads-up on whether or not you're coming, so we can have plenty prepared.

"Don't stress about it. Macy and I have it handled. I just wanted to give you a head's up because it might be a little...awkward," she says hesitantly.

"Chloe..." I whine.

Her body language shifts, and she lets out a deep sigh.

"Us three, JP, Grant, Tyler, Quinton, Crew, Cody, and Hudson."

The last thing I want is for anything to be awkward. Our family dinners are a tradition, and I don't want to be the cause of any problems. Causing drama is not my vibe. Us girls started having planned weekly dinners when we moved into our townhouse last year.

College is crazy, and schedules are even crazier. Between classes, jobs, and extracurriculars, it felt like we never saw each other, even though we lived together. Sure, we saw each other at home, but it was always passing by as someone was going somewhere or collapsing on the couch exhausted.

One Sunday night, the three of us were all home, we were actually able to sit and have a meal together. It was the best time, sitting, eating, and catching up. Real conversations happened outside of our group chat. Standing in the kitchen, the three of us were cleaning up the dinner mess when Macy suggested we make family dinners a weekly thing.

And thus, family dinners were born.

No one makes plans on Sunday nights. We enjoy a homecooked meal with no phones while we eat, and everyone chips in to help cook and clean.

Over time, our dinners were joined by some friends, and it grew. Now we keep dinners on the calendar for any of our friends who are craving "family" time or a homecooked meal. Chloe is the one to thank for the incredible food. While all of us can cook, Chloe is the one who grew up with a chef. Her dad is one of the top chefs in Dallas, and Chloe spent her time at home in the kitchen playing sous chef.

Lifting my arms up and over my head, my muscles groan at the movement, a blush heating my face. Immediately, I'm transported back into the spare bedroom at my parents', my arms above my head tangled in my shirt, Quinton's mouth devouring me.

Macy rips off my covers, slapping my ass as she stands up. "Go shower, you dirty ho."

Laughter fills the room as I stick my tongue out at her like a child.

"Damn, girls, it smells hella good in here," Jeremiah shouts from the front door.

He makes his way into the kitchen with a bouquet of the most beautiful flowers in his hand. JP always brings us a fresh bouquet of flowers when he comes for Sunday dinner. It's a sweet gesture that shows how much he appreciates the meal. Placing the bouquet on the bar, he comes over to where the three of us are finishing cooking dinner. He wraps each of us in his arms, leaving soft kisses on our temples.

"Thanks again for doing this."

Jeremiah didn't have the best home life growing up. We've gathered some information over the years and pieced some things together. He's one of five kids, and his dad left them when he was ten, forcing his mom to work three jobs to keep them fed and clothed, and a roof over their heads. Family dinners never happened, and homemade meals were few and far between. Having our weekly family dinners means the world to him, and we'll continue doing it to see him happy—all of us happy.

Family doesn't have to come from blood.

Family can come from a strong bond and a loving relationship.

We are each other's family.

"Yeah, girls, it smells so good. I'm starving," Grant adds, striding into the kitchen.

Glancing around him, my eyes scanning to find the one guy I've been nervously waiting for. My eyes land on his dark, muscular frame as he walks through the doorway. He's hesitant about what to do. Before this weekend, he would've been right behind JP leaning down and showing his appreciation with affection. Our eyes lock, both of us trying to read the other. After what feels like forever, a grin tugs at the corners of my lips. He returns the smile with a wink, turning to look at the front door that's opening behind him.

It's already changing.

Dinner is served family-style around our patio table, since it's the only table big enough to fit us all. Our townhouse has a long, fenced-in yard with a concrete patio right off the kitchen. We put a large table and extra, comfy chairs out there. The furniture isn't anything elaborate, but it works. I've been sitting on pins and needles since we all sat down. JP, Chloe, Hudson, and Tyler sit on one side, Macy and Grant sit at the ends of the table, and I'm sandwiched between Cody and Quinton, with Crew on the other side of Q. Freaking awkward.

Macy and Chloe cooked three pans of lasagna, enough breadsticks to feed an army, and a large garden salad. The boys were right. The food smells amazing, only my appetite is gone. Lasagna is one of my favorites, too.

Everyone digs in, shoveling forkfuls in their mouths. The boys carry the conversation, talking about this week's game, girls on campus, and the upcoming baseball season.

I'm so proud of them.

"Thanks, B," Grant says. Confusion must be reflected on my face, causing Grant to continue. "You didn't mean to say that out loud, did you?"

"Oh yeah, totally," I joke, winking at Grant. "But seriously, you guys are playing amazing."

"We comin' for that Natty," JP adds.

"And we'll be in the front row cheering," Macy says, moving her arms in a little cheer.

Cody slides his arm across the back of my chair, his thumb brushing my exposed shoulder. My body stiffens at his touch. It's not that Cody is touching me, that's not uncommon, our relationship is very touchy-feely. But that was before Chicago. Everything has changed in just three short days, and I don't know where anything stands.

"How did Chicago go?" Cody asks, scooping another bite of lasagna on his fork.

"Is that where you guys were?" Crew asks, joining our conversation. "I've only been once, for a field trip in middle school. Did you guys have fun?"

My gaze finds Quinton's, both of us staring at each other. My cheeks flame while a smirk tugs on Q's lips, both of us remembering last night. Grant is staring at me and Q. He gives a small shake of his head, but not before a small smile graces his face.

Grant knows. I mean, of course, he knows, he's Q's best friend.

"Umm…" I draw out. Looking past Quinton, I turn my attention to Crew. "I mean, it wasn't exactly a trip that was supposed to be fun. I had to go home for a charity gala honoring my brother and high school boyfriend who died five years ago."

As those words slip past my lips, the table goes eerily quiet.

Oh yeah, not everyone knows about the dead boyfriend.

Jeremiah's eyes widen, his mouth dropping open.

Something *actually* stunned JP into silence.

But then I watch his eyes snap to Q's too.

They all know something happened between us.

"Oh shit, Brynn," Jeremiah says as Quinton finds my thigh with his hand and squeezes in a show of support that I didn't know I needed.

"Shit," Crew says, running his hand over his beard-covered jawline. "I had no clue, or I never would've said anything."

Grabbing my glass, I take a drink of sweet tea as I try to find my voice.

"Don't apologize. It's not something I talk about. Hell, no one at this table knew about Asher until this weekend. He was my high school boyfriend who was in the same car crash that killed my brother."

Eyes searching the table, I notice that my comment killed the mood.

"It's a good thing Q was there for, umm…*moral support,*" JP adds.

Grant and Macy snort out a laugh. Leave it to Jeremiah to break the awkward silence, which I'm thankful for.

"Pass the salad," Chloe shouts, interrupting JP. But it wasn't fast enough. Cody's head whips to me.

"What'd he say?" Cody says at the same time JP says, "What? I didn't know you two kissing was a secret?"

Heat fills my cheeks for the hundredth time tonight.

When did I become such a girl?

Never have I blushed over kissing or even screwing a guy. With my eyebrows shooting to my hairline, I turn to Quinton.

Bumping his shoulder, I say, "I see someone couldn't keep his mouth shut."

He reaches his arm around my shoulder and pulls me in for a side hug, leaning down and kissing my forehead.

"I couldn't help it."

Smiling, I just shake my head and let myself embrace Quinton's touch.

"Oh shiiiit," Crew drags out. "You two an item?"

"What's with you and all the questions?" I ask Crew.

There's a grin on my face that lets him knowI'm not mad at his questions. Sliding out from under Quinton's hold, I pick up my fork and continue eating. But not before realizing that Cody hasn't said anything else. Slowly, I turn my body and find his eyes.

"What the hell happened in Chicago?" Cody asks, a chuckle leaving his mouth.

His gaze bounces back and forth between Quinton and me.

"Fucking Truth or Dare," Quinton responds, and I let out a laugh.

And for the next twenty minutes, I fill the table in on everything. From how Bryce and Asher were in an accident to the high school tribute, the bullshit gala, and Truth or Dare—leaving out what happened at the house. To say the table was silent is an understatement. No one moved the entire time I talked and cried. Yeah, seeing me cry was a shock to everyone at the table. I'm Brinley Wilder, the girl who never shows emotion. The girl who lives fast and parties harder.

But these people at this table are my family, and they deserved to know the truth. The whole truth. The good, the bad, and the very ugly.

Maybe they'll understand me a little better.

Mondays are my weird day of the week. All of my classes are in the afternoon, which is the opposite of almost every one of my friends and roommates. Instead of going to campus early and stopping at the Student Union for lunch, I head down to the kitchen to make myself a bowl of cereal, because, you know, cereal fixes everything. This giant bowl of Frosted Flakes is going to solve all my problems. In the words of Tony the Tiger, "You're GRRReat," or something like that.

It's kind of nice to go through the day without having to be *on*. I don't have to look for my friends and make small talk. I can put my headphones in and wander around campus, just going from class to class, living in my own little world. It might sound like I'm being fake with my friends, but I'm not. There are just some days where I want to be left alone with my thoughts and be up in my feels.

As much as I love being the wild, carefree girl, I've got inner demons I'm constantly in a fight with. There's a voice in my head that's always telling me that I'm not enough. As Brooke Davis told Peyton Sawyer in *One Tree Hill*, "your 'I love yous' send people to the grave." And I'm wondering if that's the same about me. Will me accepting my feelings and falling for Quinton only result in him being hurt or, even worse, dead?

I mean, how sick and twisted are these thoughts? But that's what's on repeat in my head. I'm scared. I'm scared to love. I'm scared to feel. I'm scared to get close to anyone.

Even though Quinton and I are in a state of limbo, last night I went to bed happy and carefree. Only to be brought back into my head this morning. But for a few hours, I got to be relaxed.

Finally, the weight of my past is off my shoulders. My friends know about my darkest secret and, before they left, each one of the guys hugged me, reminding me that they were there for me. It felt freeing. This morning I woke up with a slew of text messages. Quinton and Cody were checking on me. JP sent a text apologizing for ambushing the table with Quinton's *moral support*. Which made me laugh out loud.

When I left Chicago for Texas, I thought I'd be Brinley Wilder against the world. Never in my wildest dreams would I have thought that I'd find my family. We might be dysfunctional, but we are dysfunctional in the best way. Each of us carries our own baggage, but we have each other to share the load.

The alarm on my phone blares in my pocket, snapping me out of my thoughts and reminding me it's time to head to class.

Parking is a bitch when I pull in. The only problem with having afternoon classes is that the parking lot is always full. Driving up and down the rows of cars, I spot one pulling out.

It is my lucky day.

Once the car is gone, I whip into the spot before anyone has a chance to steal it from me. There's no rule that the spot is yours until you're parked in it. Turn signals don't stake a claim. It's a dog-eat-dog world in the campus parking lot.

Climbing out of the car, I pop my headphones in and turn on my *In My Feels* playlist. Hopefully, the headphones let everyone know that I'm not in the mood to talk. Walking across the brick pavement, my Monday begins.

It's a beautiful fall day in Central Texas. Exiting Rogers Hall, I walk over to a bench in the quad to sit while I wait for my next class. I slide my phone out of my backpack, opening Instagram. Scrolling through my feed, a thought pops into my head. Closing out of the app, I swipe over to my camera app, positioning it toward the quad, I take a creative photo of the trees with a few leaves gathered around the trunk. Snapping the pictures, I do a quick edit because duh, everything needs to be edited before posting. Quickly thumbing out a caption, I post the picture. The caption reads *I'm fall-ing for you,* and all I can hope is that the one person I want to see the photo sees it.

My last class of the day is a quick one. We have an exam this week, so the professor gave us a brief review of what we can expect to be tested on. Making my way out of the hall, I'm stopped by someone yelling my name.

"Brynn?" a girl asks, out of breath. Huffing and puffing, she starts talking. "Sorry, I raced to catch up to you. *Clearly,* I need to add more cardio to my workouts. A bunch of us are studying tomorrow night and didn't know if you wanted to join us."

This girl talking to me looks familiar, but I can't put a name to her face.

I really need to do a better job at getting people's names.

She's average height with killer curves. Her blonde hair is a natural balayage and her makeup is on point. She's dressed in a pink and white floral dress with brown booties. A puzzled look must be written on my face because, before I have a chance to answer, she speaks up again.

"Oh my gosh, you have no idea who I am. I must look like a total stalker. Which I'm *totally* not," she rushes out, and I interrupt her before she can continue.

"I'm sorry, I recognize your face, but I can't remember your name."

A smile breaks across her face.

"I'm Savannah Holycross. We've partied together. I'm a Delta Zeta."

"Hey, nice to put a name to a face," I say, returning her warm smile. The football team parties with the DZs all the time. I should've known her name, but again, I live in my own world. "Where y'all studying?"

"We've got a room in the library," she starts, handing me her cell phone. "Here, put your number in. I'll text you all the deets."

Grabbing her phone, I put my number in, sending myself a text so I have hers too.

"Sounds good. I should be able to make anything work. Thanks."

She walks away, and I pull my phone out to save her information. It's seven thirty and I'm exhausted. There's an NFL game tonight, so instead of heading home, I head to The Eagles' Nest for dinner and the game.

Wings, beer, and football. Sounds like the perfect way to end this day.

CHAPTER 19
QUINTON

THE EAGLES' NEST IS quiet like a typical Monday night. Grant texted earlier, saying some of the guys were heading over here for wings and the football game. The guys and I are sitting at our usual table in the side room. Grant, Harris, Riggsby, and Will are already here when JP and I walk in.

Making our way over to the table, we no sooner sit down, than the waitress is at our side. She's wearing tight, short shorts, and a tank top with the bar's eagle logo across her chest, her cleavage on full display. It's even more pronounced with the added slit she cut in the top of her tank top. Raven-black hair hangs long and shiny down her back. Her bright-green eyes find mine immediately. Pulling out her notepad, she brings it to her front, ready to take down our order, but not before pushing her boobs together. Someone is working hard for her tip.

"Hey, Q," she purrs. "What can I get you tonight?"

"I'll take a draft of Coors Light," I answer her, not sparing her any extra attention.

Instead, I reach into my pocket, pulling out my phone. She doesn't take the hint, but I don't look up from my phone. Pulling up Brynn's name, I shoot her a text.

> **Me: I can't get you out of my head.**

She doesn't reply immediately, so I set my phone on the table.

"Dude, this game is going to be crazy. Kansas City is lookin' hella good this season," I say to Grant, my attention on the pregame interviews on the TV.

"Hell yeah they are," he replies as the waitress sets down my beer.

She leans closer to me than needed. "What else can I do...I mean, get you?"

It's hard to keep the eye roll from showing. Closing my menu, I turn to her, keeping my eyes on her face, and not on her tits that she's pressing closer to my face.

"I'll do twenty bone-in buffalo ranch wings with a side of celery and carrots and an order of fries."

She jots down my order, turning to the rest of the table for theirs.

"Dude, I think she wants your bone somewhere beside wings," Riggsby says, watching the waitress saunter toward the counter where she types our order on the computer.

I follow his gaze, and that's when I spot bright blonde hair thrown haphazardly on top of her head. She's sitting at the bar, eyes on the TV as she holds her beer. Brynn is the picture of relaxed, with her body leaned back against her chair, arm draped across her chest, and knee propped against the edge of the bar, not a care in the world. I love how carefree she always is.

The guys are all discussing how the Chiefs' defense is going to stop the run game, but I can't take my eyes off Brynn. Especially now that Will has spotted her too. Scraping his chair against the floor, he gets up and saunters over toward her.

"Alright dude, spill it," JP says, bringing my attention back from what's happening at the bar.

"Spill about what?"

"You and Brynn," Riggsby says. "Two of you claim you're just friends, and then you come back from Chicago changed."

"Seriously, bro, I was the one that took y'all to the airport, and the vibe was weird. You two bang?" JP adds, picking up his beer and taking a long gulp.

Bringing my hand to the back of my head, I run it back and forth across my neck.

"Uhh, we didn't fuck, and that'd be none of your damn business." Glancing up, I see Grant eyeing me. He's waiting for me to divulge more information. "We might've hooked up, and then things got a little intense."

"Intense, as in?" Riggsby digs.

"As in, not quite sex."

"Who went down on who?" JP asks.

Grant and Riggsby laugh at his question.

I just glare, not adding anything.

"It's about damn time," Grant says under his breath behind his glass.

My eyes search out Brynn again, and that's when I see her laughing with Will. I wouldn't think anything of it, except I know those two have a past. Will stands next to her, arm grazing hers, both of them smiling. Grabbing my phone, I pull up her messages again. That green-eyed monster takes over, and I want her to know I'm here.

> **Me:** All I can think about is propping you up on that bar, sliding those pants down your legs, and you bringing me to my knees.

Hitting send, I watch her, waiting for her to pick up her phone. Setting her glass down, she reaches over and pulls her phone up. Her body tenses, and I watch as she squeezes her legs together. Before I can think about it, I'm thumbing out another message.

Me: Tell Will to fuck off for me, will you?

The message immediately goes to read. Her body turns, eyes searching the bar. She looks past the entrance to the room, before bouncing those bright ocean-blue eyes that I just want to swim in, back my way. A wide grin breaks across her face before she pulls her bottom lip between her teeth. Reaching back toward the bar, she grabs her glass, hopping down between the stool and Will. I see him appreciate the proximity of her body. My hand grips my glass tight enough that I think I could break it. But I don't. Instead, I watch my girl walk her fine ass over my way.

"Brynn!" JP yells as she enters the room.

"What's up, boys," she greets back, looking at all of us.

She's standing on the opposite side of the table from me, next to Grant.

I'm itching to touch her, but I can't when she won't come any closer.

"What are you doing here?" I ask.

I can't seem to break eye contact with her. It feels surreal to have experienced what we did on Saturday and not know where we stand today.

She thumbs her finger over her shoulder before replying.

"I was trying to watch the game with some wings and beer, but someone won't quit blowing up my phone." Her tone is light, joking.

She doesn't care. In fact, if that blush on her cheek is any indication, she appreciated that text a lot more than she's letting on.

Will comes back into the room, two fresh beers in his hand. Handing one off to Brynn, she turns to him and thanks him.

"Want to join us?" he asks her, gesturing to the empty seat next to him.

I don't say anything. I'm waiting to see how she handles this situation. For the longest time, I thought Will was going to be the one to break her series of hook-ups. The two of them have had multiple nights together. He might be a douche, but he's always made Brynn laugh and have fun.

She keeps her eyes on him.

"No thanks, I'm good over at the bar. I was just finishing up. I need to head home and work on a paper." She turns her attention back to the other guys in the room. "You guys have fun, though!"

With a smile and a wave, she turns to walk out of the room.

Wait, that was it?

She seriously just came in here, said hi, and left. What the fuck?

Our chipper waitress brings our orders. She can't take a hint that I'm not interested because she keeps dipping her chest toward me, trying to get me to react. I don't. My attention is solely focused on the girl who is standing at the bar, grabbing her purse, and nibbling on her bottom lip.

Laying her hand on my shoulder, the waitress whispers in my ear, "I get off at ten. Stick around, and I'll get you off too."

That's the moment that Brynn chooses to look over her shoulder. Her back stands taller, tensing at what she sees. Turning back toward the bar, she takes a long gulp of her beer before rushing out the door.

"I'm good, thanks," I grumble to the waitress, shrugging her hand off my shoulder. "I have a...a girl—argh—a someone."

I hate that I can't define what Brynn and I are.

Our relationship is friends, but also, possibly more than friends. Or was what happened in Chicago a distraction?

Leaning down against me, the waitress whispers, "It's okay. We've all got someone. Your secret is safe with me."

And with that, she walks away.

"Fuck man, that was awkward as hell," JP says, placing a wing in his mouth and sucking all the meat off in one bite.

"Which part?" Riggsby adds.

Shaking my head, I ignore both of them.

My mind is spiraling, but I don't focus on that right now. Instead, I focus on watching that crazy tight end for the Chiefs do one of the victory dances he's known for.

Tomorrow I'll deal with Brynn. Hopefully, it's not too late.

Hopefully that waitress didn't fuck everything up. I've spent too much time getting Brynn to trust me.

I refuse to give up until she's mine.

CHAPTER 20
QUINTON

S HE'S OFFICIALLY AVOIDING ME. And you want to know what's messed up? I expected this. This is why I have never acted on my feelings. I knew she'd run scared. I knew this, and yet, I still kissed her. All because of a stupid dare. It's not in junior high anymore. I could've walked away. Walked away, took a shot of tequila, or, hell, even gave her a quick peck on the lips. Anything but a full-blown kiss the way I did. The way I spilled all my feelings out in that kiss. And if only it was the kiss. I'm pretty sure none of this would be an issue if we hadn't fooled around at her parents'. That's what freaked her out. I know it.

And what sucks is that I swear she felt the connection between us too. She melted into that kiss like my lips were the only thing keeping her standing. And she's the one who showed up in my bedroom at her parents'. She's the one who said we weren't thinking, just doing what felt right. And her coming on my lips felt right. It felt fan-fucking-tas-tic.

"She's *mine*," I growl.

"Only she's not," Grant chimes in.

Shit, I said that out loud.

"She's not yours because you won't tell her how you feel."

"I want to give this a go, but she needs to be sure. Everything will change. Hell, it already has," I said, taking another drink of my Corona.

The guys and I are at a Mexican restaurant for Taco Tuesday. We don't normally do back-to-back nights out, but sometimes it happens. And don't think I'm not turning down the alcohol. Tomorrow's practice is going to suck, but I don't care at this point.

It's a tradition that we started halfway through freshman year when we needed some more bonding. Brynn started coming with us sophomore year, along with some of the other guys' girlfriends. She hasn't missed a Taco Tuesday since she started coming. We reserve the back half of the restaurant and fill it up with hungry football players. There's usually a handful of guys who have a competition of who can eat the most tacos. Typically, it's the linemen who do

"What did she say?" Grant nudges my arm, getting my attention to continue the conversation.

"Nothing really. Asked me if she could spend the night in my bed. Then we took things to third base. Both of us fell asleep together."

Grant's head snaps my way, eyes getting big.

"Dude, she slept in your bed? With you?"

"Yep," I answer, shoveling the last of my rice into my mouth. There's nothing better than Mexican restaurant rice.

"Hmm," Grant hums to himself. "She's never done that."

"No shit. That's why I'm so damn confused about why she's avoiding me. I mean, why now?"

"Maybe she's worried it was just a weekend thing. Maybe she has feelings for you, but doesn't want to say anything in case you don't feel the same," Grant finishes his thought just as Will slides across from the table.

"What's got you lookin' like a sad sack, Boyd?"

Clenching my jaw, I glare across the table, as I take a deep breath.

"Mind your own fucking business, Davis."

"Speaking of fucking, where's Brynn?"

He smirks. Actually smirks at me.

Pushing myself to my feet, my chair topples over, and Grant is right there in my face, holding me back. There's nothing more I want than to punch that goddamn smirk off his arrogant face. The prick.

Hands on my chest, holding me in my spot, Grant speaks low enough for only me to hear. "Walk away, Q. We're not doing this here."

Pumping my shoulders up and down, I tip my head back and forth, giving it a couple of good cracks. Deciding I'm over this night, I reach into my pocket and toss out a wad of cash, which is more than enough to cover my bill.

"I'm out," I say, turning for the door.

Heading outside I pull my phone out and order an Uber. Closing the app, I check my notifications, hoping there's a message from Brynn apologizing for being a no-show. But that's the thing with hope, it always lets you down. There's nothing from Brynn. Before I have a chance to put the phone away, my mom's face lights up the screen with an incoming call.

Hitting the accept button, I answer. This night can't get worse, might as well see what she wants.

"Quinton, honey?" my mom asks.

"Hey Ma, what's up?" I ask, running my hands down my face and over my thighs.

"What? Can't a mother call her son?"

Well of course, moms can call their sons. But it'd be nice to have a real conversation and speak to you when you're not just calling to invite me to something. I think all of that, but I wouldn't dare say it. This woman would have my ass if I actually said those things.

"Sorry, it's been a long day," I answer with an excuse.

She continues, her voice changing into an overly concerned parent.

"Baby, is Coach working you too hard? Just remember it's all going to pay off when the NFL comes knocking."

A deep sigh releases.

"Yeah, I know. Not to cut you off, but I'm calling it an early night. Did you need anything?"

"Can you come to dinner tomorrow night? Your dad and I would love to see you this week."

"No, I can't tomorrow night. We've got a mandatory study hall with the team. Can't miss."

"Studies come first, of course. How about Thursday? I think your brother will be able to come on Thursday too." Her voice gets excited.

She loves having us all at home. Which I totally get. Someday when I have kids, I want them to be around my table. But the difference is going to be that I want them there because I love and support them, not because I want to use my twisted love to brainwash them into doing what I want.

"I'll make it work. See ya Thursday," I respond, even though dinner with my younger brother is the last thing I want to do.

We see each other enough. Hell, we play football together and live together. I don't want to spend my free time with him too.

"Great, honey, see you Thursday at six," she says as a goodbye.

Abigail Boyd doesn't say goodbye. She hangs up whenever she deems the conversation over.

Pulling up my messages one last time, I fire off a text without even thinking.

> Me: Real fucking cool, Wilder. No showing. Grow a pair.

Immediately, I feel regret for sending it, but, fuck it, I can't take it back. The Uber car pulls up. After sliding in, I shut my door with more force than necessary. The driver eyes me, but no one speaks. Instead, I drop my head to the headrest and shut my eyes.

Wednesday couldn't drag on longer if it tried.

I didn't sleep for shit. My mind wouldn't shut off, and my alarm went off way too damn early. My eyes were no sooner closed and then it was five a.m.

Weightlifting sucked. Normally, I love weightlifting. I love pushing my body to its limits, seeing how much weight my body can handle. It's exhilarating. Not only do I push myself, but my music drowns out my thoughts. Only this morning, Coach wouldn't let us listen to our music. He put on some motivational podcast. It motivated me to hurry the hell up, get my reps in, and get the hell out.

Practice sucked. My head was off, thanks to a shitty morning start. I've never had any issues shutting off the outside world before. But apparently, this whole "Brynn avoiding me" bullshit is getting to me. We haven't talked since Sunday. She's posted on her Instagram Stories, but will she return a damn text message? Nope. At least not to me. And Cody. The two of us sat together in the Union for breakfast. He said she's ghosted him too. Coach was on my ass the whole practice for my shit performance. He threatened to bench me for Saturday's game if I don't get it together.

Will Davis sucked. No surprise there. I can't even remember what he did, but his arrogance and locker-room trash talk are enough to make a nun swear. But did Coach threaten to bench his ass? Nope, just mine.

And mandatory studying sucks. All I want to do is get some extra sleep and call it a day. Hell, maybe head to Brynn's to talk to her face-to-face and sort this shit out. But instead, I'm heading inside Liberty Library to sit here for a two-hour study session. It should be illegal to force people to attend study sessions, especially when said person doesn't need it. Unlike most, I take my studying seriously. I've got shit to prove on and off the field.

Reaching the top of the fourth-floor steps, I do a quick glance across the floor. That's when I see bright-blonde hair, pulled up in one of those big clips, oversized, round glasses that make her look so studious. And she's chewing on the inside of her cheek. It's a little tic she does that I feel straight to my groin.

Do I go over there? Or do I ignore her the way she's ignoring me? The inner debate starts, but I quickly push that shit aside. It's a no-brainer. That's why in the next second, my feet are carrying me to her. Stopping right beside her desk, I watch her eyes pause from her reading and glance down to my feet. Her eyes slowly drag up my legs, raking across my stomach, before coming up to meet my eyes.

"Hey, Q," she whispers.

We are in a library, after all.

"Wilder. Wasn't sure if I should approach or ignore you."

She folds in on herself. She looks defeated. And I hate that. Brynn isn't easily defeated. She's tough and strong. Independent and vocal. Not resigned and quiet. She brings that cheek back between her teeth, and her eyes well up with unshed tears.

"Shit, Brynn." I squat down so we are eye to eye, even though she's trying to avoid looking me in the eye. "I was being a dick."

"No, no you weren't," she interrupts me. "It's just a bad week, okay?"

Her eyes find mine, and so much is told in that look. There's pain, sadness, and vulnerability in that look.

That's when it hits me. It's anniversary week.

"I didn't even think." I rub my hand down my neck.

"I didn't come out and say it. After this weekend and everything that happened on Sunday night, I just needed a minute to breathe. But then Monday came, and it brought anniversary week. Chloe and Macy got into a nasty fight. It's awkward at home. And I'm just trying to survive. We had a huge exam tonight. That's why I didn't come last night. A bunch of us met here to study, and I just didn't think." She rushes out all of these excuses, and honestly, I don't need it.

I should've known that this was going to be a hard week for her and let her be.

"When I got home last night, I was going to text you, but then I saw your text. I decided I was just going to get through tomorrow, and then we could talk."

"I shouldn't have sent that text." I blurt out. Placing my hand on her thigh, I bring my other hand up to her face, pulling her chin up to look at me. "We'll talk later. I'm sorry for being a dick."

Brynn flings her arms out, wrapping them around my neck, pulling me into a hug.

"Thanks for understanding. Sorry, I shut down. It's a bad habit."

"It's all good," I answer, because it is. I get it. We all have our own way of grieving, and I'm fortunate enough to not have any clue about what's going on in her mind. I press a quick kiss to her temple before standing up. "I'm late for studying."

She smiles up at me, and I walk away, leaving behind my girl.

CHAPTER 21
Brynn

"**Y**OU DON'T HAVE TO do it, Brynn," Asher says from beside me. He's holding my hand as we stand shoulder to shoulder.

Bryce had just dared me to do a backflip off the back of the boat. And all I can think about is smacking my head off the stern.

It's the summer before our sophomore year. The weather is perfect. It's one of those summer days where it's hot but not too hot. The Nelsons picked Bryce and me up for a day on Lake Michigan. Mr. Nelson just got a new forty-seven-foot Carver yacht. He couldn't wait to get it on the water. Mrs. Nelson came over and got us, since we were home alone with Nadia.

"I'm scared," I rush out, voice barely above a whisper.

Asher places his hand on my lower back, and I swear his touch is more powerful than the sun's rays. My body instantly heats from his touch. His touches have been coming more and more frequently. We've shifted from friends to awkward teens navigating dating, and now there's a more powerful urge beneath our skin.

"What are you scared of?" he asks, eyes searching my face.

Asher knows I'll tell him the truth. I've never lied to him. Not in all the years we've known each other.

With a sigh, I look out across the lake. Bryce is floating on his back waiting for me to flip, while Mr. and Mrs. Nelson are both sunning on the bow.

"Everything," I answer.

Asher uses the hand that he's holding to bring me toward him. His other hand finds my hip, pulling me so that our bodies are flush. Withdrawing his hand from mine, he brings his hand up to my face. Cupping the side of my face, he drags his thumb across my jawline. His gaze locks on mine.

"As long as I'm standing next to you, you have nothing to be scared of, babe. I love you."

Lowering his mouth to mine, his lips find mine, locking us together in a searing kiss.

Warm tears stream down my face as I fight to hold on to the memory. Sleep is slipping from my grasp as my body tries to wake up. I will myself to fight it, the consciousness. I want to be back there. Back with my brother. Back with my boyfriend. Back before everything changed. Squeezing my eyes shut, I beg my body to give me five more minutes. I'm desperate. I just need five more minutes of hearing their laughter, seeing their smiles, and remembering what it was like to have my heart feel complete.

But that doesn't happen. My consciousness awakens, and my slumber is officially gone. Slowly, my eyes open, but the tears don't stop. Rolling over to my side from my back, I pull the sleeves of the oversized hoodie up over my hands, resting my hands under my head, as my body curls into itself.

Tears pour from my eyes like a summer rainstorm, which is only fitting since I was dreaming of our last summer together. Summer days were our favorite days growing up. No school, no homework, and no routines. The only thing we had to worry about was where we were going for the day. Bryce, Asher, and I would take turns deciding what we would get up to for the day. The three of us were inseparable. I'd give anything for one more summer together. Three months of the three of us finding crazy things to do. The crazier, the better, because we had each other by our side.

This day is always hard, but this year is even harder. I'm not sure if it's because it's been five years, and five just seems so monumental. Or is it the fact that my heart is wanting to give into whatever this attractiveness I have for Quinton, and the last time I gave my heart away, I lost the two boys that held parts of it?

My body snuggles deeper into the oversized hoodie that I wear every year on this day. The hoodie belonged to Asher. It was his freshman sweatshirt with his last name on and number twenty-two on the back. He gave it to me to wear on his first game, and I never gave it back. Whenever I'd go to his house, I'd sneak sprays of his cologne so I always had his smell on me.

His scent lingers, but only slightly, which breaks my heart even more. I dream of him and Bryce, but their features are getting blurrier. I'm starting to forget the small details that made them who they are. Their smells are fading, the sound of their laughter and their mannerisms are slipping from my grasp.

Sobs rack through my body as that realization hits me. I'm slowly forgetting them. But how could I ever forget them? Bryce was a part of me. He shared my DNA. We shared a womb. He was my mind, body, and soul. The other half that kept my heart beating. That was until I fell in love with our best friend. Asher's embrace could make even the darkest days shine bright. And oh, did they ever, that wonderful day in the hospital.

Today marks my fourth consecutive day in this room. The sounds of machines beeping has become a soundtrack I crave. Because those sounds, those sounds mean Asher is still breathing. He is still here, even though he is somewhere dreaming of better days. As much as everyone tries to get me to leave, I refuse. I am needed by his side.

Thankfully, we own this hospital. I am given the opportunity to shower in the staff locker rooms, even though I have no desire to leave his side. Those showers are the fastest showers I have ever taken. I don't want to be away from him for too long.

Mother had a cot delivered for me to sleep on, but I refuse. Each night after the nurses come in for their nightly check, I slip out of the cot and climb under the covers next to Asher, careful not to disturb the wires that he is connected to. The bed is hard, the sheets scratchy, but I didn't care because I am beside my Asher.

Losing Bryce was devastating, but I fought hard to keep myself strong. Strong for the beautiful man lying next to me. Placing my arm across his stomach, I curl into his side. Each night I share with him a story that the two of us shared.

"Do you remember our first Valentine's Day together as a couple?" I ask him, pausing, praying for a response. But one doesn't come, so I continue. "You showed up at our house in dress pants, a dress shirt, and a tie. You were so handsome in your light-blue shirt. It made your eyes pop. I couldn't stop staring at them all night. You planned the whole night, starting with having our family driver take us on our date.

"Dinner was at Steak 'N Shake because you knew I was obsessed with their strawberry milkshakes and shoestring fries with cheese sauce. I loved that you didn't try to take us somewhere fancy, even though it was

Valentine's Day. We were the best-dressed couple in that entire diner, but I loved it. I knew that things were changing between us, and we were becoming more serious, but that was the night that I knew that I loved you, like really loved you. You were always you. You didn't try hard to impress me, you just told your jokes—as cheesy as they were. You didn't judge me for inhaling two milkshakes. You were you, I was me, and we were just us.

"But our date wasn't over after dinner. Oh no, you surprised me with tickets to see The Lucky One *because of my obsession with Zac Efron. Most boys would've refused to sit through a chick flick, but not you. What was it that you told me? Something about Zac might make me swoon and the movie might make me cry, but you'd be the lucky one wrapping your arms around me—"*

"To comfort you," a raspy voice says, interrupting me.

Slowly, sitting up, I looked up and am met with dazzling blue eyes staring back at me. The arm that I had placed around my shoulders, slowly squeezes me.

"Asher?" I asked, afraid my eyes and ears are deceiving me.

"Hi, pretty girl," he rasps out, causing tears to explode from my eyes. His grip tightens and he pulls me closer, grazing his lips across my forehead. My blue-eyed beauty was awake.

Slowly sitting up, I turn to get a better look at him.

"Oh my god, Asher," I gasp out in between sobs, my lips finding his immediately.

My heart was broken, but at that moment, I feel it slowly start to repair.

Too bad I don't know what is to come in just thirty-six hours.

Leaving that memory, I get up and head to the bathroom. After re-lieving myself and brushing my teeth, I climb back under the covers, I reach over and grab the remote, flipping on my TV. Scrolling through the movie options, I find the one I'm looking for. Selecting *The Lucky One*, I let the memory fade away and let the mourning begin.

The movie is only fifteen minutes in, and my body is curled under my blankets when there's a soft rap on the door. Cautiously, Chloe sticks her head in.

"Hey, B," she starts, walking slowly into the room with a mug in her hand.

"Hi," I answer, making room on my side of the bed for Chloe to sit down.

Chloe places the mug of piping hot coffee on my nightstand.

"I brought you some coffee. I figured you were hiding away up here." Crawling onto my bed, Chloe slips under the covers, my head finding her shoulder. She reaches up, wiping the tear stains from my cheeks. "I know today is a hard day, but you don't have to hide away alone. I can skip classes, and we can hide under the covers together."

Reaching for her hand, I rest my empty hand on hers.

"Thanks, Chlo, but I just want to be alone."

With a deep sigh, Chloe stares at me.

"I knew you were going to say that, you do every year. But just know, B, I'm here for you. I know I don't know what you're feeling, but I love you, and I'm always here for whatever you need. Macy is too. And Quinton. And Cody and the rest of the guys. We hate seeing you hurt. We understand it, but we still hate it."

The two of us just lie there, side-by-side, heads together for a few quiet moments, watching Zac Efron on screen. There's comfort in the silence, in having her beside me, my head resting on her shoulder. With the arm that isn't holding her hand, I reach across our bodies and pull her in for an awkward hug.

"I love you, too," I finally say. "But I just need to be alone with them."

Her arm slides across mine, squeezing me back.

Before long, she gets up and walks toward the door.

"Call if you need anything," she responds.

With one last look at me, she leaves my room, shutting the door behind her.

I love my friends. I love how big their hearts are and how much they care. And while most people would want to be surrounded by others, I learned to grieve alone.

Most people would have their parents to help them grieve on the hard days, but I didn't. My parents were long gone before Bryce died, and once he was gone, they became nearly invisible. Each year, I'd wait for them to bring up this day. I remember my first year in college, waiting for a call from my mother to check on me. That call never came. So I learned to grieve alone.

Dedicating October twentieth as the day I mourn them both, I created my own tradition. I know that there will come a time when I won't be able to shut out the world and spend the day alone, in my room, doing my traditions, but, for now, this is how I'm spending the anniversary.

Each year on the night before, I pull out my box of memorabilia. I look at the picture albums I made throughout the years, and look at all of our happy memories—trips to the zoo, weekends on Lake Michigan, play dates in the Nelsons' backyard, first and last day of school pictures, and everything in between. It still hurts to see them, but I do have one picture of the three of us that I keep framed in my room, the rest of the memories stay buried in my heart and memory box. It's in this box that I keep Bryce's football sweatpants and Asher's football sweatshirt that I sleep in every year.

On the day of, I stay in bed all day, only leaving for the necessities. My day in bed consists of watching all of our favorite movies—*The Sandlot, Ted, Lone Survivor, The Lucky One*, and *Home Alone 2*. Bryce dreamed of becoming a Navy SEAL. I'm not sure where his fascination came from, but we would watch *Lone Survivor* over and over, and I'd watch his passion explode.

The Sandlot was the go-to movie the three of us would watch. We had it memorized, and every time we'd watch, I'd get so pissed about the whole "you play ball like a girl" line because, guess what, I could play ball, and I was damn good at it. Bryce and Asher would always challenge me in throwing competitions, and I would beat them both. It was such an ego boost for me, but they'd get so pissed.

Ted was the movie we watched the first time we smoked pot. The boys wanted to be just like Mark Wahlberg—do you see a Marky Mark trend here?—and smoke pot with a bear. We had seen this movie before, of course, but one night during our freshman year of high school, the boys wanted the full experience. Asher found a teddy bear that looked like *Ted*, and the three of us sat in our movie theater room and watched *Ted*, while smoking pot and eating all the food, with a damn bear. And yes, I kept that bear. And yes, each year I continue the tradition.

The movie I end the day with is always *Home Alone 2*. We dubbed the second movie far superior to the first. I don't want to be friends with anyone who thinks otherwise. One year for Christmas, Bryce surprised me with a turtledove, just like Kevin gave the Pigeon Lady of Central Park. And just like any kid, his wish was to go to a giant toy store and meet an old man like Mr. Duncan. He said that, even though we were twins, and even though we shared a part of each other, he wanted me to have the reminder that as long as we have our doves, we will be friends forever.

Before we buried him, I put his turtledove in his hand. Even in death, we'll still be best friends. And the day I turned eighteen, I went to the tattoo parlor to have a turtledove tattooed on the back of my neck. It's a constant reminder that, even though Bryce is gone, he's with me, friends forever.

The afternoon rolls around, and I've finished *The Lucky One* and *The Sandlot*. My stomach begins to rumble telling me it's time for sustenance. Reaching for my phone on my nightstand, I finally check my notifications for the first time. Before I check all of the text message notifications—all ten of them—I click on the Instagram app.

Clicking on the plus sign in the top corner, I scroll to my *memories* album on my phone and select a few photos of Asher, Bryce, and myself. Quickly, I throw a vintage filter on the picture and post the image with the caption, *Hope you both are giving Heaven some Hell. Up there on the gold streets crushing cans & running routes. There's not a day that goes by that I don't miss you both. Love always, B.* Hitting the share button, my first tribute photo of the three of us is out there. Yeah, I know they can't see it, but a part of me hopes God has a screen so those we lost can see all of the birthday wishes and memorial pictures we share. I just want them to know that they're never far from my mind.

The *like* notifications start rolling in, but I close the app out. Getting up from my bed, I make my way downstairs, pulling up my text messages once I get into the kitchen. Reaching into the fridge, I glance up and check the time on the microwave. Twelve thirty. Whatever, it's late enough, I pull out a bottle of beer. Twisting the cap off, I take a long pull before grabbing a leftover sub sandwich. I take my lunch over to the bar and climb up on a barstool. Now that I've got sustenance, I begin reading the messages and responding.

Roomies

> **Chloe: Just checking in. Need anything?**

> **Macy: Love you, Brynn *heart emoji***

> **Macy: I'm sorry I didn't get a chance to see you this morning**

> **Me: I'm good, Chlo. Thanks for checking *kisses***

> **Me: Love you both, so much *kisses***

> **Me: Mace, Don't sweat it. It wasn't a pretty sight.**

> **Macy: Psshh. You're beautiful, babe *fire emoji***

> **Me: *eye roll emoji* *kiss emoji***

> **Chloe: *kiss emoji***

Closing out my roomies group chat, I go to the next unread message.

> **Cody: You doing okay, babe?**

> **Me: I'm good, Cody. Thanks for checking in. *hand heart emoji***

His reply comes instantly.

> **Cody: I'm coming over after class. Don't fucking ignore me.**

> **Me: That happened one time.**

> **Cody: Yeah, and it sucked.**

Ignoring Quinton's missed phone call, I pull up his messages instead.

> **Q: Shit, Brynn. Why didn't you remind me today was the day?**

> **Q: I'm canceling plans with my parents and coming over.**

> **Me: Q, go see your parents. Don't cancel because of me. I'm fine. And I don't need them being more pissed at me.**

> **Q: I don't care what they think. You need me.**

> **Me: I promise, I'm fine.**

> **Q: See you tomorrow?**

> **Me: Duh!**

There are a couple of other messages from people I went to high school with. We might not talk anymore, but they always send a text today. I quickly *love* their messages. The next name I see surprises me, even though it shouldn't. She reaches out every year.

> **Grace Nelson: Hi sweetie, sending you all the love today.**

> **Grace Nelson: *picture of Asher and me at homecoming***

> **Grace Nelson: I found this picture the other day and thought you might like it, but I'm sure you have it. Just miss seeing you, sweetheart.**

> **Me: I don't have this picture. Thank you so much, Grace. I miss him so much *crying emoji***

> **Grace Nelson: I do too, sweetheart. But remember, he's with us. He's always with us.**

> **Me: I see him every day. He's always in my dreams.**

> **Grace Nelson: He loved you so much, Brinley. WE love you so much, sweetie.**

> **Me: I loved him too. I still do. He's got my heart.**

> **Me: I love you guys.**

> **Grace Nelson: Just promise me you won't give up on finding another love. I saw the way you and Quinton looked at each other. I recognized that look.**

> **Grace Nelson: My son looked at you the same way.**

Reading that message shakes me to my core. The tears I've been working hard to suppress since my meltdown this morning come crashing down. Hot tears stream down my face. I can't believe we are having this conversation. Not only are we having it over text messages, but we are having it on the day we lost her son. It just doesn't seem right to be talking about me loving someone else. And honestly, I don't know what the hell is going on between Quinton and me. There's no way she saw anything during the few encounters we had last weekend. Right?

My head is spinning and it's not from the alcohol. I can't have this conversation with her. Not today. Not ever. Typing out a response, I hit send and take another pull of my beer. I'm going to need another one soon.

> **Me: Grace...**

> **Grace Nelson: I know, sweetie, but love is a beautiful thing. You'll always be our daughter. Take care of yourself, sweet girl.**

> **Me: Love you *heart emoji***

I don't bother to see if she responds. Instead, I turn the "Do Not Disturb" setting on, and toss my phone away from me. My mind is reeling, the sobs racking through my body. Sliding down the cabinet, I don't stop until I'm fully seated on the floor. Bringing my knees to my chest, I wrap my arms around them as my head collapses.

I'm in such deep thought that I don't even hear the front door open and close or the footsteps alerting me that I'm not alone. Strong, tan arms wrap around me, causing me to jump out of my skin. Body jerking, I spin around to see who the attacker is, and scream.

"Jesus, Brynn, it's just me," Cody says, rubbing soothing circles on my back. "I said your name like five times. Didn't you hear me?"

"Clearly freaking not," I retort. "What the hell are you doing here?"

Running his hand through his hair, he looks me over. He must see how miserable I'm doing because his shoulders physically drop.

"Brynn," he says, pulling me back into his warm embrace. The two of us sit on the kitchen floor. "I don't want you to be alone."

"I'm fine," I answer, allowing my body to relax into his hold. "I'm good at being alone."

"But you don't have to be, B," he says, running his hands up and down my back. "Let us in. Let us be there for you."

I give in. I give in to his touch. I give in to his words. He pushes himself up from the floor, reaching his hand out to me. Taking his hand, I allow him to lead me upstairs to my room.

It's then that I notice that he has a bag in his other hand.

"What's in the bag?"

He sets the bag down on my bed, pulling out a six-pack of Shiner Bock and a baggie with two joints.

"Cody," I gasp.

"You told me one time you always watch *Ted* on this day. I thought I'd join this year," he says with a shrug. He slips off his shoes, pulling the white comforter back. "Now get your ass in bed and tell me why *Ted*."

Smiling, I do what he says. Cody hands me a joint and a bottle of beer before setting the same thing next to his side of the bed. His tall, trim body crawls in next to mine as he wraps his arm around my shoulders and pulls me in closer. His long arms allow him to open the window that's next to my bed before he pulls out a lighter. Once we are settled in, I tell him the story of *Ted*.

We stay like that for the duration of the movie. Smoking, drinking, laughing our asses off, and munching on the snacks he brought. At some point, I drift off in his arms.

Maybe he is right.

Maybe it is okay to let them in.

CHAPTER 22
QUINTON

G AZING UP AT MY parents' house, I can't help but wonder, when did everything change? When did my parents go from fun-loving parents to parents who only care about my NFL prospects?

I get it. My dad was an NFL badass. Kids grew up wanting to be my dad. They wanted to ball like Howard Boyd. And I'm the lucky son of a bitch who was born a Boyd.

But I miss everything that was before. Before the pressure. Before the constant nagging. Back when my mom cared about me, not who my agent was. Back when my dad threw the ball for fun. Before, he only cared about my stats.

At one point, this white colonial home with the burnt-orange front door felt like home. The front flower beds were full of life and welcomed you inside. It housed my greatest memories. My favorite people lived under this roof. But somewhere along the way, everything changed. Somewhere along the way, fame and success shadowed love and admiration. Jealousy and envy seeped into our bones—especially mine and my brothers'. There was a time when my brothers and I were best friends, but that changed just like everything else.

Now I envy my older brother and the life he created. I don't want to give up football, but I'm envious that my brother chose to further his education and become a doctor instead of focusing on football. My younger brother is jealous of my success on and off the field. He acts out constantly in hopes the scouts will notice him. We went from brothers who joked around with each other and who laughed at the dumb shit we came up with to brothers who barely speak to each other. We've let our parents control the narrative.

Taking a deep breath, I pull my hand from my pocket and ring the video doorbell. Yeah, I have to ring the doorbell in my own damn house. Isn't that fucked up? My childhood bedroom is still inside, decorated in navy and gray with posters of my favorite athletes and musicians, trophies line my shelves, and I still have most of my clothes here. But it's not my home—it's a house I visit.

"Quinton, baby, you made it," my mother says as she opens the door.

"Hi, Mom," I greet, stepping in through the open door she's holding open for me.

Glancing around, I notice that the decor is changing. Mom has always had good taste, but every time I come home, it's becoming more high-end. The bronze chandelier has been replaced with a crystal one, the entryway table is new with a large floral arrangement in the center, and the family photo is no longer the focal point, replaced with a piece of art. I don't know who she's trying to impress, but it feels like a showroom.

"You've changed things."

"Do you like it?" she asks, gesturing to the new pieces. "We hired a designer to come and give the decor a more luxurious taste."

"I didn't think there was anything wrong with it before," I mumble, slipping off my Air Force 1s.

Mom chuckles as she leads the way into the dining room, which is to the left of the entryway and opening to the kitchen.

"Oh sweetie, that's why you need to find yourself a woman with good taste."

I take in the dining room and notice that that, too, has changed.

"You're sayin' I need a woman who's gonna spend my money?" I ask her, following her into the kitchen.

This is a total contradiction of everything my parents have taught me. Knowing that we come from money and that there was a good chance each of us boys would end up with a large amount of money, it was ingrained in us to look out for the women that were only after our bank accounts. Those were the women we were taught to avoid. Now it sounds like that's what she wants. I swear these two fell and hit their heads.

She stops just inside the kitchen, spinning to look up at me.

"Quinton, find yourself a woman with good taste, who isn't a ho who's going to bed hop. She needs to be high-class and look good on your arm."

Fighting hard not to roll my eyes, I just agree with her.

"Okay, Mom. Thanks for the advice."

Reaching up, she places her hand on my cheek. It used to be comforting, but now it's just demeaning.

"Of course, sweetie, that's what I'm here for. I'm here to make sure you find yourself a good, strong woman who won't embarrass you. Not like that friend of yours." She mumbles that last part, but I heard it. Knowing she's talking about Brynn makes my skin crawl. She never goes without that little dig. "Speaking of that friend, we need to talk about Chicago."

"There's nothing to talk about," I state, sliding around my mom and heading toward the refrigerator.

I'm going to need alcohol to get through tonight. Opening the fridge, I look inside for anything. There's a bottle of Shiner in the back, which I grab and immediately pop the top.

Bringing the bottle to my lips, I take a very long pull of beer, draining half of it as I let the cold lager slide down my throat. It's at that moment my father walks in.

"Son," he greets. "Nice to see you're serious about your diet."

And the digs keep coming.

Pulling the beer from my lips, I use the back of my hand and wipe away any remaining liquid.

"Dad," I greet in return, ignoring the dig on my diet.

"Boys, let's go to the table. Cressida will serve us once we are all seated. Xavier should be here any moment." Mom leads the way to the dining room, and we all take our seats around the six-person table.

Dad and Mom sit at either end of the table. I sit in the seat to the left of my father. The seat to the right of my dad is reserved for my older brother. And the seat to the left of my mom is for Xavier. The seat directly beside me is always empty.

Just as we sit down, the front door flies open and Xavier waltzes in. He looks like a wreck, like something is off. But I don't have the energy to dwell on it. It's not my problem.

"There's my baby," Mom exclaims, standing from her seat and rushing to the door to hug Xavier.

Her baby is right. She's always babied him, and I don't see that changing anytime soon. The two of them have a long, drawn-out welcome. My dad and I sit at the table waiting for them to join us. The sooner we get this dinner started, the sooner we can get it over with.

"How's football going, Q?" Dad asks.

"It's goin' good. Looking forward to the game this week. Coach has been working us hard, just hoping the O-line is prepared."

"If they do their job, you should have a really good run game. Coach better be ready to put the ball in your hands." Our conversation is interrupted as Mom and Xavier join. "Son," Dad greets Xav, not bothering to get up.

"Cressida, we are ready," Mom says loudly from the dining room, calling for our maid, because we are *apparently* too good to serve ourselves.

My mood is just bitter. I'm pissed I'm here. I'm pissed this doesn't feel like home, and I'm pissed my parents don't feel like parents anymore. I'm pissed Xavier is acting strange like he's on something. And I'm pissed Brynn doesn't want me with her.

That's where my mind keeps going all dinner long. Cressida serves us roasted chicken with root vegetables and mashed potatoes. It's healthy and delicious. Dinner is quiet while we all eat. Too busy enjoying the food. Glancing around the table, I notice that everyone is still engrossed in their food. Taking the opportunity, I slide my phone out of my jeans pocket and pull up Brynn's message thread.

> **Me: I wish I was with you right now.**

I watch the message change to *delivered*, but it doesn't get read right away.

"Really? Quinton, you can't be present for one meal," Mom says, disappointment coating her tone.

"Sorry, just checking on a friend."

Xavier takes the moment to chime in. "Brynn?" he asks with a smirk.

He knows this is a sore subject.

"Yes. Today is a rough day for her."

Staring at me from across the table, Xavier doesn't let the conversation die.

"Oh yeah, I saw her post on Instagram. Something about her brother and boyfriend dying?"

"Quinton, see, that girl is nothing but drama," Mom chides.

At the same time, Dad says, "Losing them both on the same day has to be tough."

My eyes immediately snap to my mother's. "Really? That's some bullshit, Ma."

"Quinton Alexander Boyd, how dare you speak to me like that."

Tossing my napkin on the table, the rage begins to boil. "How dare I? Who says something like that?"

"Quinton, Abigail. That's enough." Dad raises his voice at the both of us, our eyes snapping to him. "Quinton, we invited you over to discuss the draft. We have an agent we'd like you to speak to. We feel he is a better fit for you."

I'm taken aback at the change of topic. I'm fuming. The girl that I'm falling for gets absolutely no respect from my parents. It's not just her who doesn't get any respect, it's me too. How dare Ma turn Brynn's tragedy into a negative attribute? And how dare my parents try to steamroll my agent's decision?

"I'm good. I have an agent."

Staring my father down, I'm inadvertently daring him to keep this conversation going. And he takes the bait.

"Your mother and I feel that by going with Prospect Agency, you'll do better financially," he adds.

"Eliza is doing a great job. She's my agent. I still haven't decided if I'll enter the draft this year or not."

I knew this dinner was a bad idea. I knew it was going to be an ambush.

Dad's face scrunches up with anger. He's pissed. His dark skin keeps the red from showing but I know that it would be as red as a cherry if it could.

"Don't be stupid. You will do as we say. Do you understand me? You'll call Peter at Prospect, and you'll sign him as your agent, and then you'll announce you're entering the draft."

That's it. I've had enough. Standing abruptly, my chair scrapes against the floor.

"No. I'm done. We're done."

Making my way to the front door, Mom reaches out to grab my elbow as I slide past her, but I jerk my arm to avoid contact. My feet slide into my shoes, and I'm out the door, ignoring my parents shouting at me to sit down.

Rage takes over my body. It doesn't feel like mine anymore. My chest heaves with anger. Slamming the car door shut, I start the car and gun the engine.

I should've never accepted the dinner invite tonight. I should've never listened to Brynn when she said she wanted to be alone. But that is about to change.

My girl needs me. And I need my girl.

Pulling into the parking lot of Brynn's complex, I turn off my car, and my body relaxes. Climbing from the car, I make my way to the front door. I give a light tap on the door, hoping Brynn answers the door since she hasn't read my message. I'm starting to worry about her. I know she wanted to be alone, but it's me. We don't ignore each other. But after last weekend, everything is weird between us.

The door opens in front of me, but it's not Brynn who answers.

"Q?" Chloe asks, surprised to see me.

"Hey, Chloe, Brynn home?" I ask.

Chloe opens the door wider for me to step inside. I toe my shoes off just like I did at my parents'. She shuts the door behind me.

"Yeah, she's upstairs with, uh, um, Cody," she sputters out.

Once again, my body feels the rage. I hate the jealousy that courses through me at the mention of his name. I shouldn't feel this way. Cody and Brynn have been friends just like Brynn and I have. But I know he has feelings for her, just like I do.

Chloe must sense the change in my mood. She looks uncomfortable, which isn't like her. Yes, she's the quietest one out of the group, but we've all been friends for years.

"Go up there, Quinton. She's going to be glad you stopped by."

Nodding my head at her, I make my way up the stairs. Pausing outside her door, I listen for anything coming from her room. The only sound is from the TV. Her door is cracked, and I slowly nudge it open. My eyes find two bodies in her bed real quick. Both of them are lying in her bed. Brynn is wrapped up in his embrace, sound asleep. Cody is just lying there, watching *Home Alone 2*. That should be me. That should've been me comforting her all day. Instead, she kept pushing me away.

Cody's gaze flicks my way, startled.

"Shit, Q," he whispers. "You scared the fuck out of me."

I don't say anything, just stare him down, my eyes bouncing from his to where his arm is wrapped around my girl. He must sense my mood. Apparently, my face is giving away every thought tonight.

"Relax, Q," he says with an eye roll. "I need to head out, I was hoping your ass would show up. Come take my spot."

Slowly, he untangles himself from Brynn's long limbs. She stirs but never wakes. While I'm waiting for him to remove himself from her bed, I take in the chaotic state of her room. There are empty beer bottles, a baggie with a joint, pizza boxes, and tissues strewn around the room. Cody slips his shoes on before pointing toward the door. With a shake of his head, I step into the hallway with him.

"How is she?" I ask.

"She's hurting. I've never seen her like this. She's just..." He pauses, looking back into the room. "Numb. Take care of our girl."

I groan at his possessive comment. "*My girl.*"

"Yeah, Q, whatever," he says, running his hand down the back of his neck. "I care about her too."

And with that, he leaves, and I make my way into her room. Sliding out of my jeans, I slip under the covers in my boxers and T-shirt. She rolls into my body immediately, her head running up and down my side.

"Quinton?" she asks in a sleepy voice.

"Hi, beautiful," I answer, leaning down and kissing the top of her head. After tasting her in Chicago, I can't keep my lips off her. I want to kiss her again. "I missed you."

Wrapping her arms tighter around my stomach, I can feel her smile against my skin.

"I missed you, too. Don't leave me, okay?"

"I'm here, baby."

And with that, she drifts back off to sleep. My girl in my arms once again. Even though she's hurting. Even though it's killing me that she's in pain. I'm going to be happy. The air has shifted around us. And right before I drift off, I feel her pull herself closer to me, snuggling into my skin, burying herself even deeper in my soul.

CHAPTER 23
Brynn

MY HAND TIGHTENS AGAINST something hard. My face isn't pressed against my soft pillow—it's pressed against something warm and hard. On its own accord, my hand tightens. A low grunt fills the room.

Last night starts coming back to me. I remember Cody and me spending the rest of the day in my bed, watching movies, devouring snacks, and me crying endlessly.

But—wait—he's not who I fell asleep with last night.

No. Quinton came. While I was sleeping, he lifted the covers, his warm body sliding next to mine. Before I drifted back into a deep slumber, I remember pulling him tighter against me. Comforting me. Bringing me back to reality. Letting me know that I'm okay. I'm always okay with him. He's my lifeline, my safety blanket, the one who always brings me comfort when I need it.

He makes another grunting sound. And oh god—that's when I realize it. Immediately my fist relaxes as I jerk up from my sleeping position. Cheeks flaming. My hand was on him. As in his morning wood.

Oh god.

Mentally I facepalm myself and want to curl under the covers.

Oops.

"Oh god, Quinton," I rasp out. "I didn't. I, uh, I didn't realize I was holding you. I mean, I knew you were there, but I—uhh—I didn't realize my dick, oh god, not mine but your dick was in my hand." Stuttering the words, I feel the heat spread from my face, down my neck, to my chest. I'm mortified.

What's with my hand always finding a dick to squeeze when I'm sleeping? Some people have comfort blankets, I have comfort cocks.

He laughs. Quinton opens his eyes and starts laughing. I don't think it's funny. Certainly not funny enough to warrant him cracking up at my embarrassment.

"It's fine, B. I thought I was dreaming."

Turning my body so that I'm facing him, I bring my legs up, crossing them underneath me. "You—uhh—have dreams like that?" I ask him as the blush comes back.

What is wrong with me? Sex doesn't bother me and talking about sex *definitely* doesn't bother me. But talking about it with Q has my cheeks flaming.

"Yeah, *I am* a guy," he answers me, bringing his arms back behind his head.

He makes no movement other than that. But I can't help but notice that, when he raised his arm, his shirt rode up. His black skin is peeking beneath his gray shirt, and I desperately want to trail my fingers down his muscled stomach. He looks content in my bed. Like he's comfortable and that we sleep together all the time.

Plot twist, we don't.

Aside from that time in Chicago. If we stay together, Quinton always takes the floor. Always.

At first, I thought it was strange, because what guy wouldn't take the opportunity to sleep next to me or any girl, but I just thought it was him being respectful. There's something so hot about a guy that has manners and treats women with respect.

Shaking my head, I pull the sleeve of my hoodie down into my palm before bringing my hand to my face, resting my elbow on my knee.

"No, not like that. I mean, I know you're a guy, a guy that likes sex. I meant a dream about me, and, oh god, never mind."

I try to hide my face, but what he says next has me snapping my eyes to his, searching his face for a giveaway that he's joking.

"Yes, Brynn. I've thought about you in my dreams. Like that."

There's no evidence that he's joking. None. The only thing I see is a pained expression painted on his face. It looks like he's hurt to finally get those words out of his mouth. I just stare at him, unsure of what to say next. Breaking our gaze, I jump out of bed, almost getting tripped up in the blanket that is still wrapped around my foot.

"I have to shower before class," I practically shout, racing toward my en suite.

Shutting the door behind me, I feel myself start to breathe again. My mind is going back to the admission that he's dreamed of me. Now factor that in with our kiss in Chicago, and I'm one confused Brynn. Does Quinton have feelings for me? When did that happen?

What do we do now?

There was that kiss outside our front door when we got back from Chicago, but I was just doing what felt right. He was the one who told me to do what felt right in the moment. And in that moment, I needed his lips on mine.

The little touches and small gestures he makes have woken something inside of me. There's a spark, a connection between us. Maybe there always has been, and I've been too blind to acknowledge it. But I don't want to fight it anymore.

Because the truth is, Quinton Boyd makes me feel alive. I don't have to find the high when I'm with him. He brings out the high that's already inside me.

Do I tell him about the shift I've been feeling? That my body hums in his presence. That I can sense him in a room before I see him.

Walking over to my sink, I pull out my toothbrush, dabbing a small amount of toothpaste on the bristles. Bringing the toothbrush to my mouth, I start brushing my teeth while my mind starts to play back over the years.

Quinton has always been protective of me, always coming to my defense when a guy gets too handsy or when slut-shaming begins for my extracurricular activities. We spend a lot of time together, but that's just what friends do, right? It's normal to spend this much time together...right?

These thoughts are making my brain hurt. It doesn't help that I have an emotional hangover from yesterday's grieving session. Factor in all the junk food, alcohol, and smoking and I'm spent. A *real* hot freaking mess.

Spitting the toothpaste out of my mouth, I rinse the brush and swish water in my mouth, before splashing cold water on my face. Stripping my clothes, I climb into the shower, letting the cold water run over me until it gets warm.

Fifteen minutes later, I'm stepping out of my bathroom with my hair in a towel and a robe covering my body. Surprise has me jumping. Quinton is still here. He's sitting on my bed, dressed in last night's clothes, scrolling through his phone. Glancing around my room, I see that all of the trash from the day before has been cleaned up, and my bed has been made.

"You didn't have to do that," I say, referring to cleaning my room.

His shoulders flex with tension. And I hate that. I hate that he was vulnerable with me and instead of talking to him about it, I fled. I'm good at that. Running when life gets a little challenging.

Glancing over his shoulder, he takes in my body. Running his eyes from my bare legs up my silk robe-covered body, snagging a little longer on my cleavage that is exposed from the opening of the robe, before making his way up to my eyes. Dark stormy eyes meet my "deer-in-the-headlights" expression. Vulnerability and sadness, and maybe a little arousal, line his features. He runs his hand over the back of his head, gripping his neck. Exhaling, I feel myself deflate.

"Q," I sigh, stepping closer to him. "I'm sorry I walked away."

My legs are next to his, and I'm standing over him as he sits. Seeing him sitting there, looking up at me with desire in his eyes does something to me. Warmth starts to spread through my body, settling in my lower stomach, nipples pebbling against the silk. He must see something on my face, because lust fills his eyes.

Quinton breaks eye contact first. Clearing his throat, he stands up. Our bodies are close, much closer than normal, especially since I'm wearing nothing except for a thin silk robe.

"Don't apologize," he says. He brings his hand to my cheek before sliding it down and gripping the back of my neck, pulling me into a hug.

I'm temporarily frozen by what has just happened, and it takes me a minute to react. Placing my arms around his middle, I return his hug. Quinton gives the best hugs. They're warm and comforting. He makes me feel strong when I feel weak. He makes me feel safe when I'm scared. Grounding me when the darkness creeps in.

Quinton Boyd feels like home. A home I've been searching for since I lost my brother.

Kissing the top of my head, he releases me. "See ya later, B."

And with that, Quinton leaves my room, leaving me feeling confused and aroused.

"Miss Wilder, can I see you in my office?" Professor Peters asks before he dismisses the class.

Cody and I exchange a glance. I knew that my outburst last week wasn't going to go unnoticed, but I was hoping Prof. Peters would be cool about it and just let it go.

"Want me to wait?" Cody whispers as he gathers up his stuff.

Putting my laptop away, I look over at him. "No, I'll see you in the Union for lunch."

The rest of the students look in my direction. I can see jealousy written all over the girls' faces. They wish they were me and were being asked to have a private conversation in Professor Peters's office. And yeah, there was a time that I wanted that too, but I don't want that anymore.

The idea of having a fling with a professor has lost its appeal. After this morning, I just want to get to the Union and have lunch with my favorite people. Quinton has been radio silent since he left my room this morning. I texted him a couple of times, but he just read them without responding. Which is annoying. Like, don't even read the messages if you're just going to ignore someone.

Tossing my backpack on my back, I make my way down the steps toward the bottom of the lecture hall and out the side exit toward the hallway that houses some of the professors' offices. Professor Peters's is the last one. The door is open, waiting for me. Knocking first, I step into his office. It's a decent size space with a desk, filing cabinets, and a small couch against the opposite wall from the desk. His walls are decorated with diplomas and motivational quotes. Honestly, I didn't expect Peters to be so stereotypical and have motivational quotes. It just seems so basic. One thing that Peters isn't.

"Ahh, Miss Wilder, please have a seat."

He gestures to the soft chair that faces his desk. And that's exactly what I do. I take a seat across from my professor.

"I'm really sorry for my outburst last week," I spit out, body slumping against the chair, once again, internally smacking my head.

Professor Peters just smiles at me as I watch his eyes rake over my body. Austin is still really warm, even though we are well into fall and approaching November. Today I threw on a distressed denim skirt and an alternative rock band tank top. Peters stares at my crossed legs where my skirt has risen from sitting down. If we're being completely honest, three weeks ago, I would've jumped at the excuse to be alone with him. Yeah, he might be my professor, but when you look this damn good, it doesn't matter. He's throwing forbidden romance vibes my way. Gosh, I sound like Chloe and one of her romance novels.

Placing both elbows on the desk, Peters leans forward.

"I should be the one apologizing," he says, looking up at me. "I'm going to be blunt with you, Brinley. I've heard about you. Hell, most of the professors at CTU know about you. Your reputation precedes you. They know about your wild ways, and you're notorious for showing up to classes hungover."

He pauses, a smirk coming over his face.

And I can't help but start to feel a little uncomfortable. His words are a shock to my system. I didn't think my out-of-class activities would pique so many professors' interests. Do I party? Yes. Do I enjoy guys? It's college. Do I have fun? Hell, yes. But what I do outside of my classes should have no reflection of what I do inside the classroom. Especially when I've maintained a 3.5 grade-point average.

Before I have a chance to interrupt, he gets up from his side of the desk, sauntering toward my side. Leaning his lower half against the front of his desk, Peters crosses his outstretched legs at the ankles, and rests his arms across his chest which makes his muscles flex. Quinton flashes into my mind and how he used his muscles to brace himself over me. Moisture gathers at my center at the memory.

Once again, his eyes pursue my body.

"It was unfair of me to judge you and put you on the spot like that. I let your reputation get the best of me and, for that, I'm sorry."

"It's no problem," I respond quickly. Wariness spreads through my body. "Let's call it water under the bridge."

I smile up at him, hoping this conversation gets over quickly.

He doesn't take the hint. Instead, he leans a little closer to me, his legs brushing my bare ones. I quickly remove them from his touch.

"Each semester, professors are allowed to ask a student to become their office assistant. After hearing your story and seeing how serious you are about getting your degree, I thought you'd be *perfect* to provide *assistance* whenever I need something. Would this be something you'd be interested in?"

And my stomach drops at the way he said *assist*. If I'm not mistaken, Professor Peters is interested in me providing assistance outside of the classroom. And that makes my skin crawl.

"Oh, um, I—" I try to sputter out a response, feeling extremely uneasy.

"It'd be a wonderful opportunity for you to learn one-on-one outside of the classroom. I have some colleagues I could introduce you to who would offer you some more experience and get you set up post-college."

Sitting up, I pull down my skirt, watching Peters's eyes follow my movement. Clearing my throat, I finally find my voice.

"Thank you so much for the opportunity. Would it be possible to get back to you?"

Annoyance and confusion flash over his face. Peters doesn't seem like the kind of guy who is used to being told "no" or asked to wait. Just as quickly as the annoyance flashed across his face, he schools his features, that flirty smirk coming back.

"Of course, Brinley. Just don't take too much time. This is an arrangement that would benefit both of us, and I'd love to get started sooner rather than later."

"Of course," I reply, and quickly scoop up my backpack, walking toward the door.

I can feel his eyes trailing my movement. As much as everyone talks about having a fling with their professor, this whole exchange has left me feeling extremely uncomfortable. Making my way out of his office, I continue pulling my skirt down. I know it's an appropriate length, but after that talk, I just feel dirty.

Quickening my pace, I push open the doors to Rogers Hall. Taking in a long inhale of fresh air, I feel like I can finally breathe again. But as I start walking toward the Union, I can't help but sense I'm being watched. Glancing over my shoulder, I see Professor Peters standing at his window, watching me. A shiver runs through me. I'm officially feeling sketched out.

Inside the Union, I go straight to the cafeteria. Skipping my usual salad, I head over to the grill. I need something fried ASAP. Deciding on the fried veggie medley, I grab a Coke from the drink machine and make my way to the checkout.

"Oh, honey, please tell me this isn't your lunch," Tina, my favorite cashier, says.

Smiling at her, I pull out my card and swipe it.

"Then I won't tell you that this is my lunch."

Tina just shakes her head.

"Are you okay, dear?"

"Of course," I say way too loudly with a wobbly smile.

Narrowing her eyes, she stares at me. Skimming my features for any crack in my mask.

"If you say so," she says. "Have a good day, hon."

"Thanks, Tina. Have a good one too."

Grabbing my tray, I scan the room for my friends. My eyes snag on Cody, who's waving his hands in the air. Instantly, I feel at ease. Dropping my tray across from Cody, I sit down in a seat next to Quinton. Picking up my straw, I hit it on the table with more force than necessary, in hopes to get it open.

"Jeez, B, what'd that straw do to you?" JP asks with a chuckle.

But I don't respond. Feeling the looks of both Cody and Quinton, my initial reaction is to hunker down in my chair and hide.

Cody speaks first. "What the hell did he do?"

The straw finally pops out of the paper, and I slip it into the lid of my fountain Coke, taking a large gulp before responding.

"Nothing. He just wanted to clear the air from last week," I lie.

Cody sees right through the lie.

"Bullshit."

Quinton hasn't said anything yet. He just stares at me, burning a hole in the side of my face. I haven't looked at him. If he can ignore me all morning, I can ignore him too. We're playing a real childish game.

"Everything is fine," I say, dipping a fried cauliflower in the ranch dipping sauce.

Cody looks at me, and then looks at Quinton.

"You're a fucking liar," he says, looking at Quinton for help. He isn't getting any from him. "What's going on between you two? Something happen after I left last night?"

I sneak a glance at Quinton as his jaw flexes. But the moment is interrupted by Macy. She slams her tray down on the table, making me jump.

"Shit, Macy," Quinton barks.

"What?" she asks, taking in the tension at the table. "Did I interrupt something?"

JP jumps in since Cody, Quinton, and I say nothing. "Something weird is happening between these three."

Macy looks us over.

"Does this have anything to do with you guys staying over last night? Oh my god," she gasps. "Did you three have a little *fun*?" Her eyebrows wiggle at her insinuation that the three of us hooked up.

All of our heads snap in her direction.

"Hell no," Cody all but yells. "I left when Q came over."

"Oh thank god." Macy chuckles. "Because that'd be awkward as hell."

"I can't believe that's the conclusion you came up with," I say. "Professor Peters asked me to stay after class. That's all."

"Hot Professor Peters?" Macy asks, with a mouth full of food. "Because damn, what I wouldn't give to get him alone."

"What'd he want, Wilder?" Quinton finally speaks up.

"Nothing, he just wanted to know if I was interested in being his office assistant this year." Before the guys have a chance to say anything, I add, "I got a weird vibe while I was there."

"What'd he do?" Cody and Quinton say in unison.

"You're weird right now," Cody says.

"Did he touch you?" Quinton adds.

Our whole table is watching this conversation.

"Guys, enough. Nothing happened. I'm going to tell him 'no.' Everything is fine," I reply, diving back into my food. "Are you boys ready for the game tomorrow?" I ask, changing the subject.

JP responds with a "hell yeah," but Q doesn't take his eyes off me. We need to talk about this morning, about the change we both are feeling.

But I'm scared. I'm scared of these feelings, and I'm scared of losing him if we aren't on the same page.

I can't lose Quinton.

A voice clears at the end of our table, and everyone's eyes snap in that direction. Monica is standing at our table. She's dressed in a pink T-shirt, the Kappa Alpha Theta letters across her chest, and skintight black leggings showing off her tiny frame.

"Hey, Brynn," she greets me.

But her eyes don't find mine. They find Cody's. Setting my food back down on my tray, I swallow the remaining food in my mouth.

"Monica!" I welcome her a little louder than needed, but I'm happy for the interruption from my thoughts. "Guys, this is Monica. Monica, this is, well—this is everyone."

She smiles at everyone.

"Cody, Monica is in our psych class."

His head pops up at that, paying Monica more attention. I watch as he trails his eyes from her face down her legs.

"Oh, awesome. Want to join us?"

Monica looks at me, and a grin spreads across her face before turning her attention back to Cody.

"Sure, thanks!"

And with the interruption of our new tablemate, the conversation turns toward her, making everyone forget about my trip to Professor Peters's office.

CHAPTER 24
Brynn

EVERYONE IS MEETING UP at The Eagles' Nest tonight, since the football team has a late afternoon home game tomorrow. I don't normally pass up a Friday night out, but I'm just not feeling it.

Truthfully, my head is all over the place. Every time my thoughts drift off, I go back to Chicago and Quinton being dared to kiss me. How he didn't hesitate and how it felt to kiss him. I thought for sure it'd feel awkward, but it didn't. And I know we went so much further than kissing, but we never would've gotten to that point without that dare. The kiss just felt so monumental.

It felt good. Damn good. My body buzzed.

And then waking up with him in my bed this morning felt so natural. And then, as if I wasn't already on edge, Professor Peters's encounter was just off-putting.

Instead of going out and getting drunk, I told the girls I was meeting a guy. Which wasn't a lie. It's why I find myself standing in front of a black door outside of the Football House. It's quiet, no loud music, and the lights are off. I don't even know if anyone is home. Before I talk myself out of it, I ring the doorbell and wait. And wait some more. Just as I'm about to turn and walk away, the front door swings open.

Quinton is standing in front of me in a pair of athletic shorts, no shirt. And my eyes trail over every muscle. They gaze over the large eagle that is tattooed across his muscled chest and the large cross that is tattooed on his right rib cage before skimming over his abs and landing on the deep V that points down to his very impressive *asset*. That same *asset* I had in my hand this morning. My cheeks flush red, and I lick my lips before snapping my eyes up to Q's. He's already staring at me, waiting for me to finish my shameless perusal of his strong, dark, and athletic body.

"You done?" he asks with a smirk.

Heat spreads across my chest, and I can only manage a nod. Opening the door wider, he gestures for me to come in.

"What are you doing here, Brynn?"

Hearing my first name on his lips instead of my last name is a shock to the system.

"I thought we should talk."

Closing the door behind me, Quinton just stares at me before turning and heading toward the staircase. This might be Quinton's house, but we never hang out in the main living area unless there's a party or a group of us hanging out. Quinton has always retreated to his room, and that's where we head.

"Yeah, we should," he tosses over his shoulder, leading us upstairs.

Following him, I take stock of the house. It's super clean, which is surprising since there are five college men that live here. Quinton has the primary bedroom that's on the left side of the house, while the other three bedrooms are on the right side. The third floor was turned into a fifth bedroom and another rec room. Quinton steps into his room first, and I'm not surprised to see his room is clean and organized. I've never met a guy as tidy as Quinton. He hates messes, which is why he's constantly picking up my room. The only things out of place are the books on his desk. Looks like I was interrupting his homework time.

"Want anything to drink?" Quinton asks, grabbing a Gatorade out of his mini fridge.

Shaking my head, I answer him, "I'm good. Thanks. If I'm interrupting, I can come back later."

He takes a drink of his lemon-lime drink and just stares at me. His eyes bore into me, and I feel exposed.

"No, we are talking. Everything is weird, and I can't take it anymore."

Making my way over to his bed, I kick off my tennis shoes and climb onto his bed. Realizing that I can't cross my legs since I'm still in my skirt, I bend my legs to the side, placing a pillow in my lap, just in case.

"I'm not trying to be weird, Q. I just—I just don't know how to be around you."

Shock crosses his face and contorts into hurt.

"What the fuck does that mean?"

Quinton doesn't join me on the bed like usual. Instead he leans against his desk, facing me.

His position mirrors that of Professor Peters. While Peters made me feel uncomfortable, all I want is for Quinton to shrink the space between us. I want to feel his hands caressing my skin while I watch his muscles flex with every movement.

"It means you kissed me. And I liked it," I whisper, looking down at my lap.

He doesn't say anything, and I refuse to look up. I can't believe I just said that. Exposing my feelings isn't something that I do. It's raw and real and feels unnatural but also perfectly natural. The pause has gone on almost too long. I sneak a glance up and see him staring at me.

Pushing off the desk, Quinton takes two large strides before he's erased the space between us. Following my gaze up to him, I see the darkness in his eyes. Before I have a chance to say anything, two large hands are grabbing the side of my face, forcing my head up to meet him. Our eyes bounce back and forth, soaking each other in, trying to guess what the other is thinking.

And then his lips are on me.

Soft, powerful lips are crushing mine. His tongue lashes out, running across my lower lip. Begging me to open for him. And I do. Our tongues meet and begin dueling with fervor. A moan slips from the back of my throat, but that only urges Quinton on more. He's coaxing my body down onto his mattress, his hand sliding in between us, grabbing the pillow I had in my lap, tossing it aside. Once the pillow is out of our way, his hand is back on me, running down my body. My legs open and his large body fits perfectly in the open space. It feels like too much. It feels passionate. It feels like we've been fighting our feelings for way too damn long.

My body feels like an electric shock from my head, down my chest, and settling in my core. Our bodies are moving together, and the only things separating us are his athletic shorts and a tiny scrap of fabric covering my pussy. The denim skirt I'm wearing is bunched around my hips. I wonder if he can feel how wet I am for him. Thank God he has black shorts on, or there'd be evidence of my arousal in his lap. Quinton pulls away from my mouth and starts kissing his way down to my neck, finding that sensitive spot below my ear.

My chest is heaving, and I'm so wrapped up in what he's doing to my neck that I don't feel his hand traveling from my thigh to my center. His pointer finger slides across the fabric. And he growls into my neck. He sucks the sensitive skin into his mouth before pulling away to look at me.

"Christ, Wilder, you're soaked." He just watches my reaction, no doubt he can see how turned on I am. "Is all this for me?"

Words are hard. My best friend just kissed me into blissful oblivion. All I can do is nod my head. Grabbing the back of his neck, I pull him back down to meet my lips. I can feel how hard he is for me. He's even harder now than he was this morning. Quinton takes his pointer finger and goes back to rubbing me. Sliding the thin piece of fabric to the side, he slips his finger inside me. A long gasp escapes my lips, and I moan. It only fuels him as he begins to pump his finger inside of me, then slips a second digit to meet the first. Using his thumb, he applies pressure to the bundle of nerves that are pulsing for attention.

"Oh god," I cry out, meeting his movement.

"No baby, it's just me," he says, going back to devouring my neck.

I'm close. So close. He must sense it too, because his movement quickens. His fingers work faster, hooking to hit that spot deep inside me, while his thumb applies more pressure to my clit.

"Quinton!" I scream, not even caring if there's anyone in the house or not. "Oh, oh. I-I-I'm coming!"

"Let go, Wilder. Come for me," he says, looking up at me.

He's watching, waiting for me to come apart. And that's all it takes. I'm coming, moaning, and screaming his name. Body shaking, chest heaving, I come back down to reality. Quinton Boyd just made me come again. Come hard and fast. And I loved it. He slides his fingers from inside me, bringing them up to his mouth and sucking them clean. I moan again, questioning if I could come again from just watching that.

His mouth finds mine again. Our lips fuse together, and I open, allowing his tongue to enter. I moan at the taste of myself. He grunts at my response before pulling away with a sexy smirk.

"You like tasting yourself on me, don't you?"

"You already know I fucking love it," I respond, reaching up to pull him back down to me.

Our tongues find each other, dueling and tasting each other.

My hand roams from his neck to his front. Grazing my fingers down the ridges of his abs, I feel him shudder beneath me. A thrill runs through me, spurring me on. Continuing my journey, I find his long, hard cock. Gripping him through his shorts, he groans against my lips.

"Fuck, Wilder," he hisses between clenched teeth.

I'm dying to repay him. I begin stroking him over the silky material of his shorts. Another moan. Another shiver. And I know what I need to do.

In one swift movement, I shove him off me and roll off the bed. Before he has a chance to speak, I'm kneeling on the floor, looking up at him through hooded, lust-filled eyes. A devilish smirk spreads across my lips before running my tongue over my bottom lip.

"Wh-what are you doing?" Q asks, bringing himself to a sitting position, legs hanging off the side of his bed, erection tenting his pants.

I chuckle before responding. "Have you never had a girl get on her knees for you?"

"I mean, yeah, but you don't have to do this. I don't expect anything in return..." he trails off.

"Shut the hell up and let me put that cock in my mouth, so I can taste you too."

"Jesus Christ, Wilder," he rushes out, getting on his feet in front of me. "Keep talking like that, and I'm going to come right now."

Without saying another word, I reach for the waistband of his shorts. Slowly, I pull them down, watching his cock spring free. Letting the material pool at his feet, I reach for him, wrapping my hand around his thick dick. My eyes watch him as I begin to pump him in my hands. Watching him watch my hand, I increase the pace. His eyes flutter before closing, and that's when I lean forward, licking the bead of precum off his tip.

A moan escapes both of us. No longer willing to wait, I take him in my mouth. His crown slips past my lips as I slowly suck him in. Working my way down and opening my throat to take all of him.

"So big," I mumble around him.

"Fuck," he responds.

I continue to bob my head as I suck and pump him with my fist.

"Shit, Wilder," he grumbles, his hand finding the back of my head. "You feel so good sucking my cock, taking me in your throat."

I moan against him as his words affect me. His hips thrust as he works my head until he's fucking my face. I continue to hollow my cheeks, sucking him as I let him take control.

"I'm coming!" he yells his quick warning before he's spurting his hot seed in my mouth.

Sucking every last drop from him, I pull away, wiping my mouth with the back of my hand.

Sitting back on my feet, I take in the man in front of me. His eyes are wide, his chest heaving, and he's a picture of a satisfied man. It's hot seeing him come undone, especially at my hands—well, my mouth.

"Thanks for the warning, Q. But I'm no quitter," I say with confidence. "And I loved tasting you."

"Shit, Wilder," he rasps out. "I'm going to be hard again."

"What's wrong with that?" I ask, shrugging.

I, uh, wasn't expecting that tonight," he admits bashfully.

Reaching down, he grabs me under my arms and pulls me so that I'm standing in front of him.

Stretching on my toes, I kiss him.

"I mean, I'm not complaining."

We both chuckle, and that seems to snap us out of our heated exchange.

"But we should probably talk."

He sits on the bed, moving until his back is resting against his headboard. Extending his arm out, he pulls me so that my back is resting against his front.

"Yeah, you're probably right," Quinton says, leaning down to place a chaste kiss on my neck.

Now that we've opened up the door, he can't keep his hands off me. I wonder how long he's been holding back on the urge to touch me. To show me his feelings. And why did it take us so long?

Sighing, he rests his head against the headboard as I burrow into his embrace.

"I want to give us a go, Wilder. It's been building, and these feelings I have aren't going away. I tried. I tried to fight them, because I can't lose you. You're too important to me."

Turning my head, I find his gaze.

"Well, it's safe to say our friendship has just gotten stronger. See five minutes ago for proof." I let out a small laugh. "But if we're going to try this, you need to be patient with me. I haven't dated in a long time, not since—not since Asher. And he was the only one."

His arms tighten around me. It feels weird to be having this conversation today. A day after the day.

"Wilder, I've been patient for two years. I'll give you whatever time you need. Just, just be mine." His expression is so wholesome, so vulnerable.

I spin, getting on my knees to face him. Grabbing his face, I lower myself to kiss him.

"Thank you," I whisper against his lips.

Before I can pull away, he stops me.

"But if we're going to give this a go, I want to be exclusive. I'm not sharing you with anyone else. You're mine, Wilder."

"I'm yours, Quinton."

THE LOCKER ROOM IS hyped. It always is on game days. I'm sitting in the training room where the trainers are stretching and taping me up before the game. Coach is going over the game plan one last time before we head on the field. A week has gone by since Brynn decided to give dating a try. And it's going fucking fantastic. I've wished for this day, and it's finally here.

"All good, Boyd," our trainer says, tapping the table, letting me know he's done taping. "Kick some ass today."

Making my way over to the rest of the team, I sidle up next to Grant. He bumps my shoulder pad with his.

"Let's fucking go," he shouts.

The locker room erupts in more shouts of "let's fucking go" and "hell yeah."

Huddling up, Harris starts our chant. "We're the best. We can't be beat!"

"We'll never accept defeat!" the rest of us shout back.

With that, we funnel out of the locker room toward the tunnel that leads to the field. This season has been epic. We're blowing out teams that should've been close. I'm getting carries that are making my stats look insane to the NFL teams. Eliza is so proud of my performance that she's feeling like a top-five pick in the draft is *really* possible. I've got my girl, and I've never felt happier. I just need to find the courage to tell her I'm not coming back next year.

The last weekend of October has arrived, which means all of our biggest games kick off next weekend. It's crucial we win and win them big.

WE WON!

We pulled off the win, making us still undefeated, which should allow us to keep the number one spot in the polls. The crowd is roaring. My adrenaline is high. Eight straight wins. Today's game was a tough one. Hartford came ready to play. Seriously, I didn't think we were going to be able to stop their run game, but, if anyone asks, I was one hundred percent confident we were going to win.

Making my way across the field, I find a few Hartford players I've gotten to know over the years and show my respect by telling them that they played a good game. Sportsmanship will be something I'm always known for. No matter how big we win and who we play, I'll always shake my opponent's hand.

Standing on the thirty-yard line, I glance up in the stands, and my eyes immediately spot her. She's standing there as the crowd disperses around her, searching for me out on the field. I take the time to admire her beauty.

Even from this far away and after a three-hour game in the sun, she looks beautiful. Her tight Levis look like they were painted on her.

Damn, her ass looks fine in those jeans.

Forcing my eyes from her legs, I take in the powder blue crop top that shows off her tight stomach. The color makes her eyes pop against her glowy skin. She's wearing her glasses, which isn't something I see often, but there's just something about her in those round tortoise shell frames that do something to me. Loose, bright-blonde tendrils fall across her face, but she doesn't care. She's too busy wearing a smile that makes my chest flutter and makes me want to run to her.

And running to her is exactly what I do.

Taking off in a jog, I keep my eyes on her. A smile spreads across my face when she finally finds me in the sea of players. I didn't think it was possible that her smile could get any bigger, but it does.

Standing on the field below her, she leans over the railing, trying to cut the space between us. My fingers twitch at my side, begging for me to reach up and grab my girl. But I'm not going to do it yet. As much as I want to tell everyone that she's mine, I don't want to scare her off. It's only been a week since we decided to go from just being friends to dating exclusively.

"Meet you at the house?" I yell up to her.

The bright smile she was wearing morphs into a deviant smirk. "Hmm, we'll see." Brynn stands up, shrugging her shoulders, playing hard to get.

Only too bad for her, I've already got her. And I'm never letting her go. Cody stands there, watching our encounter. The wheels are spinning in his head as he tries to put together the change in demeanor between us.

"'Aight then." Smirking back at her, my eyes drift over to Cody. Giving him a nod, I head into the tunnel toward the locker room.

Brynn Wilder is going to be the death of me, and I'm going to enjoy everything she throws my way.

The house is bumping when Grant and I pull into the driveway. People are spilling out of the house and all over the yard. Solo cups and cans are littering every surface. I'll have to find some freshman to get on trash duty. We don't need the cops getting called on us tonight. Not when we're celebrating. Most of the cops will turn their eyes to noise complaint calls, but there are a few that will do whatever they can to get us in trouble with the school. It's bullshit.

"Dude, you alright?" My question pulls Grant from wherever his head was.

Parking the car in the garage, I turn the engine off, and Grant opens his door.

"Yeah, something's off with my sister." He shuts the door and starts his way to the door. Grant and his sister are tight, being only two years apart, their relationship is strong. His family is the opposite of mine. The Campbells are caring, family-oriented, and loving.

Hmm, I wonder what that's like?

Making my way around the car, my strides have me standing next to him.

"Anything you need, you know I'm here?"

Grant slaps my shoulder and nods his head.

"Yeah, man, I appreciate it."

Looking up at me, he opens the door that leads into the house. Shouting over his shoulder, since the music is slow loud, "Now, let's get fucked up."

I chuckle, following him into the house.

A new rap banger is coming through the speakers and the vibe is lit. Following Grant, we head straight for the kitchen needing alcohol. Coach gave us tomorrow off, which means tonight we party.

People are grinding on each other on the makeshift dance floor. Someone hooked up the large speakers. Multicolored lights are playing in the semi-dark house. The Football House looks like a straight-up club.

Normally, I'd be Mr. Cautious, but not tonight. Not after this week.

Tonight I'm celebrating.

Taking my eyes off the crowd, I look up in time to hear someone shout my name as a beer is tossed my way. Searching the space, I see Riggsby nodding his head at me. Riggs might be a sophomore, but he's a helluva player. I'm going to miss playing with him and the other guys next season. It's weird to think that I'm not going to be here next year, especially since they don't know it yet.

"Dude, I think I'm getting hard from watching those girls dance together." Riggsby throws his arm around my shoulder. Using his other hand, he tilts his beer bottle gesturing toward two girls grinding against each other on the makeshift dance floor.

Laughing, I shrug his arm from around my shoulder. "Fuck, Riggs. Don't talk about getting hard with your arms wrapped around me."

Beer goes flying from his mouth as he belts out a laugh. "Oh god." He laughs. "Dude, I'm totally *not* getting hard from you!"

JP and Grant make their way into our conversation at the worst possible time.

"What the fuck?" JP glances from Riggs to me. "What the fuck are you two talking about?"

Bringing the bottle to my lips, I take a long pull, shaking my head at this conversation. "Lightweight over here." I point to Riggs, shaking my head.

Looking between the two of us, JP replies, "You know what, I don't need to know."

"Where's Brynn?" Grant asks, looking around the kitchen.

Shrugging, I laugh internally. Brynn usually isn't too far from me and the guys, but I haven't seen her yet tonight. Guess she wasn't messing with me when she acted like she wasn't showing up tonight.

JP nudges my shoulder, taking a long drink out of his Solo cup. Based on how glassy his eyes are, I'm guessing he skipped the beer and went straight to the liquor. Dude deserves it. He beat the hell out of Hartford's quarterback with two-and-a-half sacks.

"Trouble just entered the house."

All of our heads snap to the door.

"Ho-ly, fuuck," Riggs draws out.

"We're in trouble, boys," Grant adds.

Trouble *definitely* just walked into this house, and all I want to do is punch every guy staring at her.

Chloe, in her petite frame, is wearing a skintight, white dress with straps that look like they could be easily broken with a slight tug. Her red, skyhigh heels make her tiny legs look longer.

But it's the girl to her left that has my mouth drying, my hand sliding down my pants to subtly adjust myself. Brynn Wilder stands in my doorway with a half-empty bottle of tequila in her hands looking like sin. A leather mini skirt and black heels make her legs look endless and have me dreaming about what they're going to look like wrapped around my waist. Forcing my gaze from her legs, the rest of her outfit has me trying to keep a growl from escaping. A black, see-through, mesh shirt and a black, lace bra covers her perfect tits.

"Shit, look at Brynn." Riggs's eyes look like they're about to pop out of his head, and the thought of him ogling her has me seeing red.

"Don't!" My gaze finds Riggs. He must see the murderous look in my eyes because he spins around and heads into the kitchen.

Brynn doesn't even try to find me. She just grabs Chloe's hand and makes her way to the dance floor. Another blonde girl pulls Brynn in for a hug while Brynn passes her the bottle of tequila. I can't help but stand back and watch her. Brynn is the definition of free-spirited. From the way she moves to the music to the way she carries herself. She lives like she's the only person to make herself happy.

I envy her.

Hours pass by. The house has slowly started to thin out, and everyone is well on their way to being wasted. Except I slowed down a little while ago, and I'm feeling a nice, steady buzz. I'm just on the periphery of being drunk.

Everything is happy. A wide grin is plastered on my face. Leaning against the wall, I'm watching the girls dance to "Body" by Megan Thee Stallion on top of my coffee table. Brynn is sandwiched between Chloe and the girl who hugged her when she arrived. I've seen her around here. I think her name is Savvy, Savannah, or something.

The way Brynn is moving her body is provocative. It's got me hot in ways I didn't know were imaginable. We might be taking things slow, but the only thing I can think of is getting my girl up to my room to finally have my way with her. Her body has consumed my dreams and fantasies for two years. From over her shoulder, she finally seeks me out. Her eyes meet mine, and I tip my bottle to her. A wink is my reward as I watch her dip low between the girls, her body writhing as she makes her way back up to standing.

"Want me to have them get off the table?" Riggsby asks, shocking me out of our staring contest.

"Nah, let 'em have some fun." Placing my hand in my pocket, I keep my gaze on Brynn. "She needs it."

I can feel Riggsby staring at me, letting out a chuckle, amused at what he must see. "How long have you been in love with her?"

The alcohol has loosened my inhibitions, and, with that, my filter has slipped. "Since the day I saw her in the quad. I heard someone laughing. Looked up and saw her smiling, and it hit me in the chest. From that moment, I knew she was the one."

Mouth snapping open, Riggsby moves his body to stand directly in front of me, drawing my entire attention.

"Are you for real? Dude, it's obvious you have a thing for her, but I didn't know it was that deep."

Before I have a chance to respond, a loud crash comes from the living room. Scanning my eyes over the room, I immediately find the source of the crash, and my ears hear that laugh that had me falling in love with Brynn two years ago.

The living room table has caved in, causing the three girls to fall to the floor. But they aren't phased. With arms wrapped around each other and heads tipping backward, the girls are laughing their asses off. A smile stretches across my face. Shoving the can of beer that I'm holding into Riggsby's chest, I march toward the chaos.

"Sorry 'bout your table," Chloe says when she sees me.

At the same time, Brynn slurs, "Hope you didn't love this table."

I don't let her get another word out of her mouth. Bending down, I scoop her up and toss her slim body over my shoulder. Slapping her ass, I leave my hand there so no one gets a peek at what's under her skirt. That's for my eyes and my eyes only.

"Quinton, I didn't take you for a caveman!"

"Baby, I'm full of surprises."

And with that, we head to my room, calling it a night.

Both of us are drunk, full of laughter, and happier than we've been in a long time.

CHAPTER 26
Brynn

I'M NEVER DRINKING AGAIN.

Ha. I feel like I've told myself this before.

My head feels like Phil Collins is playing that legendary drum solo from "In the Air Tonight."

Stretching, my arm finds the cold spot next to me. And that's when I realize I'm in a giant bed, alone. Quinton and I came upstairs after my epic fall and spent the night getting more accustomed to each other. Sex still hasn't happened, but let's just say our hands are starting to know every inch of each other's bodies.

Bringing the covers up to rest under my chin, I bury myself in his spot. His pillow smells like him. And I can't help myself from inhaling his scent. A wide smile stretches across my face of its own accord.

Is this what it's like to be happy? Not the false happiness where you put a fake smile on your face while on the inside, your mind is at war with your inner demons. But true happiness where the sky is bluer, the sun shines brighter, and your body feels lighter. Because if this is what true happiness feels like, then I can get used to this feeling.

The past couple of weeks have been hard. But exploring this attraction to Quinton has helped ease the pain.

It feels like healing.

It feels like moving forward.

With one last stretch in the king-size bed, I slip out of the sheets that I could so easily spend the day under and make my way to the en suite bathroom. Inside, I find the small bag of spare personal items that I keep under the sink. Hunger pains are ripping through my stomach, and all my mind can focus on is the need for breakfast.

Glancing around the room, my eyes find a long-sleeve, button-up that's hanging on the closet door. Deciding it's a better option than going downstairs in last night's bra and panties, or even last night's outfit, I pull the icy-blue dress shirt from the hangers and slip it over my naked body, opting to go without anything underneath. It's too early for anyone else to be up. Fluffing my hair up, I take one last peek in the mirror before heading downstairs.

At the bottom of the steps, my body halts.

Oh my gosh.

The pulse through my body stutters, landing in my lower stomach like a lead ball. Squeezing my legs together, I don't take my eyes off the man in the kitchen.

Standing over the stove, with his back to me, is Quinton. He's dressed in a pair of gray joggers that hug the muscled globes of his ass. His shirt is missing, and all of his black tattoos are on full display. Every ridge of muscles is exposed, and all I can think about is running my tongue over each one, familiarizing myself with his body. I think I might die if he turns around, because gray sweatpants are a gift to all women, and I know what he's hiding under his pants.

"I can feel you staring at me." Quinton doesn't turn around to acknowledge my presence. He just stands there while my libido has been fully flipped on.

Clearing my throat, I snap my gaze away from him as my legs carry me over to the island he's standing in front of.

Placing my palms on the marble surface, I sink into a chair, watching as his muscles stretch and flex as he flips pancakes. "Did you make us pancakes?"

Finally, he looks over his shoulder and gives me a smirk that would melt the panties right off me—if only I was wearing some. Just as quick as that smirk appeared, it melts off his face, eyes darkening as he rakes over my appearance in his dress shirt, buttons not fully closed, hair wild from fooling around all night, and lips still swollen from our kissing.

"Shit," he whispers under his breath, turning around and pulling off the cooked pancakes.

Flipping off the stove, he turns toward me, eyes skimming my body again. My mouth goes even drier as I finally get a frontal view of Quinton.

To whomever created gray sweatpants, we love you. Signed, every girl in the world.

Tongue sticking to the roof of my mouth, my eyes drag over his crafted body. His light-brown skin shows every hard-earned defined muscle—hours in the weight room are certainly paying off. Scanning lower, my eyes land on the outline of his very impressive dick.

Before I know what's happening, Quinton is stomping toward me, spinning my chair away from the island. His hands find the side of my face as he tilts my face up to him.

"Good morning." His words leave his lips, and he dips down to give me one hell of a kiss that has my toes curling.

With a small hum, his tongue runs across the seam of my lips, begging for permission, which I easily grant. His tongue slides inside my mouth, and we begin dueling against each other. My legs slide apart, making room for him to step between them. He's hard already and his sweatpants do little to hide it.

One of his hands slides from my face, dragging over my neck, my arm, and my ribs, coming to rest on the outside of my thigh. He's tasting me with fervor. I never want this moment to end.

I want to live in a Quinton bubble where he wears nothing but gray sweatpants, cooks me food, and edges me to the point of orgasm just from a kiss.

The hand that was on my thigh slowly makes its way up and under the dress shirt I'm wearing. Chills erupt over my body as I fight to keep the moan from escaping. The pad of his thumb chases where my panty line normally is.

Groaning, Quinton pulls away, my lips feel lost without his touch. "Dammit, baby. You can't come down here, with the house full of men, with no panties on."

Peeking up from under my lashes, I take in his pained, lust-filled face. His dark eyes turn the color of a black hole. He's just as affected as I am, and he's trying hard not to take me right here on the kitchen island where anyone could come downstairs and find us. Why is it that the thought of being caught turns me on even more? I'm not much of an exhibitionist, but picturing Q sprawling me out over the counter is doing things to me. I can feel the wetness slicking my thighs.

Reaching for him, I cup his erection in my hand, giving him a little squeeze that I know gets him going. A growl escapes his mouth as he bends down, planting a chaste kiss on my lips before stepping back, tucking his dick in his waistband, and walking back to the other side of the counter.

My mouth drops open. I can't believe he just did all of that and just walked away. "Um, hello?"

He barely glances at me, reaching up in the cupboard and grabbing two plates for us. No more words come from him as he spreads butter across our pancakes, shakes some cinnamon sugar on mine, and pours syrup over both of our stacks. My heart warms at the gesture of him putting cinnamon sugar on my pancakes.

Bringing the plates over, Quinton slides onto the barstool next to me, digging into his pancakes. Doing the same, I take a big bite of the fluffy, sugary goodness of the fried cake.

I groan into my fork, causing Quinton to pause before muttering under his breath. "You've got to stop doing that!"

"What am I doing?" I ask, taking another bite of the delicious breakfast.

He stares at me with no emotion on his face. "You know what you're doing. The moaning. I'm finding it hard to sit here and eat our breakfast when I could think of something better I could be eating."

That does it. My mind immediately dreams up images of Quinton standing above me, my body spread out on the cool marble tile. His kisses move from my mouth, trailing down my chest, skittering across my stomach. Going lower and lower. My face flames, skin feeling like it's on fire.

Quinton knows it too. Wrapping his arm around my shoulders, he leans into me, his chest brushing my back, as he brings his mouth to my ear and whispers, "Whatcha thinking about Wilder?"

A breath I didn't realize I was holding slips out, my body collapsing into his.

Stomping feet interrupt our moment, dousing both of us with a bucket of ice water that we both needed. Quinton heads back over toward the sink, putting his hand in the soapy water to start cleaning up our breakfast mess. It's safe to say that our friendship is officially over. We are so much more than just friends.

"Sup, Brynn," Xavier greets with very little enthusiasm.

Coming into the kitchen, he plops down in the seat next to me. His head immediately finds the marble countertop.

Glancing over, I watch Xavier's hungover body collapse. He looks like shit. Little Boyd hit the bottle a little hard last night, and I can't help the chuckle that leaves my mouth.

"Morning, Xav. How are you feeling?"

He grunts his response before slowly bringing his arms underneath his chin. That's when he notices the pancakes sitting on the counter. "Bro, you made hangover cakes?"

"Not for you," Quinton answers, drying off the frying pan.

Sliding my plate over to Xavier, I nudge his arm with my shoulder, gesturing toward my plate. His eyes light up, finding mine and mouthing his thanks.

Pushing up from my seat, I decide it's time for me to head back to my place. There's a very long, very cold shower waiting for me. But I don't get very far before Quinton is right behind me, following me to his room. He kicks the door shut behind him, but I don't turn to face him. I wait for him. Even though he's been the one making all of the moves lately. It's hard for me to be vulnerable. It's hard to give myself over and love someone with all my heart. I'm scared to love him as much as I want to because everyone I love dies, leaves me, or forgets I exist. If Q were to do that, I'd never survive.

"Dammit, Brynn." Quinton moves so that his body is pressed into mine. "Would you turn that beautiful mind off for two damn seconds? Aren't you exhausted?"

Turning around, I face him, placing my hands on my hips to keep from wrapping them around his waist.

"I'm sorry," I say, dropping my head.

Placing two fingers under my chin, he forces my gaze up to him. "What the fuck for?"

He snakes his hand from my chin to the back of my neck. The movement is so powerful. It feels like he owns me. That I am his. And I'll wear that title like a badge of honor.

Sighing, I stare up at him. My eyes drink him in. "I'm scared to give myself to you. Fully. Not just as friends, but as everything."

He doesn't answer. Instead, he steps back toward his bed, his arms not leaving me, pulling me along with him. Dropping on the bed, he brings me down on top of him. Straddling him, my legs go to each side of his muscular thighs as I sit down on him. Our eyes never break connection. No words are spoken. It'd be awkward if it was anyone else. We both need time to process. And I can tell he's working through what he's about to say.

Just as I'm about to break our stare, his lips crash into mine. It isn't a heated kiss like we shared last night. This kiss is slow. It's as if he's pouring all of his thoughts and feelings into this one kiss, and I don't know how to process it. I don't get a chance to think about it for long because he's pulling away, a small smile spreading across his lips. Seeing him smile makes a smile spread across my lips.

"Go on a date with me," Quinton blurts out.

Chuckling, I shake my head. "What?"

Eyes finding mine again, he holds his gaze on me, running his hands up and down my arms. "Let's make things official. Let me take you out on a date."

"Q, we're already official. Remember? Me and you, exclusive," I respond, pointing my finger between us.

"Yeah, I know. But I want to take you on a date. Somewhere away from campus."

"Okay," I rasp out. "When?"

"Wait, for real? I thought for sure I'd have to convince your stubborn ass."

Punching his arm, I try to push off him, but he's too quick. Hands grab my hips and pull me back down. Our new position has him lining up with my center perfectly. Without thinking, I grind my hips down on him.

Groaning, his eyes find mine. "Keep it up and see what happens, Wilder."

I smirk and bring my lips to his. Immediately he opens, and our tongues begin tangling. We can't get enough of each other. He grows hard beneath me, my hips flexing involuntarily. But before he has a chance to react, I jump off his lap, running straight toward the bathroom, laughing the whole way.

"You're cruel, Brinley Wilder," Quinton shouts from outside the closed door.

CHAPTER 27
Brynn

"WE NEED TO TALK."

Four words that no one ever wants to hear. Especially as they walk in their front door. Closing the door, I make my way into the living room where Chloe and Macy are both sitting. Tension hangs around the girls like a fog on a morning in the fall. Standing in the doorway, my eyes bounce between each girl.

Chloe and Macy have been my found family for two years. Ever since we met each other freshman year, we've been inseparable.

Going off to college, especially in a new state, is terrifying. You're no longer in the comfort of your hometown where you've been surrounded by the same people since kindergarten. Now you're on this huge campus—alone—trying to make friends, declare your major, find hobbies, and get good grades, all while trying to find yourself along the way. It's freaking hard, and don't let anyone tell you otherwise.

My feet lead me into the living room while my mind swims with all the potential things the girls would want to talk about. Replaying the last week in my head, I don't recall any time that I would've pissed them off. But that's the thing with women, we don't need much to set us off. Coming to a stop on the opposite end of the couch from where Chloe is sitting on, I sit down, bringing my legs underneath me. Macy is to my right in our recliner.

Once again, my head swivels, searching for some kind of answer. "What's up?"

There's a long pause, neither girl wanting to speak first.

What the hell?

Clearing her throat, Chloe speaks up first. "Macy is moving out."

My head snaps to Macy. "What?!"

Eyes narrowing, she stares Chloe down. I'm seriously so dumbfounded right now. Not only at the fact Macy is moving out because—*what the hell is up with that?*—but that these two look like they're about to fly across the room and go all "lioness fighting over their territory."

"I'm moving in with Gregg," Macy announces, turning her attention back to me.

"Mace, I'm happy for you, but you guys haven't been dating that long. Is this what's best for you?"

A sigh leaves her lips as the corners of her mouth tip up. "Yeah, it is. Gregg and I moved fast, but it feels right."

Getting up, my feet carry me over to where Macy is sitting. Reaching down, my arms wrap around her, pulling her in for a hug.

"I'm happy for you. *I really am.* It's not going to be the same without you being across the hall."

She squeezes me back. "I'm going to miss you. But you have Quinton."

Pulling back, I smile at her. Because she's right. I do have Quinton. Never in my wildest dreams would I have imagined that my heart would be opened up for another man. Especially with Quinton, but thinking about it, the signs have been there this whole time.

"Mace, just because Q and I are dating doesn't mean that I don't still need you guys."

"I know, and I still need you guys too. But things just feel right with Gregg. We want to explore our next step."

Squeezing her hand, I get up and return to my spot. I look over at Chloe, who is staring at the black screen on the TV. "What's going on with you two?"

Chloe's shoulders deflate at my question. Her eyes leave the TV, glancing over at me before finding Macy's.

"We're just agreeing to disagree."

My eyebrows form a V, confusion lacing my face. "*About*?" I draw out.

"I have feelings for Cody," Chloe rushes out. "Macy knows. *Apparently*, she's figured it out from watching me."

I can't help the shock that comes over me. Okay now, never in my wildest dreams would I have guessed she has a crush on Cody.

Hesitantly, I respond, "Chloe, that's great. But I'm having trouble figuring out why you're mad at Macy?"

"She's mad at the way I called her out on it. I mean, it's so freaking obvious," Macy responds to the question before Chloe. Standing, she turns her entire attention to Chloe. "You stare at him like he hung the moon but you're too childish to say anything. You act like a lost puppy. Either man up and tell him, or get over it."

"How about you just worry about your relationship with Gregg and stop worrying about me?" Chloe snaps.

My head ping pongs between the two. Clearly, I've been blind to the relationship between the girls. Macy hasn't been around a lot. Between her classes, working her part-time job, and spending her free time with Gregg, we haven't seen her much outside of family dinners.

Now I'm wondering if there was more than just her being busy. But I'm not asking now. Not with the animosity in the air ready to detonate.

I'm too hungover for this, my inner voice whines.

The way these two are fighting brings me back to my childhood. There were many times when I'd be woken up in the middle of the night by my parents screaming at each other. I'd hear vases hitting the walls as my mother's voice would carry throughout the house. When we were younger, Bryce would come into my room, and the two of us would sleep in the same bed—a reminder that we were safe together. After Bryce was gone, my headphones were the only thing that would drown out the noises.

"Just go pack," Chloe yells, dismissing Macy, and snaps me out of my thoughts. "I'm done with you acting like you're so much better than me because you're in a relationship."

Macy's hands are planted on her hips, chest heaving as she stares Chloe down. It's really intimidating how she's standing over Chloe, like a parent scolding their child.

"Whatever, Chloe. Keep standing on the sidelines looking like a psycho stalker. I'm not the only one that's noticed."

As those words leave her mouth, Macy storms out of the room while Chloe sinks onto the couch.

"Chlo?"

She just stares down at her clasped hands that are resting on her lap. "Not now, Brynn."

Stretching my arm out, I place my hand on her arm, giving it a light squeeze. "I'm always here for you. I love you." Standing from the couch, I move around the table toward the stairs.

I faintly hear her say, "I love you too."

There's a shift in the atmosphere. Chloe and Macy—who were the closest between us three—now can't stand each other. And I'm falling in love. Oh, who am I kidding? I'm fully in love. With Quinton.

Here's to hoping his feelings are as strong as mine.

CHAPTER 28
QUINTON

MONDAY WENT OFF WITHOUT a hitch. There's a new pep in my step. Finally telling Brynn I'm ready to go all in removed a weight I didn't know I was carrying. Tuesday was another good day.

Practices are tough, but it's November, which is clutch time in the season. It's where the best of the best start to stand out. It's the time to fight for our chance to head to Miami in January for the National Championship.

The team's hungry.

I'm hungry. This is my last season, and I'm desperate to bring home the hardware.

The first two days of the week might've been good, but nothing can compare to right now. Wednesdays are my longest days. Weightlifting, classes, watching game films, more classes, and a mandatory study session in the library. There's barely enough time for me to eat in between everything, let alone talk to anyone. I go into ghost mode on Wednesdays. This is why I'm surprised to see long, tan legs stretched out on the hood of my Tesla.

The boys and I are heading out of the stadium after a grueling meeting going over some game film and strategizing for our game on Saturday. Riggsby is clownin' around, making the guys crack up, but I can't take my eyes off the girl on my hood.

"Uhh, Q, you know you got a baddie on your hood?" JP interrupts my thoughts.

"Is that Brynn?" Riggsby asks. Letting out a whistle, he lowers his shades to get a better view.

I hear Grant chuckling beside me before he whispers, "Dude, you've got it bad."

"Shut up," I bark back, not taking my eyes off the goddess waiting on me.

Brynn is dressed in a loose pair of fleece shorts. The lime-green color makes her tan skin look even more bronzed. Pulling my eyes from her incredible legs, my breath catches in my throat.

Fuuuuck.

Her slim figure is on full display, as well as her voluptuous breasts in her tiny corset-style, cropped, athletic tank.

This girl is going to be the death of me.

A CTU hat is covering her face—wait, it's not just any CTU hat, it's one of mine. When did she steal that? She hasn't made any indication that she notices our presence.

"Are we interrupting a magazine shoot? She looks like sex sprawled out on your car," JP says as our strides carry us toward her.

"Yeah, like that Whitesnake video," Riggsby adds.

"How do I find a girl like that?" JP asks.

"Shower," I retort.

Turning to the guys, I tell them to fuck off as I close the distance between us and Brynn. Stopping at the front of the car, I notice she's got her AirPods in, which is why she didn't notice us. Pulling out my phone, I thumb a quick text, praying her settings will have her headphones reading her text.

> Me: You tryin' to get fucked? Right here? On the hood of my car for everyone to watch?

The settings work in my favor because her eyes snap open, finding my eyes immediately.

Sliding the hat off her face, she pulls it back into its normal position. "Hey."

"Hey, baaaaby. Whatcha doiiiin'?" I drawl out.

My hands find my pockets to keep me from reaching for her and doing all kinds of wicked things that'll get us in trouble. Who can blame me? Isn't it every guy's fantasy to have a half-dressed hottie on the hood of their car? Isn't that why most rap videos have half-naked women and sports cars? Sex sells, and my girl looks like she walked right off some kind of shoot.

Sliding off the car, she brings her body flush against mine, and I pull her into a hug. "Just missed your face. Thought I'd surprise you."

"You surprised me, that's for sure."

Kissing the top of her head, I grab her hand, leading her over to the passenger side, wanting to get her in the car, knowing the guys are still watching us. Most of the guys don't know that we've made things official. But after our date on Thursday, I'm going to shout that Brynn is mine from the rooftop.

Opening her door, I watch her slide in, watching as her already short shorts slide up her legs. Tilting my head to the sky, I take a deep breath to keep from pulling her out of her seat and tossing her in my backseat to finally fuck her senseless.

"What're you thinking about, Q?" There's a hint of teasing in her voice as she asks me that question.

"You fucking know." Shutting her door, I subtly adjust myself, which seems to be a common occurrence whenever Brynn is nearby.

Throwing my bag in the back seat, I slide into my seat and slam my door, pressing the ignition button with a little more force than what was needed. Chuckling, Brynn leans over the dash, her hand finding my leg. Fingers slide up my leg slowly. *Torturously slow.*

With one last squeeze of the inside of my leg, Brynn sits back in her seat, slipping her seatbelt on. Reversing out of my spot, I head toward campus, thinking of anything to will this boner away.

It's a quick drive to campus since we only have to go around a couple of buildings to get to the student parking lot. Taking my time, I crank up the radio. It's a *me thing*. If I'm in the car, my music is on, and it's on loud. "Money in the Grave" comes through the speakers. Resting my hand loosely on the top of the steering wheel, I drive us the few minutes to the lot.

Climbing out, we both grab our backpacks, and I watch Brynn toss on some kind of jacket. A breath of relief slips out because I don't have to beat the shit out of anyone who looks at her body for too long. I'm not the jealous type, I just want what's mine to be mine without having to deal with any pricks who try to make a move.

Okay, maybe I am a little jealous.

Laughing, Brynn turns to me. "Quinton, did you think I was going to class looking like that?"

"What the hell else was I supposed to think?"

Walking toward campus, she falls in line right beside me. She's laughing at my reaction, and I can't help but smile. I love hearing her laugh. It's like sunshine rising after days of cloudy skies.

"I was just soaking up some rays while I waited on you." Her body leans in mine, and she gives me a nudge.

Making our way through campus, we fall into a comfortable silence. Until I hear someone call my name. Looking for the voice, I spot Keisha—one of the girls I slept with after our first game—up ahead. Brynn slips into her resting bitch face mask, and a wall builds right in front of me. She's tense.

Nudging her shoulder, I try to get this facade off her. "You okay?"

She doesn't even look up at me, just grunts out a "no," keeping her eyes ahead as she watches Keisha approach us. I bring my eyes up and watch Keisha, hips swaying more than needed, a look of desire on her face, and that's when it hits me. Brynn is jealous.

Reaching out, I grab her upper arm, spinning her around. She whips her head up, but before she has a chance to spout off a retort from that sexy-as-hell mouth, I dip my head down and kiss her.

My lips find hers in a searing, possessive kiss.

I claim her right here in the middle of the quad.

In front of everyone.

My hand finds the back of her head, and I pull her into me as close as I can. Right there, with all eyes watching us, I let everyone who is watching—which everyone is—that Brinley Wilder is mine.

A huge smile spreads across her lips as she brings her hands to the back of my neck, running her hand up my short hair and pulling me down closer to her. She told me she loves the velvety way my hair feels since I'm always keeping my fade fresh. Letting her take the lead, I go with whatever she wants, since PDA isn't Brynn's thing. A small moan escapes the back of her throat, snapping her out of our kiss. A bashful grin spreads across her lips as she pulls away.

"I'm yours," I whisper so that only she can hear me.

We both turn, expecting Keisha to be standing in front of us, but we only see her retreating back,

I guess she got the hint.

Will is also standing in the quad with a dumbstruck expression on his face. I guess we killed two birds with one kiss.

I don't dwell on either one but find JP coming up to us with a shit-eating grin on his face.

"I knew y'all were fuckin'!" he yells, rubbing his hands together like he just solved a mystery.

"And with that, I'm heading to class," Brynn says, pressing up on her toes to give me one more, quick kiss.

"See you tomorrow," I shout at her retreating form, watching as she turns one last time and gives me a wave with a wide grin.

Pushing the door open, I walk in the front door of Grant's townhouse. He lives alone in a two-bedroom. The guest bedroom is set up for his dad in case he ever needs to crash on campus instead of making the half-hour drive home. A half-hour drive isn't bad on a normal day, but when we get back from a game at midnight, who wants to drive when you can crash three minutes away from the stadium?

Grant and Riggsby are sitting on the couch, controllers in their hands, both in a heated game of *Call of Duty*. Shutting the door behind me, I walk over to the sectional. Collapsing on the opposite end, my body is exhausted. Wednesdays just kick my ass. I just wanted to go home and crash, but Grant said he was ordering food and playing CoD. I'm not passing up a night of killing zombies.

A knock sounds from the door at the same time JP comes into the room from the hall bathroom.

"I've got it," he says, strolling past the couch to the door.

"Good, because I think I'm dead," I respond just as Grant shouts, "Cash is beside the door."

A few minutes later, the four of us are eating the best chicken wraps around campus.

"Alright, start talkin'," JP says around a mouth full of food.

Chewing my bite, I wait to speak. Unlike JP, I've got some manners, not a lot, but some.

Swallowing, I answer, "about what?"

Six eyes stare at me, eyes narrowing like *'c'mon, you know about what.'* And I do. I'm just dragging this out. I swear, my teammates are worse than girls with their damn gossip.

Letting out a small chuckle, I answer their question. "We're together. I'm taking her out tomorrow night."

JP whoops and Riggsby gives me an "atta boy."

"Only two years in the making," Grant says, turning back to his game with Riggsby.

But JP doesn't turn back to the TV, he's still watching me. "What's he mean?"

Grant's focus stays on his game, but that doesn't stop him from answering. "It means our boy here has been in love with Brynn since freshman year. Someone got a little too drunk at a party and spilled all his secrets."

"Shut up, asshole," I say, tossing the pillow on the couch at Grant.

He just laughs as the pillow bounces off his face.

"You're good for her," JP says, turning his attention to the game in front of us.

JP has taken Brynn under his wing. He's protective over his siblings, and he's always viewed Brynn as one of them too. It's nice to have the guys on board with the girl I love. And I love that girl fiercely.

Speaking of her, my phone lights up with her name and a picture I snapped one morning while she was lying in my bed.

"Hey babe," I answer, as the guys mock me in a high-pitched voice, repeating "hey, babe."

Her laughter fills my ear.

"Hey," she greets, as she yells louder into the phone for the guys to hear, "Hey boys!"

"Make it home from the library?"

"I did. I'm just walking in now, and thought I'd call to tell you good night."

I can hear her unlocking her front door and shutting it behind her. A click sounds and I know that she's locking the door behind her.

Red fills the TV screen as Riggsby's man is killed by a zombie. Grunting in frustration, Riggsby tosses me the controller.

"I'm down at Grant's. Want me to stop by when I leave?"

Propping the phone between my shoulder and ear, I thumb through my options on the screen.

"No, that's okay. I'm just going to call it an early night. Slip out of these clothes, curl into bed, and watch that new movie with Chris Hemsworth and Miles Teller."

"Oh yeah?" I ask.

My girl has a thing for Hemsworth. And I'm not going to lie, I'm a little jealous that he gets to spend the evening with my girl while she's naked in her bed.

"Oh yeah," she answers. "Are you jealous, Quinton? It's just me, home alone, lying naked in my bed. Hands wandering up and down."

"Wilder," I grit out. "I'm sitting at Grant's with JP and Riggsby right now."

The guys' attention snaps my way.

A chuckle leaves her lips. And now I'm wanting to leave and walk the three buildings over to her townhouse.

"Hey Q?" she asks, voice taking on a more serious tone.

"What's up, baby?" Concern seeps into my voice. There's a long pause on the phone. "Brynn," I probe.

Grant's eyes dart my way, but I pay him no attention.

A sigh leaves her mouth. "I think I need to go home next weekend."

Those were not words I was expecting to hear.

"Okay," I draw out, not wanting to push, letting her control the conversation.

"It's time I visit my brother. You guys are in New York, so I thought I'd catch a flight Saturday and come back Sunday. Just a quick there-and-back trip."

"Are you sure you're going to be okay going alone? Should Chloe go with you? Or we can find a time when I can fly with you."

My mind is racing. I'm proud of her for wanting to go visit, but I worry about the emotional toll it's going to take on her.

"No, this is something I need to do. Alone."

"Okay, babe. I'll be waiting for you when you get back."

She exhales what sounds like a sigh of relief. "Thanks, Q. I don't know what I'd do without you."

Smirking, even though she can't see me, I add, "Let's not find out. I can be there in a few minutes."

"Good night, Quinton. See you tomorrow." She laughs into the receiver.

"Night, Wilder," I respond, ending the call.

Before I have a chance to set the phone down, a message dings. Clicking on the new text message, a photo fills my screen. Brynn is sitting in her bed, her white covers are barely covering her naked body, and she's chewing on her bottom lip in a way that drives me wild.

I can't wait until I get her alone tomorrow night.

CHAPTER 29
Brynn

"**D**ammnnnn, girl!" Chloe squeals, letting out a whistle as she walks into my room. "You look bangin'."

I'm applying another coat of mascara to make sure my eyes pop. Nerves consume me. Quinton and I have gone out so many times I couldn't even give you a number, but tonight is different. Tonight, we are going on a date. A date as boyfriend and girlfriend. Excitement isn't a strong enough emotion to describe how I feel.

Capping my mascara, I toss it in my makeup bag before making my way over to my full-length mirror.

"Is it too much?" Running my hands down my dress, I take one last look in the mirror.

When I picked out my outfit, I wanted to go with something sexy but still me. He's seen me in so many outfits, but I wanted to stand out tonight. And the red dress I picked out is perfect. It's tight and hugs my curves in all the right places. The girls look fantastic thanks to the sweetheart neckline that transitions into spaghetti straps that criss-cross in laces down my back, giving my skin the perfect exposure. Lifting my foot, I step into black, square-toed lace-up heels and bend down to tie them. I left my hair down in loose, beach waves with a neutral smokey makeup look. Chloe's right. I look damn good. I feel sexy.

Quinton set up our entire date. Which is such a relief. Not that I've dated, but even just planning girls' nights, it gets annoying to be the one to constantly plan every detail. Sometimes, a girl just wants to be surprised with a little "wine and dine" date. He's picking me up around six for our dinner reservations. Quinton Boyd has some weight in the city. He was able to pull some strings and get us a table at a fine-dining oyster bar and chophouse. He won't tell me what he has planned after dinner, just that there will be more to the night.

"No, Brynn, it's not too much." Chloe makes her way to stand next to me.

She's looking at me through the mirror, and I swear her eyes are getting misty.

"Don't you start crying. I'm going on a date. It's nothing big."

"I know. I'm just happy to see you happy. You deserve to be happy, Brynn." She wraps her arm around me, and I turn to hug her. "It's your time. I've been waiting on you two idiots to admit your feelings."

I laugh and pull away from her. We stare at each other. Is this something that your mom is supposed to tell you? This moment we are having, aren't I supposed to have that with my mom? It's weird to not have any relationship with the woman that gave me life. I would give anything to be able to pick up the phone and FaceTime my mom while I get ready for a date. It's been almost seven years since I've been on one.

What would my life have been like if I had a strong mother-daughter relationship? Would she have been beside me through the grieving process? Would she have seen how I blamed myself and encouraged me to move forward? Tell me that it was okay to love again? I guess I'll never know.

I shake myself from my thoughts. I don't want tonight to be tainted, not after he claimed me in front of everyone on the quad yesterday.

He must've seen how insecure I felt. I won't even say jealous, because I'm not jealous of Keisha. But hearing her call Q's name and then start strutting over to us put me on the edge. Quinton and I have a past with a lot of people on campus. I just want people to know we are now off-limits.

Making herself comfortable on my bed, Chloe settles in to watch me add the finishing touches to my outfit. I layer a simple gold necklace with my gold 'B' bar necklace, gold hoop earrings, and one more swipe of a nude shade lipstick.

"Have so much fun tonight," she says, scrolling through her phone.

Before I have a chance to respond, the doorbell chimes. A smile immediately spreads across my face.

"Oh my gosh, look at you," she says, hopping off my bed and rushing toward the door. "You're smitten."

Reaching down, I grab my clutch from my desk. "Would you stop? I'm just excited for some seafood."

"Uh-huh, I'm sure that's what you're looking forward to."

The two of us make our way down the stairs, but Chloe jogs ahead, which isn't hard since I'm wearing heels.

She reaches for the doorknob, and as she opens the door, she turns her head and says, "B, aren't oysters an aphrodisiac?"

I hear Q laugh at her, and my face turns as red as the dress that I'm wearing. Taking the final three steps, I come up beside Chloe as she finishes opening the door to reveal a hot-as-sin Quinton.

"Goddamn," Quinton rasps out at the same time I say, "Holy hell."

It's safe to say we are both very pleased with each other. Quinton is standing in front of me dressed in all black. He's like a Black James Bond. Black, skinny-cut dress pants that taper at the ankles, a black dress shirt with the top three buttons undone—sans undershirt—and a black suit jacket. Fucking fine.

"Hi, thanks for picking me up." The words fly out of my mouth quickly. Grabbing his arm, I start moving him backward. "We need to leave right now."

He resists my pushing, coming to a halt and stopping me. Warmth spread through my body, igniting a fire in my stomach as wetness pools between my legs.

"What's the hurry? We've got time."

Peering up at him, my eyes trail him from head to toe again.

"No, no we don't. Because if we stay here, I'm stripping you out of these clothes, and we will be late. And I didn't spend all this time getting ready to show up at a fine dining restaurant with sex-mussed hair."

Chloe and Quinton laugh at my outburst. We haven't had sex, yet that comment just proved how ready I am for us to take things to the finish line.

"Guess that's my cue to go," Quinton says to Chloe before follow-ing me down the steps. We don't get very far before he stops me. "You look beautiful, Wilder."

Leaning up, I meet his lips for a quick kiss. "You clean yourself up pretty well too, Quinton Boyd. Can't wait to see your fashionista style come out when you make it to the NFL."

"You'll be on the sidelines," he murmurs.

Then we are making our way to his parked car.

The restaurant is gorgeous. It's way too much for our first date, but I appreciate him putting in so much thought to get us here. The chophouse is adult-only, with its moody setting and white-cloth-covered tables that contrast perfectly against the black booths and chairs. Plexiglass is attached to each booth, giving you an even more private dining experience. For a Thursday, the place is packed. Quinton and I slide our way through those waiting, and make our way to the hostess stand.

"Good evening, welcome to Carver's," the bubbly hostess greets us. She's extremely professional in the fact that she doesn't spend any extra time on Quinton. "What is the name under?"

"Quinton Boyd."

The hostess looks over her tablet and finds our name quickly. "Right this way, Mr. Boyd."

Placing his hand on the small of my back—my body ignites from where his hand touches the exposed skin of my lower back—Quinton guides me to follow the waitress.

Eyes follow us as the hostess guides us to a booth against the wall toward the back of the restaurant. As we slide into our seats on opposite sides of the table, the waitress places our menus down in front of us.

Opening up the menu, my eyes catch on the prices next to each item. My eyes bulge like they're about to bug out of my head. I knew the restaurant was fancy, but I wasn't expecting this.

"Quinton, this is way too much."

He doesn't even glance above his menu. "Brynn, I wanted to do this for you. It's fine. Get whatever you want."

Deciding not to press the subject, I go back to browsing the menu. There are so many things that jump out at me.

"Good evening. What can I start you two off with?" our server asks.

Quinton glances up at me, raising his eyebrows in a gesture for me to go first.

"I'll take a glass of sauvignon blanc."

"Of course, and you, sir?"

"Buffalo Trace. And an order of oysters, please."

The waiter nods before leaving our table.

"Have I told you how beautiful you look tonight?" Quinton asks, taking a sip of the water that was placed on the table.

Blushing, I bring my water glass up to my mouth, taking a sip to hide the flush that paints my skin.

"Whatcha hungry for?" I ask, changing the subject. Taking compliments is hard. Like genuine comments, not the whole "you're hot" comment, but true compliments take me off guard.

"You want to share some stuff?" Quinton asks.

Vulnerability stretches across his face. Not one to wear his emotions on his sleeve, he never has, but tonight I can read him like a book. Nervous energy radiates off him. Mr. Cool and Confident is nervous tonight. As twisted as it sounds, it makes me feel good. Not because I want him to be nervous, but because it helps settle my nerves.

"I'm always down to share." Q chokes on the sip of water he was mid-drink. "Food," I rush out. "I'm always down to share food. You. Oh, hell no, I'm not sharing you with anyone."

Stop talking. Stop talking. Stop talking.

A red flag has to be waving above my head. *"Stage five clinger alert! Avoid! Avoid! Avoid!"*

His coughing fit comes to an end. Only a few heads turned our way, and I can feel my face flaming again.

"Thanks for the clarification." He laughs. I want to record the happiness that expels from him and play it on rainy days. "And just so we're clear, I don't share either."

"Good to know." I bring the water glass back up to my mouth. Where is the waiter? I could really use that glass of wine right about now.

"Since we've established you love to share." Quinton smirks at me, humor lacing his face. "What are you thinking? I can do 'turf' if you want to do the 'surf?'"

"Works for me," I answer, scanning the menu again. "Order whatever sounds good. I'm not picky."

Our waiter returns, places our drinks down in front of us, and takes our order. Quinton orders a center-cut filet with potato puree, while I order the lobster with crab stuffing and asparagus. My mouth is watering just thinking about all the food we are about to eat. Jotting down our order, the waiter leaves us to enjoy our oysters.

"How was practice today?"

Propping my elbow on the table—I know, it's not polite—I bring my hand under my chin and watch him. Seriously, I could kick my own ass for putting off these feelings that I didn't realize I was snuffing out.

Grinning, Quinton answers. "B, it was kickass. I know I've been sayin' this, but I feel like we are really going to make it happen. We're ready."

My hand reaches across the table, finding his. Turning his palm up, my hand slides over his. It's a little awkward since our hands are opposite, but it still feels right. He runs his thumb across the side of my palm.

"I'm proud of you."

It's his turn to play bashful. "Thanks, Wilder."

Dinner was perfect. Both of us are so full from the delicious surf and turf. Instead of getting back in the car, Quinton keeps walking past the parking lot.

"Uhh, Q, we parked in that lot." Hiking my thumb over my shoulder, I gesture to the lot we just walked past.

Holding his hand out, I take it. "I've got another surprise for you."

And with that, we make our trek down the road. We don't get very far before Quinton is placing his hand on my hip, sliding me in front of him, and then stopping when I'm on the opposite side of him. He's now between me and the sidewalk. I go to question him about the move, but he just looks down with a smirk and winks at me. Heart fluttering, I melt in a puddle. Right there. On the sidewalk. Quinton Boyd knows the sidewalk rule. Swoon.

It's a short walk and I thank my lucky stars. These heels are cute, but they weren't made for walking. My feet are used to the comfort of sneakers. Stopping outside of an old brick building, Quinton pulls open the heavy black door, ushering me inside. My ears are met with music. But not just any music.

Live music.

Shimmying my hips in excitement, I enter the building, throwing Quinton a subtle grin. Boy knows I love live music and dancing just as much as I love tequila shots and football games.

Sidling up behind me, his front brushes against my ass, and my senses instantly heighten. If I can help it, we won't be staying here long. Our bodies fight against the crowd in this packed bar. I'm shouldering us through as Quinton crowds me from behind.

"Well hot damn, if it isn't Brynn Wilder."

My head snaps in different directions, finding Quinton, with a puzzled look on my face. He gestures his head toward the stage—my mind realizes the voice came from the microphone.

Ecstasy is on stage.

I'm beaming from ear to ear.

"You look fine as fuck, girl. Bring your ass up here," Max says in the microphone, gesturing the mic toward me. "Make room, people."

The crowd starts looking around, trying to figure out who he's talking to.

Before I make my way toward the stage, I turn back to Quinton, searching his eyes for any clues on how to proceed. Is it bad to go up front when I'm on a date? He doesn't give me time to let my mind wander before he's nudging me forward.

"Let's go." Turning around, I start making my way to the stage. Before we get to the front, I stop and spin on my heels. "Wait," I ask. "Did you know they were performing?"

He beams down at me, and that's all the answer I need.

Quinton Boyd planned the most perfect date for me.

A guitar riff rips through the air, and I immediately recognize the tune. Ecstasy starts their version of "Scotty Doesn't Know," and my body immediately starts moving to the beat. Quinton is right behind me, not missing a step as our bodies slide together.

His hands never leave mine the whole night. Skating over my exposed skin, leaving goose bumps in his wake. Our bodies are glued to each other, his front to my back. Ecstasy is playing banger after banger. I haven't stopped moving to the beat since we got here.

Tonight has been the best night I've had in a long time. From dinner to watching my favorite band, Quinton knows how to plan a date. And now it's time to get the hell out of here. I can't take his lingering touches anymore. Either he gets me to his room, or I'm going to drag him to the nearest supply closet.

CHAPTER 30
Brynn

MY CHEEKS HURT FROM smiling. It's the best pain. I don't think I've stopped smiling all night. And my smile doesn't falter as Quinton pulls his car into the garage.

Turning my head, I stare at his profile while he puts the car in park, and then his gaze slides over to find mine. We just spent the last however many hours dancing against each other, attempting to cool off with beer. Hormones are raging, and if I don't get him inside and up to his room, I'm going to take matters into my own hands. Right here, right now, in this dimly lit garage.

Reading my thoughts, Quinton's eyes darken. His smile slowly slips into one of pure lust. Raking his eyes down my body, heat spreads wherever his gaze travels. Wetness pools between my thighs.

Chest heaving, I wait for him to make the first move.

"Wilder," Quinton rasps, searching my face. "Are you wet for me, baby?"

Nodding my head is the only response I give him, not breaking eye contact.

"Show me," he grunts out, moving his eyes down my chest while he licks his lips, gaze settling in the gap between my legs.

Slowly, I slid my hand from where it was resting on the door and let it drift leisurely up my thigh.

A growl comes from beside me. "The faster you show me how wet you are, the faster you get to come."

Eyes widening, my hand moves at a faster pace—still slow—but quicker than it was. Slipping my hand under the skirt of my dress, I move my thong to the side, letting my middle finger graze the wetness that has begun to collect there. Removing my hand, I bring it up to where he can see it, letting the illuminated light from the garage reflect on how wet I am.

"Good girl. Now suck yourself clean."

And I do just that. Bringing my finger to my mouth, I slip it between my lips. Tasting myself, I let out a moan, cheeks caving in. I'm making a real show of sucking my fingers clean before sliding them out of my mouth with a pop.

"Fuuuuck," Quinton grinds out, reaching down to adjust himself.

My eyes track his movement, and I see his hardness pushing against his zipper, begging to be released. Wanting the chase, I quickly grab my purse from the floor and push open the door. Getting out, I race toward the house. Laughter erupts from me, and I think I hear Quinton yell my name, but I don't stop. It doesn't matter, though. Quinton's long strides catch up to me in no time.

Still laughing, I round the corner into the kitchen and heads whip in our direction. JP, Xavier, Grant, Riggsby, and a few other guys from the football team are gathered in the living room playing Xbox. Pulling up, I press my lips together to keep the redness from spreading across my face. We all just freeze, staring at each other. Quinton breaks the stand-off by moving in front of me and tossing me over his shoulder.

"You really are a caveman!" I squeal. Popping my head up, I look at the room of guys. "Oh, you guys might want to put some music on."

That comment seems to have snapped everyone awake. Hoots and hollers break out. Quinton slaps my barely covered ass and jogs up the stairs.

"It's about fucking time!" Grant yells while JP shouts, "Mom and Dad finally got together."

Quinton and I just laugh.

Entering his room, he kicks the door shut before bringing me over to his bed, where he tosses me. My body bounces, a boob about slips out, and Quinton catches the movement. He stands above me at the foot of the bed, eyes trailing my body.

"Goddamn, you're a sight. As pretty as you look all sprawled out on my bed, I want you naked and coming on my cock."

I suck in a breath at his words. "Fuck me," I whisper.

"I will, baby, but first I need those lips on me."

Slipping out of his jacket, he tosses it on his desk chair before he's loosening the remaining buttons on his dress shirt. Getting the last button undone, he brings his body down next to mine. His mouth finds mine as my hands find him, pushing his dress shirt off him. Slipping his tongue in my mouth, a noise of appreciation slips out.

"Sweet and perfect," he says. "Just how I knew you'd taste."

Diving back down, he doesn't go back to my lips, he finds the sensitive spot on my neck causing my hips to jump from the mattress.

"So eager," he murmurs.

Sucking and pulling on my flesh, I know he's going to mark me. And I don't even care.

Music starts blaring from downstairs and Ludacris's "What's your Fantasy" lyrics come filtering into the room. Pausing his tugging of my neck, his eyes find mine at the same time I search him out. We both erupt with laughter.

"I did tell them to put music on."

Shrugging, I smirk down at Q. He shakes his head before finding my mouth again. Our tongues melt together, and our bodies move in sync, responding without thinking.

Skipping my neck this time, his lips make their way to my chest. His hand drags down the strap of my dress, exposing my breast, palming it. Squeezing and kneading my boob with his hand while his mouth sucks on my skin. Moving his hand to the other side, he slips that strap down and begins palming me while his mouth finds my nipple. Sucking it in between his teeth, he tweaks my other nipple while his mouth worships the opposite side.

"Oh god," I moan. I could come alone from him playing with my nipples.

Tweaking, sucking, worshipping.

"I need more." Popping my nipple from his mouth, he looks up at me.

"Patience, baby."

Groaning, I flop my head back on his pillow. "Quinton, I've been patient. It's been years. Fuck me, please."

Sliding up on his knees, he reaches his hand out for me to take. "Sit up," he demands.

Reaching behind me, he unties the straps of my dress while his mouth finds my neck again. Dragging his hands from the strings to my thighs, he pushes the dress up over my head.

"Damn, baby."

Eyes skim my naked body. Before he gets down to my thong, his eyes pop up to the new tattoo I had done last week. Bringing his fingers up to my rib, he traces the new arrow ink.

"This is new."

Nodding my head, my hands search for his body. Pushing him backward, I climb on top of him. "It is."

Straddling him, I run my hands down his abs, letting my fingers trace every muscle, stopping at the button of his pants.

"We'll talk about it later. Right now, I want you out of these pants."

And getting him out of his pants is just what I do. Sliding his button open and unzipping his pants, I slowly drag my body down his legs, taking his pants and boxers with me. I watch as his cock springs free. It's long and thick against his stomach.

All I can think about is wrapping my lips around his crown and worshipping him.

After the perfect night we just had, it's all I want.

Licking my lips, I collapse on my knees as he sits up. Taking him in my hand, I give a few pumps, watching his eyes watch me. Leaning forward, my tongue licks the bead of precum that's started leaking from his tip. I make a show of licking him from root to tip, flattening my tongue against his vein before taking him in my mouth. Then, I wrap my mouth around his head and take him to the back of my throat. He lets out a guttural groan.

Reaching his hand out to me, he gathers my hair in one fist, giving him a better view of how well I take him. He's big and thick. Tears roll down my cheek as I take him down my throat, holding my breath to keep from choking.

Sucking him turns me on. I've always been a girl who loves giving head, but giving head to Quinton, and watching someone you deeply care about fall apart because of you is dizzying.

I slide the hand I had resting on his thigh down, down, down, until it finds my core. Brushing my middle finger through my wetness, I bring it up to my clit, rubbing my fingers as I work Q with my mouth and my other hand.

Before long, I'm moaning around him. His hand begins to take control of my head, pushing me further down his cock, fucking my mouth. Slipping my finger from my clit inside me, I push in two fingers and begin fucking myself as I let him fuck my mouth.

He's close—we both are. Pushing my fingers in and out, in and out, I bring the slickness up to my clit, rubbing and working myself over. The hand I had on his cock slides down until I'm cupping his balls.

Pulling, playing, tugging. I feel him tense beneath me just as my stomach clenches. I'm going to come. But just as I think that, my hair is pulled, and my head ripped off Quinton.

"What the fu—" I start, but don't get the words out because Quinton is grabbing me by the ribs and tossing me onto the mattress, dropping to his knees.

"If you're going to come, it's going to be from me."

Sweet, caring Quinton is hot. But demanding, alpha Quinton is sexy as fuck.

His hands grab my thighs, leaving marks and spreading me open for him. My pussy is on display and my man looks like he's starved. Glancing up, he keeps his eyes on me while his mouth finds my center. His tongue flicks out, hitting my clit, and I could come from that alone. My body is primed, and it's not going to be long before I'm coming long and hard. As he sucks my clit into his mouth, my head snaps back, my eyes close.

Biting down on my clit, I gasp, finding him staring up at me.

"Eyes on me, or you don't come. Say it," he demands, a finger running up and down my slit.

Nodding my head up and down, I repeat his words. "Eyes on you. Make me come."

"Good girl," he responds, diving back down and lapping up my wetness.

Finding my clit again, he flicks and sucks it into my mouth while two fingers slide inside my pussy. Moving his fingers forward, he drives them deeper, finding that hard-to-reach spot. Working me over with his fingers and his tongue, it doesn't take long for me to come.

"Oh, oh, oh, god," I scream. "I'm going to co—" I start just as an orgasm rips through my body.

Moaning and screaming, Quinton doesn't let up, and I ride out the orgasm.

"Fuck, Wilder," Quinton grates out.

My chest is heaving, but we aren't done. Quinton finds my mouth and I taste my salty taste against my tongue which turns me on again, even though I just came. Once again, I'm pushing him on his back, climbing over him and straddling his thighs. His erection is pressed between my ass, his lips never leaving mine while his hands find my nipples.

"Lean up," he grumbles out.

Leaning up, I watch as his hand finds his cock, placing it at my entrance.

"Shit, condom," he grits out, fisting his cock.

My eyes find his hooded gaze. "I have an IUD," I respond.

Both of us search each other before he says, "I've never had sex without a condom."

Shaking my head, my eyes find his. "Me either. But I want to. With you. I trust you, Quinton."

Grabbing my face with his other hand, he brings me down for a toe-curling kiss.

Bringing my ass up, I let Quinton line himself up to me. He's big, and I know he's going to stretch me, but the pain excites me. Dropping down, I take him in one go, studying his face the whole time.

"Jesus Christ, Brinley. Warn a guy," he rumbles, hands grabbing my hips tightly to keep me from moving.

My body is going to be full of bruises tomorrow. The realization elicits chills down my spine. There's something about being marked by Quinton that does something to me. It's raw and it's possessive. I freaking love it.

Slowly, very slowly, I begin rotating my hips. His cock slides in even deeper. Grabbing my hips, he helps move me up and down, up and down.

He's close, really close this time. I can feel how close. He grips my hips, making me pause.

"Baby, slow down," he grits with his jaw clenched. "I'm trying to hold out, but you feel so fucking good."

Slowly, I rotate my hips, giving him a second while letting my climax continue to build. He's deep inside me, and I feel so full. A fire is burning low in my stomach. I'm close. Deciding I'm ready to come, I take matters into my own hands.

"So come." I let the words slip out while rocking faster, letting my clit rub against his length. "And then we can do this again."

My body starts bouncing as his hips thrust up, matching my pace.

"Touch yourself, Wilder."

I don't move. His eyes snap from where he's been watching him pump inside of me, up to my eyes.

"Touch yourself. Come again."

Lifting my hand from his delicious abs, I bring it to my center, brushing my finger over where his cock is seated inside of me. We both moan as I find my swollen bud. Applying pressure, I rub while he pounds into me. Palming my breast, he squeezes, flicking his thumb over my pebbled nipple. Moving his head he covers my other peaked nipple, bringing it to his mouth, and sucks it between his teeth. He bites down while I apply more pressure to my bundle of nerves that is pulsing with need. He flicks his tongue, and I come as I feel him pulse, spilling himself inside of me. We come together, collapsing on the bed in a heap of limbs.

Fucking perfection. That's what tonight was.

CHAPTER 31
QUINTON

H OLY SHIT. BOTH OF us are collapsed on my bed, completely spent. I knew sex with Brynn was going to be great, but that was explosive. Our bodies were in sync, and I feel like such a chump for coming so quickly. But with the combination of her tight pussy and sex without a condom, I was a goddamn goner.

Bringing myself to my feet, I head into the bathroom. Rummaging through my closet, I find a washcloth for Brynn. Running it under hot water, my feet carry me back to where she is still stretched out across my bed. Her eyes are shut, red splotches cover her body from where I marked her—hopefully, I wasn't too rough—lips swollen, and her curled hair looking freshly fucked. This is an image I want ingrained in my mind forever.

Gently, I run the warm washcloth between her thighs where my cum is leaking out of her. And dammit, my body reacts to the sight. She jumps at the contact.

"Relax," I speak before she has a chance to say anything. "Let me take care of you."

Taking care of a woman post-sex is new to me. I've never had someone sleep over after sex. It was always just a quick release for both of us. No cuddling and no sleepovers. But I want to clean Brynn up, the act feels intimate and right. She's so much more than a hook-up, she always has been. And it's time for me to tell her my plans for next year. I should've told her before we had sex, but the timing never felt right. Everything was so new and so fragile, I didn't want to risk it.

I finish cleaning her, stepping away and tossing the washcloth in my hamper.

"Thank you," Brynn whispers, a blush spreading across her cheeks. "No one has ever done that for me before."

A shy grin spreads across my face as I run my hand down the back of my head. "I've never done that before."

She stands, grabbing the extra bag she keeps in my room before rushing in the direction of my bathroom. While she's in the bathroom, I slip on a pair of fresh boxers. If I stay naked, there's no way we'll be talking. Crawling back onto the bed, I stretch out, waiting on her to return.

After a few minutes, I hear the door open as she steps out. My eyes trail over her body. She's changed into a pair of black Calvin Klein underwear and a matching bra. I watch as her legs carry her over to me. Her body finds my mattress while eyes find her new tattoo.

Trailing my finger over her smooth skin, I trace the arrow.

"I got it for you," she whispers, vulnerability lacing her words.

Snapping my attention toward her, I wait for her to continue.

"I wanted something to remind me to keep moving forward as you do. An arrow may be forced backward, but on its release, it shoots forward. My past has a way of dragging me backward, but you always bring me back to the present, encouraging me to keep moving forward. And that's what my future is, moving forward with you."

Her words freeze me. I've never felt so honored or important by such a permanent gesture. Sitting up, I move until my lips find hers. I kiss her with everything I have, hoping she can feel the words I haven't said to her.

I love you. I love you so much.

She kisses me back with the same emotion, almost as if she's saying it back.

Finding some strength, I break the kiss.

"That's really fucking amazing, Wilder." It's the only thing I think to say. I want so desperately to tell her that I love her, but it's not time.

"You're pretty fucking amazing," she responds.

I lie down beside her, my head resting on her stomach. Her fingers run over my head, and I trail soft touches over her legs.

"I'm going into the draft. I'm not coming back next year." I blurt the words out, knowing there isn't a great way to have this conversation, especially after what she just told me. The hand in my hair pauses. She's silent, and my chest seizes with worry. "I'm sorry, I should've told you sooner. The timing just never felt right."

I feel her body tense under my head before she sits up, causing my head to flop down on the mattress.

Shit. Shit. Shit.

"Quinton!" Brynn squeals. She throws her body down on me, lips finding mine immediately. I'm frozen by her reaction. Before I have a chance to kiss her back, her lips leave mine, propping her body on her elbows.

"Why are you apologizing? I'm so proud of you!"

"Yo-you are?"

"Of course I am," she answers, swatting my chest. "This is your dream. Quinton! You're going to the NFL!"

A sense of calm rushes through, instantly relaxing me. This was not the reaction I was expecting, but it's Wilder, of course she'd be proud and understanding.

"I was afraid you'd be upset I didn't tell you sooner. Especially since we just got together." My voice is quiet as I reach up, pushing fallen hair from her face.

Her head melts against my touch. Leaning down, her lips brush mine.

"How could I be upset? This is everything you've wanted. And I'm not worried about us. I know everything will work itself out."

The NFL has always been everything I've ever wanted, but that was before Brynn. Now I'm going to work damn hard at making sure I keep my girl too.

Sitting up and straddling my hips, Wilder reaches behind her back. Unclasping her bra, she lets it slowly drift down her arms. Tossing it aside, she grinds down on my hardening dick.

"Let's celebrate!"

And we celebrate all damn night.

CHAPTER 32
Brynn

BITTER NOVEMBER AIR CUTS through me as I make my way across the browning grass. I'm forever grateful that I was smart enough to remember how different the weather would be and packed my fleece-lined leggings and wool socks. Chicago in November is a lot colder than Texas in November. And Chicago is miserable today. Leaves spin and twirl as they breeze by. The sky is gloomy and overcast, fitting my mood perfectly.

Forcing one duck boot-covered foot in front of the other, I make my way over to my destination. When I arrived, I thought my memories would have blocked out the gravesite, but it must be ingrained in my muscle memory of where I was bound for. Pulling my parka tighter around, I reach up and secure my scarf closer around me to block out the blustering wind. Continuing toward my destination, I slide my beanie further down my ears. This wind is miserable. Finding the spot in the grass I hadn't visited in five years, I squat down, leaning my back against the cold stone.

"Hi, brother," I greet, rubbing my fingers against the engraving—Bryce Philip Wilder. Beloved Son, Brother, and Friend. "I'm sorry it's been so long since I've visited. Chalk it up to me being the absolute worst sister." I choke out the words, inhaling a deep breath, willing myself to be strong.

I can do this. I can do this.

I knew coming here was going to be a challenge, but I didn't realize how difficult it was going to be. But it was time. In fact, it's entirely long overdue.

The other day when I was walking across campus it occurred to me that I needed to come visit. Visiting the cemetery pops into my mind here and there, but this time it was a strong notion. It wasn't that I *needed* to, it was that I *had* to. I needed to finally grow up and stop acting like a child. It was time I came home to have a conversation with my brother.

And then one with Asher.

It's time to get closure. The time has come to close this chapter of my life and move forward. Especially if I want to move forward with Quinton. I'm not coming here to forget about them, but it's time I come here to accept that they aren't coming back, and it's okay for me to move on. I didn't die with them. It's not fair to either one of them that I quit living when I have the chance to.

Taking a deep breath, I fold my hands in my lap while tilting my face to the sky. The sunbeams warm my face, a smile breaking free from my lips. If I let myself believe it, I can feel Bryce's eyes on me. He's sending me warmth by letting the clouds part for the sun. It's his way of letting me know that he's here with me.

I hope Heaven is everything we are told and more. That it's not just some made-up place for us living to picture. I hope that he and Asher are bouncing from cloud to cloud, raising hell, and causing just enough trouble while still being allowed to stay behind those pearly gates.

Or maybe it's like *The Good Place* and both of them have found their soulmates. Gosh, I hope that's the case. I hope both of them have been given the opportunity to love—Bryce for the first time and Asher to find someone new to love, someone he's meant to spend the rest of his life with. That version of heaven is just like Earth—attending college, finding their passions, falling in love, and making new memories. Maybe there's a big screen TV where they get to sit down and check in on us still living without them.

A stream of tears slides down my cheek, and I quickly thumb them away.

"Dammit, Bryce. I freaking miss you. I miss your obnoxious laugh, your contagious smile, and your warm embraces. And I miss having you by my side. College was supposed to be me and you. Our journey together out of the clutches of Mom and Dad." A sob breaks free, and I take a minute to just let the tears pour. "I got into CTU. I almost didn't go. It didn't feel right to go without you, but I knew you would've been pissed at me. It's not the same without you, far from it, but I'm trying. I'm trying so hard to make you proud. I can't say that some of the decisions I've made over the years would have you feel proud of me, but I was doing the best I could. Which is a shit excuse, but that's always been me—full of excuses."

I pause, taking a deep breath and searching the grounds. There's a cardinal resting a few rows over. If that isn't a sign that Bryce is with me, I don't know if I could find anything clearer. "But I'm taking my major seriously. I graduate next fall before continuing on to the master's program. I want to be a youth therapist who helps kids with their grief after a loss."

For the next twenty minutes, I sit and recap my last three years at CTU for Bryce, sparing him the rest of high school. Both of us were trying to survive high school before the accident. Our minds had already traveled to what was to come next for us. Telling Bryce I'd be back, I get up and make my way over a few rows.

The shiny black marble stares back at me, Asher's name engraved on the headstone. I stand there, staring at the stone, not moving. The words for Bryce came easily. I don't know what to say to Asher. I miss him something fierce, and guilt surrounds me. Guilt for letting him take my ticket. Guilt for leaving him that day in the hospital. Guilt for falling in love with someone who isn't him. My love for Quinton came out of nowhere, but it feels so natural. It's the same feeling I had for Asher, if not stronger, and it makes me feel so guilty to have these feelings for someone else.

Finally, I force myself to move. Bending down, I sit on my knees, the words staring back at me.

"Hi Ash," my voice squeaks out. "I'm sorry I haven't been by. Truth is, guilt has consumed me, leaving me paralyzed about what to say to you." That same paralyzing feeling hits me. I don't know where I'm supposed to go from here. "I met someone," I blurt. "You'd really like him. Quinton reminds me a lot of you and Bryce. He's driven, he's caring, and he's hardworking. But I'm scared to tell him I love him. What if there's not enough room in my heart for him too? You still hold my heart like a vise. And what if my love isn't enough? Or what if something happens to him just like something happened to you and Bryce? I'd never be able to live with myself.

"I know I'm rambling. Words have never been hard between us. Hell, we both went through that dreaded junior high awkward stage together, but this just feels different."

My knees grow tired from holding my weight. I shift so that I'm leaning with my back against his stone as I did at Bryce's site.

"I guess I came here today to tell you that I love him. I love Quinton so much that it hurts. And while I love him, I'll always love you. I'll always wonder what our life would've been like. But while I'll hold on to that life, I've got to move on. It's not fair to any of us for me to die while living. And if you're watching over me, like I know you are, just give me a sign that it's okay to move on."

I let the words finish spewing from my mouth, knowing that it's a bunch of random nonsense that I'm hoping he's making sense of.

Closing my eyes, I tilt my chin to my chest and just focus on my breathing. The wind picks up, blowing my loose hair into my face. Reaching up to swipe the tendril from my face, I catch movement out of the corner of my eye.

Two cardinals are perched in a pine tree. One of them flies toward me, landing on the headstone across from me. He lets out the most beautiful chirp, and the dam breaks. Sobs erupt from my chest, streams of water pour from my eyes, and I know that was my sign from Asher.

The air is growing colder, the sun back behind the gray clouds. Standing up, I bend down and press my lips to Asher's headstone.

"I love you, Asher Nelson."

My hand slides into my pocket, and I find the photos that I had stashed away. Removing the double-stick tape from the back of the photos, I attach them to his grave. A copy of the photo Grace sent me and a recent photo of me and Quinton after one of his football games.

Making my way back over to tell Bryce goodbye, I'm just about to his gravesite when a figure appears, startling me. She's tall and thin, wearing dress slacks and a long wool coat. Glancing up, she makes eye contact with me, stopping me in my tracks, and freezing me like one of Medusa's victims.

"Mom?" I rasp out.

Carolyn Cabot-Wilder is standing in front of me. Shock doesn't even begin to describe what I'm feeling.

Clutching her hands to her chest, her eyes squint as she takes me in.

"Brinley, is that you?" Nodding my head, I slowly make my way toward her. "What are you doing here?"

"I came to talk to Bryce and Asher."

She nods her head at my answer. The look of surprise is evident on her face. For a moment, neither of us says anything. I take the moment to look at her, really look at the woman who made me. Deep lines are starting to crease near her eyes. She looks as elegant as ever, but older, like she's more exhausted than normal. I've heard that the hospital is doing well and is the number one trauma hospital in the suburbs of Chicago. I'm sure she sees a lot.

"How long are you here for?"

"I just came for the day," I answer, turning and stepping closer to Bryce's spot. "I was actually just coming back to say goodbye to Bryce."

She nods her head. That seems to be the only reaction that she gives me. Bending down, I kiss the cool stone as I did to Asher's. Pulling out another photo of me and Quinton, I attach it to his grave, hoping he can see it.

"I love you, Bryce. I miss you so damn much. Keep an eye on me," I whisper, leaving one more kiss.

Standing upright, I'm not sure what to do. To say that I'm shocked to run into my mother would be an understatement. I never would've imagined that she visited his grave, especially since she has not once visited me. Her child who is *still* alive. Pausing, I wait to see if she says anything.

Nothing comes.

I go to move around her when her hand reaches out and touches my forearm. My arm jerks in reaction, not from fright but from shock. She jerks her hand back at my reaction.

"I'm sorry," she rushes out.

"It's fine," I answer, locking eyes with her.

She takes a deep breath, and I watch as her chest rises and falls.

"I'm sorry I haven't been a good mother to you, Brinley. Actually, I've been a horrible mother for quite some time."

Taken aback by her comments, I eye her cautiously. "You have been a terrible mother," I respond.

She flinches at my response, but it's the truth. And today seems as good as any to get it off my chest.

"You acted like I was gone too, Mom. You forgot about being a mother to us long before Bryce died. When he did die, you said horrible things. You were terrible to me. You—"

"I was grieving," she retorts, cutting me off.

An exasperated sigh leaves my lips. "So was I," I shout. Tears well in my eyes, but I fight like hell to keep from shedding them. "I was grieving my twin brother and my boyfriend. And then I was grieving the loss of my parents. You told me you wished it was me. How does a seventeen-year-old come back from that?"

Tears are streaming down her face leaving a trail of black mascara.

"I've been seeing a counselor. It hasn't been long, but she's helping me deal with my problems—problems I've been facing for many, many years."

"That's great, Mom. Good for you."

And I really mean that. Quinton and I have been having conversations about me setting up an appointment with a therapist. I think everyone should find the time to talk to a professional.

Life is hard, and it's messy. It's full of challenges, and it doesn't hurt to seek help from an outsider. Even if it's just being able to speak freely with someone who doesn't know you or your history. It's healthy, and I love that so many people are finally starting to talk about their mental health struggles. Professional sports are pushing mental health on top of physical health. Maybe we won't have so many problems in the future if we end the stigma about mental health and seeking treatment—whether it be from prescription medicine or talking to a therapist.

"Do you think we can move past our issues?" Mom asks, vulnerability lining her words.

"Do I think we can move past them? No," I answer, her shoulders deflating at my response. "But I think we can work on healing our issues. It's going to take a lot of time to heal these wounds, Mom. But if you're willing to truly fix our relationship, then I'm not going to deny you. I miss having a mom." I choke out that last thought because it's true. I miss having a mom to call when I need advice or just want to share something exciting that's happened in my world.

Another sob escapes Carolyn Cabot-Wilder, and I'm shocked at the emotion she is so openly expressing. She rushes me and pulls me in for a hug. My arms stay still at my side. I haven't had a hug from my mother in ten years.

"I'm so sorry for everything, Brynn. I hope you can forgive me someday." Slowly, I move my arms up to her waist and give her a small squeeze. Our hug is short as she pulls away first. Taking a tissue from her pocket, she wipes her tear-streaked face, leaving her foundation behind on the white paper. "Be safe heading home."

"Thanks, Mom."

And with that, I turn and walk away. Leaving my mother alone in the cemetery.

I came to Chicago to seek closure from my dead boyfriend and to catch up with my dead twin brother, but I'm leaving Chicago hopeful that someday I'll actually have a relationship with my mother.

A relationship I thought was dead too.

CHAPTER 33
QUINTON

THE DAYS GO BY in a blur. Wake up, lift weights, class, film, make out with Brynn, class, practice, study, and then end the night tangled in the sheets with Brynn. And repeat.

Life is crazy busy. It's been two weeks since Brynn came back from Chicago. She's turned into a different woman. She's still the same Brynn that I've fallen in love with, but she seems lighter.

In that time, we've won the last two games, and tomorrow is the beginning of rivalry week. One more win, and we are heading to the conference championship. When we win that game, it's off to the playoffs. The National Title game is so close I can smell the blood, sweat, and tears.

My body twitches in anticipation, my mind constantly running. But Brynn is always there beside me to talk me off the ledge. The weight of all the pressure is starting to wrap around my ankles and drag me to the bottom of the sea. Anytime I sit down, my knee instantly begins to bounce like I'm on a constant trampoline.

My dreams are so close to coming true.

Every tough practice that left my muscles screaming. Every event I had to turn down because of football. It's all going to be worth it in just a few short weeks.

My parents can sense it too. They've been calling almost daily to talk about my game, but I've been ignoring them. I know that I shouldn't, but I don't need them adding any more pressure to my shoulders. My back is strapped with my own weight, the weight of the team, the weight of the university, the weight of the media, and the weight of the NFL. One wrong move could put everything in jeopardy, and I just can't risk that.

Years growing up watching *Little Giants* taught me that football is eighty percent mental and forty percent physical, which means my head has to be screwed on straight. It also means that any free time I have is spent in the team's weight room getting stronger. It's where I am tonight.

The sounds of the bars clanking together. Hearing myself grunt from the exertion. Feeling my body push itself to its limit. It all gives me peace. The weight room is my solace. The space where I can be left alone with my thoughts or the place where I can zone everything out as I let music blare through the room, leaving no room for intrusive thoughts.

Tonight, I went with the latter option.

Drake croons from the speakers while I work my legs on the leg press machine. Hitting my third rep, the music cuts off. Scanning the room, I find Coach Campbell over by the sound system. Lowering my legs to where the weight rests, I sit up, grabbing a towel and wiping the sweat that's running down my face.

"Coach." I greet him, squirting a stream of water in my mouth.

"What are you doing here, Boyd?" he asks, not moving from where he's leaning on the wall. "It's eleven thirty at night."

"Couldn't sleep, Coach."

Making his way over, Coach stops at the machine next to me, sliding his hands into his jeans pockets. "Then find yourself a piece of ass and work off steam that way. You're pushing yourself too hard."

Sitting up straighter, my eyes stare him down. "Coach—" I start but am immediately cut off.

Shaking his head, he slips his hat off and runs his fingers through his hair before sliding it back on. Coach Campbell is a great man. He's a tough guy on the field, but at the end of the day, he's like a dad to all of us. I mean, he is Grant's dad, but that doesn't stop him from trying to be a good father figure to the rest of us. A lot of the guys on the team never had that type of father figure in their lives. Most of the time, coaches stepped up to play those roles. Letting out a deep exhale, Coach sits on a workout bench looking directly at me.

"Quinton, you are one of the best running backs I've ever seen play, let alone coached. But to be excellent, you've got to know when enough is enough. I see you out there working yourself to the bone, trying to get yourself noticed. And that's great. But you've got to give your body rest too. The NFL isn't going to want someone for a year or two. They want franchise players. They want players they can invest time and money in. But you keep going the way you are, and you're going to burn out or get injured. I sure as shit don't want to see you do that."

"But, Coach," I start again before being cut off.

"No more, Boyd. I'm locking the weight room down. I only want to see you here on our required training days. And before you get any bright ideas, I'll put a campus-wide ban on any other gyms if you try those."

"C'mon, Coach?" Standing abruptly, I toss the towel I was holding to the floor. "That's bullshit."

Coach doesn't back down. Standing up, he steps toward me. Campbell might be a couple of inches shorter than me, but his energy matches that of a giant.

"Remember who you're talking to, Boyd," he starts, pointing a finger in my direction. "I need you to be healthy. I'm not risking an injury when you're in the best shape."

Pissed off and now unable to work off my steam, I reach down, gathering up my phone, water bottle, and towel. I move past Coach to head toward the locker room door, but I'm not able to make it past him before his hand reaches out and grabs my arm.

Staring at each other, eye to eye, he doesn't say anything for a second.

"Quinton, I'm proud of you. I'm being hard on you because I care. You've never used your name to get you anywhere. Who you are today is solely because of *you*. That's something to be damn proud of. And I'm proud to say that I get to coach you."

And with that, he lets go of my arm and makes his way to the exit.

I just stand there. Frozen in time.

It feels so goddamn good to be recognized like that. People on the street and in the media all want to chalk my success up to being a Boyd, to being Howard's son. But he's not the one putting in the work.

I am.

Stepping into my bedroom, I find Brynn lying on her side of the bed. Yeah, her side. Since we've made things official, I find her sneaking into my room more times than not. There's just something special about starting and ending the day by each other's sides. We still find ourselves doing our own thing. One thing about Brynn is that she's independent, and being in a relationship isn't going to stop her from doing her own thing. But at the end of the day, she's crawling in next to me.

Quietly, I drop my gym bag down next to my desk and stand there, watching her sleep. She's curled up like a cat on her side, body facing the side where I sleep. One arm is propped under her head, and the other is stretched out, searching. Searching for my body to touch. My girl isn't a cuddler when she sleeps. Thank fuck. After we have sex, she wants a few moments to lay together, but before long she's turning onto her back and reaching for her phone. She scrolls Instagram like it's a post-sex smoke. Meanwhile, I roll in the opposite direction and drift off. But just as I'm about in a deep sleep, I feel her roll over to face me. She scoots close enough to have a body part barely touch me. Usually, her foot or a hand grazes my body. But it's like her security to know that I'm still here. That I'm not going anywhere.

"What are you smiling at?" Her voice breaks me from my thoughts.

Glancing at her, I see that her eyes are still closed.

"I didn't know you were awake."

Reaching behind me, I pull my shirt over my head in one swoop before tossing it in my laundry basket. Striding over to her, I place my knee on the bed before leaning down and giving her a kiss on her forehead.

Rolling over onto her back, her hands seek out my neck. Finding it, her fingers clasp onto my neck, pulling me toward her for a long, deep kiss.

"Hi baby, I missed you."

"I missed you too," I say against her lips. "I'm going to shower."

She nods her head and rolls back over. Striding over to my dresser, I open a drawer and find a pair of loose boxers—the only way to sleep.

Moving into the bathroom and stripping out of my sweat-soaked clothes, I reach inside the shower to start the water. Climbing in, I let the water run down my body, mind replaying my conversation with Coach Campbell.

CHAPTER 34
QUINTON

THE DAY BEFORE THANKSGIVING is here, and we are three days away from our rivalry game. Tonight is the annual pep rally. Each year, CTU hosts a tailgate before the big game. Coaches talk, local restaurants cater food for people to buy, the band performs, and the players get to mingle with the crowd. It's a ticketed event, which helps keep the crowd down.

On stage, Coach Campbell stands at the microphone while some of the starting players are seated behind him, the rest of the team is off to the side. The cheerleaders are in front of the stage, chanting cheers and doing flips and shit. It's a cool event and gets us all even more hyped for the game.

As if the game wasn't big enough already, this year both teams are going into this matchup ranked number one and two. The stakes are high.

Searching the crowd, I look for bright blonde hair and piercing blue eyes. The team had to be here early, and I didn't get a chance to see Brynn before I left. Therefore, I have no idea what she's wearing. Knowing her, it's something crazy. An elbow hits my arm as I'm looking through the crowd. Tipping my head to my left, I see Grant leaning toward me.

"Dad told me he talked to you."

"He kicked me out of the damn weight room," I retort, eyes not leaving the crowd.

There are hundreds of people here. My parents are out there somewhere. Boosters, press, alumni, and other students are all here, dressed in their red, white, and powder blue. It makes finding anyone almost impossible.

But clearly, not completely impossible.

Brynn is pushing her way through the crowd with Chloe, Cody, and that girl from the Union, who has her arm wrapped through Cody's.

Grant nudges me again, getting my attention. "He's worried about you."

That snaps my head toward Grant. "What do you mean?"

Sighing, Grant glances around the crowd before leaning closer to me. "He just wants you to make it. We've been tight since we both started here. Which means Dad is even more protective of you. Not only are you his player, but you're a friend of his son's. He just wants the best for you. He wants to see you succeed."

Eyes finding him, understanding passes through me. Nodding my head, I raise a fist for Grant to bump it. Words aren't needed. I get it. It's a big fucking deal and I need to keep my head right.

Interrupting our conversation, Coach Campbell turns toward us. "And now let's meet some of the team."

The crowd erupts. Cheering and clapping ring out as the band fires up a quick beat. Campbell goes down the row of players, introducing us to the crowd. We stand when our name is called and wave to the crowd. Once he announces Will—the douche—as the last player up here, the cheerleaders take over.

"E-A-G! L-E-S!" Chants echo through the crowd, our sign that our time here is done.

Climbing the stairs off the stage, I find my parents waiting on me.

"There's our boy." I hear my mom as she comes up to me, wrapping her arms around me for a hug.

"Hi, Ma."

Hugging her back, I look over her shoulder for the one girl I was hoping would be waiting for me. Releasing me, my mom steps aside, only for my father to take her place.

"Son." He stretches his hand out for a shake.

"Dad," I respond, gripping his hand in a firm shake.

Did I grip him a little stronger than necessary? I'll never tell. But I will say, I'll never look weak in front of this man. Xavier and Damien are standing next to Dad, and all three of us give a nod in greeting.

"Your father and I can't wait for Saturday. Our baby is going to kick some major ass." Mom says, drawing my attention back down to her.

"There's a few people here I want you to meet, son." Dad gestures toward the opposite end of where we are standing.

There's a pop-up tent with men in suits with CTU-colored ties. They don't look like men who I want to introduce myself to, not tonight.

"Not tonight, Dad. Tonight is my night," I respond, reaching up and gripping his shoulder. Leaning down, I give my mom a hug. "See you tomorrow for lunch," I whisper in her ear, and then I walk away from my family.

Walking through the crowd is a challenge. People clap me on the back, wishing me good luck this weekend. Spotting Brynn and Chloe sitting on a table, I change my direction to get to them. I'm just about to them when a little boy steps in my path. I almost run him over, but my hands reach out to grip his shoulder on instinct to make sure he doesn't fall over.

"Whoa, dude, almost didn't see you there."

"Holy shit," the kid gasps. "Quinton Boyd just called me dude."

A woman slides up beside him. "Tanner, cuss word."

Looking up at what appears to be his mom, the boy—Tanner—rolls his eyes.

"Mom, it was warranted. It's Quinton Boyd." He gestures to me, his mom following his hand to see who he is pointing at.

Sheepishly, she looks at me with a little embarrassment. "I'm sorry, Tanner has been so excited about this event all week. I didn't think he'd track you down and almost tackle you."

Laughing, I smile at the woman before squatting down to the little boy. "All good. So, you're Tanner?"

He just nods his head, a tinge of pink spreading across his cheeks. Reaching my fist out to the boy, I wait as he bumps it back.

"How old are you, Tanner?"

"Se-seven," he stutters out.

"Seven is a sweet age."

Looking down at his hands, I notice he's holding something.

"Want me to sign your jersey?"

With his eyes bugging out, his energy skyrockets. "Oh my god, that'd be so cool. I seriously didn't think I'd meet you tonight. Oh my god, Mom," Tanner rushes out, looking up at his mom, pure excitement written all over his face. "Mom! Mom! Get the marker out!"

His mom reaches into her small bag and starts moving items around, searching for her marker. It takes her a couple of minutes, then her face falls, and moisture lines her eyes.

"Tanner, baby, I forgot it."

His body immediately deflates, disappointment written all over his face.

Looking up past Tanner, I see Brynn watching our interaction, admiration written all over her face. Bringing my hand up, I make a writing gesture that she immediately interprets, giving me the sign for one second.

"Hold on, buddy. I've got you."

His eyes instantly widen as Brynn makes her way over to us.

"Does someone over here need a marker?" She holds out the marker, looking down at the boy.

Throwing his arms around Brynn's waist, he mumbles into her, "Thank you, lady."

She pats his back with a smile on her face as Tanner steps back, handing me the marker. Brynn doesn't leave us. She just stands off to the side, continuing to watch our interaction.

"You're my favorite football player. Like my absolute favorite." Tanner shares while I take the marker and jersey from him. "My dad was a huge CTU fan, but he died, so now I'm trying to be the biggest fan ever, for the both of us."

My hand stops writing, and Brynn gasps as my eyes bounce between Tanner, his mom, and Brynn. Tears line the mother and Brynn's eyes.

Clearing my throat, I finish signing. "Well, Tanner, I'd say you're our biggest fan. What other dude is going to run into the star running back?"

He blushes. Brynn's eyes shine bright with something I can't quite put my eyes on.

Admiration? Lust? Love?

She clears her throat, waving her hands around. "You guys all stand together, and I'll take your picture!"

Looking at Tanner's mom, I wait for permission.

"Ar-re you sure?" she asks.

Brynn chimes in before I have a chance. "Of course, he's sure. It's no problem."

The three of us move toward each other.

"Is she your girlfriend?" Tanner asks, moving in between his mom and myself.

Glancing from Tanner to Brynn, I watch as a shy smile appears on her lips.

"Yeah, dude. That's my girl."

Tanner looks from me to Brynn. "She's a hottie," he says.

"Tanner!" his mom scolds, tapping him on the back of the head. "Apologize to—uh—"

"Brynn!" Extending her hand out, she reaches for Tanner's mom. "Brynn Wilder. It's so nice to meet Quinton's biggest fans."

The woman takes Brynn's hand in a quick handshake. "Kari. Kari Sander." Stepping back, she stands next to her son with a small smile on her face. "It's really nice of you both to take time to do this for him. It's been a rough year."

Brynn gives her a nod in understanding, the corners of her lips turning up slightly, eyes dropping to a beaming Tanner, whose energy is bursting at the seams.

"Alright. Let's get you guys a picture!" Slipping her phone from her pocket, she adjusts a couple of settings before she's pointing the camera at the three of us. "Say 'Go Birds'!"

"Go Birds!" the three of us say, smiles stretching our faces.

Squatting down, I start up a conversation with Tanner while Kari gives her number to Brynn for the photo. While talking to Tanner, I learn that he's from Texas, in the second grade, wants to grow up and be a professional football player or a bull rider, and that his dad didn't make it back from Afghanistan at the end of 2021. After a few minutes, we part ways.

Instinctively, my arm wraps around Brynn's shoulders, pulling her into my side.

"You were amazing with him," she tells me as we watch Kari and Tanner walk away. "Like watching you with him. You were so sweet. And understanding. It was so hot."

Shaking my head, I lean down and plant a big kiss on her forehead. "Only you, Wilder, only you."

Tipping her head back, our lips find their way to each other. But we keep it short because of the fucking press. Standing to my full height, I take a moment to let my eyes glide down her body, taking in tonight's outfit. A small chuckle escapes my lips. Only Brynn could pull this outfit off. She's wearing a pair of dad sneakers on her feet, baggy straight-leg jeans, a cropped red tank, and an oversized retro Eagles jacket. Her hair cascades down her back in her signature loose waves.

"You look like an NFL wife." The words escape my lips as soon as they pop into my head. She laughs. That perfect laugh that I could get lost in. "What's so funny?"

Chloe appears out of nowhere, chiming in. "She spent an hour on Pinterest this morning searching for 'NFL wife aesthetics' and 'what do NFL girlfriends wear?'"

My gaze roams over her body, my hand drags across my mouth. "Well, you fucking nailed it."

Our little group is joined by Cody and the same girl that I saw wrapped around him a little while ago.

"'Sup," Cody greets, sticking his first out for a bump.

Dabbing him back, I give a nod. "'Sup, man." My eyes find the girl, reaching out a hand, I introduce myself. "I'm Quinton."

She giggles. There's a vibe radiating off her that I just don't like. I recognize it immediately. This is the type of girl who latches on and doesn't let go. Her hand finds mine, a seductive grin slides across her lips.

"I know who you are. All the girls do. I'm Monica." Her voice purrs her words and I cringe.

Yep, she's the thirsty type.

Beside me, I can feel both Brynn and Chloe cringe. Something's off with this chick. My eyes find Cody's as I let go of Monica's hand. He's watching her with a smile on his face. Lust and attraction mirror his face. Does he not get the same vibe that we all do? He's a baseball star, he should be able to sense a cleat chaser. Homegirl is screaming cleat chaser.

Monica turns into Cody, running her fingers slowly, down his chest. Peering up at him through her lashes, she runs her tongue across her lips, and he follows every movement.

"Cody and I are going to head out now that you've found Quinton. My roommate is home for the break."

Cody wraps his arm around her and spins her so they're shoulder to shoulder. "Kick some ass Saturday, Boyd," he says to me before his eyes slide over to Brynn. "See you Saturday morning at the house, B."

"Be ready to party," she replies, voice getting louder with excitement.

He grins at her, giving us all a nod, before turning him and Monica around and walking away.

"What the hell was that?" I ask, pulling Brynn closer to me, eyes going from her to Chloe.

Chloe is standing there stock still. Cody didn't even say goodbye to her. I know the two of them aren't that close—not like him and Brynn—but Cody has manners. He always says goodbye to everyone. But there's something else there. Her face is almost white, moisture clouds her eyes, and she just seems defeated. Brynn catches me watching Chloe, and with a nudge into my side, I look down at her. She gives me a tight smile before shaking her head. That shake tells me not to push it.

"You girls ready?" I ask, sliding my other arm around Chloe.

The press would have a fucking field day if they saw this. *Quinton Boyd leaves pep rally with two very attractive girls under his arm.*

But let them talk. I know who I am. I know when a friend needs to lean on someone. And tonight, my girlfriend's friend needs us.

Squeezing Chloe's shoulder, I get her attention. She looks up at me as a lone tear slides down her cheek. Pressing her lips together she gives me a tight smile. Returning the smile, I lower my head for only her to hear.

"We've got you, Chloe."

CHAPTER 35
Brynn

T HANKSGIVING DAY. A DAY to celebrate all the things that we are thankful for. I always hate getting asked at dinners what we are thankful for. And since I have no idea what to expect from Quinton's family's Thanksgiving, I start making a mental list of things I'm thankful for, just in case the topic arises.

This year I'm thankful for:

My health and spirit.

Chloe and Cody—my besties that always have my back.

The football boys for welcoming me into the crew, even more than I already was.

Going home to see Asher and Bryce.

Truth or Dare.

This year I'm so thankful for the stupid game because, if it wasn't for some girl from my past daring Quinton to kiss me, I don't know if we would have given in to our attraction. I'd like to think that we'd have eventually woken up on our own and seen it, but I don't want to take that chance.

"You're going to hurt yourself," Quinton says from the driver's side of my Mercedes, interrupting my thoughts.

Head snapping toward him, I find him staring straight ahead. I can't help but admire how handsome he looks in his camel-colored sweater and dark-washed jeans.

"How so?"

Glancing my way, he takes his right hand and pulls my bottom lip from where I was worrying it between my teeth—I didn't realize I was nibbling on it.

"From thinking so hard. Relax, babe. It's going to be fine."

"Easy for you to say," I scoff, turning back toward the window, eyes watching the landscape pass by. "Your family doesn't hate you."

A long breath passes through his lips, his gaze burning holes in the side of my head.

"They don't hate you, Brynn," Quinton says, reaching his arm across the console and settling on my thigh.

He takes his thumb and rubs tiny circles on my exposed skin from where my skirt has ridden up.

"They might not hate me, but they certainly think I'm not good enough to breathe the same air as you."

We both know the truth. His mom can't stand me. She's never gotten to know me, but she already assumes I'm not good enough for her son. I don't know why Quinton tries to deny it when the words have actually come from her mouth. She's written me off as a gold-digging ho—her words, not mine—even though I have my own trust fund. I don't need Quinton's money. I can easily support both of us if he ever decides that a career in the NFL isn't what he wants.

My eyes slide down to where his thumb is rubbing tiny circles, the ones that always seem to calm me down. But instead of appreciating his touch, I'm questioning my outfit choice for the millionth time today.

An explosion in my room would have done less damage than what I did this morning. I think I changed my clothes twenty different times before I settled on a tweed skirt with an ivory and brown grid pattern, a golden-brown colored turtleneck, and my white Lucchese cowboy boots. When I sat down to do my makeup, I made sure to keep it very neutral, nothing too dark or too heavy, with a simple nude lip.

Quinton told me I looked beautiful when I finally emerged from the bedroom. He was waiting downstairs since he stayed over last night. Without planning, our outfits complimented each other, making us look like a cute matching couple. *We'll have to take a cute picture for Instagram.*

But I don't think it would matter what I picked out. Abigail Boyd will always find a fault, and I'm thinking that the skirt I picked out is too short. I forgot to check the length when I sat down. It looked fine standing, but now I'm sure it'll garner some kind of comment once I'm seated.

Up ahead, I spot their property. Quinton navigates us through the gated, paved drive that leads to the beautiful, white colonial home. Where my parents' home is warm and traditional, the Boyds' is cool and modern. Bringing us to a stop, Quinton turns off the ignition before turning to face me.

Eyes searching my face, I know he can see all the worry lines and the missing lipstick from where I've worried my lips the whole drive. He brings my hand to his lips, kissing my fingers.

"You're beautiful, Wilder. Don't let my parents get to you. I don't care what they think and neither should you. I love you, and that's all that matters."

Wait, what?! What did Quinton just say? Did he just drop the love bomb parked outside of his parents' house?

"Wha-what did you just say?" My eyes search his face for any regret.

There's none. Earnest eyes stare back at me, and a tiny smile spreads across his face. Gripping my face, he holds my head still while I stare at him.

"I said, 'I love you and that's all that matters.' I love you, Brinley Wilder. I have since we first met. There was something about this spunky, wild girl that caught my eye, and I knew that I was going to fall in love with her."

Before I can even process what I'm doing, I'm flinging myself toward him. My body slides up on the console in a very awkward, very uncomfortable position, but I don't care. I need his lips on mine. I need to feel his love.

Slowly, pulling away from his kiss—even though I didn't want to—we both sit there, staring at each other, goofy grins painting our faces.

"I love you too," I respond, Quinton's smile growing even wider.

Our moment is interrupted when someone knocks on Quinton's door. The two of us separate, and I reach down into my purse and pull out my lipstick. Reaching up, I pull down the visor, open the mirror, and reapply my freshly kissed lipstick. Quinton opens the door and steps out. Damien stands there, stepping back to make room for Quinton to stand up outside the car.

"Hey, Brynn." Damien waves before turning to face Quinton. "You two done sucking face?"

"Shut the fuck up."

Reaching out, Q pushes his older brother in a joking manner before the two of them are embracing each other in that handshake/hug thing guys do.

"'Sup, bro?"

"Ready to get this shit show over with," Damien responds, both men making their way over to my side of the car.

I'm closing the visor, slipping my lipstick inside my purse when my door is opened for me.

"That's supposed to be my job," Quinton grumbles, hand in his pocket, while Damien opens my car door.

Grabbing my purse from the floorboard, I slip it on my shoulder as I slide out of the car, thanking Damien.

"Breathe, Brynn," both men say at the same time.

I chuckle.

As chaotic as Quinton's family dynamic is, Damien and Quinton are the closest. There was a time when envy toward his brother ran through Q's veins, but they've both been working on their relationship. It's really good to see both of them smiling and joking with each other.

Look at us. Both growing up and dealing with our shit.

There was a time when Damien just stood back, quiet and broody, standing outside the group. The outsider of the family, he never pursued any type of football after high school. There was a lot of damage done between Mr. Boyd and Damien because of that decision, but as a true outsider of the family, it was the best decision Damien could've made.

The three of us head toward the house. Damien led the way, with us right behind him, walking hand-in-hand into the lion's den. Or should I say lioness' den? Damien presses the doorbell while Quinton leans down and gives me a kiss on the cheek. My eyes stay straight ahead, waiting for the door to open. The burnt-orange door slowly opens, and there stands Abigail.

A wide smile touches her lips as she looks from Damien to Quinton, and then her eyes find mine, her smile dropping, her lips curling down at the corners, before she quickly pastes a fake smile on her face. But it was too late. We all saw it. Tension radiates from all of us as Abigail opens the door wider for us to enter.

Delicious scents filter in from the kitchen, welcoming us with more warmth than the mother of the two boys in front of me. I stand there, feeling incredibly awkward, as I watch the exchange between mother and sons. She reaches up, kissing each boy on their cheek and wrapping them in her arms for long hugs.

Someone who doesn't know the Boyds would think this is a sweet loving family. But I know the truth.

"Don't let her get to you," a voice says next to me, making me jump.

I didn't see anyone slide up next to me. Removing my eyes from Quinton, I look to my side and see an adorable older lady. She's dressed in purple trousers, a silky, black top, and an oversized, matching, purple button-up. Her eyes aren't watching the exchange, but looking right at me.

"Excuse me?" I ask the lady.

I'm assuming she's Quinton's grandma, but I'm not positive.

She laughs. "I'm the old one who's supposed to be hard of hearing, not you. Maybe you should stop listening to so much live music and get your ears checked."

I'm taken aback by the old woman who has jokes.

"Grandma Cleo?" I ask, trying to figure out who she is.

I'm assuming she's Q's Grandma Boyd. He's the closest with her. Her frail arm slides under the crook of mine as she escorts me away from the entryway.

"Come, we need a drink if we're going to make it through this dinner. And call me Grams."

I do as I'm told, letting Grams lead me down the hallway toward the living room. As I'm walking, I glance over my shoulder. Quinton is staring at us with a smile of adoration on his face. I smile back.

Before long, we are gathering around the dining table. It's an elegant table that has been lengthened with leaves to accommodate most of us. Some of the younger kids are seated at the table in the eat-in kitchen. Quinton pulls out my chair for me to sit, both of us looking at each other with hearts in our eyes. He loves me. Quinton Boyd told me he loves me. I still can't figure out how I got so lucky.

Grandma Boyd—I learned I guessed correctly—hasn't left my side. She's hilarious and a terrible influence. I'm already on my way to a *really* strong buzz, and we've only been here an hour. Grams, on the other hand, is heading straight toward drunk. She's a tequila drinker, which means I love her even more. She's been making us Palomas, which I didn't think I would like since it's grapefruit, and the only grapefruit I like is a grapefruit hard seltzer. But I've learned, if Grandma Boyd wants you to do it, you do it.

Speaking of Grams, she slides into the seat next to me, giving me a wink. Internally, I chuckle. Here I thought this little old lady was some frail thing, but it just turns out she's a tiny enabler.

I feel his breath against my skin before he says anything.

"I see you've hit it off well with Grams." I smile, dragging my glass up to my lips for a small sip.

"She's freaking awesome. Why haven't you introduced us sooner?" I asked quietly. Well, I thought it was quiet, but Grams hears us.

The woman doesn't miss anything.

"Yeah, why haven't you brought me around her before, Quinton?" Grandma chimes in, interrupting us. "You ashamed of me? Or is the honey pot too sweet to leave?"

Choking on my drink, I begin coughing as Quinton's face turns bright red.

"Christ, Grams," he barks out.

"Cleo, for god's sake," Abigail tsks in disgust.

"Oh, lighten up, Abigail. He's a grown-ass man in college. He's having sex. Maybe you need to remove that stick from up your ass and get laid every once in a while," Grams retorts.

The whole table goes silent, watching the two women stare down.

I'm doing everything in my power to not burst out laughing, my eyes staying fixed on my place setting. I know if I look up at Damien, who is seated right across from me, we're all going to lose it. I see from the corner of my eye that Quinton is trying his damnedest not to laugh too.

But Quinton makes the mistake and looks at Damien. They erupt in laughter, and I follow suit with Marcus, Quinton's uncle, following along.

"That's enough," Mr. Boyd barks out. "Mom, enough."

Her eyes leave Abigail's as she turns to her son. "Mind your manners. Don't forget who raised your wild ass. There was a time I was chasing hoes out of your room. At least Quinton took the time to find a good one."

Clearing her throat, the caterer stands in the doorway. Abigail turns to her, nodding her head.

"Lunch is ready, let's just eat."

She ignores the dig Cleo slipped in.

I might not have Abigail's stamp of approval, but I have Grandma Boyd's, and that's like winning the lottery.

Grams means the world to Quinton.

So if she approves, then I can rest easy.

CHAPTER 36
Brynn

LUNCH IS SERVED FAMILY-STYLE. Platters of delicious food line the table. Smoked turkey, honey ham, sweet potatoes, mashed potatoes with gravy, cornbread dressing, green bean casserole, and cranberry sauce are all placed in front of us.

Everyone helps themselves to the food in front of us, and the conversation goes back to normal.

"So, Brynn, what are your plans after college?" Mel, Marcus's wife, asks as we are halfway through lunch.

"I'm studying psychology with the intention of being a youth grief counselor," I answer.

Eyes seem to find mine from around the table while Quinton's hand finds my thigh, rubbing those damn tiny circles on my exposed skin.

Dabbing her mouth, a look of appreciation coats her face. "Wow, that's amazing. I imagine that would be a really hard field to go into."

"But you have experience with that, don't you?" Abigail chimes in. *What a bitch.*

It's not that she's saying it in a nice way, it's almost like a dig. Well, fuck you very much, Abigail. It's not a goddamn dig, and I'm about to make you look like a fool at your own damn table.

"Ma," Quinton scolds, his head snapping toward her.

Finding his thigh, I give it a squeeze. His eyes find mine.

"It's fine," I tell him before turning my attention to Abigail.

"Having a dead twin brother and dead high school boyfriend definitely counts as experience."

Gasps elicit from the table. Grams's head snaps toward Abigail. My eyes never leave hers, and hers never leave mine.

"Oh honey, I'm sorry for your losses," Mel says with a solemn expression. "How long have they been gone?"

"You don't have to talk about it," Quinton whispers in my ear.

Shaking my head, I whisper back. "It's okay. I'm done running from it, they deserve to be talked about."

Turning my attention back to Mel, I tell them the story. Every little detail gets shared. How long it's been, how I've harbored guilt for five years for sending Asher in my place, and how my relationship with my family changed drastically. Mel has tears in her eyes. Grams finds my hand on the table, giving it a pat.

"Seems everyone you love dies," Abigail mutters into the napkin she's brought up to her face.

Every head whips in her direction.

Damien is the first to speak. "What happened to you?"

"Excuse me?"

"You heard me. What happened in the last few years to make you such a bitter bitch?" Damien spits at her.

No one else at the table says anything. It's tense. It's awkward as fuck, but I'd like to actually hear this answer.

Her eyes shoot straight to her husband's. They lock on each other in a stare-down. Both dare the other to either speak first or keep their mouths shut.

Minutes seem to fly by when, in reality, it's only been a few seconds of awkward silence. Damien is the first to break the silence.

"Whatever, I'm out." He places his napkin on the table before scooching his chair backward. "It was good seeing everyone. Happy Thanksgiving."

And with that, Damien heads out of the dining room. The sound of the front door closing snaps everyone back to reality.

Quinton follows his lead, sliding his chair out from the table. Before he gets the chance to stand, his mother's attention snaps to him.

"Sit your ass down. Lunch isn't over."

He continues to rise, placing his hand on the back of my chair. Helping me push my chair back, I begin to rise too.

"Nah, this family lunch is over."

"Let them go, Abigail," Howard barks out. "We never should have had this lunch."

Tension radiates off Abigail. Chest heaving, she flips her hand out, gesturing us to leave. Grams grabs my arm before I can walk past her, causing Quinton to bump into my back.

"I had fun today with you, honey. Don't be a stranger." She grins at me before finding Q over my shoulder. "Don't let this one go," she says with a wink, and Abigail scoffs.

I force myself to ignore her. I would love to share words with this woman, but I respect Quinton too much to cause any more drama.

With a final goodbye to everyone, we get the hell out of there.

Thanksgiving didn't go as planned, but I finally got to meet Grams. And for that, I'll always be thankful for this Thanksgiving dinner.

"God, baby, if I would've known *that* was going to happen, I never would've taken you."

Quinton and I made it back to my townhouse some time ago. Both of us were stuffed from the incredible meal but mentally exhausted from the tension. We went straight to my bedroom, stripping out of our dress clothes. I slipped on an oversized, Imagine Dragons concert tee, while Q just stripped down to his boxers, both of us climbing into bed for some Thanksgiving Day football.

Rolling into Quinton's side, I prop my hands under my head, resting them on his chest. I let a finger trail over the feathers of the eagle he has inked across his chest.

"Don't apologize, seriously. I knew what I was getting myself into."

"But you shouldn't have to. I'm done with them."

"Quinton, they're your parents."

"So what? Parents aren't supposed to act that way."

No, they're not, I think. Parents are supposed to support you and love you unconditionally. But I'm not one to judge, my relationship with my parents is complicated. Who knows if I would've spoken to my mom had I not run into her in Chicago? I mean, I haven't even received a 'Happy Thanksgiving' text. Q's parents might be judgmental assholes, but at the end of the day, they care enough about their kids to reach out to them.

What's that say about my parents?

What's that say about me?

A hand reaches out and slides to the nape of my neck. Gathering my hair in his first, he grips it. Hard. He pulls my head back, and a small moan escapes my lips as he fists my hair.

"Get out of your head or I'm going to fuck the thoughts right out."

"Is that supposed to be punishment?" I quip, running my tongue across my lips.

His eyes track the movement. I feel him harden beneath me. A smirk tugged on my lips as I lift my eyebrows in question.

Before I know what's happening, I'm being flipped to my back, and his lips are devouring my neck. His hand still grips my hair, and he uses the fisted strands to tilt my head, exposing my long, lean neck for him to devour. Sucking my skin into his mouth, he bites down. A moan escapes me as he slowly releases it. Arms bent on both sides of me to help hold himself off me, his head pops up, finding my eyes.

"I love you."

"I love you too." Grabbing his neck, I bring his lips to mine.

We spend the rest of Thanksgiving devouring each other like the pumpkin pie we never got to have.

We fall asleep, limbs tangled together, drifting off in a happy, blissed-out state.

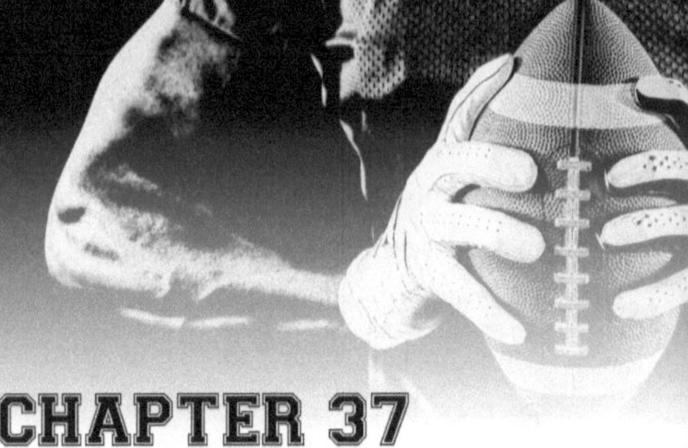

CHAPTER 37
QUINTON

"**F**OURTH QUARTER. LESS THAN fifteen more minutes, boys!" Coach Campbell yells in the huddle.

It's the fourth quarter in the Lafayette game, and we are down by two touchdowns. It's been a fucking battle since kickoff.

Both teams have so much on the line this year. For me, I've got everything on the line. It's my last chance at winning my third conference title, my last chance to go to the playoffs, and my last chance to win a National Championship.

"We've got this," Harris yells out. "This is for all the two-a-days, all the weightlifting, early mornings, and aches and pains. Let's go out there and kick some Gators' ass!"

"Eagles on three!" I yell.

"One."

"Two."

"Three."

"Eagles!" the team yells as we turn and run onto the field.

Valor Stadium is a sold-out, white-out game. It's fucking sick to look up in the crowd and see nothing but white shirts and white towels waving in the air. Crowds of people are on their feet, screaming and cheering us on.

Smacking his hand on my helmet, Harris pulls my attention back down to the field. "Stay focused. You've got this, man."

Taking my place on the field, I line up to the right of Tyler. Xavier did a helluva job with his kickoff return, setting us up on the forty-five-yard line. Only fifty-five more yards 'til we score.

Harris calls for the snap, and it's perfect. He takes a step back before handing it off to me. Running toward the left sideline, I pull up quickly, eyes searching down the field. The offensive line is securing the line, blocking anyone who tries to get to me. A hand flies in the air, and I pull my arm back before snapping it forward, launching the ball into the air. It's a playbook throw, spinning in a perfect spiral and landing perfectly over Grant's shoulder.

He gives one shimmy before he fakes out the safety.

He's down to the fifteen-yard line.

Ten.

Five.

TOUCHDOWN!

Running all the way down, I join in on the celebration. Our trick play was textbook. Grant is hitting the Griddy before he turns, finding me. Jogging toward me, he motions up with his finger, and we both jump up, sides hitting each other.

"Fuck yeah!" I shout.

"Fuckin' perfect throw!" he says, both of us jogging off to the sideline as we wait for the extra point kick.

Energy radiates off us, especially when the defense makes another epic stop to keep Lafayette from scoring. Five minutes flash on the scoreboard, and we are still down by a touchdown. I can't stand still, bouncing from foot to foot on the sideline, my nerves frayed.

The punter for the Gators kicks the ball high in the air. All of us are standing still on the sidelines, silence among us as we hold our breath, waiting for Xavier to catch the ball.

Catching it with ease, he takes off in a sprint, following the blockers in front of him. A hole appears out of nowhere, and Xavier blasts through it. He hits the twenty-five, thirty, and thirty-five before being tackled at the thirty-eight-yard line. Another great return.

Xav is having a hell of a game, and my chest booms with pride.

I make my way onto the field with the rest of the offense. The stadium is loud, man, it is loud. It makes hearing Harris difficult, but we make it work. Grabbing the snap, he steps back and finds Riggsby, our tight end, open for a short pass. Riggsby digs in and makes it another five yards before being taken down.

On second down, Harris finds Grant down the field for another big play. Grant picks us up another twenty yards, putting us inside the fifty-yard line with a fresh set of downs.

Lining up behind Harris, I wait for the snap. It comes, and Harris turns immediately, handing the ball off to me. A quick jab to the left, and my legs explode to the right. Dicing and cutting, sliding past the defensive line, I power my legs forward, getting another ten-yard run in.

The clock is winding down, and we up the tempo even more, going no-huddle. Everyone gets set, and a quick snap has Harris finding Riggsby near the sideline. He runs for a couple of yards before stepping out of bounds to stop the clock.

Three minutes and ten seconds remain, and we still need twenty yards. Once again, I line up in the backfield, only this time, I'm to the left of Harris. Snap, catch, step back, pitch, and I'm exploding forward. Finding a hole, I kick it into another gear, diving toward the goal line.

Slam!

A brick wall slams into me, my vision blurs, and my body goes limp.

Holy fuck!

CHAPTER 38
Brynn

I'VE BEEN ON THE edge of my damn seat this entire time. The beer guy has been staying close to us, he knows where the money is. Drinking has been the only thing to calm my nerves during this game. I've really just needed something to keep my hands busy, but the alcohol does help too.

The Lafayette Gators came to play, just like we all knew they would. This kind of rivalry is what football is all about. Both teams *hate* each other. There's absolutely no love lost between the two teams. And if you don't win the big game, be prepared to hear about it for the next three-hundred sixty-five days.

Central Texas has won the last eleven meetings. And I have been sending all the good vibes to whoever is listening to give us this win. Honestly, I don't care about the win for the team, I just want it so bad for Quinton. I'd give anything to see him finish his season with a Natty.

Glancing over, I watch as Chloe is on her feet, screaming away too. The two of us spent the morning hopping from tailgate to tailgate, drinking more beers and shots than I can count. I was smart enough to remember to hydrate in between. There was no way I was blacking out before this game. Uh-huh, I was staying conscious.

The energy is palpable. Everyone is on their feet as we watch the minutes tick down and pray for a miracle.

I have faith in our boys. They've been working so hard all season. I watch as Tyler hands the ball off to Quinton, fisting my hands, I bring them up under my chin, holding them there as nerves rake through me.

But there's a gap. Holy shit there's a gap. I see it. And oh my god, Q sees it too. He jukes out the last defender before he's heading downfield.

"Go! Go! Go!" I'm screaming, jumping up and down as I watch Quinton slice and dice through the field.

As he dives toward the end zone, my arms fly up in the air, but then I see a safety for Lafayette coming out of nowhere. The safety drops down and dives toward Quinton.

Crack!

The nastiest sound is heard throughout the stadium. Quinton drops to the ground, body across the goal line, hand outstretched, still gripping the ball. The referees must signal a touchdown, but my eyes won't peel away from Quinton. He's just lying there. Not moving.

"Get up," I whisper to myself, arms going out to grasp onto something, anything. I think they find Chloe and Cody's arms. "Get up. Get up."

But he doesn't.

Grant is the first to see it, and he goes running from the opposite end of the field and sliding down next to Quinton. It feels like slow motion from that point on. Medical staff and coaches rush the field, but he still hasn't moved. Nausea swims through my system and I feel like I'm going to be sick. My body collapses in my chair as I watch a medical cart navigate across the field as the staff works to load Quinton onto a stretcher before he's rushed out of the stadium.

Gaze snapping from the field where I watch my lifeless boyfriend to the jumbotron, I wait for the thumbs up—the recognized sign that a player is okay.

"Come on, come on."

But it doesn't come.

The next few minutes go by in a blur. The team is huddled together, but I don't watch. Cody is busy getting me out of my seat, pushing me through our row of people. Students move immediately when they see me behind Cody. "He's going to be okay," "he's got this," and other words of encouragement filter in as we pass by people. I don't acknowledge anyone.

This is all my fault. Two days ago, I told my boyfriend I loved him. We made love that night, sharing tender kisses, and talking about the future, and we were happy, so happy.

Maybe everyone is right. Maybe Abigail Boyd had a reason to hate me. My love sends people to the grave.

Reaching the last step, we hit the concourse level. Cody's arm wraps around my shoulder as he ushers us through the few fans while he thumbs through the contacts on his phone. Finding the one he wants, he brings his phone to his ear.

"Eric," Cody barks into the phone. "I'm with Brynn." He pauses. "Q's girl. Where are they taking him?" He listens to whatever Eric has to say before thanking him and hanging up. "They're taking him to General. I'll drive you guys."

"N-n-no," I stutter. "I just want to go home."

Those words cause Cody to stop at the gate.

"What do you mean?" Chloe asks.

Shock covers her face, and I'm not sure if it's shock that I don't want to go to the hospital or shock from what the hell just happened. Either way, I don't ask. Cody looks down at me and searches my face for something. He must find whatever he's looking for because he just turns us to the gate, shaking his head.

The drive to the house is quiet. I rest my head on the window, keeping my eyes locked outside. Cody keeps glancing my way, but he doesn't say anything. He knows what I'm doing. I'm shutting down. He can see that I'm running. I might not be physically leaving the area, but my mind is on a one-way ticket to Bumfuck, Egypt.

Bon voyage, see ya never!

Punching in the code on our front door with more force than necessary, I blow into the house and head straight toward the freezer. Tugging the door open, I reach in and grab my bottle of El Jimador Silver. Closing the door, I turn on my heels and make my way toward the stairs. Chloe slides between me and the stairs.

"Move, Chloe," I bite out.

"No."

"Just give her some fucking space," Cody snaps.

Both of them have a stare-off that I'm not even touching on right now. She drops her arm from the railing and I blow past her, taking the steps two at a time. Footsteps pound the stairs behind me.

I don't stop until I'm flinging my body onto my bed, the bottle of tequila still in my hand. Cody sits down next to me, reaching over me to grab the bottle. My eyes shoot to him. If he's going to tell me I'm not drinking, he's got another thing coming.

"Relax, you're not drinking alone. Now give me the damn bottle." He wiggles the fingers on his outstretched hand. "Has anyone ever told you that you have a fucked-up way of dealing with shit?"

I hand him the bottle and watch as he unscrews the cap.

"No, because I'm great at dealing with hard stuff."

The bottle pauses near his lips, and he shakes his head.

"Not what I was talking about," he mutters. "See fucked up."

Cody only takes one pull from the bottle, grimacing, before handing it back to me. He sits there and watches me take swig after swig, not saying a word.

I know where I should be right now. I should be sitting in a waiting room, making sure my boyfriend is okay. But that's too déjà vu for me. It wasn't that long ago that I was sitting in a waiting room, my brother and boyfriend in surgery. I can't go through that again. The waiting. The unknown. The turmoil.

Instead, I'm cowering in my room like the asshole I am. But I can't sit and wait for bad news again.

I guess I haven't changed like I thought I had. Same Brynn. Same selfish person. Same situation.

Sometime later I wake up, even though I don't remember falling asleep. Darkness has settled over the city, much like it has me. My clothes are still on, but my shoes are off, and I'm lying on top of my covers. Dragging my arms behind me, I push up off my bed and sit up. I instantly regret the decision.

Shit, how much tequila did I drink?

One of my hands finds my forehead as I begin rubbing, the hangover already settling in. I drop my head forward, resting it against my palm while my arm rests against my bent knee. Reaching with my other hand, I search for my phone. It's plugged in, charging, on my nightstand.

Oh, Cody Jacobs, you are the best.

The screen is way too bright, and my eyes squeeze shut immediately. Slowly, I force myself to open them as my pupils get used to the brightness. Thirty-seven text messages and twenty-two missed calls. Sighing, I place my phone back down on the table.

Right now, I'm forever grateful to the me from this morning who prepared my nightstand with all the post-drinking essentials. A water bottle, electrolyte packet, and migraine medicine sit on my nightstand. Little did I know that my hangover would be from drinking myself stupid instead of celebrating. I don't even know if the team won or not. Hell, I don't even know if my boyfriend is okay.

Groaning, I collapse backward, my head finding my pillow. Lifting my legs up, I reach down and drag the covers up over me before drifting off to sleep again.

CHAPTER 39
QUINTON

THE SOUND OF BEEPING wakes me. The scent of antiseptic consumes my nostrils.

Fuck me, my head hurts.

My eyes refuse to open, but I'm alert enough to know that I'm lying in a hospital bed after one of the worst hits I've ever received in my entire football career. The stupid dickhead knew what he was doing.

I know that my leap started way before he even thought about tackling me. I remember the impact, the awful cracking sound that the helmet-to-helmet collision made, and the pain. Oh god, the pain was instant. I thought my head was going to explode. But it didn't. I'm alive. Even without opening my eyes, I know I'm alive. There's no way Heaven would have the sound of beeping and this pungent stench. Clean or not, antiseptic should smell a helluva lot better than this.

Plus, I picture Heaven would welcome you with a moist towelette to clean off your past life. Maybe even some leis and a tropical drink. It'd be like arriving in Hawaii. Yeah, the afterlife would be like a tropical oasis. And this hard bed and this scratchy blanket are not it.

Voices pull me from my thoughts of Heaven. They're hushed, but there's a harsh tone to them.

"I told you, Howard," I hear my mom say.

"I'm sure there's a reason. Calm down," Dad says, annoyance flashing through his words.

They sound close, but not next to me. Maybe by the doorway.

"Her reason is that her meal ticket got hurt and she bailed. I told him. I told you all that she's just a gold-digging ho who wants our money."

"Enough, Abigail. She's from a wealthy family. She doesn't need Quinton to pay her bills."

"Oh, please. Her family left her, so she's clutching on to the first person who has shown her any promise of fortune. It's been three days and she hasn't shown up yet."

I hear Dad sigh, but I don't have the energy to open my eyes. "What's your problem with her? She's the first girl who has ever caught your son's eyes for longer than a hook-up, and you have never given her the time of day. Instead, you're spewing hatred every time you're around her."

Mom's voice goes icy. A shiver erupts across my skin. It feels like we have just been transported to the Arctic.

"And why do you constantly defend her? You got eyes on her? She remind you of all the hoes lining the sidewalks, waiting for you to give them the okay to crawl into your bed? All the hoes who you slept with while I was home raising your boys. I gave up my career to be your wife and raise your kids, and what'd you give us? A roof over our heads was all the payment we got while you slept with every girl with a pulse," she grits out.

Holy shit, holy shit. Mom just dropped some major truth bombs. Eyes, stay shut. I repeat, eyes stay shut.

"That was ten years ago, Abigail," Dad bites out, his voice getting closer. "We worked through our shit, went to counseling, I gave it all up too."

And then silence stretches through the room. A noise comes from beside me—magazine pages turning and Dad sighing.

Do I wake up now? Has it been enough time to act like I didn't just hear all of that? I've been out for three days? And what does she mean "she hasn't stopped by?" Is Brynn okay?

I need answers.

I will myself to open my eyes. They try to fight me at first, but slowly, they begin to flutter open. Once I open them, I blink a few more times, trying to get them adjusted to this bright light. Who puts lights as bright as the damn sun inside hospital rooms?

"P-pops," I rasp out, my gaze finding him sitting in a chair next to my bed, thumbing through an issue of *Sports Illustrated*.

He pauses, not moving. His gaze seeing my open eyes, he lets out a breath of air. "Son." His eyes fill with unshed tears. "It's damn good to see your eyes open."

My mouth is as dry as the Sahara. I try to wet my lips, but it only makes things worse. Taking the hint, Dad stands up and grabs the pitcher of water sitting next to the bed. He pours a cup before bringing it to my lips.

"Slow," he instructs.

I resist the urge to gulp down the cup of lukewarm water.

"What happened?" I croak, my voice raspy.

"A lot has happened, son." He chuckles, but it isn't full of humor, it's almost like a sad chuckle. "You were blindsided by an illegal hit. The safety was kicked out for targeting, but somehow you held on to the damn ball and scored the touchdown." He pauses, beaming down at me with a proud smile before he continues. "The extra point was good, tying the game. Lafayette miffed the kickoff. We recovered. Coach made some smart decisions—I'm talking shit you don't see until the pros. And Grant caught the game-winner."

"Hell yeah, he did," I respond, not the least bit surprised.

Coach Campbell is a helluva coach. I don't know why he's still coaching college and not in the NFL yet. Dad's and my moment is interrupted when Mom comes through the door. She stops dead in her tracks, mouth gaping open.

"Quinton," she says my name, running toward me. "Oh, my baby. It's so good to see those chocolate-brown eyes."

"Hi, Ma," I grit out. Her voice is loud, and my head is killing me. She releases me from her hold, but her hand finds my arm.

Dad stands from his chair. "I'm going to grab the doctor," he says, head down, avoiding eye contact with us.

Mom just stands there staring at me, tears welling in her eyes. It's hard for me to look at her though. I'm trying hard to play dumb about the conversation that they don't know I overheard. A few minutes later, Dad comes in with an older gentleman—I'm assuming he's the doctor—and our team doctor Dr. Anderson.

"Quinton, I'm Dr. Patel. How's the pain, on a scale of one to ten?" he asks, scanning over my chart.

"A seven," I answer. I don't know. I hate when doctors ask you to rate your pain. There isn't a definition for each number. I'm more than a little uncomfortable.

"Seven is certainly to be expected with a head injury like the one you sustained. You suffered a moderate concussion, but we have no reason to believe there are any other brain-related injuries," he adds.

Thank fuck it isn't anything severe. I can deal with a concussion. What I can't deal with is a brain injury that's going to keep me from playing.

"What about football?" I ask, bouncing my eyes from Dr. Patel to Dr. Anderson.

Dr. Anderson takes over the conversation, resting the chart he's holding in front of him. "You won't be able to play in the conference title game—"

My body immediately reacts to his statement, trying to sit up higher in the bed.

He raises a hand, stopping me from speaking.

"But as long as things go well over the next week, and given we win on Saturday—"

"Which we will," I mutter.

Dr. Anderson gives me a small grin before continuing. "And *when* we win, we don't see any reason why you won't play in the playoff game."

A relieved breath escapes my lips.

"We'll let you get some more rest," Dr. Patel states, turning to leave.

"Wait," I add before the doctors have a chance to leave the room. All eyes look at me. "Why'd it take me so long to wake up?"

"Your body needed the rest," Dr. Patel answers. "Your body was just exhausted, so it let your mind rest a little longer. There were times you'd stir and we thought you were awake, but your eyes never opened. We monitored you closely, and no red flags popped up."

Nodding my head, I accept the doctor's answer. The two men leave the room, leaving me with just my parents, who are avoiding each other, staring only at me.

"I-I I'm going to get some rest."

"You do that, son. We'll be back later to check on you."

They both stand, Mom kisses my forehead and Dad squeezes my arm.

And with that, my eyes drift shut again. The last thing I see is my parents leaving the room. But it's the last thought that keeps me from drifting into a deep sleep: where's Brynn?

It's not long, or at least I don't think it's long before I'm stirred from sleep. A sense of someone watching me washes over me, and all I can think is that Brynn is here. Eyes slamming open, I see the faces of some of my teammates, my best friends, my brothers. Grant, Tyler, and JP are sitting in chairs, scrolling on their phones.

"Don't you fuckers have a game to get ready for?"

Heads snap to me.

"Oh shit, he is awake," comes from Tyler.

Then JP is chiming in with his own comment. "We missed your ugly mug too much."

We all chuckle.

"Pshh, you know I'm fly as fuck."

"How bad is that brain of yours?" Grant jokes back. And we all laugh before a somber moment stretches over us. "Dude, don't pull that shit again," he adds.

The severity cloaks the room.

"It's not my fault that dickhead hit me illegally."

"Run faster," JP quips, and I toss up my middle finger.

"Man, fuck y'all," I add before finding Grant. "What's going on with Brynn?"

All three guys look at each other, no one wanting to answer. Staring at them, I just wait.

It's Grant who pipes up first. I knew he'd be the one to tell me. "She kind of just shut down. We've all been trying to check in on her, but she's a mess."

I think back to my time on the field, after I got hit. I'm trying to piece everything together. I remember being semi-alert. I could hear the trainers talking to me, both Grant and Tyler telling me, "you've got this," but then it just gets kind of fuzzy after that.

"Di-did I give a thumb's up?"

Grant just shakes his head.

Fuck.

She had to have been scared shitless, and I know seeing me get hit like that would've triggered her past trauma she's been working so hard to heal. I mean, we just told each other we loved one another, even though I've been loving her from afar for years.

"Q, I've never seen her like this," JP whispers.

Head snapping up, my eyes bore into him, but he just looks as worried as I'm feeling. "Explain."

"Quiet, reserved, lost in her head. Cody's picked her up from the bar two nights in a row, blacked out in a booth," JP explains.

"Sunday night, I found her in their backyard, sprawled out on her back in the grass, smoking a bowl with a bottle of tequila half drank next to her," Grant adds.

"And I passed her on campus yesterday. Her hair was in a mess on top of her head with bloodshot eyes and dark circles lining her face. Dude, she was in the baggiest pair of sweatpants and sweatshirt I've ever seen on her. I don't know how she managed to keep them up," Tyler says, eyes trained on his folded hands in his lap.

I did this to her.

And my mom's haunting words come rushing back to me. *"Seems everyone you love dies."*

The color drains from my face as my eyes slide over to find Grant's. He must see what I'm feeling, because he reaches beside him to grab the wastebasket just as a bout of nausea hits me. Grabbing the wastebasket, I empty whatever is in my stomach.

"We're watching her, Q. We're trying to bring her back to herself. She might think she's alone, but she's got us," Tyler says, squeezing my leg.

Our conversation is interrupted when Coach Campbell comes striding into our room. He sees me holding the wastebasket.

"Need me to get a nurse?"

I just shake my head. He nods and makes his way over to the bed.

I don't even listen to what he's saying. All I can think about is getting out of the goddamn hospital and finding my girl.

CHAPTER 40
Brynn

IT'S BEEN FOUR DAYS. Four excruciatingly long days since Quinton went into the hospital. *'Seems everyone you love dies'* plays over and over in my head. The only way I can get the words out of my head is when I'm high or drunk. When I'm faded, I can pretend that Quinton's right beside me, drifting through the clouds. But as soon as that high wears off, I'm snapped back to a reality where I don't know if my boyfriend is going to make it. I don't know if I've killed another person who I love. So instead of staying with those thoughts, I reach for the bottle of tequila.

Classes drag on, and I barely make it through each day. As soon as class ends and I'm outside, I reach inside my purse and pull my vape pen to my lips to chase that high again. Everyone keeps checking on me, and it feels suffocating. I'm going through the motions. Wake and bake, Uber to class, smoke, come home, lay in the grass, smoke and drink, pass out, and repeat. I'm a zombie, but a life without Quinton is a life I don't want to be a part of.

I'm lying in the grass, cold pizza next to me. I've finished my bowl, and I'm just chilling here looking at the sky. Tears stream silently from my eyes.

I see him.

See his light-brown skin, eyes that want to drink me in, and a dazzling smile that always makes me happy. We're running through the sky, running away from reality. It's just the two of us, running hand in hand. He pulls my arm, and I spin into him. Gripping my face, he's just about to kiss me when dirty-blonde hair and crisp, moss-green eyes stare back at me.

I see his lips moving, but I can't make out what they're saying. It's not until I'm being flung over his shoulders and carried into my house that I realize it's Grant Campbell.

"Jesus, Brynn. You're a fucking mess."

He doesn't stop once we're inside. No, he continues to carry me up the stairs and into my bedroom. Pushing my bathroom door open with his foot, he carries me until he's dropping me into my shower.

"Grant, what the fu—" I start, stopping as he reaches beside me and turns the nozzle. Cold water hits my fully dressed body, and I gasp from the shock of it. "What the fuck?!" I scream, scratching at his forearm, the one that was holding me under the water spray.

"Dammit, Grant. That's not what we talked about," Cody says, walking through the open bathroom door.

Grant doesn't let go of me, he just lets the water beat down on me while his other hand slowly turns the water toward the warmer setting.

"I don't give a shit. I'm sick and tired of her pity party. Quinton's awake and asking for his girlfriend."

"Quinton's awake," I gasp out.

Grant's icy stare finds mine, and his expressionless face stares down at me. He's pissed. He might not be showing it, but I know him well enough to know that he's so far past pissed right now.

"Yeah, Brynn," he grits out. "Quinton's awake, and you'd fucking know that if you'd quit self-medicating long enough to answer your goddamn phone. We've all been worried about Quinton, and you've gone and put more worry on us by self-destructing. You've been acting like you've already been to the wake when he's been alert for almost a day now."

My body sinks down the tiled wall, collapsing on the shower floor. He's awake.

He's alive. Sobs erupt from my body, my shoulders shakes as I let myself finally feel. Cody's pushing Grant aside, climbing into the shower next to me.

"A little fucking harsh, man," Cody grits out, wrapping his arms around me.

"She needed to hear it," is the only response Grant gives Cody. In the next instant, he's dropping into a squat, reaching out to grip my chin, forcing my eyes to his. "Get cleaned up. Get sober. And be ready by eight o'clock tomorrow morning for me to pick you up. I'm taking you to see Quinton."

I just nod.

Sometime after Cody leaves, I climb into bed after spending way too long in the shower scrubbing my body of all the guilt and idiocy. I pull my phone from where I stashed it in my nightstand drawer and power it on. So many text messages light up my screen. I don't have the energy to open them all, but I stop on a few.

> **Cody: Answer your phone!**

> **Cody: Heard from Grant. Quinton's awake! Pick up!**

> **Grant: He's awake and asking for you.**

> **JP: Girl don't make me come track you down. Come see our boy!**

But it's the last one that has me pausing, tears start streaming down my face.

> **Quinton: I'm okay, baby. I'm awake. I'm okay.**

> **Quinton: I love you, Wilder**

I fall asleep with my phone clutched to my chest. Tomorrow, I get to see my favorite person again.

Right at eight, the doorbell rings. I knew Grant would be right on time. I mean, he's almost always on time, but today I knew he'd be on time to prove a point. Sighing, I fling open the door.

"I just need two seconds," I greet, reaching down to zip up my brown ankle boots.

With one last look in the mirror, I check out my outfit—denim shortalls with a multicolored pink plaid shirt underneath and my brown suede ankle boots. It's cute and casual, making it look like I've got my shit together when, in fact, I'm severely hungover. My hands keep finding my hair, tousling the long blonde strands. My hands keep shaking, I'm so nervous.

"Brynn. Brynn," Grant says, trying to get my attention.

My eyes find him in the mirror.

"You look fine. Quinton is going to be happy to see you. Now let's go."

Nodding my head in acknowledgment, I grab my keys and sunnies from the bowl on the table. I grab my purse as we head out the door.

The drive to the hospital is quiet. It's awkward, neither one of us know what to say to the other after last night. I'm a little pissed at the way that Grant showed up and went all caveman. The only time I like for a man to go all caveman is when he's about to worship my body, not throw my ass in a fucking freezing cold shower.

While I'm pissed at him, a part of me is glad that he showed up to knock some sense into me. Usually, it's Quinton, but that just shows how good a friend Grant is. He risked pissing me off to get me to his best friend.

"Thank you," I finally say, still not looking at Grant.

He grunts. And we're back to awkward silence. "I'm sorry for being a dick about it," he finally says as he pulls us into the hospital. Grant doesn't find a parking spot but follows the driveway toward the main entrance, stopping under the overhang.

"You're not coming in?" I ask, finally looking at him.

"Nah, you two need a minute."

With a small, tight smile, I open my door and step out.

After speaking with the receptionist in the lobby, I'm told Quinton's room is on the tenth floor, room 1004. I make my way to the elevator and wait for the doors to open. When they do, I step inside, and as the doors close, anxiety swells in my stomach. A bell chimes when I reach the tenth floor, and I step out once the doors open.

The floor is buzzing with nurses doing their morning checks. There's a cart with trays of food that's being delivered to each room. Slowly, I make my way to room 1004. A guy with a tray in his hand is about to knock on the door.

"Excuse me," I say before he has a chance to know. The guy turns his head to me. "Do you mind if I take the tray in? He's my boyfriend," I supply when he looks at me with a questioning look.

He nods his head before handing me the tray. I give a light knock before stepping inside. Sunlight streaming in from the cracked blinds is the only light illuminating the room. Quinton's lying in his bed, head toward the TV where I hear the NFL Network's *Good Morning Football* coming from the speakers. He hasn't noticed me yet, so I take a moment to take in the room. Q is in a medium-size room. There's a small couch, chairs, and a counter with a sink, and his bed is in the middle. Tubes and wires hang all around him with a monitor next to his bed.

Slowly, I creep toward his bed trying like hell not to drop his tray, my hands shaking like crazy. "Morning, handsome," I say as my way of greeting, pausing beside his bed.

His head whips in my direction, shock filling his face. "Brynn?" he questions, searching me from head to toe. "Damn, baby, I missed you. Get over here."

I don't hesitate, I drop the tray onto his rolling table and rush him. His arms open, and without hesitation, I dive into them, being careful not to wrestle him too much.

As soon as I feel his arms close around my body, I can't keep the tears at bay. I know as soon as he feels the sobs rack my body because he's pulling me in tighter.

"I'm so sorry I wasn't here," I cry into his chest.

Shushing me, he starts consoling me. "You're here now, and that's all that matters."

Looking up at him, I search his face for any hint of anger or resentment, but all I see staring back at me is love.

"I love you so much," I say on a sob.

"I love you too, baby," he answers, lips finding mine. "Are you okay?" Quinton asks when he finally brings himself to pull away from my lips.

"Am I okay? Quinton, you're the one I should be asking that to."

"I'm fine," he answers. "A little banged up with a moderate concussion, but I'll be back on the field in no time."

Narrowing my eyes, I examine his face for any hint he's not telling the truth. And of course, there isn't one.

"But I'm more worried about you. Uhh, the guys might've filled me in on how you've been this week."

"Traitors," I say with a sigh. "But I'm fine. Really. I might've been in my head, like, really bad, over the last few days. I may have been suppressing those feelings with whatever I could get my hands on, but I'm fine now. I'm fine because you're okay." Lowering my head onto Q's chest, I soak in his warmth before whispering the last part. "And my love didn't kill you either."

"Look at me," he demands, but I don't move. "Dammit, Brynn, look at me," he demands again, only this time he brings his hand under my chin and tips it up. Umber eyes bore into me, and I swear he is imprinting himself into my soul. "Your love is not toxic. Your love will never kill me. And I'm tired of you feeling that way."

"How can I not feel that way when your own mother thinks so," I scoff. "And then we finally say 'I love you,' and then *bam*, down you go. How am I not supposed to feel like my love is cursed?"

"Your love is a goddamn gift, and anyone who is blessed to feel your love is the luckiest son-of-a-bitch in the world. And as for my mother, it's not a 'you' thing, it's a 'her' thing."

"Oh yeah, I'm so sure about that."

"Would you stop being so fucking stubborn? Christ, woman." I can't help the chuckle that escapes. I missed this. I missed the combative conversations that get both of us fired up. And then the next thing I know, we're both fighting with our bodies and not our words.

"Are you thinking about me ravishing you right now? Is that why that beautiful golden skin I love so much is tinged pink?"

I just nod. He groans, reaching down to bring my face to meet his lips. But we don't get too far before a knock interrupts us as someone is opening the door.

"Ah, I'm interrupting," an older Indian man says. "I'm Dr. Patel. You must be the girlfriend?"

"Yes, I'm the girlfriend," I answer the doctor before sliding off the bed and adjusting my overalls.

"Good news, Mr. Boyd. You can go home today," Dr. Patel announced.

Quinton finds my hand and gives it a squeeze. "It's about damn time, Doc. I've got a lot of time to make up with my girl," Quinton replies as a blush coats my skin.

A chill spreads down my entire body before landing at my core. And I swear my pussy lights up like fireworks on the Fourth of July.

CHAPTER 41
QUINTON

FOUR WEEKS HAVE GONE by. Our semester ended, we won the conference championship game easily, and Brynn and I have been inseparable.

It took a little while to get back to normal after I was released from the hospital. She was in a vulnerable state, and I was focusing on my recovery. Her ghosting everyone, especially me, really hit me.

I love her. There's never been any denying that, but there's always that worry in the back of my mind that she's just going to up and leave because she's scared something is going to happen. But we're working on ourselves in the midst of everything else we have going on.

We're on Christmas break, and I'm still insanely busy with football, especially since we've got playoffs approaching. Brynn is doing an apprenticeship at a local youth counseling program. It's been exciting to come home after our long days and watch her body light up when she tells me about her day. She hears a lot of bad things that happen to kids, but seeing her get excited to help kids who are struggling is pretty remarkable. There are days, though, when she'll come home and crash into my arms, letting tears fall from some of the stories she hears.

I wish there would've been someone in Brynn's corner when she lost Bryce and Asher, encouraging her to get help. But I think helping others is helping her heal.

Not only is she doing her apprenticeship, but she's been hanging out with Kari and Tanner, the mom and son duo from the pep rally. She spends time with them, helping Tanner work through his grief. After Brynn sent Kari that photo, the two of them continued their conversation, hitting it off. It's been really good for Brynn too. She's able to work through some more of her shit while helping Tanner.

Christmas is tomorrow, and this year, we decided that we would spend it with just the two of us. Mom was pretty pissed when I told her. It led to an even bigger conversation, one that I wasn't going to get into with her. But it came down to either she backed off and accepted that Brynn was going to be the girl that I married, or she risked losing me forever.

The ultimatum pissed her off, and we haven't spoken in almost two weeks. She'll either come around or she won't, but it's time that I start living for me and not being influenced by her, or my dad's decisions.

"Hey babe," Brynn says from the doorway of my room.

Turning, I find her a bright, chaotic mess. I could live off her beaming smile, never needing to see the sun again. She's my sunshine, the light on my darkest days, the little spark that brings me a hit of serotonin. Her arms are full of bags—an overnight bag, shopping bags with wrapped gifts spilling out of them, and grocery bags. Tendrils spill from where her hair is gathered in a large clip. Her face is flushed as her chest heaves. She takes my breath away.

"What's all this?" I ask, standing and striding toward her, reaching out to take some of the bags from her.

Shrugging, she lets me take her overnight bag. "Just some stuff to get us through the weekend." She carries the rest of the bags over to my bed, dropping them when she gets close enough. "Holy shit, that was heavy."

"You could've called me," I suggest. "Or you could've taken two trips?"

"Two trips are for pussies," she states, turning her back to the bed before collapsing onto my mattress.

Chuckling, I come up to lean over her. And then collapse on top of her, arms catching my weight before crushing her. Finding her mouth, I give her a searing kiss. "Missed you," I say, pulling back. "Merry Christmas Eve." Planting one more quick kiss on her lips, I pop up.

"Merry Christmas Eve," she replies, sitting up on her elbows, watching me riffle through my drawers.

I need to change out of my sweats and into something a little nicer. Tonight, we are celebrating with some of our friends.

Coach gave us Thursday through Sunday off for Christmas. Since our season is extending—thank God—he wanted to make sure everyone had plenty of time to celebrate Christmas with their families. But come Monday, all of our asses better be at the training facility by five a.m. ready to get focused. Our first playoff game is on New Year's Eve in Atlanta, with the National Championship game being in Arizona nine days later.

Grabbing a pair of underwear, I head into the bathroom for a quick shower. Pausing at the doorway, I glance back to a sprawled-out Brynn, eyes closed. She looks sexy as fuck all laid out for my eyes to wander. Dressed in tight brown plaid trousers and a cropped sweater, I can't help but stare at the skin that's exposed at her waist from her arms stretched over her head.

"Wanna join?" I ask.

"Maybe later," she replies, eyes never opening.

Thirty minutes later, we make our way downstairs. Our cleaning lady came yesterday. She must've been feeling a little festive because she added some Christmas flare to our dining table. The guys and I don't decorate for Christmas. I mean, we're guys. In college. And the house is always hosting a party. Shit would just get destroyed.

Xavier and JP are sprawled on the couch playing Madden. JP glances at the two of us, a whistle leaving his lips. "Damn, you two look spiffy."

"Thanks, Jer. You don't clean up so badly either," Brynn says, heading into the kitchen to check on the food.

I called Hog Heaven Barbecue and had our dinner catered. Less stress for everyone means more people will come. And who can turn down barbecue? I don't follow her, instead I make my way over to one of the plastic fold-out chairs we set up.

The doorbell rings before being pushed open. Grant walks in, but he's not alone. Stepping aside, a woman walks in. She's tall, only a few inches shorter than Grant and he's six-one with a toned, athletic body which she shows off in a skintight, V-neck, burnt-orange sweater dress. Long brownish hair is pulled up in a ponytail.

"Goddamn, who's your friend?" JP asks.

Grant's eyes close into slits as he looks at JP. If looks could kill, JP would be six feet under. "My sister," he answers, making his way farther into the house.

"Addy, these are the guys." Grant introduces the room, pointing each one of us out. "Quinton. His brother, Xavier. JP. And I'm sure Brynn's around here somewhere. She's Q's girl." Pausing, he stares at us. "This is Addy. She goes to Arizona. *Don't* even try anything. Oh, and she has a boyfriend."

"'Sup, Addy," Xav says, turning to go back to the game.

"Hey there," she replies.

"Brynn's in the kitchen." I point Addy in the direction of the kitchen.

She nods her head in appreciation before walking away.

Grant makes his way over to where I'm sitting. "Your sister's home?"

Sighing, he drops into a chair next to me, running his hand down his face. "Yeah, she got in last night."

"I bet Coach is happy to have her home."

"Something's off with her, I just don't know what it is yet. She just seems…I don't know, different." Both of us look up, the sound of laughter spilling from the kitchen.

"Brynn will get her out of whatever funk she's in."

"Yeah, maybe," he says, exasperated. Grant and his sister are close. They're two years apart. Last year he was really bummed that she wasn't coming to CTU. Instead, she chose to go to Arizona, nine hundred miles away.

The front door flies opens and in walks Riggsby. He's carrying a bottle of tequila in one hand, a bouquet of flowers in the other, and a bag from a local bakery on his arm.

"Hey guys." He nods toward the room while he kicks the front door shut behind him before walking toward the kitchen.

"Whatcha got there, Riggs?" Grant asks, curiosity written all over our faces.

He pauses right before he gets into the kitchen. "Got Brynn tequila and flowers for hosting and cheesecake from my favorite place for all of us," he says, shrugging like it was no big deal.

"Wait, you got my girl flowers? I'm the one who's hosting," I chime in.

"Correction, we are hosting," adds JP, pointing to Xavier, me, and himself.

"Whatever. We all know it was Brynn's idea." And with that, he turns into the kitchen.

Dinner is amazing. There's a reason why Hog Heaven is my favorite. The meat just melts in your mouth. After dinner, we all break out the cards and start playing drinking games.

Before she gets too drunk, Brynn goes upstairs and carries down one of the giant bags that she had brought up there earlier in the day. She passes out small gifts to everyone, except Addy since she didn't know Addy would be coming. She apologized over and over before running upstairs and finding an unused gift card for Starbucks. Addy kept assuring her that it was okay, but Brynn wouldn't have it. She said it was either that or one of the gifts she got me, with a wink, she told Addy should choose carefully.

Brynn enjoyed her bottle of tequila, almost polishing off the bottle, but she did have help with it. Addy and Brynn hit it off just like I knew they would. Chloe joined the night a little later. The three girls drank and danced while us guys played more drinking card games.

The evening wrapped up a little after eleven, and everyone headed home before Christmas. Brynn and I went up to our room, I mean, my room, hell, who am I kidding? It's ours. She has so much shit in here that it's like she's moved in.

Before she let me get ready for bed, Brynn walked over to another large bag and pulled out two small bags—one for me and one for her. Unwrapping the gift, I pulled out a pair of Santa-themed boxers with white fur trim. I loved them.

Brynn ran into the bathroom with her bag. And when she emerged, my mouth fell open. There stood Brynn in a red-laced thong and a satin bow wrapped around her breasts. She looked fucking delectable.

I peeled that bow from her chest and spent hours worshipping her body before both of us rolled over in a heap of satisfaction.

CHAPTER 42
Brynn

THE FLIGHT TO ARIZONA was full of Eagles, not the real bird kind but the CTU kind.

That's right, baby! The Central Texas Eagles have landed in Arizona for the National *fucking* Championship!

Twenty-twenty-three started with a bang. CTU played the Eastern Carolina Coyotes for the late-night playoff game. It was a nail-biter. Eastern Carolina came out looking to take us down. They tried hard and almost did, but we were just that much better. Just like in the Lafayette game, Quinton leaped across the goal line for a game-winning touchdown.

Watching him leap across that white line gave me major PTSD flashbacks, but Damien was there beside me keeping me calm. After the debacle of Thanksgiving 2022, Damien and Quinton have really been working on mending their broken relationship, which means I've spent a lot more time with him.

The two of us have definitely gotten closer and I'm glad he flew out to Arizona with me. Chloe wasn't able to make it to the game. She needed the hours at her job. I tried to buy her a ticket, but she wouldn't have it. Macy has been MIA since moving in with Gregg. She and I still text, but our friendship isn't the same. I understand and accept it. At the end of the day, we know that we're always there for each other.

When I was debating on going solo, Damien said he'd fly with me. I had no reason to be nervous about flying alone since our whole flight was Eagles fans. The Pilot even came across the speakers as we got close to Arizona and started the Eagles chant. Everyone on the plane was chanting along. It was freaking awesome.

The two of us are heading to baggage claim before heading to the hotel to meet the team. The team arrived on Saturday, but Damien and I decided to fly in today. The game is tomorrow night, Monday night prime time.

"E-A-G," Damien yells, hand cupping my mouth.

My head whips in his direction, my mouth falling open. Straight and narrow, Dr. Boyd is starting a chant in the middle of Tuscan International.

"L-E-S!" Erupts around us.

I can't help the laugh that escapes me. The airport is lit. And as we grab our bags and head toward the exit, it's getting even crazier.

Party buses, town cars, shuttles, and Ubers line the street. We follow a crowd toward one of the party buses. A girl bumps my shoulder pushing me into Damien. She spins around on her heels.

"Sor—" she starts before her eyes bug out. "Brynn!"

"Savannah!" I shout back as she flings her arms around me. Savannah and I have gotten closer over the last couple of weeks. *Now that I've put a name to her face.* We spend a lot of time together at the library studying and when we aren't studying, she joins me at a party. I never would've thought that this preppy Kappa Delta would love to party as much as I do. "You guys have a ride?"

"Just going to grab a shuttle," I answer, pointing over my shoulder.

"Nonsense, c'mon," she says, sliding her arm in the crook of mine. Savannah leads us over to a blacked-out party bus. "This will be way more fun than a shuttle," she says.

The driver is standing near the door with the bottom compartments open. We hand him our bags, following Savannah up the stairs. The bus is spectacular. Blue LED lights trace the outline of the bus, two stripper poles are in the middle of the bus, gray leather seats are placed along the perimeter, and the bus is packed with students from CTU. I recognize a few faces and we greet each other as I follow Sav toward the middle.

Glancing over at Damien, I see that he's making himself right at home. Somehow he managed to get a beer in his hand and a girl on his lap. These Boyd brothers. They're something else.

The thirty-minute drive is an absolute blast, and I'm bummed when we pull into the parking lot of the hotel. Savannah and I make plans to meet up tomorrow before the game.

"Hey, I, um, I'm going to go back to her room for a bit," Damien whispers in my ear, pointing toward a girl waiting for him at the bottom of the steps. "You good?"

"I'm good. Have fun," I reply before leaning closer. "Need any condoms?"

"I'm good, thanks," he replies with a smirk. And then he's standing and following his new friend into the hotel.

Gathering my bag, I wheel it inside the hotel finding the concierge desk.

"Welcome to the Hilton, checking in?" the concierge asks.

"Yes, the room is under Brynn Wilder." Answering her, I scan the lobby.

It's a good mix of Eagles and Commanders fans. Excitement fills my veins, but I can't help the nerves that are settling, especially now that I'm in Arizona. Tomorrow is just going to be worse. I might have to find a local dispensary and get some gummies to get me through.

"Here's your key, Miss Wilder. You're on the eleventh floor, room 11122. Enjoy your stay." Taking the key, I grab my suitcase and head to the top floor.

Sliding my keycard against the magnetic strip, the green lights flash, unlocking my door. Wheeling my bag inside, I place my card on the dresser and grab a bottle of water before heading straight toward the window to open the blinds. Reaching for the drapes, I fling them open letting the Arizona sunlight shine in. And there she is. State Farm Stadium is just a few blocks over. I stand there, staring at the arena and throwing up a silent prayer for Quinton.

Turning around, I start to head toward the bed. "Ho-ly *fucking* shit!" I scream, hands trembling as I bring them to my chest. "You scared the shit out of me, you jackass!" I toss the bottle of water at Quinton who was lounging on the bed. "What the hell are you doing in here?"

"Hey, baby, nice to see you too," he retorts. "And this is my room. Or should I say our room?" He waggles his eyebrows up and down at me.

"Coach Campbell approve of this sleeping arrangement?" I ask, hands finding my hips, slowly sauntering toward him.

"He did." Quinton reaches out and grabs my hips, tossing me up and over him. Landing on my back, he immediately rolls on top of me. "I missed you," he says, leaning down for a kiss.

CHAPTER 43
QUINTON

T ODAY IS WHAT DREAMS are made of. I've been dreaming of this day since I was seven years old. That year, my dad was on assignment for ESPN, and he surprised Damien and me—Xav was too young—with tickets to go with him to the National Championship where Loganville and Colorado played. The game was in Dallas, and we had seats in a box. Damien and I had no connection to either team, it was just so cool to be there. Mom didn't go on that trip, instead, a friend of my dad's went with us. She looked out for us while he worked.

When the final seconds on the clock ticked by and confetti filled the air when the buzzer went off, I knew I wanted to be a part of that moment. I wanted to be in the middle of the field with confetti raining down on me, my team's band playing, and holding the National Championship trophy.

And thirteen years later, here I am. Standing in the middle of an NFL stadium getting ready to play in the National Championship. Dreams really do come true when you pour everything you have into achieving them.

Coach has had us up and moving since eight o'clock. He didn't want us lounging around all day and getting tired. The team met in the hotel dining hall for a private breakfast. I wasn't sure if I was going to be able to eat, but thanks to last night's endless rounds of sex, I worked up quite the appetite. Thank God Brynn was on board to let me use her body to work off all my stress.

We fucked until she finally told me that her pussy needed a break. I could ravish that tight body for days on end, but I agreed with her. I didn't want her to be sore for today and it was getting close to lights out. Coach agreed to let me stay with Brynn, but he threatened me with bed checks. My girl likes to sleep naked, and I didn't want to give Coach a reason to come into our room and embarrass him or Brynn.

After breakfast, we rode on buses over to the stadium for a light workout and team meetings to go over any last notes on our game plan. Before we left, Coach had everyone come out and take in the field.

Standing at the fifty-yard line, I take in the field. The stands are empty right now, but it won't be long before sixty thousand people make their way to their seats. Somewhere, a little boy is going to be witnessing a National Championship game tonight and a dream will be planted inside him.

"Feels pretty fucking crazy, doesn't it, man?" Grant asks, flinging his arm around my shoulders.

"I can't believe we're here," I answered.

"Well believe it," Coach Campbell interjects. "Believe it, men," he shouts for the rest of the team to hear it. "Stand here, soak it in for as long as you need for it to sink in. You're here because you've worked your asses off to get here. You've conditioned yourself for this. You've listened to me ride you for months now. And I know you thought I was being a dick, but I cared. I saw that this team, this team right here deserves to be in the National Championship. It's been a helluva season, but we've got one more in us."

"Hell yeah, we do!" I shout back to Coach.

"Now do whatever you need to do. Be dressed and ready on the first-floor conference room. I recommend taking the stairs, there are a lot of us, and the Eagles mob will be waiting at the elevators. We'll gather there, walk through the lobby together, and board the buses."

And with that, Coach Campbell walks toward the exit.

It's not long before the rest of us are making our way back onto the buses.

Brynn is in our room when I get back. She's curled under the covers with her eyes closed. Glancing at the clock, I see it's just after one in the afternoon. Pulling my phone out of my pocket, I set my alarm for an hour before swiping the "sleep" mode. Placing my phone on the nightstand, I toe off my tennis shoes, rip off my shirt, and slide my pants down. In only my boxers, I crawl under the covers bringing Brynn into my body. She startles at first, but then she relaxes into me.

For the next hour, I get some rest. Dreams fill my head, but they're dreams of celebrating our win tonight with my girl in my arms.

The alarm on my phone goes off. Leaning over, I switch it off. Rolling onto my back, I bring my arms above my head and stretch them out. Brynn wakes up too, sleepy eyes finding mine.

"I'm proud of you," she says, her head propped on my chest.

Lowering my arms, I wrap them around her. "Thanks, baby. Couldn't have done it without you by my side."

"Don't," she scoffs.

"I'm serious. You've been my biggest believer, my biggest supporter. You've let me unleash stress onto you when you didn't deserve it, but most importantly, you've always been there for me. When I need to talk or when I need to have some fun to unwind, you've always been in my corner."

She beams up at me. "I love you."

"I love you too. Now go hit the shower, and I'll lay your clothes out," she says, pushing off me, but not before she gives me a quick kiss.

Stepping out of the bathroom, steam escapes with me, but what I find waiting for me takes my breath away. Brynn is standing in the tiny living area with a tray of food in front of her. She's laid out my freshly steamed burgundy suit with the tapered suit pants, a white button down, and a burgundy and white checkered tie. On the floor by the bed are my black dress shoes and on top of the clothes are my black aviators and headphones. As much as I appreciate her getting my outfit together and ordering me food, it's Brynn that has my full attention.

"Is this outfit okay?" she asks.

I just nod my head as I take her in. I feel myself start to grow hard as I take in my girl wearing my jersey. Brynn is standing in front of me wearing my white CTU jersey, the one with BOYD across her back in big block letters. Her long, tan legs on display look even leaner in her favorite white Lucessees. Somehow while I was in the shower, she had time to curl her hair in the long beach waves that she always wears. It's the red lipstick that has me wanting to push her down on her knees and take me in her mouth, painting me with that red.

"Sexy as hell," is my response. "Wait 'til you see what's underneath," she says with a smirk, dropping into her chair and slowly spreading her legs, just wide enough to be a tease, before she crosses one leg over the other.

I drop my towel to the ground, she eyes my erection. *Two can play this game, baby.* Striding over to the bed, I pick up a pair of tight boxer briefs and slowly—very slowly—slide them up my legs, tucking my boner in the waistband. Once my boxers are on and my situation is secured, I take a few steps and sit down behind the tray of food. Both of us eat in silence, my mind focusing back on the game.

When I'm finished eating, I stand up, walk over and give her a kiss on the cheek before slipping on the rest of my clothes.

At five till five, both of us gather up our things—I grab my phone and headphones and Brynn slips on her oversized denim jacket and her clear purse. Stepping aside, I usher her in front of me as we head out of the room. Once she gets in front of me, I notice that the denim jacket is one she had customized. The light denim-washed jacket has a picture of an eagle with its wings spread across the back, it's artistic and cool as fuck, but my name and number are also stretched across her back.

"Cute jacket." I hear from behind us. Brynn doesn't stop walking, just turns her head over her shoulder, giving a smirk and a wink to whoever was talking to her.

"Looks like someone is ready to become Mrs. Boyd," Grant whispers in my ear, stepping in line beside me as we head down the stairs.

I just flash him a wink and his mouth drops.

The crowd is huge. There are so many people lined up just waiting around to cheer us on as we make our way to the bus. Walking by people, I stick my hand out and high five whoever is lucky enough to be within my reach. A high-pitched voice captures my attention. "Quinton! Quinton!" I search the crowd. A small boy with blonde hair and a CTU Eagles jersey is staring up at me.

"Tanner, my man!" I shout, pausing beside the crowd.

"Kick some ass!" Tanner screams, putting his fist up for a bump. His mom is standing next to him, shaking her head at Tanner's use of the curse word.

"Tell your girlfriend thank you for everything," Kari says. Confused at why she would be thanking Brynn, I just nod my head.

"I've gotta catch the bus," I say, pointing at the team that's waiting outside.

"Good luck!" they both shout. I smile down at them, nodding my head as I turn and quickly make my way to the bus.

Piling onto the bus, Coach silences us once we are all seated. It's game time. It's time to focus.

Multicolored confetti rains down from the ceiling, players are dropping to their knees, and I just stand there in shock. I... I can't believe it. I can't believe it's all over. Everything I've worked for since I was seven years old just ended. The long days of pushing my body to its absolute limit, feeling like my body is going to give out if I do one more rep. The mental game of not measuring up. The parties I missed out on because I was hitting the books, working hard to be more than just a jock.

But it was all worth it because I'm a National fucking Champion!

"We fucking did it!" Grant screams, jumping on me, breaking me out of my shock. My arms fly in the air, and I scream until my lungs feel like bursting. "We fucking did it!"

Our entire team is on the field celebrating. Fans are jumping over the railings and rushing from the stands. My head is spinning, looking all over the place for the blondie in my jersey. Before I can find her, she finds me. Leaping into my arms, I catch her with ease.

"You fucking did it, baby! You fucking did it!" Brynn screams into my ear as her arms wrap around me, hands tangle around my neck.

I squeeze her middle, lowering my hand to make sure her jersey hasn't ridden up to expose whatever it is underneath. But knowing Brynn, it's something lacy and tiny. She pulls back just enough to give me a kiss on the lips before she's wiggling in my arms.

I bring her down to her feet before I'm wrapping my arms around her shoulders and pulling her in for another hug. That's when I notice the camera crew approaching us.

"Quinton Boyd, how does it feel to be a National Champion?" the news anchor asks as Brynn steps away from the camera.

"It feels fu—freaking amazing!" I correct my answer quickly. "It's like a dream come true. The whole team has worked so hard this season, our whole goal being the National Title."

"And how are you feeling after that nasty hit in the Lafayette game?"

"I don't even remember it," I joke. "But seriously, I feel great. This win feels great. I'm just, wow, I'm just kinda in shock that we're here."

"National Champions, baby!" JP screams beside me.

"Have fun celebrating." The news anchor walks away.

And celebrate, we do. Tomorrow we are flying home with the National Championship trophy.

CHAPTER 44
Brynn

Three Months Later

Kansas City, MO

APRIL IS UPON US already. Spring is in the air in the Midwest. Birds are chirping and flowers are starting to bloom. Spring is when everything begins to live again. Or at least I like to think of spring as starting over.

Finals wrapped up a few days ago. I couldn't feel more relieved. This semester was tough. Not only was I taking high-level classes, but I was taking eighteen credit hours. I overloaded my schedule this semester, and I'll do it all again in the summer and fall semesters. If everything goes as planned, I'll be graduating in early December. Graduating early means, I'll be able to be reunited with Quinton a semester early.

Speaking of Quinton, it's Draft Weekend. The three-day event kicks off Thursday and runs through Saturday. If all goes as planned, and what Eliza has told us, Quinton will go easily in the first-round top five. The two of us flew into Kansas City late last night. We have all day today to do some sightseeing before Quinton has a few media interviews tomorrow morning. I'll find something to keep me busy, I'm going to have to get used to doing things on my own if I'm going to travel with him when he plays.

"Hey, Wilder." Quinton gets my attention.

I've been watching people while we've been sitting at a patio table outside a little coffee shop.

"Yes?"

"Would you ever get married without getting engaged?" he asks.

My head tips in confusion. "I'm confused."

He chuckles. "There's nothing confusing about it. Would you get married without being engaged? For example, we go on vacation and find the perfect little chapel. The idea of getting married pops into your head, but we aren't engaged. Do we get married right then, or do you wait until we're engaged?"

"Hmm." I bring my black coffee up to my lips for a sip. "I don't need to be engaged first. And I don't even know if I'd want a big wedding."

"Really?"

"Really. I mean, who would give me away? I have no relationship with my dad. My brother's dead. The closest guys to me are you or Cody. And I'd obviously be marrying you."

"Obviously."

"So I guess finding a little chapel would be all that I'd need. No plan, no proposal, just doing it in the heat of the moment."

He nods his head, going back to drinking his coffee, scrolling through the articles on the ESPN app. I just stare at him, puzzled at where his line of thought just came from. While he reads on his phone, I go back to watching people pass by.

My thoughts quickly go back to him asking about weddings. Honestly, I wanted a big wedding. The one where you're surrounded by all your loved ones as you walk down the aisle, in the beautiful white gown. And as your dad hands you over to your groom, a tear slips from his eye because he's giving away his baby girl. Of course, that's what I wanted. Don't all little girls want that?

But when my life changed, so did my dreams. And I'm okay with that. Honestly, I don't want a fancy wedding with the perfect dress. I want the perfect man. And I've already found him. A grin finds my lips as my eyes find him again, but instead of his phone, he's watching me. Tilting my head, I watch him watch me.

"What's on your mind, Q? Nervous for tomorrow?"

He shakes his head. "I'm not nervous about tomorrow. I know whatever is going to happen, will happen and where I'm drafted is where I'm meant to be."

"Wise words coming from you, Mr. Boyd."

"It doesn't matter as long as I have somewhere to play. And with you in the stands watching."

"I'll be by your side."

"I know you will," he says, sliding out of his chair and standing up. He reaches out his hand for me. "Come on."

Drinking my last sip of coffee, I stand up and let Quinton pull me up before grabbing my purse and following him out of the patio fence.

He leads me down the street for a few blocks. Neither one of us say anything, just enjoy the stroll walking hand in hand. Glancing up at him every once in a while, I notice that there's something on his mind. But I don't press him.

After a few more blocks, Quinton stops outside of a spa. He walks around me and heads toward the front door. Opening the door, he gestures for me to walk in.

"What is this?" I ask, looking around at the luxurious spa.

"This is my gift to you. You've worked really hard this semester, you deserve some time to unwind," he says, placing his hand on my lower back, ushering me to the front desk.

"Hello." The hostess speaks in a calm and quiet voice. "What's the reservation under?"

"Quinton Boyd," Q answers, reaching into his pocket for his wallet. He finds his credit card and slides it over to her.

She swipes his card, handing it back to him. "Miss Wilder will be ready in three hours."

My eyes bug out. Three hours. I didn't come all the way to Kansas City to sit in a spa. I came here to explore with my boyfriend. To support him and to soak as much time that we have together before his NFL career takes over.

He senses the tension radiating off my skin. Leaning down, he kisses my forehead. "Relax and trust me. I'll have a car waiting for you at noon." And with that, he turns and walks away, leaving me alone with the hostess.

"Right this way, miss." She ushers me to the right side of the lobby. I follow her and she instructs me to go into a dark room, strip off all my clothes, and lie down on the bed with the blanket on top of me. I'm about to have an hour-long massage before a facial, manicure, makeup application, and a blowout.

I can't stay mad at him for too long. This has been the best three hours of my life. Walking out to the waiting town car my body feels light as a feather and there's a calmness around me. All of the stress from the last couple of months has melted off me.

The driver takes me back to the hotel. He opens the door for me, I make my way to the hotel room. I scan the keycard and push the door open, my shoulders slumping as I'm met with an empty room. The only noise is alternative music coming from the television. Inhaling a deep breath, I spot a gift box on the bed. It's a white box with a blue bow attached. There's a note attached to the ribbon. Lowering my purse to the bed, I sit next to the box staring at it. This day has been the strangest since coffee this morning. Picking up the note, I spot familiar handwriting.

Wilder,

I'm living out all my dreams this weekend. There's just one more thing I need to do to make them all come true. Open the box, put what's in it on, and meet me downstairs in an hour.

Love Always,

Q

Slipping the ribbon off the box, I slowly open the lid. A gasp leaves my lips, and I drop the note to the floor.

What does Quinton have in mind?

CHAPTER 45
QUINTON

"AND WITH THE THIRD pick of the 2023 NFL draft, the Colorado Colts select Quinton Boyd, running back, Central Texas," the NFL Commissioner announces.

Brynn and I watch on the TV from the waiting room inside Union Station as my name is called. Tears spring into my eyes, and I grasp for Brynn immediately. She turns, hugging me and bringing her hand to my face and a grin spreads from ear to ear. Bending down, I give her a quick kiss before I'm ushered down a hall toward the stage.

Brynn's the only one here for me, aside from Eliza, on this big day, and I wouldn't have it any other day. She's the only one who has supported me my entire college career. She's encouraged me to do what I felt. On my darkest days, she has been the light at the end of the tunnel. It was her cheering me on, encouraging me and motivating me that helped land me here. Do I wish my parents were here? Of course. But for the past year, they've done nothing but push their agenda on me. At the end of the day, they wanted what would look best for them, not what was best for me. The only one I wanted here was Brynn.

The camera stays on me my entire journey. I keep my head down, but I can't get the grin off my face. I did it. Me. Not anyone else. I secured a first-round draft pick, and it was in the top five. Hell, it was number three when I was expecting a number five pick. Elated doesn't even begin to describe how happy I feel.

I'm almost to the end of the hall when someone on personnel hands me a flat bill Colorado Colts hat. Looking in the mirror, I quickly place the black hat with a blue bill on my head and tug it on so it fits snugly.

And then I'm walking out on stage. Holy shit! My arms stretch out to my side. A little celebratory sound comes out of my mouth. I begin waving my arms up and down, bouncing on my feet as I make my way over to the Commissioner. We give each other a high five, he pulls me into a hug, slapping my back. He congratulates me before handing me my jersey. In my hands is a black Colorado Colts jersey with silver letters and BOYD printed across the back. We stand together as the cameras flash over and over. With one last handshake and congratulations from him, I move to walk off the stage.

I step down into the hall again and am immediately directed toward the left instead of straight. It's a media frenzy down here. Cameras are set up all over the room with an NFL Draft 2023 backdrop. Scanning the room, I find Eliza and Brynn waiting at a high-top table. Brynn has a glass of champagne in her hand and a megawatt smile stretched over her face. She looks stunning tonight. She always does. But tonight, she has on a gold thin strapped, deep V-neck formal gown. The gold in the dress brings out her golden skin and ocean-blue eyes. And the sequins that are sewn into her bodice make her shine.

Gold dresses are her color. My mind goes back to our trip to Chicago and the gold minidress she wore. It was the night everything changed between us. I took a dare and made a move on my girl. Six months later, my heart is overflowing with love for her.

Stopping in front of the backdrop, I smile for the cameras, holding up my jersey. Erica Adams, an ESPN reporter, steps up next to me.

"Congratulations, Quinton. You are the newest member of the Colorado Colts. How does it feel to be heading to Colorado?"

"Erica, I couldn't be more excited. It feels amazing to even be drafted, let alone in the top three. I've never been to Colorado, but it sounds a lot like home."

"Colorado is coming off a tough season. Does that impact you at all?"

"C'mon now, Erica." I chuckle. "Nah, I'm fired up. I'm so happy to be a Colt. I'm looking forward to getting out there, getting settled, and winning some football."

"Alright, Quinton." Erica chuckles too. "You're looking well-dressed tonight. I see you're sporting some new ice. Tell us about it." Erica points out my chains and the diamond studs in my ears.

"The chains came from my grams. She dropped them off before we flew out here," I say, referencing the gold chain with the diamond-encrusted cross necklace. "And my wife surprised me with the studs this morning."

"I'm sorry, did you just say wife?" Erica asks, mouth dropping open. A smile takes over my face.

As I tip my head in the direction of Eliza and Brynn, the cameras spin to her. Brynn lifts her champagne flute in a salute, flashing her engagement ring—a six-carat oval cut diamond surrounded by a row of smaller diamond accent stones. Below that rests her wedding band, a diamond eternity band. The rings shine beautifully on her dainty fingers.

Erica turns her head back to me. "Well, I guess congratulations all around. Good luck in Colorado, Quinton."

With a final goodbye to Erica, I step around the cameras and stride over to my wife. Leaning down, I give her a hard kiss that has her clenching her thighs. Eliza clears her throat. Without removing my lips from Brynn's, I slide my gaze up to meet Eliza. She just shakes her head, a tiny smirk on her lips.

"Congratulations, Quinton," she says. Standing back up, I reach my hand out to Eliza.

She smacks it away and throws her arms around me. Squeezing me tight, she whispers in my ear. "Thank you. Thank you for taking a chance on me."

"I had no doubt you'd get me here," I whisper back as we both pull away. "Thank you for everything. I wouldn't be an NFL player or have a wife if it wasn't for you."

She leans down and gives my blushing bride a hug. I hear her wish Brynn congratulations. Stepping back from the embrace. Eliza's eyes bounce between the two of us. "Now that the big surprise has been dropped, have fun celebrating you two. Be smart and be safe."

I hold my hand out and my wife takes it, the two of us head out of the room. There are Draft parties happening all over the city tonight and I'm ready to show off my new bride.

This weekend my dreams came true. The NFL wants me. And my best friend became my wife. Here's to all of the unknowns. No matter where life takes us, we'll always be together as husband and wife.

She was the late hit I didn't see coming.

EPILOGUE 1
QUINTON

Three Years Later

FLASHES OF LIGHTS GLEAM around me. I did it. Three years ago, I was walking across a stage in Kansas City, shaking hands with the Commissioner of the NFL, and today, today another dream comes true.

Standing at the fifty-yard line, my body slowly turns in a circle. Seats are beginning to fill. The atmosphere is palpable. Black and blue jerseys are scattered throughout the stands. My number is plastered across people's chests.

I made it.

I made it to the Super Bowl. Not only am I playing in one of football's biggest games, but I'm hoping to join a class of some of the best players. And if I have anything to say about it, today I'm becoming a Super Bowl Champion.

It's been a trying couple of years. My rookie year was tough. The NFL is no joke. There was quite an adjustment period. Practices that seemed endless as we worked out new plays. Strength and weight training that pushed my body to the limits. Working with a nutritionist to develop and maintain strict diets. Endless meetings with the media, upper management, the team, and sponsors.

Then when you think you're done, there would be mandatory events from PR. Of course, the events were for charities, and I didn't mind attending, but there were nights when I just wanted to go home to relax and mend my pained body.

On top of everything, there's navigating Colorado's atmosphere which is severely different from Texas. So many times I thought I was going to pass out on the field as my lungs adjusted to the thinner air. Not only was there an adjustment period for my body and the game I love, but I had to do it alone.

A part of my goddamn soul was missing. It was crushing. Some days felt impossible to get out of bed. I was beaten, broken, and alone. No one tells you about the isolation. About self-doubt. The fleeting feelings of inadequacy.

But then, on my hardest days, the days I question everything, her name would flash on my screen.

My Wilder.

Her voice always calms me immediately. A year apart while she finished her degree felt impossible. She is truly my best friend, and I didn't realize at the time how much I relied on her. How seeing her smile would change my entire day. How having her wrap her arms around me would make me feel whole. But it was only a year. A year we could do while she finished her degree.

Even when she wasn't with me, knowing she was mine made things easier. Knowing that she was walking around CTU with my ring on her finger. It felt primal. It felt like I was beating my chest, even hundreds of miles away, telling every guy on campus that Brynn Wilder—Brynn Boyd—was *mine*. Marrying Brynn in Kansas City was the best decision I have ever made.

A few weeks prior to the draft, this all-consuming feeling swept over me. and I knew that KC was going to be the right time. She was asleep in my bed, wrapped in my sheets, and I couldn't take my eyes off how peaceful she looked. With the families we both of us came from,

I knew it was always going to be Brynn and me against the world. Her eyes fluttered open, surprise crossing her face as she found me staring at her.

"Hi baby," escaped her lips in a whisper, a slow smile spreading across her kissed-swollen lips, her hair a mess from being fucked into exhaustion, and she never looked so beautiful.

Once she dozed back off, I reached for my phone, finding Eliza's number. Quickly, before Brynn woke back up, I typed out my plan for Kansas City. My agent thought I was crazy, but she arranged everything.

In the last three years, we've navigated long-distance marriage, adjusted to marriage in the same state, and learned how to handle a marriage where I'm on the road for half the season. It's been a challenge, but life with Brynn wouldn't be any other way. A lot of healing has occurred over the last three years too. Brynn and her mom have been working on their relationship. Carolyn and Brynn see each other a few times a year, both taking turns flying to see each other. Their relationship isn't perfect, but it's so much better than it was. Brynn's relationship with her dad is still nonexistent, but her relationship with her mom has always been more important to her.

I wish I could say that my relationship with my parents is better, but unfortunately, we had to cut that cord. After confronting my parents about the conversation I overheard while I was in the hospital, I discovered that my dad wasn't the dad I thought he was. The game he took Damien and I to was one he went with his mistress, not someone who worked with him. Needless to say, that memory was completely ruined.

My mom filed for divorce and latched on to the president of the credit union where she worked. I guess she was the one we all had to worry about being in it for the money.

While my parents' marriage fell apart, my brothers and I turned to each other. Damien followed us out west and he lives in the city, not far from our condo. In his last two years of college, Xavier really buckled down and got serious. He's now a rookie in the league and plays in Boston. The three of us get together as much as our schedules allow. Damien has his sight set on a nurse he works with. Maybe there'll be a wedding for him in the future.

"Boyd!" a tiny but mighty voice sounds from the sideline, pulling me from my thoughts. Eliza is standing in a blue pantsuit with a black Colorado Colts T-shirt underneath.

Nodding my head in acknowledgment, I leave my spot on the field and make my way toward her. The closer I get, the wider her grin spreads across her lips.

"You made it," she says, clutching the folders tighter against her chest.

"I couldn't have done it without you, Eliza. None of my dreams would've happened if it wasn't for you and all of the hard work you put into making them come true."

"Now don't get soft on me now. You've got a ring to win." She pauses, looking around the stadium. A look passes over her face as the smallest amount of moisture gathers in her eyes. "Thank you for taking a risk with me." Clearing her throat, she continues before I have a chance to respond. "Now go kick some ass."

"I second that!" my favorite voice exclaims from beside us. I turned to find my wife making her way over to us.

A low growl escapes my throat—Eliza chuckles—as I take in my wife's appearance.

Her long blonde hair is curled in waves, pulled up in a high ponytail. The blue and black jersey is customized with my number thirty-one stretched across her chest in Swarovski crystals. Yeah, somehow, I managed to keep my high school number through college and into the NFL. It's pretty exhilarating.

My eyes continue trailing down her body, landing where the jersey stops mid-thigh on her tan legs. Bright blue cowboy boots cover her feet, but I can't take my eyes off where the skin of her legs is exposed.

"Fuck, baby," I rasp out.

She smiles, a blush taking over her cheeks. She throws her arms around my middle and I wrap my arms around her, pulling her in as tight as I can with my full pads on. She lifts onto her tiptoes, I move my mouth down to meet hers. Our lips find each other, and I can feel the nerves escape me and flow into her.

That's the thing about Brynn. She's a feeler, always taking on what everyone else is feeling.

Ending the kiss, I look down at her, still so lucky that I can call her my wife. "I love you, Wilder."

"I love you too," she says, grinning back up at me. "Now go kick some ass."

Leaning down, I brush my lips against her forehead one last time before turning and jogging away. But before I get out of arm's reach, a hand slaps against my ass. Looking over my shoulder, I find my wife with the biggest shit-eating grin on her face.

"Love you, thirty-one!"

Goose bumps erupted over my skin while moisture lined my eyes as one of the country's biggest performers belted out the National Anthem. It was chilling to stand on the field before the game, but nothing compares to how I feel right now, mere minutes away from kickoff.

"And the home of the bra-a-aaave," the country singer finishes, just as a roar of F-16 engines rush overhead causing the stadium to rumble. Hands start slapping my shoulder pads as we turn to huddle up on the sideline before kickoff.

Hands dropping to my side, I shake out my limbs, opening and closing my hands. I tilt my head from side to side, cracking the bones. I take one last glance up in the stands toward the suite where I know my family is watching. Bringing my fingers up to my lips, I blow a kiss toward them while our team awaits the kickoff.

The Minnesota Grizzlies kicker sails the ball, but our returner is able to easily catch the ball. He takes off like a rocket, dodging and weaving through the mob of players rushing toward him. Following his blockers, he makes it to the twenty-seven-yard line. And just like that, my first Super Bowl game is underway.

The offense makes our way out onto the field. I find my position to the right of our quarterback. Clapping his hands, he waits for the snap. Dropping back, he finds one of the best receivers in the league for a quick fifteen-yard gain. In the huddle, he looks at me and gives me the play.

Breaking the huddle, we rush to find our spots. I wait for the snap and once our QB has the ball, I take off to my left, running behind him as I await the handoff. The offensive line holds off the defensive, and I pick up a quick seven-yard run.

Slow and steady, we take our time making our way down the field. Our team is good, damn good, but so are the Grizzlies. The game plan is to take advantage of the clock as much as possible. Short runs to pick up quick yards. It's working as we find ourselves inside the five-yard line after taking five minutes and clicking down the clock.

Once again, I find myself lining up to the right of the quarterback.

"Hike!" our quarterback yells, stepping back and waiting for the play to start.

Starting toward my defender like I'm going to block, I quickly drop back to receive the ball. Juking right and then propelling to my left, I cut and weave until I'm inches from the end zone. The defense is closing in, but not fast enough. Stretching my body out, the hand holding the football crosses the goal line before I'm brought to my knees.

Touchdown!

Jumping to my feet, I'm met with the rest of the offense. Finding our quarterback, I point my finger toward him in a show of respect, thanking him for giving me the ball. Helmets smack together, cheers erupt, and the vibe is celebratory as we make our way over to our sideline.

The rest of the first half and the third quarter go off the same way with us taking a slow and steady approach to the game. The Grizzlies are looking to make it a fast-paced game, their strategy isn't working for them. In fact, it's making them flustered. The Grizzlies have three interceptions and two fumbles, yet they're still within a touchdown of tying the score.

Halfway through the fourth quarter, there's an electric current running through our sidelines. The fans can feel it too. We are up by two touchdowns with six minutes left. Coach gathers us around.

"All right, boys, you ready?"

Grunts of agreement envelop us.

"Good. Listen, we aren't changing anything up. Keep the pace. Make smart decisions. We are sitting good. Let's not get cocky yet."

And with that, we rush out to the thirty-seven-yard line.

Confetti shoots out from cannons around us as the clock winds down to zero. Reaching up, I unhook my chin straps before removing my helmet. The smile that breaks free consumes my face, and I can't help but let the tears form.

I fucking did it.

We fucking did it.

Teammates rush the field. Grown men have tears in their eyes and are celebrating like kids at a carnival. Today, dreams were made.

A high-pitched voice pulls me from celebrating with my team. "Daddy! Daddy!" comes the voice. My head is on a swivel looking for the owner of the precious voice. "Daddy!"

Pushing their way through the crowd is my baby girl in my Wilder's arms. She's dressed like her mama in a custom jersey dress and denim jacket, much like her mom wore for my National Championship game. Only this time instead of an eagle on the back, it's a bucking colt. Her beautiful tan skin is the perfect mixture of my black and her mom's white skin tones. Beaming blue eyes that match her mom's stare up at me. Her curly light-brown hair is pulled back in a high ponytail and my sweet two-year-old looks beautiful.

Our eyes find each other, and she stretches her arms toward me. Grabbing her out of Brynn's arms, I toss my girl in the air.

"Cleo!" I shout as she squeals.

Pulling her into my chest, I reach out and pull Wilder into me. Tears are streaming down her cheeks and a look of pride is plastered on her face.

Throwing her arms around my neck, her lips seek mine out immediately. All sounds fall away around us as I savor this moment. Cleo wraps her arms around me as she buries her head in my neck. Brynn kisses me over and over, my sweat and tears mix together with her tears. After what feels like an eternity, she pulls back. Her eyes find mine and she searches my face. I'm not sure what she's looking for, but I let her soak it all in.

"I'm so incredibly fucking proud of you!" she screams over the crowd. "We are so incredibly proud of you!" She steps back from my embrace and I watch as her hands move from my neck and land on her stomach.

My eyebrows draw in, confusion crossing my face. My eyes bounce from her face to her hands on her stomach and back up to her face. A wide grin spreads across her lips.

"The three of us are so proud of you."

My knees buckle as I digest the words that Brynn just said.

The three of us.

"B-Brynn," I stutter. "What are you saying?"

But that grin never leaves her face. "You ready to be a daddy again, Mr. Super Bowl Champion?"

With the arm that isn't holding Cleo, I lift my wife off the ground and spin them both. "I love you so much, Brinley Boyd. You keep making my best days even better."

"I love you, too, Quinton."

I thought winning the National Championship was the best day of my life.

I thought getting drafted into the NFL was the best day of my life.

But at this moment, celebrating another dream coming true, with my wife, my beautiful daughter, and now another child. It's by far the best day of my life.

And we're just getting started.

EPILOGUE 2
QUINTON

When they say the days are long, but the years are short, man, they really weren't playing. It's been eight months since I won my first Super Bowl ring, and Brynn announced that we were extending our family again.

At thirty-nine and a half weeks pregnant, I find my Wilder girl in our son's nursery. She's sitting in the glider with a sleeping Cleo wrapped around Brynn's beach ball-sized belly. My two girls look peaceful as B sings a soft melody into Cleo's curly hair. When she was expecting Cleo, Brynn discovered a song about a mother's promise always to have their child's back. After learning the lyrics, it's been her go-to lullaby to comfort our daughter.

Standing in the doorway, I refuse to disrupt their moment; instead, I just watch them. With her swollen face, ankles, and dark circles below her eyes, Wilder only gets more beautiful as the years pass. Motherhood looks good on her. And as I watch her rub her side where our wild son is no doubt kicking his mother, I think of all the ways I'm going to try putting another baby in my wife. There's something about seeing her swollen belly and glow from pregnancy that makes me go a bit feral.

"You going to stand there or join us?"

Erasing the space between us, I lean down and kiss Cleo's curly head before placing a chaste kiss on my wife as I rub her tight belly. "How are you feeling?"

"It won't be long." She sighs. "I heard Cleo moving around while I was pacing the house and couldn't resist snuggling her."

"It won't be long, and you won't be able to do that."

"You shut your mouth, Quinton Boyd. I have two arms for my two babies."

"Alright, alright," I say, raising my arms in defense. "What's going to happen when I put another baby in you and another one after that and another—"

"Slow your roll, Daddy. Let's just get our son here, and then we'll talk about all the babies you're going to put in me. And all the fun we're going to have making them."

Groaning, I stare up at the ceiling before I decide to take my woman right here. "Let's go to bed, wife."

"Fine." She rolls her eyes as I reach down to scoop up my daughter.

"Daddy," Cleo's sleepy voice whispers.

"Hi princess, let's get you back to bed."

Brynn places her hands on each side of the glider as she tries to push herself up. My son can't get here soon enough. Between chasing our almost three-year-old around and all of the pregnancy symptoms, I can tell she's really starting to feel the exhaustion. Our son has been her longest pregnancy so far.

Cleo arrived four weeks early in a rapid and slightly terrifying way. Luckily, Brynn was with me in Colorado when her water broke, but with me still being new to the area, finding the hospital was a bit of a challenge. It didn't help there was a couple of inches of snow on the roadways, which led to me managing to get us lost not once but twice, and after being on the phone with the hospital, I thought I was going to have to deliver my daughter on the side of a mountain. Luckily, we were able to find the hospital in time, but she delivered within forty-five minutes of us pulling into the parking lot. With how fast delivery came, she was unable to have any medication, which made me admire my wife even more.

With an outstretched hand, I grab onto Brynn and help her stand. My lips find her temple and I just hold my girls in my arms. Becoming a dad was never on my mind. But now I can't imagine my life without Cleo. She's everything I could've asked for in a daughter, with her sweet and caring nature. My girl is wrapped around my fingers.

As Brynn moves out of the nursery and down the long hallway to our bedroom, I walk across the hall and place Cleo in her princess bed. My daughter is in her fairy tale era. A princess movie is always on our TV, and she carries a plush Moana doll with her wherever she goes.

"Night, my princess." With a kiss on her head, I watch as she rolls onto her side and cuddles her doll.

Latching her door behind me, I walk down the stairs and do a quick check to make sure all of the doors are locked, and the alarm is enabled. I did this same walk a few hours ago, but my mind can never have too many safety checks.

Bret's black and white border collie, Chase, is asleep in his bed which is in our large laundry room. And yes, he's Bret's dog. I don't have the time for one, but she found him at a shelter and refused to leave him. Now, the two of them are besties, and I have to constantly kick the mutt out of my bed when I'm home. Chase eyes me as I check the lock on the garage door. He's probably waiting to see if I leave so he can take his spot on my side of the bed. Bastard.

Satisfied that the house is secure, I climb the grand staircase to our second floor, where the bedrooms are. The oversized mountain home is too big for just the three of us. It's a contemporary two-story home on a half-acre lot with brown rustic wood siding and warm stonework around the bottom of the exterior. Inside are eight bedrooms between the second story and the basement, which is great since we always have someone popping in for trips to watch me play football. However, our guest rooms will slowly diminish in the next few years.

"Q!" Brynn shouts my name, and I take off running up the stairs. She meets me at the top of the stairs, eyes wide, hair a mess, but a wide smile is pasted across her face. "It's time to meet your son."

Whoosh, it's as if all the air has been sucked from my lungs as I lean back and grab ahold of the railing.

My son.

Tears well in my eyes, and I watch a glossy sheen fall over hers. "Let's go meet our boy, Wilder."

Leaning up on her tiptoes, Brynn's hands wrap around the back of my neck as she pulls me into her. Our lips meet, but only briefly before she pulls away. Letting out a groan, she clutches her stomach and waits out the contraction.

"Did you wake Carolyn?" Brynn nods. Her mom has been living with us for the past five weeks as we've all been patiently waiting for baby boy's arrival. Carolyn Wilder being in my home was not something I thought imaginable when Brynn and I first said 'I do' three and a half years ago. But with a lot—and I mean, a lot—of therapy, Brynn finally has a relationship with her mother.

While helping Brynn walk down the stairs, my mind is in a blur of all the things I need to make sure we have. Chase meets us at the bottom of the stairs, whimpering. "It's okay, sweet boy. Mama is about to have your baby brother." She pets the mutt's head and scratches behind his ears while I glare at the beast.

Slipping into a pair of sneakers, I get us loaded in the car, double-checking that our bags are still in the back of the SUV. Starting the engine with the push of a button, I'm reaching for the gear shift when soft fingers land on my hand.

"Relax, baby." Her words are nurturing, as if she were talking to our daughter after she hurt herself. Brynn leans over the center console as best as she can as her lips find my neck. She sucks the skin into her mouth above my pulse, and I groan.

"Wilder," I grit through my teeth. "We do not have time for me to fuck you right now."

Her giggles fill the interior of the SUV while my heartbeat pumps in my ear. "No, we don't, but it got you to relax, didn't it?"

"No, because right now I'm fighting a hard dick as the thought of taking you in the backseat is all I can think about."

"Quinton?"

"Yes, wife?"

"Let's go have a baby."

And have a baby, we do.

Bryce Alexander Boyd was born November sixteenth at three fifty-seven AM, weighing eight pounds six ounces and a whopping twenty-two inches long. He's got plans to be as tall as his daddy.

Brynn did an incredible job birthing our son with a surprising, all-natural birth. She said she did it once and that she could do it again. My girl can do anything when she sets her mind to it. After a brief twenty-four hours in the hospital, the three of us arrive home. I cannot wait for my baby girl to meet her new brother.

Reaching for the handle, Brynn stops me, much like she did the night we left for the hospital. "I love you, Q."

"I love you, too, Wilder."

"Thank you for making me the luckiest woman in the world. I don't know what I've done to deserve this life you've blessed me with, but I just want you to know how grateful I am for everything you sacrificed for our family."

Tears pour down her cheeks, and I lean over the console and kiss each one of them away.

"This family of ours is the best thing that has ever happened to me. Thank you for loving me and for showing me what love without strings attached looks like."

My lips find hers, and the saltiness of her tears mixes with her natural sweetness. But our kiss is kept short as our daughter opens the garage door and holds her Grandma's hand. Carolyn looks at us with a sheen to her eyes.

Stepping out of the car, I walk around the back of the SUV and open Brynn's door. Gently and much to her annoyance, I help her get out of the vehicle and guide her toward her mother. "I can walk," she grumbles, but I just kiss her temple before turning back and opening the back door where our son sleeps.

Bryce's complexion is darker than Cleo's, more like mine, while he takes after his mom in the eye department. His eyes are currently a bright ocean blue, and I hope they stay that way. He's a handsome devil, much like his dad, if I do say so myself. Unlatching the carrier, I trail after my family as Carolyn leads Cleo into the living room with Brynn on their heels. While Chase is sitting in his bed watching the chaos unfold.

"Hey, baby girl."

"Daddy! You have my baby?" Cleo asks in her imperfect toddler speech.

Sitting Bryce down, I crouch in front of Cleo, who is sitting at the end of the couch next to her mom. "I do. Promise to sit on the couch like a big girl and be really gentle?"

"Pwomise." Her sparkling eyes stare back at me, and I'm blown away that we made this perfect girl.

Brynn helps Cleo get situated with a pillow underneath her arm while I unclasp Bryce's harness. Pulling the tiny bean out of his seat, his body instinctively curls up as his knees draw toward his chest, and his tiny hands form little fists. His face smooshes as I gently place our son in the arms of our waiting daughter. Cleo lets out a tiny squeal as Brynn gives her words of encouragement. Bryce arches his back as he wiggles in her tiny arms until he nestles into her.

With a quivering chin, I let the happy tears roll down my face. My whole world is sitting there on our couch in the home we built.

"You did good, Quinton." Carolyn places her arm around my back and pulls me in for a hug. It's a warm embrace, the kind of hug only mothers can give.

"Thank you," I whisper.

"No, thank you, Quinton. Thank you for making my girl the happiest girl in the world."

I choke on a sob as my heart explodes with more love than I know what to do with.

"Oh my gosh, would you two knock it off," Brynn calls. Glancing at my wife, I watch as she doesn't fight the tears streaming down her face. "I'm the hormonal one, and now I'm not going to be able to stop the waterworks."

Carolyn chuckles before pulling away. "Quinton, honey, go squat by the arm of the couch and let me get a picture of the whole family."

My whole family.

That is until Brynn lets me put another baby in her.

"Quinton Boyd, I swear I can hear you thinking about another baby." The words come out harsh, but when I look over at her arm helping support Cleo as she holds Bryce, I can see the desire swirling in her eyes.

"I love you, wife."

"And we love you."

THE END

Not ready to say goodbye to Quinton and Brynn?

Please keep reading for a special bonus scene of their wedding.

Want to know more about their family?

Download a special bonus epilogue. Visit authoralexisbuxton.com/extras and get a glimpse at their future!

BONUS SCENE: THE WEDDING
Brynn

Wilder,

I'm living out all my dreams this weekend. There's just one more thing I need to do to make them all come true. Open the box, put what's in it on, and meet me downstairs in an hour.

Love Always,

Q

Slipping the ribbon off the box, I slowly open the lid. A gasp leaves my lips, and I drop the note to the floor.

Before me, something is folded delicately in half, covered in the most delicate lace. Reaching inside, I pull out the material and hold it before me. My eyes rake over the beautiful ivory and white lace dress.

Quinton Alexander, what do you have planned for us?

Laying the dress flat on the bed, I continue unwrapping items in the gift box. It seems Quinton has thought of everything. I pull out a lingerie set to wear underneath the dress, two boxes of jewelry, and a shoe box with white heels with a bow across the ankle strap. I'm utterly speechless as I try to wrap my head around everything.

Tears gather in my eyes at the realization that I am marrying my best friend today. Fanning my face, I will the tears to go away and not ruin the makeup I just had done. How did we get here?

From competing against each other during the first week of college to becoming fast friends, two kids with unsupportive parents found support with each other. We understood each other on a deeper level, allowing our love to take root. Slowly, those roots grew stronger over time as our love, passion, and connection grew.

I never imagined that a trip back to my childhood home would cause that love to bloom into what it is today.

Will some say we moved too fast? Of course. Society has this pre-conceived notion of how long someone must date and be engaged before marriage. But the truth is, if it feels right, why wait?

I've learned how fleeting life can be from firsthand experience, not once but twice. Everything you know can disappear and leave you alone in the blink of an eye. But one thing I've learned, with the help of Quinton, is that it's okay to live. It's okay to be happy and chase dreams. Just because I've suffered loss along the way doesn't mean that I have to lose out on life, too.

Today, I'm marrying Quinton Alexander Boyd, and as the realization keeps settling deep in my bones, I've never been more excited for my future.

Unable to wait any longer, I begin slipping out of my clothes. Picking up the delicate strapless lace corset, I notice the small flowers embroidered in a pale blue thread.

My something blue.

God bless this man.

Once my lingerie was in place, I couldn't help but admire the dress on the bed. My heart felt like it was going to burst at the seams as a small number of nerves started coursing through my system. In the dimly lit hotel room in a city far away from the home we'd created with our friends, it was time to slip on my wedding dress.

Standing before the mirror, I admire myself in the elegance of the dress. I feel like a princess in a long-forgotten fairytale. One who thought her happily ever after was over.

The sheer floral lace formed a graceful overlay atop the nude liner, creating a magical essence. The long, sheer sleeves with eyelash-trimmed cuffs and the off-the-shoulder neckline added a touch of enchantment with the refined crochet lace details. The dress hugged my figure perfectly, with the sculpted bodice creating a tailored contour as it slipped down to meet the fitted waist, which sculpted my silhouette. The A-line mini skirt fell around mid-thigh and drew attention to my long, graceful legs.

As I slipped on the silver, tear-drop earrings and clasped the dainty necklace around my neck, I couldn't help the dreamy smile that spread against my peachy, nude lips as I admired the woman staring back at me. The makeup artist at the spa had painted my face in a natural look. The corner of my eyes was slightly smoked in a deep brown, while my lids had a golden shimmer against thick black liner. My entire face was incandescent and bronzed as my long, platinum blonde hung down my back in soft, tousled curls. Half of my hair was pinned back in a simple updo with a delicate rhinestone hair clip that resembled floral branches.

Happiness looks good on you, Brynn Wilder.

Tightening the strap of my heels around my ankles, the hotel phone rings.

"Hello?"

"Hello, Mrs. Boyd, your car is here waiting for you," the receptionist informs me.

Mrs. Boyd.

Holy shit, I'm becoming Mrs. Boyd today.

"Thank you, I'll be right down."

Hanging up the phone, I stand for one final look in the mirror before reaching for the small clutch I packed for tomorrow night's Draft.

The ride in the town car didn't take long. While Quinton was absent from the ride, his agent, Eliza, was waiting for me. The two of us made small talk, but she refused to answer some of my burning questions: how did Quinton organize all of this? Did she know where we were going?

She only smiled and complimented how I looked and how happy the two of us seemed together.

The driver parks in front of a concrete sidewalk that leads to a large brown building with gray columns. It's a pretty nondescript structure, which still hasn't answered my question about where we are going.

Eliza leads me up the walkway, past luscious flowerbeds, and through wooden doors that she holds open for me. A blast of cool air hits me as the sound of my heels clicking against the stone flooring hits me. The space opens up to a large welcoming room with two oversized floor-to-ceiling stone fireplaces sitting opposite each other. Eliza moves us through the room and out the sliding automatic doors to the rest of the property.

Luckily for us, it's a beautiful spring day in Kansas City, with temperatures in the seventies. The concrete and brick-outlined walkway leads us deeper into the gardens, past sculptures and brick walls where succulents grow between the bricks. The property is stunning, and with each step, nerves and excitement continue to build deep inside my soul.

We pass wood benches where people sit and watch us pass by as the walkways lead us around a pond. Sitting atop the pond are water lilies and the sound of fountains fills the air. I'm mesmerized by the spectacular view. But Eliza doesn't stop here.

"Eliza, honey, I love everything you've done for Quinton, but if you don't tell me we are getting close, I might kill you."

She chuckles. "Not too much longer, Brynn. I guess we should've thought through the shoe situation a little better."

"You think? My feet are made for boots, not heels."

"I promise it'll be worth it, and I'll even arrange another morning at the spa if you'd like."

"You're a goddess, and I take back the threat of killing you."

Finally, after what felt like an eternity, a beautiful one nonetheless, we approach a gigantic triangular-shaped wood building.

My breath catches in my throat as my heart races. I find myself grabbing my chest with sweaty palms as tears of happiness well in my eyes. Eliza stops short in her tracks and turns to me. Placing her hand on my back, her soothing voice interrupts my thoughts. "Are you okay, Brynn?"

I nod. Seeing the chapel standing before me in all its glory makes this moment feel surreal, almost as if it's been a dream this whole time.

"Take a deep breath, honey. In for two and out for three." I follow Eliza's instructions and slow my breathing. Not for one second am I second-guessing my decision to get married today, but I'm overwhelmed with the burst of love that has consumed my entire being.

"Let's go get me a husband."

"Thatta girl." Eliza takes my hand, and with a few quick squeezes and a warm smile, she leads me up the walkway.

Oversized pots filled with overflowing greenery line both sides of the enormous wood doors. Glass windows line both sides of the wooden entry, which allow you to see right through the chapel and out the back as both sides are entirely covered in glass. The exterior is intricate, and I'm dying to see the inside. Reaching into her trouser pockets, Eliza taps something on her phone before placing it back in her pocket.

"Ready to become Mrs. Quinton Boyd?"

"More than anything."

With my admission, the doors open from the inside, and two gentlemen step outside, holding the doors for our entry. Pale wooden aisles line both sides of the aisle, and ornate architecture fills the room. The triangular peaked roof is completely open, allowing the beams to run from the floor to the peaked ceiling. Gray stone flooring will lead me to where my eyes land on my soon-to-be-husband.

Quinton turns around, and I see the moment his attention lands on me. It's as if both of our breaths catch at the same time. Waiting for me, dressed in a tailored burgundy suit with a black tie and black dress shoes, is my best friend.

Too busy taking in everything around me, music starts to filter in as I realize Eliza has moved off to the side and found her seat in the front pew. Two photographers are inside the church, one facing me and the other facing Quinton, as they capture our moment.

Tears well in my eyes as my heart swells with the notion we are about to take the next step in solidifying our relationship for the rest of our lives. With one heeled foot in front of the other, I slowly make my way down the aisle to 'Can't Help Falling in Love With You' playing in the background. The rendition Quinton selected is breathtakingly beautiful, causing goosebumps to break free under my lace-covered arms.

Wise men might say fools rush in, but Quinton and I have spent years getting to know each other—years of learning from each other and letting each other grow into the people we are today. My heart is his, and his heart is mine.

Licking my lips, I smile softly as Q's gaze tracks every movement. Moisture glistens in the corner of his eyes, and I smile wider, thinking that he's just as affected as I am. Finally, standing before him, he reached his hand out to help me climb the three steps so I could stand on the same level. A man dressed in a black suit stands before us with a bible in his hand.

I can only imagine that the view past the glass windows is as spectacular as the rest of the grounds we passed on our way to the chapel, but I can't look away from the man in front of me. With my hands in his, Q leans forward and kisses my cheek. "You look stunning, Wilder."

"Quinton," I whisper his name. "I can't believe you planned all of this."

"I love you." My face softens and more tears gather in my eyes as one lone tear slips down my cheek. Quinton is quick to gather it with his thumb. "Don't ruin your pretty makeup."

The pastor clears his throat as he smiles warmly at us. "Welcome. Quinton and Brynn, today we are gathered here to recognize the love you two share in the most intimate way. As we are gathered in this chapel with the serenity of nature surrounding us as we celebrate the love that surrounds us. Allow today to be a reflection of how far you have come and how strong your love has grown and will continue to do so."

I tune out the pastor as my eyes lock on Q's. He mouths, 'I love you' as I mouth, 'I love you too.'

"Quinton has prepared his own vows."

"Wait, you prepared vows? I didn't have a chance to do that."

He winks. "Wilder, there was a time in my life when all I wanted to do was play the game of football. That's all I had ever wanted in life. Eat, sleep, and run the ball. And then, during an icebreaker game our freshman year, some high-energy blonde decided to wage war against me because she couldn't keep her competitive streak in check. Little did I know that ball of spunk would become my best friend. But our story didn't end there. For years, I've witnessed a girl who was unapologetically herself embrace life in the messy hand she was dealt.

"You showed me there was more to life than running a ball down the field to score touchdowns. You taught me how to cherish the little moments, to find laughter in the every day, and to embrace the mundane as if it were our last moments on earth. With you, I learned I had a whole new dream to achieve, and that dream was to make you my wife."

Reaching in his pocket, Quinton pulls out a linen handkerchief, which I use to dot the tears seeping from my eyes. Of course, he'd bring me to tears in his speech.

"All my life, I've only ever known an overbearing and dysfunctional family. But you, Wilder, showed me that fairytales can become reality. With your trust, love, and immense support, you showed me that I can have my happily ever after as long as you're by my side.

"Today, I make the promise always to love you. Always cherish you and put us before anything else our future has in store for us. Tomorrow is never promised, but the one thing I promise to do is love you with my whole heart until the end of my time. You are my dream, Brynn Wilder—I mean, Brynn Boyd—and I can't wait to spend the rest of my life with you."

Shaking my head, a soft chuckle leaves my lips. "How am I supposed to follow that?"

"Listen to your heart, and the words will come to you," the pastor instructs.

Staring up at warm chocolate eyes, I take a deep breath and do as the pastor says. "Quinton, when I met you, life was all about floating through the motions of endless parties and chaos while wearing a mask to hide the immense amount of grief and guilt I felt. No one knew the reasons for my wild ways, and while I pushed most people away, you fought to stand next to me. You never gave up on me, even on my darkest days. With you by my side, I learned that family didn't have to come from blood, but from the bond people make. The family we created at CTU will always hold such a special place deep within my heart.

"You saw past the façade and helped me face my grief. And with that support, our love bloomed. For so long, I fought the pull between us because everyone I loved left me or chose not to reciprocate my love for them. I was terrified I'd lose you too. But you showed me that wasn't living. By ignoring my feelings, I was doing a disservice to Bryce and Asher. Q, you showed me the real meaning of love. That it is patient, and it is kind. Love is supportive, and it heals. You showed me that I'm worth loving when there were days when I didn't love myself.

"Quinton, I vow to be your partner and to support you as you've always supported me. I know our days of facing challenges are far from over, but we'll face them together, side-by-side. I love you, Quinton Alexander Boyd."

His large, warm hands envelope both sides of my face as his lips crash against mine. The pastor chuckles as Q's lips leave mine.

"Sorry, man, I think I did that out of order."

"It's quite alright, young man. Do you have rings?"

"I—" my words are cut off as Quinton reaches inside his pocket, and Eliza walks next to me. She reaches her hand out, places a ring in mine, and sends me a wink. "You seriously thought of everything," she says.

The pastor says a quick, silent prayer over the rings that we are holding before looking at both of us.

"Do you, Quinton, take Brynn to be your lawfully wedded wife?"

"I do." Quinton smiles down at me as he places a diamond-encrusted white gold band on my finger and then reaches back into his pocket.

The ring he pulls out has me gasping for air. He slides a six-carat oval cut diamond surrounded by a row of smaller diamond accent stones onto my finger, and I admire the sparkle that shines from the natural light.

"It's beautiful, Quinton."

"A beautiful ring for my beautiful wife."

"Do you, Brynn, take Quinton to be your lawfully wedded husband?"

"I do." And with the ring, Eliza slipped into my hand, I slid the black tungsten ring with gold outlines onto Quinton's third finger.

"With the power vested in me, I now pronounce you husband and wife. Quinton, you may now kiss your bride."

And kiss me, he does. His lips meet mine in a breathtaking display as all the words we've spoken in our vows come pouring out in our kiss, reassuring our love.

"I love you, wife."

"I love you, husband."

Not ready to leave CTU?

Ready to watch tension swirl between CTU's star baseball pitcher and the girl he can't seem to avoid? Check out **The Change Up**, a frenemies-to-lovers, forced proximity, slow burn romance!

https://mybook.to/changeup

Want to learn more about Macy and her decision to abruptly move out of the townhouse? Check out The Christmas Scramble, an emotional holiday novella.

https://mybook.to/christmasscramble

If you're craving more, join the Facebook group, Heartfelt Huddle Hub, for lively discussions with fellow readers and an exclusive behind-the-scenes look!

Thank you so much for reading Quinton and Brynn's story! If you enjoyed it, PLEASE consider leaving a rating/review on Amazon and/or Goodreads.

Acknowledgements

Well, friends, I did it! I wrote the damn thing! I can't believe that I wrote a book and it's out in the world with you. Never in my wildest dreams would I have imagined that I would publish a book. Let's just say, a lot of tears were shed in the making of this book. I mean, who's surprised? I'm a very emotional person.

I couldn't be more grateful that you took the chance to read my debut novel. Seriously, it means the world to me that you picked up The Late Hit.

The Late Hit wouldn't be possible without the love and support of the following people...

To my husband, Brad – This book wouldn't be here without you. Your love, support, motivation, and positivity means everything to me. On the days when I feel like giving up, or imposter syndrome takes over, your positivity encourages me. You are always the glass half full to my glass half empty. I love you more than words can express and I'm so thankful to have you in my corner cheering me on. There's no better feeling than you telling me how proud you are of me and how you get so excited to see me light up when I'm talking about something I'm passionate about – writing and becoming an author. Oh, and thank you for reading excerpts of my novel even though you don't like to read. I love you!

To my kids, Henry and Eleanor – Thank you for both for letting mommy focus on this crazy dream of mine. I hope by watching me work towards this goal of mine, you'll have the desire to fight for all of your dreams. Henry, I loved hearing you ask about "mommy's book". It made everything feel so real. You both are my world and I love you dearly.

To my sister, Natalie – Where do I even begin? Thank you from the bottom of my heart for being at my beck and call whenever something would pop into my head. I got so damn lucky with having you in my life, because you're more than just my sister, you're my best friend. Once again, this book wouldn't be here without you. From answering every call and text with enthusiasm when I had a wild idea in my head and needed someone to talk it through, no matter the time of day or night. To watching the kids when I needed to hit a deadline, you helped make this happen and I love you so much!

To my parents – Thank you for all that you have done for me over the years. Your endless love. Your endless support. Your endless encouragement. You both are the best parents a girl could ask for. Thank you for passing on your drive, your passion, and your hard work ethic. I love you both so much!

To my Grandma Drumm – Thank you for passing down your love for reading. Thank you for giving me the free spirit to never stop chasing my dreams and following my heart. I've always loved browsing your bookshelves and discussing my "brain candy" books with you.

Amy – I could not have done this without you! From our daily voice messages that rant and ramble, you were my brain dump, my emotional support, and my guiding light. I'm so glad we got to go through the journey of writing our debut novels together.

Mel – Thank you for creating such a beautiful cover for The Late Hit. It's been such a joy working with you to create stunning covers for the CTU Eagles books. Thank you for bringing my visions to life.

To my sweet Booksta Babes After Dark Girlies: *Aileen, Alexa, Brook, Lauren, Lindsay, Jessica* – I love you girls so much! Your support and always willing to share my posts means the world to me. I'm so thankful that Bookstagram and our love of smut brought us together. Oh, and of course, our daily sending of Instagram model posts *cough cough* *Christian*.

To my family – Thank you for letting my writing, stress, and excitement consume our conversations over the past 6 months. I appreciate and love you all so much!!

To my friends – Thank you for kidnapping me for nights out for drinks and for sending me all the bookish reels. I know that not all of you love reading like I do, but I love you all for always supporting my love of books.

To my Alphas: *Allison, Carlene, Jasmine, Madeline, & Stephanie* – You girls got the hardest job, deciphering the roughest copy of this novel. I know it wasn't easy, but your feedback no matter what it was helped make this novel stronger. I appreciate you all so much!

To my Betas: *Allie, Amy, Lindsay, Sara, & Teri* – Thank you so much for spending hours critical reading, giving feedback, and answering my questions. Your feedback made this book possible!

To my Street Team & ARC Team – Every like, comment, share, and review moves me to tears. Seriously, I appreciate your support and getting my book out there with your friends, family, and followers.

To Harlow James & Jenn McMahan – Girls, thank you for constantly talking me off the ledge when my mind spiraled with analysis paralysis. Seriously, your words of encouragement and telling me to take a deep breath saved me so much. I appreciate your guidance, your encouragement, and your support.

To Ellie & her team at My Brother's Editing – I'm sure you cringed every time you saw me pop in with another email, but Ellie, I appreciate all of your help. This was such a new avenue for me and I appreciate you being so willing to answer all of my crazy questions. Also, I'll eventually figure out my tenses and how the heck to use a comma!

Thank you everyone for reading! I'll always be grateful for you.
 My heart is so full!
Love Always,
Alexis

About the Author

Alexis Buxton is an avid reader turned author. A lover of all things love, Alexis enjoys reading all varieties of romance novels – the steamier, the better. Writing has always been a passion of hers and with the encouragement of friends and family, Alexis decided it was time to follow a childhood dream. She enjoys writing romance novels with damaged characters who need a little extra love and leave you *feeling all the feels*.

Born and raised in Ohio, Alexis currently resides in a small, lake town in Ohio with her husband and two small kiddos. Alexis is a small-town girl, through and through.

An avid sports fan, when she doesn't have a book in her hand, you can find Alexis watching sports. She prides herself on being a Cleveland Browns fan, even on the hardest days (or years). She also enjoys going on camping adventures with her family, visiting breweries to try new craft beers, attending races at her local dirt track, and supporting local businesses and restaurants.

Alexis runs on coffee, craft beers, and chaos, but she wouldn't have it any other way.

Stay in Touch

facebook.com/authoralexisbuxton

instagram.com/author_alexisbuxton

goodreads.com/alexisbuxton

tiktok.com/@authoralexisbuxton

9 798988 226475